Thieves World™

Enemies of Fortune

TOR BOOKS BY LYNN ABBEY

Thieves' World™

Enemies of Fortune

Edited by Lynn Abbey

TOR®

A TOM DOHERTY ASSOCIATES BOOK
NEW YORK

THIEVES' WORLD™: ENEMIES OF FORTUNE

This book is printed on acid-free paper.

A Tor Book
Published by Tom Doherty Associates, LLC
175 Fifth Avenue
New York, NY 10010

www.tor.com

Tor® is a registered trademark of Tom Doherty Associates, LLC.

Library of Congress Cataloging-in-Publication Data

Thieves' world : enemies of fortune / edited by Lynn Abbey.—1st ed.
    p. cm.
    "A Tom Doherty Associates book."
    Contents: Introduction / Lynn Abbey—Widowmaker / C. J. Cherryh & Jane Fancher—Deadly ritual / Mickey Zucker Reichert—Pricks and afflictions / Dennis L. McKiernan—Consequences / Jody Lynn Nye—Good neighbors / Lynn Abbey—Gathering strength / Selina Rosen—Dark of the moon / Andrew Offutt—Protection / Robin Wayne Bailey—Legacies / Jane Fancher & C. J. Cherryh—Malediction / Jeff Grubb—The ghost in the phoenix / Diana L. Paxson & Ian Grey—The man from Shemhaza / Steven Brust.
    ISBN 0-312-87490-1 (acid-free paper)
    EAN 978-0312-87490-2
    1. Fantasy fiction, American. I. Title: Enemies of fortune.

PS648.F3T47 2004
813'.0876608—dc22

2004049575

First Edition: December 2004

Printed in the United States of America

0 9 8 7 6 5 4 3 2 1

Copyright Acknowledgments

This volume of Thieves' World™ is, as always, dedicated to the loyal fans and followers of life in Sanctuary.

Everyone is invited to "browse" on over to http://groups.yahoo.com/group/thieves-world to join in the on-line fun.

Contents

Thieves' World™

Enemies of Fortune

Introduction

Lynn Abbey

The guards at the Prince's Gate hassled Cauvin each time he led the stoneyard's mule cart between them, the same as they'd hassled him from the beginning. They hassled him by name now—

"Hey, Cauvin—what've you stolen this time—?"

"Stand aside, Cauvin, and let us take a look inside that cart—"

"Frog all, Cauvin, what's the point in hauling rocks *into* Sanctuary—?"

He supposed recognition was an improvement, so long as he remained Cauvin, the sheep-shite stone-smasher from up on Pyrtanis Street with a reputation for brawling and, yes, raiding the old abandoned estates beyond the walls for stone that was a cut above any rock that could be dug out of the city's ruins. Cauvin wasn't the most common name in Sanctuary, but he had enough namesakes that someone could—might—wonder which Cauvin was which. His life—the life of a competent mason in a city built from mortared stone—would fall apart if lunk-headed puds from the guard ever got the idea that Cauvin the stone-smasher was the same Cauvin who'd turned up as one of Arizak's more trusted advisors.

"You know how it is," Cauvin said as he led the mule off the beaten path for inspection. "Some nabob wants to add a room, he doesn't want to add it with common Sanctuary stone, he wants it out of matching stone from some dead nabob's garden."

The tallest of the guards pulled the canvas back, exposing an assortment of wedges, chisels, two mallets, and about a hundred-weight of fine-grained granite with most of its old mortar chipped away. He shoved a chunk or two, just enough to assure himself that there wasn't something truly interesting underneath all that rock, then turned back to Cauvin with his hand discreetly cupped for a bribe.

"Can't expect Wrigglie puds like you to earn an honest living."

Cauvin shrugged off the insult. Never mind that he and the guard shared the same nasal dialect, same mongrel features—middling-brown hair, hazel eyes, and a thick hide that darkened like old leather in the summer sun—the guard made it clear that he fancied himself as a son of the Rankan Empire with a gods given right to lord it over lesser folk, which in Sanctuary meant Wrigglie folk, folk who didn't always know who their parents had been, much less their grandparents.

Frog all, Ranke had pulled out of town nearly forty years ago and most of its thirty-eight Imperial cities were in worse shape than Sanctuary. The smart money—the nabobs' money, whether they were swarthy Wrigglies or golden-haired Imperials—had shifted over to the Ilsigi Kingdom which, after a few centuries of inbreeding, had surprised itself and spawned a clever, ambitious king.

On the other hand, when it came to lording it over Sanctuary, nothing compared to a dyed-in-the-wool Ilsigi nobleman slumming in the city his ancestors' runaway slaves had founded. Bad as "Wrigglie" sounded through an Imperial Rankan accent, it sounded that much worse in Kingdom tones.

"We Wrigglie puds do what we have to," Cauvin replied, matching the guard's inflection because he was a decent mimic and he hadn't changed all that much from the brawler he'd been a scant year ago.

He dribbled four padpols—the going rate for common contraband—into the guard's palm, then he clicked his tongue and the mule started for the gate. The guard muttered one of Sanctuary's earthier epithets, but neither he nor his companions got in Cauvin's way.

Once through the gate, the fastest way to his family's stoneyard on Pyrtanis Street was through the 'Tween and up the Stairs. The long way—the mule's way—was down the Wideway to the Processional. Being a smart mule with a good memory, that was the way Flower intended to go. Cool water, fresh hay, and a patch of shade awaited her in the stoneyard. She had no interest in the 'Tween and no intention of plopping her hooves down on its tangled streets. When Cauvin signaled his intention to head toward the Stairs, Flower let loose with one of her attention-getting brays and rooted herself to the ground.

A lesser man—lesser in stubbornness and strength—might have given in to his mule's wisdom, but not Cauvin. He gave Flower a shove in the shoulder that got her and the cart pointed in his chosen direction, then strode into the 'Tween ahead of her. She brayed a few times in protest before giving herself a mighty shake and following her wayward master.

Cauvin scratched Flower's long ears when they were again within reach. He bought a melon from a dozing vendor and gave the larger half to his mule, earning her forgiveness. His own portion Cauvin held in his hand until they were deep in the tangle, then he righted a bashed-in barrel, propped it up between a shaded wall and a fence that was more hole than slat. With a nod to the mule, Cauvin settled in to savor his fruit, like any other workman stealing a few moments for himself.

The melon was sweetly delicious, but it could have crawled with maggots for all Cauvin noticed it. His attention was on a storefront squarely visible through the battered fence. The faded signboard above the open door proclaimed that the shop belonged to one Meerash who sold olive oil suitable for cooking and preserving. A pyramid of glass cruets and ceramic bottles filled the open window. From his vantage point behind the fence, Cauvin counted four spiderwebs connecting the pyramid to the window frame.

A halfway observant man could easily conclude Meerash wasn't selling much oil this summer. A man with access to the officers of the watch and guard knew that Meerash wasn't selling *any* oil because watchmen had fished his body, with a garotte still knotted around his neck, out of the harbor a month ago.

The knot had snagged someone's curiosity. That someone had cut the cord without damaging it and passed the length to someone else, who'd passed it to someone else again and again until it wound up in Arizak's hands.

This mean anything to you? the Irrune chieftain had asked, giving Cauvin a good look at the stiff, stained cord.

Arizak hadn't been asking for Cauvin's personal opinion. As far as the Irrune chieftain was concerned, Cauvin by himself was still a sheep-shite stone-smasher, but Cauvin had fallen heir to Molin Torchholder and been inexplicably engulfed by the memories of a lifetime not his own when that old pud had finally died. There wasn't much about Sanctuary that the Torch didn't have squirreled away in his memories. So, when Arizak turned to a stone-smasher for answers and advice, what he truly wanted was for Cauvin to immerse himself in a dead man's past.

Cauvin had conquered the disorientation that accompanied an upswelling of another man's memories. He froggin' sure didn't *like* it, but the process no longer nauseated him. The dead Torch's memories were no help with the knot, though, which was a bit of a surprise, and a bit not. Molin Torchholder might have cleaned Dyareela's minions out of Sanctuary, but he'd never known the bloody-hungry Hand of Chaos the way Cauvin, who'd grown up in their orphan pits, did.

Maybe, Cauvin had answered Arizak, hedging his bets. *Let me do some checking around. I wouldn't want to be wrong,* he'd said, when the froggin' simple truth was he was afraid to be right.

Arizak had seen straight through Cauvin's dodge. The man might be rotting away from the leg down, but his wits were sharp and he knew how to rule a people who didn't want to be ruled by anything or anyone—which described Arizak's own Irrune tribe as well as it described Sanctuary. The chief had told Cauvin to take his time, and said it with eyes that were heavy with warning.

Cauvin had backtracked the knot to Meerash's shop. He'd kept his eye on the place for the last month, and he still wasn't sure he had all the pieces in all the right places. Or, maybe, he just didn't want to. When it came to spying, Cauvin was a froggin' lubber. His inherited memories were no use: The Torch never dirtied his hands collecting scuttlebutt; he had a web of informants, a web that had slipped through Cauvin's fingers months ago. Soldt, the one person Cauvin trusted with his own questions, had taken off two months ago on a commission to assassinate some Ilsigi wizard. That left Cauvin with only his own wits for the job; and, shite for sure, he was the first to admit that his froggin' wits weren't the sharpest.

As best Cauvin could figure, the new owners of Meerash's shop were selling protection and enforcing it with a gang of thugs, three of whom emerged onto the street as Cauvin watched. The trio were all of a type, the same type as Cauvin himself: brawny young men with big hands and thick skulls. He sized them up reflexively: He could take any one in a fair fight, any two with a stave from the barrel he was sitting on, but if all three took exception, he'd froggin' have to run.

Cauvin glanced at the cart. Soldt had been giving him sword lessons for almost a year now, but he'd feel most comfortable with a steel-head mallet leaning against his thigh. He thought about retrieving it; that would mean leaving his spyhole. Maybe it was sheep-shite stupid to set himself up in a tight corner the way he was, but there could be no doubt that it would be doubly stupid to call attention to his froggin' self rattling around in Flower's cart, so Cauvin stayed put.

He kept his eye on the trio. Two of them bore a jagged tattoo, like sideways lightning or the oncoming profile of a hawk in flight, on their left forearms. The third probably had a similar tattoo, but his shirt was long-sleeved. Cauvin knew the tattoo as the mark of the Kintairs, an old 'Tweener gang he'd tangled with a few times before crossing paths with the Torch.

In those days the Kintairs—the name was a shortening of *sikkin-tair,* the dragons of Ils the Thunderer—had answered to Saluzi, a onetime sea captain and full-time troublemaker. Cauvin hadn't seen Saluzi since he'd started spying on Meerash's shop. If he'd had to guess, he'd say Saluzi had met the same fate as Meerash because, shite for sure, Saluzi hadn't taken over Meerash's little shop. Unlikely as snow in summer, the shop had been taken over by a woman and the Kintairs were taking their orders from her.

Her name was Cassata; at least that was the name she used here in the 'Tween. Her dress was slovenly—draped and hitched around her until it was impossible to decipher the shape of the woman beneath. She wore a foreign sort of headdress with flaps that squared her face and fell across her shoulders like ragged, striped braids. The headdress covered all her hair except for a careless, mud-brown forelock. A bloody wen the size of a froggin' walnut swelled on her jaw to complete her portrait. Beauty wasn't everything, but women who looked like Cassata were more apt to beg for a living than give orders to thugs, leaving Cauvin to suspect that Cassata couldn't possibly be the woman she seemed to be.

And then there was the knot . . .

Cauvin could have duplicated that knot with his eyes closed: When the Hand taught an orphan a lesson, even a sheep-shite stupid orphan learned it down to his froggin' toenails and never forgot it, either. The Dyareelan priest who had taught Cauvin how to tie that knot was dead; Cauvin had watched the aptly named Strangle die. And all but a very, very few of the other orphans who'd learned that particular lesson were dead, too, but one of them . . .

Froggin' gods, one of the surviving orphans had been Leorin and Leorin had been Cauvin's wife for a few short hours last autumn, for the few hours it took to betray him to what remained of the Hand hiding out in the tunnels beneath Sanctuary.

Cauvin had escaped from the Hand a second time that night and Leorin had escaped the Irrune wrath he'd called down upon his captors. He'd hoped—because, though he couldn't forgive his erstwhile wife, his heart still ached when he thought about her—that she'd have the sense to live her life far from Sanctuary. Far from him.

His wife had been beautiful—golden, curling hair, honey-hazel eyes, curves and grace—but she was about the same height as Cassata and had the same habit of twisting a bit of string between her fingers as she talked. The wisdom of his inherited memories said habits mattered more than appearances.

Appearances didn't matter to the Hand—or, rather, appearance didn't matter unless it was useful. A beautiful Leorin had been useful when no one knew who she worshipped. With that secret unmasked, beauty had become a liability—a beautiful Leorin could never have returned to Sanctuary.

The only questions worth asking were, Who had sent his wife back to Sanctuary? And why?

Cauvin had half a mind to walk right into the froggin' shop and ask her. He hadn't given in to that half . . . so far.

The trio concluded their business with Cassata and walked away from the shop, two headed off together and one headed toward Cauvin. He scooted silently over to the mule and had her walking when the Kintair thug came abreast of him. The two men gave each other the once-over and kept going.

Cauvin led Flower past Meerash's shop. The mule was between him and the open door, and he was careful not to look into the shadows, but she'd see him—remember him—if she looked out, if she was Leorin . . . his wife. Cauvin told himself that he was, in his own way, warning Leorin—warning her that he knew who she was and that she needed to pack up and leave Sanctuary, this time for good.

The problem was, Leorin hadn't gotten the message the last time Cauvin had led Flower past her shop, or the time before that; and Arizak wanted answers, results. Frog all, Cauvin didn't want to stand in front of the Irrune chief and admit that he knew who had tied the knot around Meerash's neck, where she was, and what she was to him. He didn't want to say anything to anyone until he could say that Leorin was *gone*.

The mule and Cauvin rounded a corner and headed back to the Wideway. With each step Cauvin cursed the luck that had brought Leorin back to Sanctuary while the one man he trusted completely was out hunting wizards. Frog all, he cursed the luck that had left him with a dead man's memories, but not the wit to use them; and the sheep-shite luck that had brought him to birth in Sanctuary in the first place.

Widowmaker

C. J. Cherryh and Jane Fancher

"Sail ho!" the cry was, and Capt. Jarez Camargen of the *Widowmaker* climbed to the masthead himself with his best glass, sweeping the dawn sea.

A day and night of treacherous shifts and tricks, and now, with the wind off the starboard quarter, the *Widowmaker*'s best sailing point, there she was, their chase, the Yenized ship *Fortunate,* sail above the horizon.

"Ho, Cap'n!" came from his lieutenant, below. "No longer quite as *Fortunate,* eh?"

Camargen grinned, a wicked and wolfish sort of grin. *Widowmaker* was, to put it in the very best light, a pirate. Her prey had run her every trick in a thick old book, and here they were again, out of the isles and onto the southern coast.

They were a Yenized polacre xebec themselves, the *Widowmaker*—
at least Yenized-built, before they'd taken her in the Isles. Capt.
Camargen had liked the look of her: long, low-waisted, a pretty set
to her lateen sails fore and aft, her bastard mizzen, which gave her
power, and quick, oh, much better in his able hands than in the
hands of the fool that had left her largely unmanned and anchored
off Keina's Head. Her former captain had been taking on water on
that island when they'd seen black smoke billowing up from the harbor and their sweet xebec standing out to sea under all sail. The
Happy Isle, she'd been, under a fool; but *Widowmaker* she'd become, and she had a nose for treasure—had a sure, keen nose, these
days, wizard-guided, since they'd met up with old Hada Korgun and
his grievance, and used him for a weathervane.

There he was, out under the bowsprit, incorruptible, as good a
guide as a pirate's instinct to the whereabouts of the *Fortunate.* They
didn't check him often, but he was there, arm outstretched, glassy
eyes open, mouth still stretched wide with his dying curse, and where
he pointed, there they sailed.

There was a Yenizedi wizard on board the *Fortunate,* likely in
better shape. And they'd tried the soft approach—used *Widowmaker*'s Yenized-built outlines and her old Yenizedi flag to get close
to the *Fortunate* the first time, but that trick would never work
twice. Hada Korgun had laid his curse, burst his heart doing it, and
now forget all the old bastard had said about duty to the king of Enlibar and the pardon they'd get if they only got his treasure back.
A dead wizard didn't keep promises any better than a live king, and
Camargen never had liked that part of the bargain.

The *Fortunate* carried a number of items along with a scoundrel of
a Yenized wizard, a man after Camargen's own heart, who'd stolen
this treasure from Hada Korgun by an act of hospitality betrayed . . .
clever man, who had a very well-known ruby, the Heart of Fire, along
with a book of spells and a gold-headed wand.

The Enlibrite, Hada Korgun, had lost his court job over that theft,
the ruby being the property of the king of Enlibar. He desperately

wanted his king's property back, along with the head of the offender, that being the condition of his reinstatement. He'd approached them in the free port of Anbec, offered them considerable inducement to pursue the fugitive—for starters—and claimed the magical ability to track this prize.

All this was useful until they had the ship in sight and Korgun tried some rite or another attempting to link the two ships. He died in the magical backlash—died, or something like it. The crew had lashed him to the mast and kept him there four days, in the hopes he'd come around and blast the ship that now ran them a merry chase. His arm moved. Where that ship went, when it tacked or wore, it tracked, no matter the weather. But he'd begun to have an effect on the crew, just standing there in the way of hands on business, and it seemed less and less likely he'd come to and be himself again.

So they'd lashed him under the bowsprit, down where hands bound for the head could look out and wish him a good day, if they wanted. At night he had a wan kind of bluish glow about him, and for his part, Capt. Camargen would just as soon cut him free for fish bait, being averse to wizardry from the start and convinced by a long shot he didn't need a wizard-compass to run down a bloody great Yenizeder merchantman in the middle of the ocean.

But the captain of that vessel was a right seaman, no question. They'd used all their tricks on each other, setting out decoys at night, muffling up their wizard-compass with sailcloth and dousing all lights to creep closer on a following breeze. They'd gotten the most of every wind that would serve, crept through a maze of islands and chartless reefs, turned tricks of light and weather, and all he'd done had kept the bastard from any civilized port, at least. Run as he would, every time he came close to land, he'd gotten between and chased him out to sea.

They'd be rich. The law of the Brotherhood was share and share alike, and they'd be rich when they ran that beggar down.

So the crew put up with misery, put up with a chase that dragged into days and weeks, into calms and blows and heat and frozen, deadly rigging. The deep calms had set them in sight of one another, the weed growing thick on both their bottoms, until they both sailed like slugs, and no time for either of them to heave down and scrape clean. The chase took on a nightmare slowness at times, every scrap of sail aloft and the log running slower, slower, while they blazed away at one another with Yenized Fire, and flung glass bombs, trying to set sails or pitch-soaked wood ablaze. Crew were scarred with burns, to a man.

Then they reached latitudes where storms grew deadly icicles in the maintop, that plunged to deck and dented the planks, where men took horrible falls, and thus far survived them. " 'Cause he's dead, we ain't," was the common wisdom, and the crew didn't want to look at their wizard—all frozen up with icicles, one report said, but still moving—but they had acquired a superstitious belief that old Korgun was their luck as well as their compass.

A sensible captain might have called it enough. *Widowmaker*'s situation had gotten desperate, running them low on provisions and on water, the bitter latitudes wearing the already thin sails and rigging to a perilous state. At times they thought they'd have lost their quarry, and Captain Camargen began to think of ordering the *Widowmaker* to some wooded shore, some foreign port where they might forget the foolishness and get it out of their blood.

But there was that damned wizard-compass up under the bow, their figurehead. And just when they thought they'd lost her, there was the thrice-damned *Fortunate*. At times a glass showed her clearly, let them see that cursed Yenizedi wizard walking around, talking to the crew, sometimes just lingering back by the stern and watching them, just watching, silver hair streaming in the wind—a live wizard, to their dead one.

"We can find other prey," Capt. Camargen had said. Even he had a conscience, and when water itself ran short, when they could take no time to send boats ashore: "We're down to a ton of water," he told the assembled crew, "and even the hardtack is running slim."

"We ain't et all the rats, yet," the crew shouted back. "We're goin' on, Cap'n!"

The log itself had gone strange. What Capt. Camargen thought he'd written turned out written differently when he checked his course. His charts showed frayed and lost lettering just where it might have been most useful.

But now they were closer than they had been in weeks. The *Fortunate* was hull-up, and lagging, the wind deserting her sails as she bore close to a shore where the charts warned of reefs and shoals, another of her tricks, but not one she could play to great advantage: The *Widowmaker* could skin through channels where the *Fortunate* risked her bottom, and a xebec's sails gave her much more maneuverability in the tricks of wind.

Around a headland, skimming close, close to shore, and now there seemed to be a spot on the lens. Capt. Camargen closed the glass, polished the lens with his cuff, and tried again.

Not a spot, after all. A spot of bluish haze, the sort of color that ought to belong on the horizon, but that had set down on the sea, right near that coast, and the sea beyond it all wrinkled with wind.

Camargen snapped the glass shut and glared, not needing a glass now to see that situation, the dog.

They had the wind off their starboard quarter, carrying them along at a good rate, no danger of a lee shore while this wind blew, but that riffling of the blue water out there was a white squall of the sort infamous in the southern sea, a brutal shift in the wind, in this case bearing right toward the coast, and the *Fortunate* sailing right along that coast. The *Fortunate* had that squall in their sights, too. Had it in their sights, bloody hell! That blackguard wizard might have stirred it up as a favor to the captain.

Hammer and anvil, the coast for the anvil and the squall for the hammer, and them a good long ways behind. The *Fortunate* was meaning to skin through, pass by that deadly rocky headland before the squall came sweeping down on that coast, and leave them in her wake. It intended the squall to cut them off, to force them to veer out to sea and sail wide of the weather.

They were both short of water and short of rations, damn them, and if the *Widowmaker* had to turn out to sea, she had as well turn around and go back to the Isles, her prey escaped, all this long chase for nothing.

That or a long, thankless search in every cove and inlet on this impoverished, treeless coast, for a ship taking on water.

Crew had seen it too—exhausted crew that had been hauling up glass bombs and fitting the cables to the catapult. Some tried to point to the situation.

"Carly!" Camargen yelled for the bosun. "All aloft. Mizzen royal, storm trysails! Gunners, shift everything forward!"

Carly stared at him half a heartbeat, the whole intention implicit in those orders. The pipe shrilled. There was a moment's awful hesitation, old hands knowing full well what the game was: It was in their eyes. But then they howled with one voice, "Camargen or the devil!" and top hands swarmed aloft to spread all the canvas she had, while gunners worked like devils to shift their light catapults to the forecastle to back up the bowchasers.

Camargen dived down to the xebec's little cabin for another look at his charts. The shore was notorious for its hidden reefs. In sight of the shoreline, he had his landmark in the headland itself, and he set everything in memory well as he could, because they might sail on their wind right across the teeth of that squall, much faster than the *Fortunate* on this point of sailing, and they were going to have to run up the *Fortunate*'s backside and come under fire from that towering deck in order to clear that space of coast before the squall swept them onto the reefs. The crew saw their prize; they cheered the choice they saw. They knew they could overhaul that bastard. If they could withstand the fire she could throw long enough and not sink her, they could board and take her.

The crew was mad with desire, seeing gold for every man jack of them; and now he might have caught the contagion himself . . . hell, if he'd fall off now and let that Yenizedi dog skin past, laughing at them. Wizard or no wizard aboard that ship, they had old Korgun up there for a charm, and they were going to take that Yenizeder bastard this time.

He ran up on deck, already feeling the difference in the ship's motion with the new sails abroad, and hoping their weather-worn canvas held . . . that was the devil in it, because if something carried away, they might not have the speed to make it past that squall. Fool, something said to him, reminding him there was still escape. Fool, no treasure is worth it. But there was no hesitation in the crew at all, who worked like madmen. Catapults brought to the forecastle were bowsed up to the fine, fair view of a square-rigged ship coming closer and closer, as the *Widowmaker*'s full spread of canvas hurled her along the fine line between that squall and hidden rocks.

Thought I didn't have the charts, did you? he asked his enemy. Thought we'd not have the nerve? The *Widowmaker* ripped along, rigging singing, the whole deck humming. Old Korgun was getting a soaking up there, the bow wave sending up continuous spray, so that the gunners had to canvas their catapults' cables and shield their slow-matches from the wet.

Closer and closer, with the white squall a haze on their larboard bow, and the *Fortunate* towering up ahead of them. No need for the glass now. A blind man could see the tall stern of their enemy, could see one head and another take a look at them over the taffrail— could see activity back there and know that they were preparing their own rain of fire and missiles, and their deck so high they didn't have to worry about the spray. A silver-haired man leaned on the rail up there—Yenizedi, no question, and their wizard. Wind caught that hair and spread it like a banner.

"Off covers!" Camargen shouted at his gunners. "Fire at will!"

Canvas came off. Bombs were heaved up and settled into their padded slots, their fuses set alight, and *thump-thump-thump!* the catapults cut loose, two at once and the others close after, the glass bombs flying. One smacked against their enemy's stern-post, one fell in the sea, and others hit near the rail. Silver-hair vanished for a moment and reappeared.

The gunners worked like fiends, angling up for maximum loft, winching back, no longer in unison. It was a race, and the first went off, then two and three so close they made one *thump,* sailing up and over the enemy's rail, spreading fire. The fourth hit the rail itself, right where Silver-hair was standing. The heavy bomb splintered the rail and spattered fire.

Silver-hair's robe caught. He made a futile gesture to put it out, turned in a sheet of fire, and in a gust of wind, lost his footing and fell, his black robes and pale hair a downward trail, a small flutter of fire amid the dark cloak.

"Ha!" the gunners crowed.

"Get that bugger!" Camargen roared to midships, and junior officers and spare gunners rushed to the rail to seize up two of the xebec's long oars from their stowage. They ran them out, while the gunners kept lobbing bombs at their target, and now bombs came back, belated fire from a towering great merchantman. Bombs burst on the deck and made puddles of fire that spread in the watery sheet of spray as crew ran to dowse them and wash them overboard.

Camargen dodged between two such and saw the wretch hauled in, half drowned and snagged between crossed oars.

Silver-hair it was, but not the old wizard, not wearing any great ruby, but a young man, a drowned duck of a young man who coughed up water and had to be hauled up to his feet, streaming water.

"He's not the one," Camargen said as the thump of catapults went on and an enemy missile exploded off the mainmast. "Search him for valuables and pitch the bastard in the hold."

"Fool!" the drowned man cried. "You're caught, we're all caught, we're all gone mad! Turn back! Turn back now or we're cursed, all of us are cursed!"

The hands had their superstitions. "Wot curse?" one asked, shaking him.

"There is no curse," Camargen said, grabbing the wretch by the front of his icy shirt to shut him up.

"Curse there is," Silver-hair said, teeth chattering, lips turned blue. "We've been years at this, years, now, and we're both caught in it. Cut Korgun free and fall back or we'll all be caught, forever. It's not a natural storm! We've all run mad, and there's no end to this chase!"

"Cap'n!" the lookout cried. "Cap'n!"

The merchantman ahead of them half vanished in a blinding gust of windswept spray. From a mile away the squall swelled up between one breath and the next and drove down on them in a blinding mist.

There was no time for fools. The gale rushed on them. "Helm!" Camargen shouted, seeing that the helmsman was struggling. "Hargen, Cali, to the helm!" A solid wash of spray broke over them, and he struggled aft, to make his orders heard. Their chase was aborted. They were, with the merchantman, fighting to get through, if they had gained enough headroom around that point of the coast. "Shorten sail!" he yelled, under a wash of water. Sea and sky began to mix, and the air was a steady roar as he turned.

Their prisoner had escaped. Silver-hair was hand-over-handing his way forward, toward the catapults and their glass bombs.

"Damn it to hell!" Camargen ran to stop him before he got to fire that would float and burn. "Stop him!" But Silver-hair had dodged past the gunners, struggling to secure their pieces and their fire-globes, ran the length of the forecastle and clambered up onto the bowsprit as Camargen gave chase. Metal flashed in Silver-hair's right hand as he clasped the bowsprit with both legs and his left arm, cloak let fly to the storm, shirt soaked, hair streaming comet-like against the storm.

"Damn you!" Camargen pushed past the startled gunners and seized a hold on the bowsprit himself, saw Silver-hair forge farther and farther out, toward the end of the bowsprit, where the mainstay held, the stay of not only the mainmast, but all the masts, Silver-hair with this shining metal in hand, and no good intention.

Bent on killing them all, on killing the whole ship. If that stay went, they were dead men, all.

Water, fresh and salt, mingled in the air. Camargen swarmed outward on the bowsprit, got hold of Silver-hair's leg and hauled, and Silver-hair half lost his hold, turning with his back to the gale and his free hand lifted, holding not a knife, but a wizard's wand.

"The hell you do!" Camargen shouted against the wind, and hauled with all his strength, for life itself.

A violent gust hit them. The *Fortunate* completely vanished behind a great mountain of water, and the *Widowmaker* nosed down, her bowsprit aimed at the trough. He seized a fistful of trouser-leg and hauled with all his strength, to get his hands on Silver-hair himself.

Silver-hair slipped further, and grabbed him. "You don't understand," Silver-hair shouted at him. "Let me get us through!"

He had a grip on Silver-hair's belt now, hauled him against the bowsprit only to get his hand on his throat, and as he did, Silver-hair slipped, dragging them both over, dragging them right down where rope and chains held waterlogged old Korgun. With a crack like a catapult, the bowsprit shook.

Canvas had ripped, a tattered streamer of the lateen foresail blowing over their heads, trailing its sheets. Then, sickening shock, the great cable of the mainstay parted a strand, and another, unwinding before their eyes.

Crack! again, and something had given way. The whole mainstay parted, the mainmast pulled violently aside, and death was taking them apart, trailing canvas. Cables and canvas frayed and parted as if sudden rot had taken them. Camargen had Silver-hair by the throat now, and vengeance was all he had, vengeance for his crew, for the *Widowmaker* herself, for all the long sorry chase and the end of it in a watery grave. Old Korgun looked on, blue-lit in lightning and spray, and Camargen kept his grip, kept it while the timbers parted in a series of sickening cracks and lost-soul groans, and the whole fabric of the ship came undone. They went under together, tangled in each other, and while he drowned, he kept strangling the one

who'd done it to them, in hatred more precious than his last-held
breath.

"Where did you get this?" Bezul held the necklace in front of Kadithe's face and Bezul's sharp gaze raked him up and down.

Kadithe Mur ducked his head and mumbled: "I made it."

The little bell rang over the Changer's door and Bezul's strong fingers grabbed his arm, pulling him into a little room just inside the
shop's warrens, closing the door behind them.

"Sit!" Bezul hissed and Kadithe hunched on the edge of the wooden
chair facing the small, cluttered desk. Bezul threw himself down in
the desk-side chair and laid the necklace, gently as if it were a butter-
fly wing, on the table between them. "You tell me and you tell me
straight, boy, *is that stolen?*"

"No."

"I don't deal in that sort of thing. You know I don't."

"I tell you, *I didn't steal it!*"

Bezul's wife, Chersey, cracked the door and asked, was everything
all right.

"Fine, my dear," Bezul answered quietly, and Kadithe scowled at
the floor.

She nodded, once, and disappeared from the door, her point
made.

"All right, boy, start talking, and fast. You say you made it. Out
of what?"

He shrugged, resentment rising. "Stuff. Shite lying in the gutter,
under the scrap from th' fires. Lotsa bits left lyin' 'round iff'n ya
opens yer eyes."

Hell, half and more of Bezul's stock out in that warehouse he
called a store came from the same source, just better stuff, gang-
scavenged.

"Who taught you?"

His eyes dropped. He'd been a fool to come here, or rather should
have stuck with the odd repair job Bezul had for him. The new bits

and bobs, *his* work, only raised questions he dared not answer. Secrecy, more, anonymity, Grandfather had always said, was their only safety.

"Just . . . give it back," he said sullenly and reached for the piece, only to find Bezul's square-fingered hand covering it.

"Not so fast." Nothing could hide from those keen eyes. They bore past pretense and saw:

"Kadithe. Kadithe . . . Mur?"

He jumped. He'd never given the name. *Never.* But Bezul nodded slowly.

"Mur. Aye, you have the look of his boy." He sat back, taking the necklace with him, and said, almost to himself: "I thought the line had died out."

"Just . . . *give it to me.*"

"Grandson?"

He set his jaw.

"Where is he, boy?"

Counting the necklace lost, he darted for the door, only to run headlong into Bezul's wife.

"Here, now." She caught his arms, and gentle but firm, made him lift his head. She *tsked* softly and wrapped a kind arm around his shoulders.

Kind. So why did he still feel like a prisoner?

"What's going on, Bezul?" she asked, over his averted head.

"The boy here wanted to trade this for a shirt and a blanket. Take a look. Tell me what you think."

She made him look up again. "Promise me you won't run?"

He swore, his voice breaking, and threw himself back in the chair. She picked the necklace up; lamplight caught the moonstone ring on her finger, making it glow with life. A beautiful stone . . . with a setting that failed to do it justice. All urge to escape faded in the face of that beautiful stone, how *he'd* set it, given half a—

Chersey exclaimed softly, then moved over to the lamp, and all thought of the ring vanished. If he hadn't been terrified, the look on her face would have made him happier than he'd been in . . . a very long time.

"Beautiful. So very delicate. I haven't seen work like this since . . ." Her voice trailed off and her eyes lifted to meet her husband's. Then she turned to Kadithe, lifted his face with a finger beneath his chin, then brushed his hair back from his eyes to study him the same way she'd studied the necklace. "Where is he, child? We heard his shop was ruined, burned to the ground, that he died."

He said nothing, only wished desperately that he could leave.

She chuckled softly, the way Grandfather chuckled when he recalled his time in the palace. "He was always so *proud* of his bronze-work, his statues. He never appreciated . . . Of course, it wasn't stylish. Large, ostentatious, that's what the nabobs wanted. But the jewelry he made was for his daughter-in-law. She was small, delicate." She smiled at him; he shuddered. "A lot like you, child."

He ground his teeth. *Delicate* wasn't something he wanted to be. Delicate didn't survive what he'd survived these last years. No way. No froggin', shite'n way in hell.

"He says *he* made it."

"Does he, now?" She took his hands before he kenned her intent, studied them from all angles, touching the calluses, the tiny pricks and cuts the metal left, apologized when she inadvertently pressed a still-raw burn, then smiled and placed the necklace in his hands before releasing him altogether. "He's taught you well." She settled on the edge of the desk. "So, husband, how are we going to help this talented young man?"

"What about the shop?" Bezul asked.

"We're out. Says so on the door. Don't change the subject. He's not, I take it, a member of that annoying guild."

Bezul raised a brow at him; he shook his head. He didn't know what guild she was talking about, but he shite'n sure wasn't a member.

"Thought not. He's far too young. They have all those *rules*. As if that necklace shouldn't be evidence enough."

"What . . . rules?" he whispered, before he could shut his fool mouth. It was a dream she offered, not reality. He'd just wanted to exchange the damned necklace for a blanket.

"You must put in your time with a master—"

"Meaning you have to pay someone who's paying huge sums to the guild for the privilege of being slave labor for at least five years."

Pay for the right to make things? He shook his head. "Impossible." Not even if he had the money.

"There must be some way around it. Look at this, Bezul. He's done his time. How long, child? How long have you worked with Harnet?"

His eyes went funny, his head light. He hadn't heard Grandfather's name in over five years. Had learned not even to *think* it. *Secrecy, Kadithe. It's our only chance.*

"S-since I was four . . . five . . ." He couldn't remember the first time he'd sat next to his grandfather, high on a stool, a tiny mallet clutched in his hand. "Something like."

"There. You see?"

"And where is he? Harnet's been gone for five years and more. Is he a paying master, boy?"

He shrugged. Shook his head.

"But he's still alive." His wife persisted.

Bile rose in his throat. Fear such he hadn't known for many long years. He began to shake, tried again for the door, and found himself ensnared in her arms.

"Please," he whispered, in the hoarse voice that was all he had left these days, "please, may I just have the blanket. It—" He choked and got the words out, owing these people who spoke fondly of Harnet Mur at least that much. "It's for my grandfather."

She set him back on his chair. "Why didn't you just say so? Pride is a shortcut to hell, child." She picked up a slate and began writing. "Blanket. Shirt. What else?"

"You'll trade then?"

"Wasting time, young man. What else?"

Bezul nodded and slipped out the door, evidently counting the deal closed—or in the hands of a master.

"P-pissing pot?" he whispered, his face hot as ever it could get, and she added it to her list with only a hint of a twitch to her kind mouth. One by slow one, he added those small items they'd done without for so long, waiting for her to stop him, unable to believe the necklace could possibly be worth as much as she was allowing. When he asked, hesitantly, for an iron skillet and she agreed, he began to suspect charity, and closed his mouth, firmly, resenting the position she'd put him in, wondering what her angle must be.

"So," she said, scanning the list. "Fair enough, though if you'd used anything better than agates in it, I'd owe you. Think you can carry all this at once?"

"Safer if I made more than one trip."

Safer was not lost on her. Bezul's shop was in the Shambles, opposite the Maze. Safe was a concept she well understood.

"I'll get Ammen or Jopze to deliver it. Where do you live?"

"I'll come back," he said firmly. No way he was leading these people to home.

Again, that gentle smile that saw through him. "Good enough. I'll get it ready."

As she left, Bezul returned, carrying something in his hand. It was a spool. A spool of fine, copper wire.

"You know what to do with this?" he asked, and Kadithe, unable to take his eyes from that treasure, nodded. "I want you to take it. Make beautiful things. Bring them here to me. I don't want you or that grandfather of yours wanting. Ever. You need something, you come and ask. We'll work it out. Understand?"

Understand? He understood nothing except that he'd betrayed Grandfather's trust. And yet, as the numbness in his mind eased, somehow . . . some god must be smiling on him, because it was just possible that it would all work out for the best.

Still not altogether certain he wasn't dreaming, he gathered up the beautiful wire, stammered something he hoped was thanks, and escaped.

He was home before he remembered the two bundles lying beside the doorway of Bezul's Exchange.

The rocky reef had one high point about the size of a ship's boat when the tide was in, one rock a man could sit on that was above the fetch of the waves with a south wind driving. So Camargen sat, sodden down to his boots. A man could freeze, in such a wind, even under the burning late-summer sun.

Flotsam went by from time to time, washing past the reef, and he had snagged a few boards, but nothing yet of a size. Cordage had washed up, a kind of a garland on the seaward side, and it was gray and rotten, as Camargen's clothes were grayed and aged and his sword and dirk were rusted. He was not aged. He was sunburned. His hands, ripped bloody from the reef rocks when he had washed up, were still young hands, and his jaw had only the ordinary stubble of beard.

Sorcerers. Sorcerers, sorcery, and magic flung about, insubstantial and unseeable until it hit a ship and the wood rotted in an instant. He was through with sorcery, had no future use for the whole sorcerous breed—but then, he had no future at all, so far as he could see, alternately freezing and baking on this cursed rock, the outlines of which he knew down to a nicety, low tide and high. Today there was a dead fish floating in the garland of cable, if he wanted to get that desperate for moisture and food. He was not a fastidious man, but he was not yet at his limits. A piece of the *Widowmaker* or the *Fortunate* big enough to carry him to shore might yet come along— shore was just hazily visible on the horizon as a line of surf, so close he sometimes thought he might swim it. But where there was shipwreck, there were scavengers and predators, and sharks figured in his hesitation. Being a blue-water sailor bred and born, he was not that good a swimmer, and the fear of sharks and suchlike monsters being well-engrained, he stayed put.

So he watched planks go by, and snagged another one before it escaped, wood almost gone to punk from rot. While he was off his rock and soaking his feet, he hauled the rotten cordage a little higher on his diminished shore, seeing it as a means to tie the whole together. He would make a raft, if enough bits and pieces bumped up against his little refuge.

Of his crew, or the *Fortunate*'s, no sight nor sign, not unless one counted a scrap of cloth or two.

A barrel went by, a mostly empty beef-barrel, it might be, but too far to reach, damn it all. He watched it go.

Then his eye shifted to another thing, a small boat, a scrap of sail, hazy in the distance, inshore of the reef. He watched it. He took off his coat and waved it like a banner. And that boat tacked and came closer, working up the wind, a long, slow process.

There were fishing villages hereabouts. And that was what he saw, as the boat came closer, a small, single-sailed fishing boat, not even a two-man vessel, clumsy and broad of beam, lumbering this way and that as it came.

He stood waiting, finally, as it nosed gingerly up to his perch, riding cautiously where there was water enough to keep its keel off the rock. An old man managed it.

"Cast me a line!" Camargen said, an order—it was habit, and he tried to mend his ways. He saw he'd startled the old man, who sat with his hand on the tiller and his sail swinging back and forth, slack, and the boat just too far to reach. The old man mumbled something unintelligible in the rush and suck of water, then stood up and flung him the line.

Camargen caught it and pulled, the two of them working the boat closer to the rock until it bumped and he jumped aboard, instinctively finding his footing in a slovenly tangle of rope and net.

The old man said something about a ship, a wreck, he made that much out. And then the old man picked up a pole in a menacing way, and held out his hand palm up.

The hell, Camargen said to himself, and several things occurred to

him: one, that this man wanted money, which he had; that the old
man had a weapon he might then use, having said money; and third,
that this was a perfectly serviceable, if stinking, boat.

He grabbed the threatening pole in one bloodied hand, grabbed it
with the other, and wrenched over hard, which carried the startled
old man overside.

He strode aft and grabbed the tiller, hauled the rope in, and
watched the old man splash toward the boat. He let the wind back
the boat off a little, and the old man turned and splashed toward
the rock, where he hauled himself up, dripping, onto the sole safe
refuge.

"I've started a raft there," he called to the old man. "Good luck
to you."

"Damn you," he thought he made out for a reply, but he'd been,
overall, polite. He bowed, and turned the boat before the wind, bringing the sail close, and sailed away, sweet as could be, with a wind off
the quarter and a lubberly old boat that could even sing a bit, once the
wind got behind her.

There were the fishing villages—not necessarily a good thing, to
come sailing into such small places with another man's boat—but
there was plenty of coastline to choose from and there was net and
line. He'd not starve.

But as the shore came nearer he saw a smudge of smoke, smoke
which proved to cover a broad spot on the horizon.

A signal fire, he thought. Was it a smoky signal fire, someone sum-
moning other survivors?

He aimed the little craft for it, and sailed, even kicking up a little
spray from the bow as the wind blew inshore. He was wet. He was
cold, and the wind grew colder as the boat ran, so that he sank down
as much into shelter as he could get, and wrapped a dirty tarpaulin
about himself, leaving only his hand on the tiller and his face exposed to the chill.

The smudge came clearer, as the haze above a settlement, but such
a settlement. He saw other boats, and kept clear of them; and he saw

taller masts, and a huddle of buildings big enough to been seen from a distance through the haze.

It was no village. It was a whole damned town. A city, where no city ought to be.

Anonymity was possible, in such a place of size.

But his charts had been wrong. There was nothing here. There could be nothing.

He sailed closer, no longer quite trusting his senses—his charts, he had greater faith in, but they had proved false. He sailed closer and closer, beyond a short breakwater, to a ship-channel and what was a fair-sized deepwater harbor, with quays all brown, weathered board and precious little paint, the town rising, all brown boards, beyond it. He felt far from conspicuous as he nosed his stolen boat up to the side of a long, sparse boardwalk, tied onto a piling beside a boarding ladder, and climbed up onto the level of the town.

People came and went. Chimneys gave out smoke. Nobody's clothes were in much better case, his having lost most of their color. The harbor stank of fish and the dockside was as scurvy a place as Pirate's Rest up in the Isles. It felt, in short, like a homecoming of sorts.

He walked, still sodden, but no longer quite so cold, down the boards and onto the stony walk of solid ground, walked with a sailor's roll to his step, but not the only such hereabouts.

A harbor with room for ships of size, though he saw nothing larger than a channel-runner in port at the moment in this back-water place. The *Widowmaker* was lost, taking with her the best crew a man could ask, but he was alive, he had gold in his pocket, probably more than adequate for a start in this town, and he could live, gather a small crew about him—and wait for a likely ship to come in. He'd buy new charts, too. Damn the mapmaker.

All around him he heard the fisherman's accent, a handful of words discernible and those few uninformative. He could read signs, spelling as indifferent as any in the Rest. One sign marked an inn, as he took it. It said, THE BROKEN MAST, with a piece of cracked spar above the door.

If a man was looking for fellow seamen, that looked apt enough. Broken Mast it was. He needed a dry place, food, and a bed.

He walked into the mostly deserted inn at this hour, picked the scarred table nearest the fire, and threw himself into a creaking wooden chair.

"Wan drink?" the bartender yelled, and something that sounded like *come here*. Every man in this damned town talked with marbles in his mouth—a dialect, and a muddy one, like the town itself.

There was, however, a universal shortcut. Camargen felt at his waist for his purse and, among its currency of various climes and kingdoms, extracted a coin of small size . . . gold, however. It winked in the general gloom of the place.

"You want this?"

The barkeep drew a big pewter mug and brought it to the table.

"Room," Camargen said, keeping converse to small words, and the barkeep made a try at the coin. "Food," Camargen insisted, retaining it.

They made do with few words, which turned out to involve a small roasted fowl, nondescript greens—welcome, after months at sea—and a bowl of grayish duff, not to mention an upstairs room for an indeterminate number of days, all for the same small coin.

Left to his own devices, Camargen wedged the chair in front of the door, pitched the filthy sheets onto the floor, and slept, rusty sword in hand, for a good number of hours.

Deadly Ritual

Mickey Zucker Reichert

Dysan awakened to sunlight streaming through a high window, dust motes swirling in the beam. He yawned and stretched luxuriously across his pallet of piled straw, enjoying the soft touch of a knitted blanket against his naked flesh. Though a small room, barely three paces across, it seemed like a mansion to him. It still carried the sawdust and mortar scents of new construction, and he could faintly hear the sounds of movement and light murmurs of conversation in the other rooms of Sabellia's haven. He had no furniture, just his two sets of clothing lying in neat piles in each far corner, a chamber pot, and a bowl of water for washing. He could never remember feeling so content, so fabulously wealthy. All this, and the five ladies who spread Sabellia's word, every one of whom he called "Mama."

For the first time, Dysan appreciated the disease that had damaged him in the womb. Its effects, combined with the poison he had unwittingly consumed along with the other Dyareelan orphans slated to die, had stunted any chance he had ever had for normal height. The size of a seven-year-old, he passed for one without much difficulty, though he was already a decade older. The priestesses babied him and worried that he never ate enough to pack weight onto his skinny frame. Someday, they would notice that he never grew at all and begin to wonder about his true age; but, for now, he intended to enjoy their pampering for as long as possible.

Dysan wriggled out of bed and dressed in his regular clothing. Though patched and faded, his tunic lacked the filthy crunchiness to which he had become accustomed; his mothers insisted on regular washings. Thin and soft, it barely kept out the soggy dankness that defined Sanctuary, but it no longer scratched or abraded his skin. He appreciated far less the frequent scrubbings that finally seemed to have banished the mites and fleas that had plagued him most of his life. Though no part of him had properly matured, tooth gritting and mental distraction could not dispel the unholy thoughts that assailed him whenever the youngest of his mothers, SaKimarza, washed certain places.

Dysan pictured her now, her fine Rankan features softened by a cascade of russet hair with just a touch of gold, her body soft and curvy in all the best places. Thoughts of her stiffened him, and he cursed the affliction he had cherished just moments before, the one that allowed this one awkward remnant of adolescence to blossom in an otherwise childish body. She was only five years older than he, yet as unattainable as the goddess herself. He called her "Mama"; she thought he was seven.

Regaining control of his nether regions, Dysan used the chamber pot, then pulled on his leggings. He opened his door and stepped onto the landing of the two-story building that now stood where his ruins once had, on the Promise of Heaven. The upper level held their private bedrooms, the library, and the study. Downstairs, the women cooked, washed, and met with clients, most of whom came for solace, to learn of or admire the goddess, or for advice. His mothers happily entertained anyone who chose to visit, spreading the word and love of Sabellia to the women of Sanctuary, performing with a selfless goodness he had never before experienced. It had all happened so fast; and, even half a year later, he found himself awakened by nightmares that his past had found him despite his mothers- and goddess-protected haven.

As Dysan headed toward the stairs, a grunt of frustration exploded from the library. He changed direction in midstride, effortlessly, and knocked at the door.

He received no answer.

Anyone else would have taken this as a warning, a plea for solitude; but small talk and custom tended to elude Dysan nearly as completely as counting. The infection had warped his mind, damning him to a life without numbers or social competence, even while it made him a raw genius with sounds and language. The Dyareelans had manipulated and pounded that instinctive ability into a talent. Dysan could stare at a bird for an hour and might not recall its size or color when he looked away, yet he could reproduce the exact pattern of its calls and whistles, as well as any conversations that had flowed around him at the time. Anything he heard, with or without intent, remained forever lodged in memory.

Dysan pushed open the door. "Mama?"

Again, he got no answer, though he could clearly see the leader of the order, the Raivay SaVell. She sat in the room's only chair, her back toward him, hunched over a desk covered with an array of books. She wore her steel-gray hair functionally short, and it fell in uncombed feathers to the nape of her neck. She stiffened at his entrance but gave no other sign she heard him.

"Mama?" Dysan trotted toward her.

Finally, SaVell dropped her quill and glanced at Dysan over her shoulder. "Not now, please, Dysan. Why don't you go downstairs? SaShayka can make you some breakfast."

Curious, and oblivious to the edge in her voice, Dysan walked right up to the desk. Two scraps of paper lay in front of SaVell, one badly crumpled and covered with hasty scribbles, the other blank. He stared at the written one for several moments, at first seeing only oddly angled lines and squiggles. Then, his talent kicked in, and the scrawlings arranged themselves into proper words. "What are you doing?"

Apparently resigned to the realization that Dysan was not going away, the Raivay sat back in her chair. She turned her attention onto the boy, her aristocratic features set in irritation. "Dysan, please. I'm trying to do something very difficult, and I'm not having any success. I'm frustrated with the whole project, and I really do wish to be left alone."

"I understand," Dysan murmured, finally getting the point but now too caught up in the writing to obey. "I . . . just wonder . . ." He met the woman's piercing yellow gaze. ". . . what business a good priestess of great and loving Sabellia has with the Bloody Hand."

SaVell's eyes went round as well-minted coins. Her nostrils flared. "What?"

Dysan retreated a step. He did not usually shy from sudden reactions, the way most of the survivors of the Pits did. He had only gotten whipped once and had only felt the first blow land before unconsciousness claimed him. The Dyareelans had known better than to risk their frail, young spy, with his uncanny verbal skills, at least until they found a better one.

"I'm just wondering why you would have such a thing here." He pointed at the wrinkled paper, battling memories that threatened to overtake him, like they had so many times. He would give up his room and comfort, all five of his mothers, to avoid any further interaction with the cultists.

The Raivay did not bother to follow his gesture. "Dysan." She rose from the chair. "Are you quite sure these writings come from . . . them?" She spoke the last word with clear disdain.

Dysan focused on her voice, which kept him lodged in the present. Feeling queasy despite his mental victory, Dysan nodded, his thick black hair barely moving. No matter how often the women combed out the tangles, they always returned by morning.

Still staring, the Raivay SaVell lowered both hands to the desktop. "I've been trying to interpret it all night and morning."

Knowing what the paper contained, Dysan did not understand. "Why?"

"Because a young man brought it here. He said it was priestly writing and promised a generous donation if I translated it for him."

Dysan knew his mothers accepted almost any hard-luck case that came their way. The women had arrived in Sanctuary with money, but he had stolen and spent it in a vain attempt to evict them from his ruins. Now they relied on donations, including the coins Dysan sneaked anonymously into the till from pickpocketing and his thus-far rare hirings. He had no idea how close he had come to replacing what he had pilfered. Five was the highest number he could reliably count, and he knew his mothers would not approve of what he did if they knew it consisted of thieving and spying. "Sanctuary has a linguist. Heliz Yunz—"

SaVell interrupted. "Our visitor says he tried the linguist first. Distractable fellow, apparently, and not particularly agreeable. Our client used more colorful language, but I get the idea that Heliz tends toward . . . let's just say . . . condescension."

Dysan did not mention that he had observed the Crimson Scholar in the Vulgar Unicorn and overheard talk of him as well. The linguist of Lirt maintained a dangerously haughty and arrogant attitude for a man of little size and no martial skill; most dismissed him as an overeducated fool who would not last long in Sanctuary. Dysan's ears told him much more. In a dark corner of Sanctuary, a city well known for its shadows, Heliz had once displayed a magnificent magical power harnessed from words themselves. Like many of the folk in this scummy, backwater town, Heliz Yunz was not what he appeared to be.

The Raivay brought the conversation back to the point. "Dysan, how do you know this writing bears the taint of the Bloody Hand?"

Dysan leaned across the desk to point at the lettering, though he would not touch it. He understood little of magic and worried that the paper might have some ability to suck him into itself, to hurl him back into the years of horror and madness. For an instant he considered placing his fingers upon it for that reason alone. He had despised the life he had barely escaped ten years ago; but, at least then, he still had his beloved brother. "See here." He indicated the upper part of the page and read: "All who inhale when the last in-gredient is added will gain the strength of the blood-eating goddess for a fortnight. Rise up and slaughter thine enemies with thine mighty, bloody hands." He ran an aerial finger down the list. "Here: the in-gredients of the spell and, down below, the order and proper pro-curement . . ."

Suddenly realizing the Raivay had gone preternaturally still, Dysan stopped talking to glance at her. She sat in stunned silence, her hands curled on the desktop, her jaw limp.

When she said nothing, Dysan spoke again. "What?" Defensive-ness colored his tone. He worried that Raivay SaVell might explode. *Now I've gone and done it. I've lost everything.* His head drooped, and the dark tangles fell into his eyes. The past half year had seemed too good to be true; and, now, he believed, he would pay the price.

Finally, the Raivay managed speech. "Dysan, my dear. As long as you've been with us, how come this is the first I knew you could read?"

Dysan shrugged. "No one ever asked."

"Of course no one ever asked." SaVell looked down at the paper, her regal features screwed into an uncomfortable array, as though she had taken a bite of bitter fruit. "One makes assumptions about a child who can't count his own toes. You are a mass of contradic-tions, young man; and I wonder if we will ever find you under all of those layers."

Only glad his oldest mother did not seem angry, Dysan smiled.

"Can you also write?"

Dysan flushed. "Not . . . well." It was an understatement. Though quick and agile when it came to movement, he lacked the fine finger coordination needed for such a task. He could swipe a purse or other object with considerable skill, but his letters came out smeared and wobbly. He interchanged languages without meaning to, much as he had verbally when first learning to speak. He had overcome that flaw with time and assistance. He suspected he could learn to write with enough training, but he had no wish to battle through the frustration and effort.

SaVell turned back to the paper. "What tongue is this in, anyway?"

Dysan's blush deepened nearly to scarlet. "I . . . don't know."

She looked up quickly.

"I don't get it, either," Dysan admitted. "Don't try to make sense of it, Mama. It'll tie your brain in knots."

SaVell laughed, a throaty sound Dysan did not believe he had ever heard before. She had always been the most serious and intent of the group, the most committed to the order, the one who kept the others focused and in line. "Forgive me testing you, but I need to know for sure before I accuse a man of ties to Dyareela." She shoved a book in front of him. "Read this."

This time, the letters took shape much more quickly, as the more familiar Rankene script leaped into bold relief. He read a line carefully, watching Raivay SaVell from the corner of his eye. She studied the words over his shoulder, saying nothing. Not that Dysan needed any encouragement. His language skills were the only thing that had never failed him, and he would trust his own rendition of what the writing said more than even Heliz the linguist's.

At length, SaVell pushed the book aside. She ran a finger along her lips, then tapped them twice. "Remarkable."

Dysan said nothing.

SaVell yawned, rising. "Well, I suppose I should tell our young visitor that we couldn't make sense out of this." She reached for the paper.

"No." The word escaped Dysan's mouth before he realized he intended to speak.

Once more, the gray-haired lady looked at him, awaiting clarification.

"We need his money."

SaVell sighed. She could hardly deny it. A favorite saying of hers was "Food may grow on trees, but you only eat if you own the tree." The Sisters of Sabellia were often so eager to perform good works that they forgot to request payment even for services that demanded it or people who promised. Things loaned out often never returned. A huge Irrune mercenary named Kadasah had twice offered to treat the ladies to meals, then skipped out on the tab. Dysan could not count, but at least he had the business sense to collect on monies promised.

"There's a principle here, Dysan. I'd rather go hungry than spend money tainted by evil."

Ideas floundered through Dysan's mind. "Then skip the donation this time. Once word gets out that the order will translate for pay, other customers can make up the difference."

"Dysan—"

"So we should lie, then?" Dysan knew the suggestion would inflame. His mothers lectured him extensively on the virtue of and need for honesty.

SaVell cringed. "I can tell him the truth, that we don't assist in the workings of evil. That I could translate for him, but I choose not to."

This time, Dysan could not stop the flood of memories that assailed him: mindless children with empty, soulless eyes ripped apart; a screaming, weeping woman with the savagery of starved dogs; a priest triumphantly clutching a severed head over an altar, scarlet rivulets twining down his arms to mingle with a swarm of tattoos. Those visions, and so many more, had left scars more painful than anything the womb disease had inflicted upon him. "They're dead," he forced through gritted teeth, his voice a hoarse whisper.

SaVell dropped her own volume to match his, and her tone gained a touch of gentle and sympathetic magic, the kind that drew out painful confessions like pus from an opened abscess. "Who's dead, Dysan?"

"Them," he said, with venom, battling innocent rage and deep-seated agony. "The Hand. They were all executed. Every . . . single . . . one." He looked at his oldest mother, feeling as vulnerable as he looked. "Right?"

It would only take a single syllable to quell Dysan's fear, but the Raivay SaVell could not voice it. She would not lie to him. Instead, she gathered him into her arms, her words still pitched to soothe. "That's what they say, sweet darling boy."

Dysan was neither sweet nor darling, and he was not a boy any longer. He knew the truth, that nothing so evil ever truly dies. Some-where in the deepest bowels of Sanctuary, a spare few or, perhaps, massive clots of Dyareelans laid low, awaiting their chance to wreak their malicious and brutal form of worship upon the citizenry again. He had heard the buzz in the Bottomless Well, in the Vulgar Uni-corn, in every filthy, sodden alley and every slimy dive throughout the city. He heard everything, whether he wished to or not, and even the complicated and changing verbal codes of those who dwelt in the deepest of Sanctuary's shadows could not escape a talent that sometimes seemed more like a curse. "Mama, you have to do the translation."

The embrace ended in an instant. The Raivay held Dysan at arm's length, as if to read his intentions from the expression on his face. Not for the first time, her eyes seemed to bore through flesh to his very soul. "What?"

"You have to do the translation." This time, Dysan managed to sound self-assured and doggedly certain.

"Why?"

She did not immediately deny him, which Dysan took to mean he might still convince her. "Because we have to know what this man plans to do with it. We have to know if the Hand still exists; and, if so, where."

SaVell nodded awkwardly. Dysan could not read her mood, he rarely could; but he sensed clear reluctance. "Then, I'll translate in-completely. Get an ingredient or two deliberately wrong."

"No!" The word was startled from him. Sweat trickled suddenly down Dysan's back, and a flash of heat prickled through him, followed instantly by ice. He forced his eyes wide open, focused wholly on the single shelf fastened to the wall that held the few books not already on the table. To close his eyes or look at SaVell would bring images of his mothers assaulted by hordes of foul-smelling tattooed men, raped on the altars and dismembered in the name of Dyareela, their screams lost amid the savage cheers, their blood staining the altar. "Please. They will know. Do not cross them." His next words emerged in a pant as he strained against memories he dared not relive one more time. "They . . . will . . . come . . . here . . ."

"Sabellia will protect us."

Dysan wanted to shake her. He wished he could open up his memories to her of innocent priests and priestesses dragged from their prayers by masses of torture-crazed and vicious children who knew only violence, to watch grotesquely tattooed men and women fornicate and defecate upon their altars in Dyareela's name. Those holy men and women died in an excruciating, slow agony, their wits and bodies drained at the same time, their begging and crying only spurring the cultists. Instead, Dysan pointed toward the single window. "Don't you see what remains of the Promise of Heaven? Crumbling, defiled ruins, all of them." He guarded his tongue. "I love Sabellia for all she has brought me, but her temple was not spared."

SaVell sighed deeply. "Dysan, I've seen the scars." He believed she referred to the marks his single beating had stamped permanently upon his back and shoulders. "Gods only know what you went through or why, but surely there are better ways to root out whatever remains of that hideous, disgusting cult."

The old wounds on Dysan's flesh were nothing compared to the ones burnt deep into his psyche. He had never been normal, could never be so, but the Bloody Hand had seen to it that he never forgot his anomalies and weaknesses every moment of every day, and even into sleep. "Write down the translation as I tell it," he begged. "Or I will." It was an idle threat he had little hope of fulfilling.

"And if I do," SaVell said, still staring at him with grim, yellow eyes. "Who will see to it that the ritual written here is not consummated?"

Dysan hoped he sounded more confident than he felt. "Leave that part to me."

Hunkered on the floorboards in the upstairs study, Dysan watched their young male client pace through a knothole in the planking. From his angle, he could not assess height, though it did not seem extraordinary. In fact, nothing about this man seemed remarkable, and that bothered Dysan. He forced himself to take careful note of every detail, using verbal descriptions so they might stick in his memory. It was a trick his Dyareelan handlers had taught him. He could not recall the specifics of objects he saw unless he dissected them down to words. That worked exceedingly well, but he had to choose those particulars carefully. Otherwise, he found himself constantly mumbling, talking his way through everything.

The other had hair as dark as Dysan's own, though not nearly as thick and much sleeker, pulled back into a horse-tail. He wore a tunic and leggings so deep in their blue they might just as well have been black. As if to deliberately offset them, a brilliant cerulean sash encircled his lean frame, and the band that held back his hair matched it perfectly. He wore a sword at his hip and at least one dagger. His walk seemed almost mincing, as though he was concentrating on hiding a natural cocky swagger that eluded his efforts at intervals. Nevertheless, his booted feet made no sound on the floorboards. The awkwardness could not hide a natural, or very well-trained, dexterity. He moved like a cat.

Missing things struck Dysan most. The man's arms bore scars and his palms looked callused, but he did not sport a single tattoo. Despite those work-hardened hands, he dressed well, almost flashily, in garb Dysan could never hope to afford. Only a few years older than Dysan, he would have been a child no older than nine at the time of the Dyareelan purge. If Dysan looked upon a member of the

Bloody Hand, he was a recent recruit, a fact that made Dysan more, not less, uneasy.

The door below swung open, and SaVell stepped inside with the stranger, her face a mask of displeasure. Beside him, her ivory features looked pallid, her gray hair colorless. Only then, Dysan noticed the swarthiness of the man's skin, his thick brows, and well-shaped features. Everything Dysan noted, he transformed into words in his mind. He would not allow himself to forget this man.

"I've brought your translation," the Raivay said.

The man barely nodded, though, when he spoke, he sounded gracious. "I've brought your payment."

"Keep it," SaVell said, her voice a warning growl. "I want only two things from you." She held the papers in a firm grip.

The young man's eyes went from the paper to her face.

"A name. *Your* name. And a promise that you will not use our work for evil."

The man's lips set into a grim line. Dysan wondered if he struggled for the first request or the second. In Sanctuary, a man's past and intentions belonged to no one but himself. "I would not use what you have given me in good faith to harm the decent folk of Sanctuary."

It was a promise full of holes. SaVell had some small magics, but Dysan doubted she could compel the man to keep his word. Dysan held his breath.

SaVell waited, still holding the paper.

"And I am called Lone."

The name brought the last scattered pieces into place. Dysan had seen this man before, in some of the same dark corners he also preferred. He had learned that the youngster, also known as Catwalker, was a thief of great competence and growing renown. Dysan also heard things he should not, things whispered in places honest folk would never dare to go, things that simply knowing could get a man killed. Lone was, some said, the reincarnation of the infamous Shadowspawn. Sources Dysan trusted more claimed he simply apprenticed to what remained of that notorious burglar, a crippled old man long past his second-storey days.

In either case, if men who knew the inner workings of every rat-hole and palace of Sanctuary masterminded the revival of the Dya-reelans, all seemed already lost. *What have I done?* Abruptly Dysan desperately regretted talking his oldest mother into handing over the means to the city's destruction. He had fallen prey to his own pride, believing he could single-handedly stop the resurgence of a maliciously immoral cult that had warped and slaughtered men, women, and children in droves. It had taken the combined might of so many magicians and warriors to unseat them. He wondered what madness had made him think he could deal with this problem alone.

Yet, now committed, Dysan did not hesitate. He hurried down the ladder as the papers changed hands and rushed to follow the young thief into the city. He opened the door a fraction of an instant after Lone exited. As swiftly as Dysan had moved, as prepared as he believed himself, he found the Promise of Heaven empty.

Muttering epithets his mothers would never believe he knew, Dysan headed back inside to grab some breakfast before putting his plan in motion.

Dysan made his way through the Shambles, down Wriggle Way, to the gate of the shop yard of Bezul. This late in the day, any goose the Changer might have forgotten to pen should already have made its presence known. Nevertheless, Dysan tripped the latch with caution, listening for a faint rustle, the light snap of a twig, the coarse honk of an irritable goose. Barely reassured by the silence, he shoved the gate open and stepped into the yard. When nothing feathered charged him, he breathed a sigh of relief and made his way to the shop with quiet and practiced stealth.

Dysan found Bezul alone in the shop that also served as his home, humming while he shifted objects from one dusty shelf to another. As always, the room contained a wide assortment of necessities, strange objects, and sundry bric-a-brac that changed every time Dysan entered. Not wishing to fill his mind with a clutter of details he would have to reduce to words, he did not bother to look around any further than it took to assure that nothing could imminently harm him. Instead, he fixed his attention directly upon the proprietor.

Bezul ceased humming at the sight of Dysan and turned him a welcoming grin from beneath a mop of sandy hair nearly as wild as Dysan's own. He seemed particularly happy, apparently a good day for trading. Dysan was just pleased no other patrons competed for the Changer's attention; and that his two massive temporaries, Jopze and Ammen were not with him. Dysan liked Bezul's wife, Chersey, but making small talk with more than one person at once taxed his limited abilities. He avoided those situations as often as possible, though he knew that, in itself, seemed rude.

As usual, Bezul spoke first. "Good day, Dysan. What can I do for you?"

Dysan breathed a faint sigh of relief, glad the Changer had obviated the need for chitchat. "I . . . was just wondering." He found the words harder to speak than he expected and wished he had rehearsed them.

Bezul dipped his head, encouraging.

Worried someone else might come into the shop, Dysan forced himself to continue. "That man I saw in here, a while ago. Pel, you called him."

"Pel Garwood. The healer. Yes."

"Yes," Dysan repeated, shifting from foot to foot. He let his gaze wander over a shelf of neatly stacked crockery. "You do sell him his . . . flasks and vials and such." He dodged Bezul's gaze. "Don't you, Bez?" He cursed himself for further shortening the man's name. That only encouraged the Changer to do the same to his, and he hated when anyone called him Dys. It reminded him that his name started with the same syllable as the Bloody Mother, Dyareela. He added lamely and too belatedly, ". . . ul, cleared his throat, and put it all together. "Bezul."

Bezul regarded his single patron more intently, squinting, the grin growing slightly. Dysan trusted no one fully, but he relied on Bezul more than anyone else in Sanctuary. He had no way of knowing whether or not the Changer had ever cheated him, but he always managed to buy the things he needed here. When he laid a handful of coins on Bezul's counter in payment, the Changer rarely claimed all of it. "It would seem so, yes. When I have it, I sell or trade him what he needs."

Dysan could not imagine Bezul ever not having anything. No matter what he wanted, he found it here amid the clutter of junk and finery, even the time he sought snakes, rats, and mice. "If I were buying a cure from him today, what would he put it in, do you think?"

For an instant, the Changer's dark eyes showed a spark of curiosity, but he did not ask Dysan's purpose. He never did. Instead, he turned, walked to the opposite side of the room, and perused his inventory. He tapped a finger over generous lips. "A large or small amount of . . . cure?"

The recipe had demanded a single dose of "a treatment for buttocks boils distilled from tamarask bark." It was the only difficult item in the brew, so poorly described that it would take an expert with potions to create it. The other objects, such as salt and red dust, a vat of soured wine, a specified number of rat hairs, the blood of an orphan and a virgin, could come from almost anywhere. "A small amount."

Bezul rummaged through crockery. "So long as there isn't anything that reacts with clay, he would use . . ." His head disappeared among the wares, his toned, round-cheeked bottom swaying as he shifted through the mess for the right piece. He pulled it out and turned simultaneously. ". . . this." He held up a well-cast bottle. "And he'd wrap it in this." He dangled a dingy triangular pouch by the strings.

Without bothering to examine them, Dysan moved to the main counter, mostly free of disorder. He tossed his own small purse onto the top as Bezul came over with his finds. As usual, Dysan dumped the entire contents for Bezul's perusal. Padpols spilled out, more than five by Dysan's crude form of counting. Bezul claimed three, shoved the rest toward Dysan, and handed him the bottle, now swaddled into the pouch. Dysan swept the remaining coins to his purse, tying both at his left hip.

"Dysan."

The young man looked up cautiously, anticipating some sort of warning. Bezul would not question, but he might remind Dysan that the new healer performed an important service for Sanctuary. He would not want to do anything that caused Pel to change his mind about coming to ply his trade in this mudhole. But Bezul said only, "Be well."

Dysan nodded, heading toward the exit. The healer was not his concern. He worried for the future of Sanctuary itself, for the return of the murders and maimings. He could not risk his new mothers; they came from an imperial world where the politics had more to do with money than survival. They opened their hearts and home too easily, and they trusted men whose own fathers would not dare share a confidence. Pel was a stranger to Dysan, one who bore a striking and terrifying resemblance to a cultist Dysan had once known. That likeness kept him a cautious distance from Sanctuary's new healer and the Avenue of Temples, though a neighboring street to his own. The many shattered buildings in the area gave him plenty of places to hide and watch the patients who came and went from Pel's growing building. Not all of them seemed innocent or wholesome.

Dysan headed there now, trotting down streets that grew more familiar daily, choosing a route that took him through as many darkened alleys as main thoroughfares. He changed his manner from habit as he entered each one: winding congenially through the regular masses or slouching through the puddled shadows of the alleys. Feigning focus allowed him to appear deaf to the conversations, though he heard, and inadvertently memorized, every one. It allowed him to dodge the small talk that usually defied him and the cutpurses seeking larger and easier prey. He stopped only once, to partially fill his new-bought bottle from a washerwoman's tub.

At length, Dysan reached the home and shop of Sanctuary's

healer, every bit as new as his own, yet not quite finished. The Sisters of Sabellia had prepaid for the stonemasons and builders with a large amount of money that came from their temple in Ranke. Pel, on the other hand, had had little coinage, forced to barter his trade for the work and materials to rebuild a crumbling temple bit by bit. Like Dysan, Pel had suffered Sanctuary's dark and icy winter without adequate protection, but Dysan believed he had a lot more experience. Now, they both had four solid walls and a roof that shed the rain, though Pel's was not yet completed.

Well-hidden in a dense patch of greenery that had sprang up amid the wreckage of Ils's temple, Dysan watched people come and go from Pel's apothecary. Some approached boldly, others limped or came steadied by friends or family, and one woman sneaked to the door beneath the cover of a dark hood, mincing every step as if stalking the building. Pel took them all inside in turn, nodding his head and shaking his long, white-veined hair. Some left empty handed, others with a hidden bulge at their waists or clutched tightly beneath their cloaks. A few openly carried bottles that looked much like the one Bezul had sold to Dysan. Fewer still threw guilty or nervous glances around the neighboring wreckage before slinking, red-faced, from the apothecary. No one visited after nightfall, but Dysan continued to watch until Pel extinguished the last candle, leaving his newly built home as dark and hulking as the ruins all around it. Only then, Dysan realized he had eaten nothing since breakfast.

Swiftly, he headed home. His mothers rarely questioned his comings and goings anymore, but they would force food upon him. He did not intend to protest.

Dysan resumed his vigil just before sunup the following day, pressed deeply into a tiny crevice of a mostly toppled wall that had once served the followers of Vashanka. His handlers had taught him how to twist, stretch, and bundle his undersized body into holes more fit for rats than men. He found the tight quarters secure and surprisingly comfortable. Though he had tried to sneak out without awakening his mothers, SaMavis had beaten him to the larder and forced a midday meal upon him. It now lay, still wrapped in a tattered rag, near the shambles of an altar. Smashed artifacts studded the mushy ground, long ago looted of anything valuable. Nervous excitement kept Dysan's stomach in knots, and he regretted the few bites of breakfast he had managed to swallow.

Wedged into his hiding place, Dysan watched the comings and goings of Pel Garwood's patients through the morning, seeing patterns where none had previously existed. He noticed many of the same people who had left with nothing the day before now held bottles in their hands or concealed in folds or sashes, their purses flatter. The elderly widow Sharheya, who owned the northside lumberyard, arrived with her son-in-law, the surly sawyer Carzen. Pel opened his door and waved them inside; but, unlike the others, Carzen did not comply. The three exchanged words, not wholly civil by their expressions and gestures. Then, Pel shut his door and led the other man around his shop and home, indicating a large area of his roof completely devoid of planking. Only a thickly oiled sheet of canvas protected Pel and his valuables from the elements, and that would not last long in a place as stark and damp as Sanctuary. Already, the wind worried at the edges, tattering them into streamers. Only half the roof had secure boards in place, and not a single tile had yet been laid. Carzen nodded grudgingly.

Again, Pel opened his door for the pair, and, again, Carzen refused the invitation. Pel entered alone, swiftly returning with a large bottle in a rough-sewn pouch. As famed for his discretion as his potions, clearly unaccustomed to handling transactions on his doorstep, Pel looked more nervous than his clients as he handed the pouch to Sharheya. No money exchanged hands, and the pair left, the woman clutching her potion like a gleeful toddler with a new doll. Those two had not visited the day before, and Dysan guessed they had a standing order that Pel delivered weekly or monthly to ease some chronic discomfort.

Still Dysan waited, seeking some sign of Lone among the healer's other patrons. He had assumed the young thief had gone straight to Pel after disappearing from Dysan's view, transacting his business in the time Dysan had shopped with Bezul. He doubted a cure for buttocks boils would prove that exotic or difficult, though a man might not wish for others to know of such ills. He doubted shame would hold Lone back, though; payment bought Pel's silence as well as his wares.

A worrisome thought struck Dysan. In some cases, the healer might deliver his potion the day of its request. Perhaps Pel kept some on hand or the customer waited while he mixed the order. *What if the whole transaction went down yesterday? What if, at this very moment, the worshippers of the froggin' Bloody Mother are already mixing their vile concoction?*

The thought spiraled a chill through Dysan, and he suddenly felt trapped. He eased from the crack in the construction, seized by an urge to run. Screams and sobs filled his ears, broken images of steaming entrails tossed onto stone-cold altars, the overpowering stench of blood and sex and death. He had never left the confines of the ironically named city. Despite all he had heard, he felt caged within Sanctuary's borders, as if the world beyond was only a figment of men's imaginations. He pictured himself sprinting in frenzied circles while Dyareela consumed the entire city in an enormous blood-flooded, shite-stinking repast.

No! Dysan screwed his eyes and mind shut. *It's still early. Lone may still come.* He wished the Raivay had not trusted him so much, wished he had not sounded so confident when he said he could handle the repercussions of giving over the proper translation of the old Dyareelan scriptures. As much as he needed the women's mothering to rescue him from the barbarity the Hand had battered into him nearly since infancy, they needed his experience and suspicious mind to save them from their own instinctive kindness, which often bordered on naiveté.

Dysan melted back into the shadows of the ruin. Banishing the past from his thoughts, he concentrated on trying to predict Lone, a task that seemed nearly impossible. From what he understood, Shadow-spawn had selected his thefts with care. A notorious cat burglar of astounding competence, he rarely if ever stooped to common thievery. To follow in the master's footsteps, Lone would have to pattern that behavior. Serving the will of the cultists seemed beneath him.

Yet, Dysan had become jaded enough to believe that money might drive any man to serve the will of evil. Perhaps Lone did not understand the slaughter that could result from assisting Dyareelans, or he did not care. Curiosity was a capital crime in Sanctuary, where silence and secrecy cost less than tangible goods. Men who asked too many questions did not live long here.

As the sun sank slowly toward the horizon, Dysan continued to wait and watch. Color touched the sky, dimmed by Sanctuary's infernal dampness. Dysan's gut finally rumbled, and he slipped from his new hiding place to claim the wrapped parcel SaMavis had given him. It contained a veritable feast: crusty bread soaked in last night's grease, dried fish twisted into a cheerful braid, and two shriveled apples. Dragging the food to his vantage point, Dysan spied a tall, wary-looking man dressed in a cloak too warm for the season slithering from the apothecary with a bottle-shaped pouch at his belt. With only a swift glance left and right, he headed into the deepening twilight.

A moment later, another figure emerged from the fog, a creation of mist and shadow that appeared to arise from a shattered wall and hurried along the Avenue of Temples. Dysan recognized him at once, though his utter darkness muted into the gloom: black clothing and buskin boots, ebony hair, darkish skin. *Lone.* Dysan had missed whatever exchange had occurred between Pel and the thief, apparently in those sparse moments when he had dared to unwrap his meal. Dropping the fish, Dysan padded soundlessly into the twilight, attention fixed unwaveringly on Lone. His quarry had disappeared on him once and never again. Dysan could not afford to lose Lone now that he carried the most difficult of the Dyareelan's ingredients. Once mixed, that potion had the potential to destroy Sanctuary again, to initiate another rampage of murder.

The gray dank of evening deepened as Dysan followed Lone through the city. Both men moved as soundlessly as the shifting shadows, Lone with natural ease and Dysan from desperation. Twice, Lone paused, melting into his surroundings as if sensing his tail and seeking him among the regular stalkers of Sanctuary's roads and alleyways. Both times, Dysan found a ledge or crevice that fully hid him from the other man's view. Neither attempt lasted long. Apparently intent on a goal of his own, Lone clearly did not have time to ferret out his tracker in the filthy, wild tangle of streets.

So focused on his own target and the terrifying concern that he might lose the young man to darkness, Dysan did not notice the cloaked figure until Lone came directly upon it. The same man who had most recently left the apothecary now stood momentarily still in a place of silent darkness, measuring his path in the twilight. Agile as a cat, Lone slipped up beside him. Few would have noticed the fingers that dexterously untangled pouch strings from the other's belt; but Dysan, trained to notice exactly such things, did. Lone had skill, though he clearly lacked practice. Dysan followed every nimble motion, using the distraction to carry out a theft of his own. Freeing his pouched bottle from his sash, he sneaked to Lone's side and made the exchange.

The cloaked man gave no sign that he noticed either of the thieves.

Lone moved faster than thought. He spun toward Dysan, catching a handful of hair in a strong fist. A blade pricked Dysan's abdomen, impaling his tunic and drawing a drop of blood. Had Dysan stood the proper height for a man his age, Lone's hand would have his throat, and the knife would have threatened his left kidney. Startled more than hurt, Dysan loosed a screech and dropped the bottle. It thumped to the ground, rescued from breaking by the cloth pouch.

The cloaked figure swung around at the sound. He pawed at his waist, then dove for the fallen pouch. "Hey, you thief! That's mine!"

Dysan tried to run, but Lone's grip tightened, and he shoved. Dysan's back slammed against a wall. Pain shocked through him, and he bit his tongue hard enough to draw more blood. Dazed, he barely had a chance to sag before Lone caught him properly by the neck, the dagger still menacing his vitals.

The cloaked figure glanced at the two only an instant before snatching up the bottle and sprinting into the night.

Dysan stared into Lone's face, trying to hide his terror. The grim black eyes revealed nothing, and he had the predatory features of one accustomed to murder. Dysan knew he was going to die and horribly. He had seen that expression on the faces of the other Dyareelan pit-slaves, before they tore a man to pieces, laughing and howling with glee. His mouth went painfully dry, and he could feel his heart pounding like a hammer against his ribs. The situation, the rabid features, jogged a memory. Dysan abruptly realized he knew this man, and not only from the rumors writhing through the underground. Ten years ago and longer, this young man had shared the Pits of Dyareela with him. The Hand had called him Flea-Shit, one of many charming names they gave the children they trained to bloody service and also used as sacrifice. Lone had never claimed another name, so the orphans called him Nil, because where he clearly stood, they might find nothing an instant later.

"Nil," Dysan managed hoarsely. "Is that . . . you?"

Lone's expression hardened, and he examined Dysan in the failing light.

Dysan tried to look brave, uncaring. Fear often inspired carnivores to blood frenzy, driving them to attack. Courage where fear should be made them cautious.

Finally Lone spoke, "Dysan?" When he did, his grip and expression relaxed slightly. Though not a happy reunion, at least Lone no longer seemed intent on tearing out Dysan's throat or slicing up his vitals. Neither wanted any reminder of their time in the Pits. Lone added coldly, "Don't call me that. Not ever again." He released his hold so suddenly, Dysan fell to the muddy ground.

Scrambling to his feet, Dysan clutched his own throat and nodded.

With a silent swirl of black cloth, Lone turned his back, the ultimate gesture of disdain. When a man so wary makes himself vulnerable, it is only because he knows the other is too weak or incompetent to harm him. "You have no idea what you just did."

Dysan believed he might, if he only had a couple of answers. "That paper you had translated. You stole that from still-living Hand?"

"Yes." Lone glanced over his shoulder, giving Dysan a hint of credit. "But they already had the potion mostly done. Once I knew what they needed, I realized they would send someone for that last ingredient, the one that required a healer to make."

Suddenly, it all came together. Dysan felt like the worst of fools for believing Lone himself worked for the cult. "The cloaked man."

Now, Lone turned back to face Dysan. He held a stance of supreme confidence, as if the entire world would bend to his whim, if he only asked. "I relieved him of that necessary ingredient. Then you, you . . ." He bit back whatever insult had nearly left his lips. Calling another pit-child sheep-shite stupid would only make him sound like the despicable masters they had escaped. ". . . you gave it back!"

"No." Dysan displayed the other cloth-wrapped bottle, the one he had stolen from Lone. "It's safe. It's here."

Lone took the parcel from Dysan's hand, pulled out the bottle, and studied it. He returned his attention to Dysan, his assurance only a trifle wilted. "This is . . ."

"The potion." Dysan smiled. "I switched it when I thought you carried . . ."

Lone opened the bottle and took a cautious sniff before dumping the contents into the sodden murk of Sanctuary's alley. Only after the entire potion lay splattered in the mud, Lone asked, "So . . . what was in the other bottle? The one the Hand will pour into their brew and inhale?"

"Nothing special." Dysan shrugged. "I just wanted the ritual to fail. It's only water from a bleaching vat."

"A bleaching vat?" For an instant, Dysan thought he saw a sparkle pass through those flat-black killer's eyes. "A bleaching vat?" Lone huffed out an unexpected laugh, a sound clearly unfamiliar to his usually deadly and serious repertoire. When a confused Dysan did not join his mirth, Lone explained, "The other main ingredient in that . . . mix of theirs is a vat of soured wine."

Dysan knew that. He had made the translation. "Yes."

"Do you know what happens when you mix bleach and vinegar?" Lone laughed again, this time with clear pleasure. "Deadly poison. One whiff, Dysan. That's all it takes."

Dysan imagined the priests calling upon their hideous, twisted Mother, their hands mottled and sticky with tattoos, red ink, and blood. As the last ingredient entered the pot, they all sucked in a deep breath, seeking strength and finding only the death they had inflicted on so many others. He only hoped it was a painful way to die. He looked to Lone to ask him, but the other man had already melted into the growing shadows. Where he had once stood, Dysan saw nil, nothing.

A smile on his face, Dysan ignored the pain still throbbing through his neck. His mothers would wonder about the tear in his tunic, the scratch on his belly, the bruises in the shape of fingers across his throat, but they would accept whatever explanation he gave them.

Then, they would feed him.

Pricks and Afflictions

Dennis L. McKiernan

Two words of many meanings . . .

Glog!

The wave shoved Rogi down again, and a great bubble exploded from his mouth as he spat the oath underwater: *"Thshite!"*

Rogi fought his way upward, yet even as he broke through the surface—*thnk!*—the box slammed into the back of his head.

Down went Rogi once more, the little hunchback now caught in the undertow and dragged along the mud and silt and sand.

In spite of his panic, in spite of clawing for purchase even as the powerful riptide slammed him repeatedly into the bottom and rolled him and tossed him somersaulting, *Ith thith the end of Rogi?* he wondered.

Just moments before, as he'd stumped along the western shore of the White Foal and swatted mosquitoes and shooed away gnats and picked off leeches while he hunted the rats who frequented the fringes of the Swamp of Night Secrets, rats that occasionally came out from the reeds to the shoreline to hunt small crustaceans and perhaps lick salt from the rocks, as the sinking sun hung low in the sky, Rogi had "thspotted a chetht" tossing to and fro in the white-caps and tricky currents 'round the Hag's Teeth, there where the furious rush of the White Foal met the cold surge of the sea. He saw the curious markings—runes mayhap—carven into the sides, and he guessed that it was something "thpethial." Perhaps the rumors were true about the strange wreck out on the Seaweal Reefs; maybe this chest had come from there. Quickly, Rogi had stripped off his clothes, pausing momentarily to admire his dragon, and then he had plunged headlong into the heavy waves yet cresting from a blow somewhere far out to sea. The shock of the cold water shrank his dragon down to minuscule proportions, but Rogi persevered, swimming an ungainly sidestroke against the white-crested billows rolling in from the south, and the swirling, gurgling river current rushing down from the north. With water cascading over him and the long red hair growing only on the right side of his head whipping about in the currents, gasping between crests, he made his way outward to fetch this curious artifact . . . or so he hoped it might be. After all, if it were "thomthing thpethial" his "mathter" would reward him handsomely . . . perhaps even enough to visit the ladies above the Yellow Lantern and make his dragon happy.

But then a breaker had smashed him under and a swell had lifted him up and he had been hit in the back of the head by the box, and another roller had hammered him under again, where the undertow had grabbed him and hurled him along the bottom. And he had no air, yet needed to breathe, but could not, deep down as he was. And as he tumbled, the swift-running undercurrent crashed him against the skeletal ribs of the rotted remains of a long-drowned hulk, its keel deeply buried in the muck.

Desperately, Rogi grabbed at the wooden beam and managed to hang on, and then, as if climbing a tree, he shimmied his way up the curved member, his diaphragm pumping hard against his clenched-

shut lips, seeking to draw *anything* into his lungs, whether it be air
or not. And with black spots swirling before his eyes . . . all of a
sudden was free of the seaward pull of the deep tow.

Now hastily scrambling upward, but still clinging to the sunken
ship's paling and with darkness sucking at his mind, at last his head
broke free of the water, and—*ghuuuuh!*—he sucked in sweet, sweet
air, though with the offshore breeze blowing out from the swamp,
others might not call it "sweet." Yet to Rogi, nothing else in the
troughs between combers had ever been so precious as the odiferous
stench he sucked into his burning lungs.

With waves yet crashing over him, Rogi tried spotting the chest,
the little hunchback scanning about in the surge. "Dogths ballths!"
he shouted—*glug!*—as another billow washed by, "I've lotht it!" for
he could see nought of the box tossing among the foaming crests.

Turning loose of the hulk's rib, Rogi began awkwardly side-
stroking in the direction of the tops of the waving reeds he could
now and then see above the billowing whitecaps, and, struggling, at
last he reached footing, muddy silt and sand though it was.

Waves knocked him down several times ere he gained the shore
and, drenched, water runnelling from his completely hairless left
side but sopping his extremely hirsute right, he made his way toward
his clothing.

Rogi dressed quickly against the chill, for though the summer air
was warm, the waters of both the ocean and the White Foal were
startlingly cold. Even as he pulled on his breeks, he paused momentarily to mourn over his poor wrinkled dragon, but then hauled the
pants up to his waist and cinched tight the rope he used for a belt.
Throwing on his shirt with its too-long sleeves, he plopped down
and slipped into his floppy-topped socks, one of his toes seeking
freedom through a hole. At last he slipped into his shoes, with scrap
leather stuffed inside to make him taller than his considerably short
four foot six, though, hunched over as he was most of the time, he
seemed more like three foot four. Finally, he flopped a great length
of his long red hair from the right side of his head over the bald left

side—the mother of all comb-overs, someone at the Vulgar Unicorn had called it—and jammed on his ear-flapped cap, tying the cord under his chin.

As he turned to take up his blowpipe and drugged darts, "Vathan-kath'th member!" he cried, for in the fading light and washed ashore not ten feet away lay the rune-marked chest.

Hâlott looked up as the sound of a timid tap tapping came down the stairs from the weatherworn, heavy-planked, iron-bound door. "Rogi!" he hissed, his whispery voice sounding much like that of dead leaves stirring in a cold wind.

Moments passed and the familiar scuttle of Rogi's waddle did not come.

"Rogi!" again Hâlott called out, if a hoarse rasping can be said to be a call.

Tap-tap came the soft knock.

Still Rogi did not respond.

"Pah." Hâlott set aside the long, thin-bladed flaying knife and stepped away from the half-skinned corpse on the table and headed for the stairs leading up to the first floor.

Tap-tap.

With skeletal, black-nailed fingers, Hâlott lifted the latch and swung the door inward. Just beyond stood a woman in a dark brown, coarse-spun cloak held tightly 'round.

She cast back her hood. "My lord—" she began, and looked up into Hâlott's face, and gasped and recoiled, half turning as if to flee. But then she mastered her panic, though not her rapidly beating heart and once more she faced this reputed necromancer. Before her she saw a tall, gaunt, cadaverous, dried-up, dark-robed being; perhaps he had once been a man, but no longer it seemed. He had parchmentlike yellowish brown skin stretched tightly over his completely bald skull, his face nought but sunken-in, hollow cheeks and a narrow, desiccated, hawklike nose, and his eye sockets covered with the skin of eyelids sewn shut. Even so, false eyes he had—painted in kohl—and the young woman flinched at the sight of them, for they reminded her of the markings on a death's head moth. Long, bony, grasping fingers he had, and bony limbs from what she could see of his wrists and arms jutting out from partly rolled-up voluminous sleeves. And when his cadaverous whisper came—"Well?"—she was certain she was speaking to a corpse.

Hâlott on the other hand saw before him a young woman, and surely a lady, for beneath the coarse-spun cloak she wore the quality and cut of her garments told a tale. Too, her ginger hair was well coifed and in the latest style, and she was quite clean. Her nails were well manicured, and she wore a ruby ring on a finger of her right hand, a ring Hâlott recognized.

"What brings you here from the court, my lady?" Hâlott whispered.

She gasped. "How did you—?"

"I am Hâlott," replied the necromancer, as if that explained all. "Won't you step into my—"

"No, no," she blurted, drawing back from this, this *creature*. And she twisted the ring from her finger. "Lady Na— um, my mistress commanded me to bring you this." Her hand trembled as she gingerly held out the ring, the circlet tentatively grasped between thumb and finger, the maiden no doubt hoping against hope that she wouldn't come into contact with Hâlott's withered digits. "Though I can see nothing wrong with it, my mistress says it needs repair. Yet when I suggested Thibalt the Rankan—Thibalt the Jeweler—could mend any ring, she said it must come to you. And so . . ."

Hâlott's blue-tattooed lips twitched in what was perhaps meant to be a grin, but appeared more like a grotesque facial tic instead. Again his hollow whisper sounded: "When?"

"My lady says she needs it two days hence, for she would wear it at the courtyard gathering three days from now." In spite of the repellent being before her, the young woman's face lit in anticipation. "We are celebrating the visit of per-Arizak—he usually stays up in the hills, you know—and just about everyone will be there, and my mistress would wear her bloodred stones."

"Bloodred. How fitting," said Hâlott, and again he smiled, this time more widely, his rictus exposing yellowed teeth.

The woman flinched back.

Hâlott held out his hand, palm up, and said, "Come back at this time two days hence. Tell—tell your mistress it will be ready by then."

With relieved smile on her face, for she did not have to touch the yellowed and no doubt dead skin, the young woman dropped the ring into Hâlott's hand and turned and fled.

At the palace, Nadalya, the golden-haired second wife of Arizak, stood in an alcove and whispered to fair-haired Andriko, and from the cast of his face and hair he, like Nadalya, was clearly of Rankan blood. The tongue they spoke was neither Rankene, Ilsigi, Irrune, nor even the bastardized Wrigglie. Instead in hushed tones they spoke Yenizedi, a language not likely to be understood by anyone else in this part of the palace.

"Driko, I would have you ride into the hills and find me a hornet's nest, or that of wasps," she murmured as the setting sun shone through a nearby casement and cast a ruddy light over all. "Make certain that it is plugged or contained in some manner so that they cannot escape, though I will need a means to set them free."

"My lady?" Andriko's blue eyes widened in disbelief. "A hornet's nest? Oh, 'tis the season, and I've seen one out in the hills, but hornets, wasps?"

Momentarily, Nadalya's face flashed in ire, but then she smiled and said, "Yes, Driko. I would have the nest, a large one at that, with many of the stingers inside. It is for a . . . demonstration I have in mind."

Andriko shrugged nonchalantly, though a bit of a frown of puzzlement yet lingered on his face. "I can get a small wooden cask or box and enclose a nest therein."

Nadalya nodded, but then her eyes lit up. "Better yet, Driko, seal them in a clay jar, one that is easily broken."

"A clay pot when broken, my lady, makes a sound."

"Oh, Driko, you are right. Perhaps a box is better."

"Yes, my lady," said Driko. "When do you need this—?"

"No later than early morn three days from now, Driko."

"The day of the courtyard affair?"

"Yes, Driko. Then."

Twilight fell and great clouds of mosquitoes and gnats rose up from the swamp. And on its fringes and dragging the chest by one of its brass handles, Rogi struggled along the west bank of the White Foal, now and again forced into the racing water by a stubborn out-jut of reeds. And every time he had to do so, the rush of the current nearly tore the prize from his grasp. *"Blathsted thwamp!"* he muttered, his long, long tongue causing his incurable lisp. Often he stopped to swat at the "bloodthucking petht" buzzing about, and to pick off a leech or two, but at last he reached the end of the reeds, where he paused momentarily to rest. As he stood panting, he knuckled away sweat runnelling down his hairless left brow and into that eye; as well, he flicked sweat from his single, hairy eyebrow—the only one he had, and that over his right eye—and he looked at the rune-marked box. Some mere three feet long, two feet deep, and two feet wide, it didn't look all that heavy. Still, Rogi recked that it was at least twice his own weight. And though the handles were brass and the bottom was brass plated, the bulk of it seemed made of gilded wood. Perhaps what was within was what made it so heavy, yet Rogi could find no lock nor latch nor lid nor anything else by which to open it. "My mathter will know how to get inthide."

After a short rest he took up the journey again, dragging the chest after. *If the White Foal wathn't tho thwift, I could float thith boxth nearly all the way to my mathter'th tower.*

But the waters of the 'Foal *were* swift, and so Rogi dragged the chest toward the ford. Reaching it at last, gasping and struggling, he hauled the box into the knee-deep flow, but halfway across he stumbled and fell, and lost his grip on the container, and it bobbed off downstream. "Oh, no, you don't, you pieth of thsheep-thshite!" shouted Rogi, rising up and floundering after, falling—*glug!*—rising up again, falling once more, but finally catching the case in the swiftening current just ere it reached the narrows where it deepened beyond his head.

Struggling, Rogi managed to gain the shallows, and, with water runnelling from him, he drew the floating box through the ford until he came to the upstream end of the crossing, and there he dragged it onto the bank and rested once more. At last, he took up the effort again, and began hauling the container overland, following the White Foal northerly, until he came to the trace that led toward Hâlott's tower.

At that juncture and in the darkening dusk, a young woman in a brown cloak going the opposite way came hurrying down the trail, and before Rogi could catch his breath and offer to let her see his dragon, she veered wide of him and shrieked, "Get away from me, you ugly little thing!" and fled toward town.

Shrugging, Rogi grabbed a handle of the chest and dragged it along the faint path toward the tower. Finally he reached the door and pushed it open. Grunting, dripping, he hauled the box into the darkened chamber, then splopped about, his shoes squishing as he lit lanterns—for although Hâlott with his painted-on eyes seemed to need no light to see, Rogi was not as fortunate. And so he struck strikers and filled the dusty chamber with luminance, all the while shouting, "Mathter, Mathter, come and thsee what it ith I have dithcovered! It'th a thecret boxth! A thecret boxth! Come quick and open it!"

When Rogi awakened the next day, still his "mathter" had not managed to find the way to open the chest. Hâlott had spent all night trying to discover the secret, yet he had failed. Even so, he had seemed overly excited when he had first seen what it was that Rogi had dragged in, if a tensing of his corpselike body could be said to be uncontained excitement. And he had traced the runes carven into the wood, or whatever it was the case was made of, all the while muttering in an arcane language under his breath, a language Rogi didn't know, and given Rogi's lengthy life's experiences, it was rather odd that he hadn't a clue to what this tongue might be.

Finally Rogi, exhausted from his labors and unable to sustain the excitement of what might be in the chest, had left Hâlott to his unsuccessful attempts and had gone down to his dank quarters in the fourth sub-basement under the tower and had promptly collapsed into sleep.

But that was last evening and now it was midday, and Hâlott still hadn't managed to open the box, though somehow he had managed to get the heavy container up on a table.

"Perhapth it takth a thecret word to open it, Mathter," suggested Rogi, clambering up onto a stool to observe. "Have you tried a thecret word? I know theveral thecret wordth, and—"

Hâlott made a sharp gesture of dismissal.

"Did you try to thlip thomething under thomthing elth? I have thome thkinny knivth that we could—"

Again, Hâlott made the gesture, only this time he whispered a hollow groan of sorts, a groan that Rogi knew represented a growl of rage.

Still— "Did you try prething thomething and then thomething elth? I could preth on thomething while you preth on thomething elth and—"

Hâlott's whispered groan got louder.

"We can alwayth thmack it with a thledge hammer," suggested Rogi. "One really good thmack with a thledge hammer and I bet it would—"

The necromancer whirled on the little hunchback, and how Hâlott managed to glare with painted-on eyes Rogi did not understand, nevertheless a glare it was.

"Yeth, Mathter, I'll be thilent." Rogi got down long enough to fetch a piece of bread and a hunk of cheese from the cupboard. He was the only one of the two who seemed to take any sustenance, though he suspected that Hâlott did something with the corpses he seemed always to be cutting into or dismembering or flaying or draining of blood or raising up in a ghastly semblance of life. Maybe Hâlott drank the blood, or ingested some other bodily fluid to keep life flowing through his own collapsed veins. Regardless as to whatever it might be that Hâlott did, Rogi would just as soon dwell in ignorance than to truly know.

Rogi waddled back to the table and clambered up onto his stool, and, in spite of his promise, as Hâlott pushed and prodded on the case, Rogi grunted and sucked air in between clenched teeth, and moaned, and fluttered his lips, and—

"Rogi," hissed Hâlott, jerking his head toward the little hunchback, dried muscle and sere tendon and ancient bone creaking like twisting rope, "You will go now into the woods and forage for the *kastor ricinus*."

"Thothe little brown beanth that made me thshite and thshite until I thought my thtomach wath going to oothe out of my athend . . . and I only ate one? Thothe beanth?"

"Yes, those beans. Bring me a handful."

Rogi shuddered and sighed but said, "Yeth, Mathter."

He hopped down off the stool, and, stuffing the uneaten remainder of his bread and cheese into a pocket, he took up a small empty pouch and his blowpipe and poison darts, and he set off out the door and stumped 'round the tower and into the hills, heading toward the last place he had found the poisonous bounty.

As Nadalya came into the chamber, the coterie about Naimun suddenly fell silent. She smiled sweetly at the various members, and then at her eldest son. Some among the group bowed, while others merely canted their heads, depending on whether they saw her as a lady of Ranke and wife of the current ruler of Sanctuary—as she was—or merely the fair-haired daughter of a well-to-do wine merchant and not of royal lineage, or as a degraded woman, degraded because she had become the number-two wife of an uncouth, Irrune outlander, king though he was.

Fair-haired and handsome in a coarse, heavyset way, Naimun's thick lips curved upward in a smile. "Mother," he said.

"La, my son," said Nadalya, her tone merry, her hazel eyes atwinkle. "Take care, for if you and your group fall silent when one outside your circle enters the chamber, why, one might think you were plotting."

Even as she laughed in blithe unconcern, still her gaze took in every nuance of the group—*Some of those fools actually looked away.* But one of them, Nidakis, held his composure and stepped forward and deeply bowed. As the young man straightened and brushed his black hair from his dark eyes he said, "We were merely stunned by the light of your presence, my lady."

"Oh, my, a flatterer, I see," replied Nadalya, smiling. "Beware this one, Naimun. He is like to turn your head."

To one side, ginger-haired, freckled Caliti quickly glanced at Naimun and then looked down at the floor.

"Mother, where are you off to?" asked Naimun.

Nadalya sighed. "Your father seems rather pained by his leg this day, and I go to cheer him and to beg him to be at the courtyard gathering in two days to help us celebrate the visit of per-Arizak, the Dragon. Seldom does Ariz come down from the hills, and I would have him know he is welcome in his father's house."

"Indeed, my dear lady," said Nidakis, "an event that Lord Arizak should attend, can his health permit him to formally welcome his eldest son. And so, let us not cause you to tarry, as pleasant as that might be."

Nadalya grinned and tilted her head. "Naimun, 'ware my words, for this second son of Lord Kallitis is a wily one and likely to charm you blind."

With that she stepped on past the young men and into the corridor beyond, where her merry mood vanished, and her gaze grew hard. *They plot to set Naimun on the throne, and therefore they plot against Raith. For that they will pay, though but one at a time. And Nidakis: the chief schemer, that one, his smooth words those of a serpent, a seducer of minds, including Naimun's. Should Naimun gain the throne, instead of my beloved Raith, Nidakis would stand in the shadows and whisper in Naimun's ear and thereby actually rule. Well, we shall see about that. Indeed, we shall see.*

In his tower, with a disgusted grunt—if a whisper can be said to resemble a grunt—Hâlott finally gave up on the chest. It was beyond his skill to open. Nevertheless, there were some in Sanctuary who might succeed where he had failed. He considered several:

Tregginain? No, too incompetent.

Dysan? Too young. No experience with puzzles and locks, I think.

Spyder? Some say he moves like a cat burglar, but there is an aura about him that does not speak of thief. I will have to look into him one day. —Ha! Look into him. Hâlott's blue-tattooed lips twitched in what was for him a grin at his unintended double entendre.

Pegrin the Ugly might do, even though he seems to have given up his thieving ways, now working as he does for a steady wage at the 'Unicorn. Still, it might be that he will take on a commission, even though he seems appalled by my appearance.

Then there is that young one known as Lone, though perhaps he is nought but a cat burglar.

Ah, wait. There is one even better. I will send Rogi to fetch him.

Satisfied with his decision, Hâlott patted the chest and then turned to the ruby ring. It was time to begin that commission.

Rogi scrambled up the thorny slope and over the crest, and down into the grassy vale beyond. In moments he had come to the stand of *kastor ricinus* plants. At the first of them, a rather tall one, he pushed aside the large, bronze-green star-shaped leaves, some of them with a purplish tint down their centers, and he looked for the spiny, seed-bearing pods. Since the warm season was upon them, surely there should be some. Yet, after long examination, it seemed there were none.

Rogi moved further into the stand of the smooth-stemmed shrubs, and once more failed to find any bean pods.

A bit farther in, he spotted a number of the spiky husks yet clinging to the inner branches, and Rogi pushed through to get them.

He had nearly filled the small pouch, when he heard the sound of a horse coming over the rise and down into the vale. Rogi froze so as not to be seen, for oft had he been harassed by bravos looking for a bit of sport, but for Rogi it was maltreatment. Of course, the moment they discovered that Rogi was Hâlott's lackey, the torment immediately ceased, such was the regard for the *thing* Hâlott was, though no one was certain just what that thing might be. However, if there were a rider astraddle the oncoming horse, then whoever this rider might be, perhaps he did not know of Hâlott or that Rogi fetched for him. And so, Rogi remained concealed among the leaves and limbs of the *kastor* plants.

When the horse and the man rode by—for it was a man on a horse—he passed heedless of the little hunchback within the foliage.

Rogi watched, just in case he had to run, yet the rider seemed to be following something, for his eyes were focused on a point in the air. What that might be, Rogi didn't— *Oh, wait, it'th a flying inthect of thome thort. Well I'll be thshite upon; it'th a wathp or a hornet. Why would thomeone follow a wathp?*

Curious, Rogi slipped out from under the drooping branches of the *kastor* plant and, at a distance, trailed after.

It was not long ere the man stopped beneath the limbs of a large, wide-branched tree.

Rogi flopped bellydown in the tall grass.

The man cautiously backed his horse away from the tree, and dismounted and tied the reins to a sapling. He then unlashed a small, latched wooden box from the rear saddle cantle and sat down beside the horse and waited. And as he lingered, he tied one end of the rope 'round the box and the other end to his belt.

The scant remainder of the day slowly passed, and Rogi watched the man as the man watched the tree. As dusk descended, the man stood and took up the box and walked to the tree and looked up. After long moments, he somehow seemed satisfied and began climbing, one end of the rope yet fastened to his belt, the other yet tied to the box sitting on the ground.

Rogi frowned in puzzlement, but kept an eye on the man.

Finally, with the rope yet affixed to his belt, the man reached one of the large middle limbs and stepped onto the heavy branch and carefully sidled outward. He finally stopped and straddled the limb and warily moved a bit more outward. He then drew up the box and unlatched a hasp and opened the lid and cautiously raised it and swiftly—

What the thshite? He'th thlipping it over a horneth' netht!

The man quickly latched the hasp and then slowly lowered the box. As soon as it was on the ground, he swung down from the tree. In moments he rode away with his prize lashed to the back cantle.

What the thshite did he want that for: a boxth of angry horneth?

Shaking his head, Rogi got up from his concealment and, weighing the bag of *kastor* beans in his hand and deciding he had enough, he set off for the tower, hoping to arrive before dusk turned to dark. . . .

He didn't make it, and blundered in just ere mid of night.

Carefully, Hâlott, down in his laboratory, twisted the minute augur into the minuscule denticle, barely widening the hollow running its length. Then he augered even tinier holes thwartwise through the sides of the tooth. Finally, he carefully rasped the widest end of the tiny, conical dent to flatness. He examined the work in total blackness, the lack of light notwithstanding. The bone was, in fact, the minute tip of a wee serpent's fang, now no larger than the point of a pin with a tiny length of shaft, hollow end to end with three additional infinitesimal flutelike holes along the insignificant span.

"Good," he whispered in the darkness.

"Rogi!" he called, though it sounded more like groan.

There was no answer.

"Rogi!" he groaned again, somewhat louder.

There was still no answer.

Hâlott went back up the stairs and began examining the rune-marked, gilded box. He was still prodding and poking it well into the night, when at last Rogi came stumbling in.

"I wath lotht, Mathter," he said in the dark, "elth I would have got here thooner." Rogi began lighting lanterns.

"Have you the *kastor ricinus*?"

"Yeth. Quite a few, Mathter."

Hâlott held out his hand, and Rogi dropped the pouch into it.

"There wath thith man, Mathter, and he put a large horneth' nctht into a boxth."

"Did he see you?"

"No, Mathter. You told me to avoid being theen when I collect the beanth."

"Good." Hâlott stepped away from the table and headed for the stairs to the lab. But then he paused and said, "I want you to go and find a man they call Chance. He is a man with black hair and dresses in black and limps and carries a cane." Hâlott seemed to glance at the box, though how Rogi could tell is a mystery. Perhaps he had come to know Hâlott's ways through long association, for they had been together through many years and across many countries and through many escapes and flights from angry mobs and enraged rulers and other such. Regardless, Hâlott slightly twitched his head toward the box and said, "Tell him I have a commission for him. You might find him at the Bottomless Well."

"But Mathter, they throw me out of the Bottomleth Well."

"Tell them you are on *my* business." Without further word, Hâlott turned and descended the stairs.

With a sigh, Rogi got another chunk of bread and a wedge of cheese from the cupboard and then left, heading for Sanctuary, all the while mumbling about "having to thtumble about in moonthadowth with a bag of beanth, and nobody theemed to care that he needed retht and needed to get thome thleep, and what'th more it'th

the middle of the night, and robberth and muggerth would be lurking in alleywayth and . . ."

Andriko stood in the light of the moon above and waited.

A slim, dark figure came slipping through the shadows.

"You have it, Driko?"

"Yes, my lady." He canted his head toward the latched box. "It's
a rather large one. White-faced hornets."

"White-faced? Not yellows?"

"The whites are very aggressive, my lady."

"Well and good. I need them placed in the courtyard sometime ere
the gathering, unseen, of course."

"Yes, my lady. The day after tomorrow."

"I need them to be unnoticed, and I need a means for loosing them
wherein I will not overly suffer from stings."

Andriko frowned in puzzlement but said, "I will arrange for both."

"Thank you, Driko."

With mortar and pestle, Hâlott ground the husks of the *kastor* beans
to a fine powder. Then he added a bit of liquid from a vial, and another bit from a second vial. He was not overly cautious while doing
these things; after all, why should he be? Poisons, toxins, venoms:
None had an effect on him, not even elixir of *ricinus*.

Stirring the admixture, Hâlott's brows twitched in a frown. What
might the rune-marked box contain? And he wondered whether
Rogi had yet found the man called Chance.

Grumbling to himself, Rogi stumped away from the Broken Mast
along the docks. Several fishermen had paused in their worry about
the oncoming storm season long enough to jeer at him, but they had
made no move to plague him further. After all, he *was* Hâlott's man.

Before going to the Mast, he had tried the Bottomless Well, the
'Unicorn, and the Yellow Lantern, but in none of those places was a
man in black, no man with a cane. But now he was headed for the

Golden Gourd, a place said to be a brothel, though they always threw Rogi out before he had occasion to see for himself.

Rogi finally reached the tavern. Stepping through the door, he immediately spotted a black-haired man in black clothes sitting at a table. A rather heavy hardwood cane hung on the back of his chair. Across the table was a black-haired woman dressed in drab, rather shapeless garments. It was Elemi, the S'danzo woman who had read her cards for Rogi and had told him that as a newborn on two separate occasions he had been deliberately cast into the sea and had been twice plucked therefrom. She and the man in black seemed to be in deep converse. Other than those two, there were but a handful of patrons within.

"You little shite!" called Prall, starting 'round the bar as he added, "I told you to never show your face in this—"

"I am thent here by my mathter Hâlott," yelled Rogi at the barkeep. "I am here to thee a man named Chanth."

Prall glanced at the man in black, who shrugged and nodded.

"All right, pud," said Prall, waving Rogi forward. "But keep a froggin' civil tongue in your head." Then he looked at Rogi and laughed uproariously and managed to gasp out, "As if you could keep that long lapper of yours inside your mouth."

Rogi scuttled over to the table where the man sat and looked up at him. In spite of the man's black hair, he appeared to be in his sixties. "Are you the one called Chanth?"

The man nodded.

"I am thent by my mathter who wanth to give you a commithion."

"A commission?"

"Yeth."

"And it is for . . . ?"

"He didn't thay."

Chance shook his head. "I take no commissions these days, Rogi."

Rogi's eyes widened in surprise, for the man knew his name even though Rogi had not until now ever spoken with this person called Chance.

Still, the man seemed to be intrigued, and he glanced over toward a dark corner where sat a young man. Rogi looked, too, and saw a youth also dressed in black, though a red sash splashed a bit of color across his waist. His black hair was pulled back in ponytail, and he wore a sword at his side and an upside-down dagger strapped to a forearm. *A dangerouth perthon,* thought Rogi.

Chance interrupted the small hunchback's observations: "Rogi, have you no inkling whatsoever as to what this commission might be?"

Rogi glanced at Elemi. The young woman stared back at him, her dark, dark eyes glittering in the lantern light, her gold hoop earrings gleaming as well.

"You can trust her," said Chance.

"I think he wanth you to open a boxth."

"Open a box?"

Rogi nodded. "A thecret boxth."

Chance smiled, and then called to the youth in black. "Lone."

Lone stood and crossed the common room, his walk like that of a swaggering cat, his jet ponytail swinging in counterpoint.

Near dawn, Hâlott filled the minuscule fang with a minute amount of the *ricinus* elixir, and then he sealed the flat end with a insignificant amount of wax. Just as he took up the ruby ring, he heard a shout: "Mathter, Mathter, I bring you thomeone to open the boxth."

Lone looked about the chamber and shook his head. Not only had he seen that the square-based tower was a ruin—with vine-covered rubble about its foundation, the top two levels but shells, with partial walls here and there and stairs leading up to dead ends or gaps—but now that he was inside, the ground-level floor seemed nearly a ruin itself, even though it was intact: barely livable, it was all but dead of neglect. Rogi set the lantern on a dust-laden table then went about lighting candles, while still calling out "Mathter, Mathter, thomeone to open the thecret boxth."

Lone's gaze went to the rune-marked, gilded box sitting on

the table. There seemed no latch, no lock, no lid. He smiled in anticipation.

And then Hâlott walked into the room, and Lone turned, and for
the first time the youth saw Hâlott up close and personal. Oh, he
had seen Hâlott in the 'Unicorn now and again, yet always at night,
and always from across the room. But now he stood no more than a
stride away from what seemed to be the desiccated remains of a living
corpse, and Lone wondered, *What the frog has my mentor foisted
upon me now?*

At dusk, once again came a light tapping on the door. When Rogi
answered it, he saw the young woman who had called him an ugly
little creature and had fled.

Even as she recoiled once more, Rogi smiled and looked up at her,
the irises of his eyes such a pale, pale blue that the whole of them
looked dead white . . . white with black dots where his pupils were.
Rogi began fumbling at the rope at his waist. "You would like to
thsee my dragon, yeth?"

She huffed and said, "I would see your master."

Rogi's shoulders slumped. He turned and called out, "Mathter,
thome woman to thsee you."

A hollow whisper came from the adjacent room, and Rogi responded.

In moments, Rogi exchanged the ruby ring for a small but fairly
weighty pouch, and the young woman fled once more.

Rogi sighed, and closed the door, then untied the pouch strings
and fished out from among the coins two rather large and squarish
silver ones—shaboozh—and one small gold piece—a royal—and
pocketed them for himself. After all, he had worked hard for his
wages: Not only had he found the "boxth," he had wandered around
in the shadowy woods in the moonlight with a bag of "beanth," and
he had searched all over town to find Chance and Lone and had been
jeered at by fishermen and had nearly been thrown out of the
Golden Gourd and . . .

From nearby and for perhaps the hundredth time came Lone's frustrated shout: "Frog! Froggin' chest!"

Dressed in white and wearing her ruby jewels, Nadalya, smiling, sauntered among the crowd of personages gathered in the courtyard to celebrate the visit of per-Arizak, known as Ariz to some and, because of his fiery temper, as the Dragon to others. Big and brawny and brown-haired, as were most of the Irrune, he was a man who clearly had gotten his height not only from his father, but also from his mother, Verrezza, Arizak's first wife. In the courtyard to greet his eldest son was Arizak, who sat in a chair with his damaged left leg propped on a pillowed footstool. Tall, gray-haired Verrezza was there, too, for certainly she would not miss an event where the "one true" heir to the throne was present at court. Naimun, first son of Nadalya and Arizak, stood off to one side surrounded by his coterie of plotters, many of the young men laughing over something that their own pretender to the throne had said, or at some gaffe by Ariz, an uncouth but dangerous boor in their eyes, living in the hills with the bulk of the savage Irrune people as he did. Red-haired Raith was elsewhere among the crowd, the second son of Nadalya and Arizak. At seventeen, Raith was lithe and of a middling height, taller than his petite mother, shorter than Naimun, and certainly shorter than Aziz. Raith was the brightest of the lot, or so his mother deemed, and would make a better ruler than either of the two other contenders.

Additionally, there were merchants and their wives from Land's End, powerful in their own right, as well as ladies of the court and daughters of various guests, all hanging on the words of so-called men of power or of their sons, especially those of Aziz, Naimun, and Raith. The smarter ones, though, sought out Verrezza or Nadalya, for that's where the true machinations of the court as well as the progression resided.

Nadalya wove her way among the crowd, pausing here to jest with a youth, stopping there to speak of the tide and times with a merchant, lingering at another gathering to compliment the gems or hair or dress of some lady. Across the courtyard, she espied Andriko and caught his eye, and he nodded toward a cloth-draped table on which sat casks of wine used by the servants to replenish pitchers they bore through the gathering to refill goblets and glasses held by the guests.

Slowly, working her way outward, Nadalya eventually came to the table and casually and without notice found the box beneath, a cord tied to the hasp of the latch.

She tapped on the wine casks, as if measuring their fill, and at the same time, she repeatedly kicked the box below, the sound of one covering for the other. Then she took up the hasp-string and pulled the lid open, then stepped away toward Naimun and his circle of friends.

In moments, screams signaled that the enraged hornets had found their way out from under the cloth-covered table and were attacking anyone or anything that moved.

As men batted at the angry insects, women screamed and ran for the doors of the palace. Verrezza and Ariz got Arizak to his feet, and, with him hobbling, they headed for the palace as well.

Nadalya turned the ring 'round her finger until the gemstone was toward her palm, and she twisted aside the ruby and stepped to Nidakis and cried, "Oh, Nikki, there's one on you," and she slapped him on the back of his neck, then grabbed Naimun's arm and headed for the palace, and was most pleased to see that Raith was before them and moving with the crowd.

The next day, Nidakis developed a cough, which by the following day turned into an endless hacking along with nonstop diarrhea. On the third day, a fever came upon him, and he could not keep any food on his stomach—vomiting until he was empty, and then retching nought but greenish bile thereafter. Even water would not stay down, nor juices of any kind. By that evening he had fallen into a coma, swiftly followed by death. The healers were puzzled, including Velinmet, the best of the lot . . . until postmortem they examined his body, and embedded under the skin in the back of his neck they found . . .

After four days of repeated and frustrating attempts, Lone, who had stubbornly determined that nothing could or would defeat him, at last opened the gilded box. It took twenty-seven separate moves of sliding panels in just the right sequence to unlatch the thing, and inside he and Hâlott found a carefully wrapped bronze bust of a woman. Beautiful she was, with a long, elegant neck and high cheekbones and graceful lips and a narrow chin and a long, straight nose. She had a high forehead and shell-like ears, and she wore what seemed to be a crown of sorts, or perhaps a strange, tall hat. The hat itself was marked with an ankh, like the one Hâlott himself wore. But strangest of all was that her eyes were outlined in a similar manner to Hâlott's own painted-on eyes of kohl.

Lone was disappointed, for this was no treasure he wanted—no gems, no gold, no silver, no coinage or jewelry of any sort—and he had expected riches worthy of the puzzle of the box. But Hâlott was devastated, and he howled at the sight of the bust and sank to his knees and buried his withered face into his bony hands and sobbed inconsolably, though no tears whatsoever ran down his desiccated cheeks.

Lone drew away from the living dead man, and muttered something about coming back for his fee, and then he was out the door, leaving the grief-stricken necromancer behind, who now and again whispered the name Meretaten between howls of anguish.

For the next several nights, the guards at the Gate of Triumph reported seeing that dreadful person Hâlott wandering through the graveyard just beyond their post. What he was doing there, none knew, though one reported that he seemed to be weeping.

Rumors and whispers flew throughout Sanctuary, in the taverns and inns—the 'Unicorn, Yellow Lantern, Broken Mast, Six Ravens, and the many other establishments—over back fences, in alleys, down at the docks, and perhaps in the palace itself. No matter where, whenever men and women got together, inevitably their voices dropped and they whispered conspiratorially:

"That Nidakis, he's not the first one of the court to have died in this manner."

"A mysterious ailment, I hear."

"Yar. Like the ones before: terrible fever, can't keep anything down, coughing endlessly. They say their whole insides died—guts, lungs, hearts, livers, kidneys, all of it—and that's what killed 'em."

"That don't sound like no snakebite to me."

"Snakebite?"

"Yar. From one o' them beynit snakes. Kill you in moments, they will."

"Pah! Wasn't no snakebite killed Nidakis."

"Wull then, just how do you explain the fact that the healers found a tiny snake tooth stuck under the skin in the back of Nidakis's neck?"

"I hear it was found in his mouth."

"Bit him in the night, I hear."

"Ooo, gives me shivers, it does, terrible snakes slithering through the dark."

" 'Fit were a snake tooth, a beynit snake, then the Beysibs are back."

"Small, they are, I hear, and brightly colored."

"The Beysib?"

"Nah, the snakes. The Beysib, though, eyes of a fish they have, them women."

"Mayhap they're gathering again."

"Might have somethin' to do with that ship what was wrecked."

Rumors flew, whispers flew, and soon it was told that a huge conclave of the Beysib were plotting somewhere deep in dank tunnels beneath the city, and they would one day come forth en masse. It would then be a case of the devil you know—the savage Irrune—versus the devil you once knew—the fish-eyed Beysib.

Nadalya was quite pleased with this turn of events, for even some at court were caught up in the Beysib rumors. It was a nice bit of misdirection, Hâlott having used an embedded serpent's fang to slowly deliver the deadly toxin. She would have to pay him a bonus. And because Nidakis had first sickened a full day after the courtyard gathering, and then had died three days beyond that, there was nothing to connect the gathering with his untimely demise. Yet even had there been, nothing could ever be proved. Regardless, Nidakis was dead—"Isn't it sad, that poor youth, and he had seemed so healthy, too?"—and so she had temporarily cut off the head of that particular set of scheming serpents surrounding Naimun. Perhaps now the rest of the snake would die, and Raith would be safe from their plotting.

Little did Nadalya know that she had merely eliminated an insignificant member of a much larger cabal conspiring together for power. For, depending upon who was pacing it out, a mile or two northeast of Sanctuary in a closed room on a rich estate at Land's End Retreat, powerful men gathered to speak of this latest assassination at court, and what they might do about it. Aye, though the conniver Nidakis was dead and his sycophants leaderless, the true head of that particular serpent was still very much alive.

None of this bothered Rogi at all, for he lay with an extremely well-satisfied lady of the evening in a room above the Yellow Lantern. His rather impressive and considerable dragon was very happy that night.

Consequences

Jody Lynn Nye

Pel held the compress on Tredik's right biceps until the bleeding stopped, then dabbed at the deep slash with an antiseptic wash. The fair-haired carter's lad watched him work, the pain dulled by a very small amount of poppy in a large slug of willow-herb tea. Pel wanted him conscious so he could appreciate what he was going through.

"Don't tell my mother," Tredik pleaded, as Pel sewed up the slash.

"That you've been brawling?"

The young man—old enough to know better—reddened. To his credit, he didn't make a sound as the sharp needle went in and out of his flesh. "Not exactly brawling. We were having our own tournament, see? We're training up for next time. That Tiger lady, she shouldn't have bested everybody in Sanctuary so easy."

"Why not? If she was well trained, hale, and aware, she had as much chance as any fighter here."

"But it's not right, a stranger taking the prize in our own city. One of us ought to have defended it properly. I think it was witchcraft. If that old Torchholder had been around, well, he'd have spotted her for what she was. I mean, what she must be. A witch, I mean. No outlander ought to be that good."

Pel smiled. He doubted that during the years of the Bloody Hand, or even the early times of Irrune rule, that anyone would have been invoking civic pride, but it sounded as though Sanctuary's youth felt something for their troubled and fate-trodden city.

"Well, it's too hot to battle like that," Pel said gently, winding bandages over the now-clean wound. "Infection grows in temperatures like this."

"Oh, so we should wait until winter rolls around again?" Tredik asked, rolling one mud-brown eye to meet Pel's bright blue gaze. Pel had to laugh.

"There's no right season for stupidity and high antics," the healer said. "You'll do what you do. It's not up to me to stop you. I won't tell your mother . . ."

"Gods bless you!"

". . . If *you* do."

"Ser Garwood!"

"You can't hide what happened to your clothes, can you?" Pel reminded him. "Those rips and all that blood? Take your time over the matter. You can pick your moment to tell her the truth. But she must hear it. What if you'd been killed? If you're going to fight like a man, you must learn to take precautions like a man, and your medicine afterward. Speaking of which . . ." He produced a small clay bottle with a chunk of wax-soaked rag for a stopper. "One sip of this three times a day, dawn, noon, and nightfall. You haven't got an infection at present. This will keep one from appearing."

Tredik pulled his torn tunic back on over his head. "I'll be a man, all right. What do I owe you?" His face turned red again. "I haven't got much money. Everyone's been telling me they're broke and asking me to wait. It's getting so my father is telling me to ask for goods to settle the bills."

Pel sighed. Actual cash had been growing very short for him, too. Admittedly, the quality of wares offered in exchange for his services were becoming more interesting since the wrecked ship had been found, but there were items for which he must pay in coin. Bezul had been kind about exchanging some of the oddities, but none of the merchants could hold out indefinitely. Pel felt as though there was a wall somewhere, and all of the money of Sanctuary was disappearing behind it. The wall must be broken down, or the economy, key to rebuilding this wounded city, would collapse. He slapped Tredik on the back.

"My next workday is this coming Shiprisday. Percaro traded a patch of land he inherited to Bezul for a new plow blade. I took it off his hands for a herb garden. It's full of rocks in all the wrong places, blocking the sun. There'll be at least three of you helping me to lay out the plot. If you haul the stones out, you can have them, trade them to Cauvin if you wish. I don't need them. I need the space for plants."

Tredik gave him a grateful glance, both for finding a non-cash solution and for treating the debt seriously. He was of a man's size, but still remained a boy in so many ways. Pel couldn't remember having been that innocent. Tredik tucked the small bottle into his torn tunic, and made his escape.

He was the last of the brawlers to seek out Pel's assistance. Mioklos's son Nerry wouldn't lose his left eye, but it had been a near thing. He was going to have one impressive scar, though it would never look as though it belonged upon the round and cheerful face that bore it. His sister Las was probably to blame for the entire mock tournament, whipping up their newfound patriotism into a frenzy. She had come out of the battle without a wound, and, Pel was sure, was lying her heart out regarding her involvement. The boys half admired and half resented her, seeing her as a pesty younger sister, but also, maybe, a future Tiger in her own right. Pel had known plenty of brave and fierce women who had fought for the Bloody Goddess. *Please*, he thought, *may Las be a force for goodness—real goodness*. He admired the Irrune for calling such a tournament, allowing any fighter to come forward and try their skill.

Pel had had few dealings with the Irrune since his return. The largely Rankene and Ilsigi population of Sanctuary had gone on with their lives as usual, trading and cheating, raising children, making love, building, eating and drinking, gossiping and arguing. It was splendidly normal in his eyes, a life he would never have foreseen taking joy in. Blasphemers, brutes, thieves, philanderers—so many would have merited death or punishment by Dyareela, but Meshpri— Meshpri loved them all. Pel had to work hard to live up to his new goddess's altruism. But that was why she was a goddess, and he a poor, flawed mortal.

Maybe a roughed-up mortal if he didn't pay attention to his potions! He went over to the altar where he had a beaker simmering over a candle. This medicine relieved the tightness of a weakening heart. It took two long days to prepare. Two pinches of heart root into the potion caused the liquid to foam up the sides of the ceramic beaker. As the bubbles subsided, the brew turned a bright red. Pel breathed a sigh of relief.

An answering exhalation made him jump. Heart root dust flew everywhere. He had been so intent on his preparations that he had not noticed the muffled shape just inside the door of the temple.

"Forgive me!" he exclaimed, hastily putting down the bottle of powder.

He glanced down into the beaker. A miracle that he had not accidentally dumped in more of the powerful ingredients. An over-measurement would have caused the potion to thicken and overflow spectacularly; plus, the stain would have been difficult to get out of the smooth stone surface of the altar. All was well. He turned his attention to his visitor.

The shape stirred slightly, and a pair of deep amber eyes rimmed with kohl looked out at him through the shadow cast by a fold of silky bronze cloth.

"You concentrate so deeply," a husky female voice said. Pel didn't recognize it. This was not Kadasah dressed up in camouflage. "I have been watching you. You are very careful."

"Not so careful," Pel said, with rueful humor. "I don't normally ignore customers, M'sera . . . ?"

But no name was forthcoming. She was an Irrune; the accent was unmistakable, and she was tall. If he had been standing beside her, the top of her head would have been level with his mouth. The eyes studied him deeply.

"We . . . I . . . need someone who takes care of others. I hear you can keep a secret. Is it true?"

"I promise it," Pel averred. "If you ask for my services, I will not tell anyone what passes between us. You pay for both treatment and confidentiality."

"Under pain of torture or death?"

Pel eyed her, but the amber gaze didn't waver. She wasn't joking. "I have vowed to care for the sick and injured, though I hope not to have to suffer to help others. How may I aid you?"

The honey-colored eyes held steady for a long moment, as though making a decision. "I am not your patient. If you choose to come with me you must tell no one where you have been or what you have done. Do you swear?"

"Not to you," Pel said. "To my patient, whoever he or she may be, and whatever it is the patient wants kept secret."

A nod. "Then, come."

"Wait," Pel held up a hand. "I can't bring my entire pharmacopaeia with me. What am I to treat?"

Another hesitation. "Infection."

The sun had fallen behind the buildings. Long shadows dropped cool darkness upon Pel's shoulders as he followed the woman between buildings. The last legitimate deliveries were being made, such as beer and provisions to the taverns. Pel caught a tempting scent of roasting meat wafting out of the door of one establishment. A patient of his, a fragile young woman whose persistent cough he had cured, raised a hand from the table she was clearing in greeting to him. He waved back, tilting his head toward her with an unspoken question. Before the young woman could respond his escort shot out a long, narrow hand from inside the folds of cloth, and grabbed his arm, pulling him into the shadows.

"Please do not speak to anyone," she whispered. "No one must know where you are bound."

Pel forbore to remind her he didn't know where they were bound. "They will think I am behaving oddly if I don't pass the time of day with them," he told her, reasonably. "Walk ahead of me a few paces so we're not seen together. I'll keep an eye on you."

The woman fell silent, then nodded. "All right."

Pel hefted his sack of herbs and medicines, and wondered whether he was walking into a trap. His guide was not a young woman, and the rich fabrics spoke of someone who was well-connected at court. Everything about the silent shadow who flitted ahead of him in and out of lantern-light made him believe she was a noble, even royal. She was intelligent, too. She had picked a moonless night, one cooler than the last several, ensuring that most of the folk who would otherwise be sitting on their doorsteps or on stools outside of the inns moaning about the heat would have fled indoors.

His guess had to be at least partly right. Though the alleyways and narrow streets through which they passed were not ones Pel normally traveled, he knew they were approaching the palace. Naturally, she did not advertise their arrival by marching up the long approach to the well-guarded gate. Instead, she joined the slow-moving queue of suppliers and workers who trudged toward the dimly lit postern gate and the kitchens. Pel would have thought that one among them would have turned to notice the bundle of bronze silk among them, as distinctive as a jewel on a burlap sack, but not one of them looked up from his or her burdens. Either they were well schooled with beatings or threats to ignore the sudden presence of their betters, or she carried some magical device on her to conceal herself. No, it wasn't magic, he realized, as he shuffled forward in between a barrowload of cabbages and a herd of goats hoping to get at the sweet-smelling green globes ahead of them. It was fear. He'd heard of the Irrune response to those who failed to heed their customs. Pel could almost scent the waves of dread as the silk-clad figure pushed by, heading for a corridor that led off the main passageway to the right. He was well-familiar with the smell, having inflicted it on hundreds, if not thousands, of sinners during his life as the embodiment of Wrath.

A flash of gold in the flickering torchlight, and his guide slipped out of view around the corner. Pel pulled his satchel out of the mouth of a flat-faced goat, who was chewing vigorously on the strap, and hurried after her. He had taken only a few steps into the sudden darkness when the door behind him shut with a loud *clang!* All light was cut off. Pel spun back and tried to pull it open. The heavy latch had snapped behind a heavy bar. His fingers fumbled over a sharp-cut keyhole, but no key. He was trapped!

For a moment the events of his past life shot through his mind like an evil children's picture book. Had he been lured here to join his former associates in humiliating and painful death? He fumbled in his satchel for the vial of poppy. He might have time to down it, and float off to eternity in peaceful oblivion, before they dug out his eyes and sewed him into a sack.

In that moment, he became aware of a soft blue light beside him no brighter than the phosphorescent glow of rotting fish. The glittering eyes regarded him above a palm-sized globe from which the gleam emanated. They looked amused.

"Stay close," she said. The blue glow floated away into the blackness.

Willing his heart to slow down to a normal pulse, Pel obeyed.

Rumors of secret passages riddling the many levels of the ancient palace were proved true as the quivering light led Pel along narrow corridors of stone, up unexpected flights of stairs, and down ramps with low ceilings he never saw until his forehead impacted with one. Blinking stars of pain out of his eyes, he hurried to catch up with the will-o'-the-wisp who guided him. Far away he could hear noises and hollow voices like ghosts, but they never encountered another living creature. The rats avoided these passages as much as humans did.

After an eternity in the cold, damp darkness, he emerged suddenly into a warm, stifling blackness in which smoldered the red-gold coal in the heart of a single brazier. The blue glow vanished. Another smell, that of putrefying flesh, caught at Pel's throat and made him cough.

A low voice, near to the fire, chuckled.

"Makes you sick, eh? I'm attached to it, can't get away from my own stink." The accent was Irrune, coarse and hearty.

"Who . . . ?" Pel began, but his own voice failed him.

"Call me . . . call me Dragonsire," the man said. The joke appeared to please him. He chuckled some more. A pair of slender, fair-skinned hands appeared near the faint light and poured dark liquid from a slender-necked pitcher into a heavy goblet. Another hand, dark in contrast to the woman's, reached out. The cup disappeared into shadow. "Ahhh! Wine, ser?"

"Er, thank you," Pel said, realizing how dry his throat was. A cup was pressed into his hand by the unseen server. It was surprisingly heavy. Pel guessed that it must be made of gold. The rough shapes of stones studding the bowl scraped his fingers. He hesitated before drinking. "Er, how may I serve you?"

"Right down to business? Good." The figure sat up. Pel thought he knew what to expect as the firelight touched its face, but he still gasped out loud. Arizak. "Do not fear me. Heh! If anything, I have more to fear from you."

"What, ser?" Pel asked. Sweat filmed his face and palms. He had to grasp the big cup in both hands to keep it from squirting away from him.

"I don't fear pain. No Irrune does. I don't fear death. We welcome a good death. But this!" Arizak gestured at his leg with a disgusted hand. "This is not a good death. I am disgusted by it. It's not a clean battle wound, an ax through the neck, a sword in the belly, a dagger tearing out your heart. No! It's like being eaten alive by slugs. Look!"

He pulled a cloth off his lap. Beneath his left leg lay outstretched, the end propped up on a painted stool. There was no foot.

As nervous as Pel felt suddenly facing the ruler of his city he was taken even further aback by the limb the Irrune chief now revealed to him. The original wound must have been a fearsome one, but it had disappeared in seeping pillows of flesh that had been a healthy pink and had turned an angry red, even going black in small patches that Pel knew would grow. He sucked in his breath. The rot would have to be cut away if the limb was to be saved—if it could be saved at all. The leg must have been very painful. When he looked up, Arizak's gaze held his, strong, confident, and weary.

"I have three sons," the Irrune lord said. "Each wants to rule after me. My eldest is the strongest. He is not often here. He does not like Sanctuary. I don't like it much myself. He came here at my behest this week—you may have heard. The greatest product of this place is talk. Everyone talks to everyone."

"Yes, lord, I knew."

Arizak slammed the heavy goblet down on the arm of his chair. "He did not show decent respect. I will not take that, not while I draw breath. I want to be whole again, healer, as whole as I can be. I want to ride out and teach my miserable offspring the truth about the name he bears. If he survives, well, maybe I'll let him rule one day. When my time is over. But my time is not over yet. Not yet." The face grew more craggy as from a throb of pain.

"Why me, my lord?" Pel asked, full of pity. "You have healers and magicians in plenty. The best in the land."

The shrewd gaze met his eyes and locked them in place. "You must have been born in a basket, man," he said. "They are all corrupt in this city, men and women alike. It comes from living inside these rotting walls. If you had the clean air all around, you'd have to be an honest man. Here, you can hide your sins."

"He is honest," said the soft voice of the woman who had guided him. Pel looked around for her, but the brazier's light fell short. The shapes he saw beyond it could have been curtains or pillars or tapestries. The blue light reappeared, rising until it was between Pel and the unseen woman. "The stone affirms it. No great faults here—fewer than most men, as though he was a young child. I wonder why. Perhaps he *was* born in a basket."

Pel opened his mouth and closed it again. To correct her he would have to explain his rebirth, and that admission would cost him his life. He knelt over the wound and prodded it gently. Every poke made the flesh twitch, but the Irrune lord said nothing. He had impressive self-control. He had to be in agony. Most of Pel's patients moaned and cried over splinters in the thumb.

"Can you do anything?" Arizak asked, after a time. "You can say no, man, and leave here with your skin. I just want truth, that is all and everything to me. If you can cure me I will reward you well. If you cannot, I will be glad of your candor. I am so weary of the shite-eating hypocrites in this city, it would be worth a bronze wristlet to hear an honest answer."

"I can try, lord," Pel replied. The stink of the rotting flesh made his throat tighten. "Such a wound has to be treated inside and outside. If your constitution is hale enough, you may be cured, with Meshpri's aid."

"Pah!" The Irrune ruler spat a wine-tinged gob on the floor. "Keep your false godlings to yourself, Wrigglie. If you've got any skill in your fingers Irrunega put it there."

"I apologize," Pel said, and went back to his examination. Meshpri aid him, indeed! He had never seen such decay in a wound on a living being. Yet, he felt the flesh. In spite of the cold he felt warmth in them, and when he pinched a patch of intact skin down near the tortured ankle, the color rushing back to it was visible even in the poor light. Automatically he felt behind him for his pouch. Without his having to ask, the unseen serving woman came forward with the blue ball in her hands. Its illumination increased to a pure blue like a cloudless sky, easy for Pel to distinguish which herb packet was which.

"What do you need?" the soft voice of his guide asked from the shadows.

"Water and wine," Pel replied, untying packets. "This will take more than one treatment, probably many. Best would be water drawn from an open stream under a waning moon, to assist in closing the injury. But we must heal the infection first, not shut it away inside your flesh."

"Shut away, like me in this frog-filled city," Arizak growled. "Go ahead, then."

He sat back in the big chair. Pel could now see that it had been carved out of a single piece of wood, a master's work. Dragons reared their heads under each of the ruler's big hands, and another loomed up to form the chair back. From all accounts that was the way Arizak lived: surrounded by dragons, not one as benevolent as the wooden ones who supported him. Perhaps his truest supporters were here: the silent serving woman and the gold-eyed lady who waited in the dark.

The serving woman brought him a small table, and set the pitcher of wine upon it. A small metal pan, bronze by the glints of light the fire struck off its sides, was placed on the brazier to heat. Pel willed himself to concentrate, to allow his mind to step away from this dark and troubled place, to the hamlet where his life had started over. Instead of the Irrune ruler, he pictured a farmer whose leg had been sliced by his plow blade, and had been too stubborn and too busy with the planting to come in to have it seen to until his wife forced him. He glanced up into the golden eyes of the woman waiting by the wall, and guessed that this case was much the same.

Pel stood up and exercised his long back. Arizak had drained the cup of medicine he had mixed and was watching him with speculative eyes.

"What do you make of it, healer? You've eased some of the pain. Good start. Can you *cure* my frog-rotting leg?"

Pel opened his mouth to speak.

"Yes," a woman's voice interrupted him, at the same time a young man's voice said, "No."

Surprised, the healer looked around for the speakers. The ruler lifted an eyebrow.

"A mummer as well, you can throw your voice in two different directions. Give me a straight answer, and keep your ventriloquism to amuse those shite-eaters in the Maze. I want a straight answer."

"I don't know, ser," Pel replied, getting his own voice back. "But I will try."

"Good enough." Arizak turned to the woman with the golden eyes. "Take him back."

All the way through the dark streets, Pel wondered whence had come the voices that had spoken out in Arizak's chamber. Once the bronze-clad lady had illuminated the room with the globe she now held shielded in her hands he could see no one but the four of them. The old man had seemed surprised but not alarmed, so it was no one concealed behind the walls. Clearly, Arizak believed Pel had manifested them.

Pel had a different interpretation, though he scarcely dared even to think it: Meshpri and Meshnom had spoken, there in the small stone room. The healing gods had watched over him, and given him the ability to heal, this he knew, but they had never before manifested themselves. What did it mean? In the gentle goddess's eyes, all patients were the same, with rank, age, wealth having no impact upon her gift to them. Yet not only did the gods speak out regarding this patient, but they disagreed on his prognosis. It meant to Pel that Arizak was at a turning point, neither too ill to recover nor guaranteed to live, and that his life must impact the health and well-being of many others.

The Avenue of Temples was silent this dark night. Voices and footsteps rang from the depths of the surrounding city. Only the soft brushing of their feet on the stones could be heard. Pel paused. Was that another set of feet behind them?

He couldn't tell. When he stopped, they stopped. It might have been an echo in the man-made valley of stone. If she heard, his guide made no indication. Just before they reached Pel's shop, he thought he saw a very small figure, darker than the darkness, slip in between two of the ruined buildings. A spy? A would-be thief? A patient in need of Pel's services who did not wish to reveal him- or herself yet?

Inside, the woman set down her blue stone. It glowed gently, then faded.

"I leave this with you, healer," she said. "When my lord has need of you, it will burn with the blue fire. Follow where it leads. It may not be to the same place as tonight—I do not know. Will you come?"

"I will," Pel promised.

"And no word?"

"None."

She inclined her head, and slipped out into the moonless night.

Shiprisday bloomed bright and hot. Pel toiled as hard as any of his patients paying their debts; harder than some, of course. Once again, Miskegandros, fabric merchant and sufferer from gout from his overindulgence in the foods he loved and could afford, lounged at the side of the field shouting orders as though he was the master here. Pel should have insisted on cash from the Rankan, but Miskegandros was disinclined to part with any for his weekly dose, and, truthfully, Pel thought a day's hard gardening would do the man more good.

"Up, good ser," Pel said, playfully, urging the merchant to his feet with the flexible tines of the rake that the man had discarded. "By my reckoning you have five hours to go."

"But it's only four hours left in the day," the Rankan pouted. "The others say they're leaving by late afternoon."

"And they've been working since midmorning," Pel explained, with a friendly expression that brooked no disagreement. "Come along, you're still several yards short of a suit."

Grumbling, the Rankan lumbered to his feet and went back to raking. The pile of stones grew on the perimeter of the field where a small group of girls were fitting them into the gaps in the ragged wall. Once this had been a noble's pleasure garden, Bezul had relayed from Percaro, the most recent of the land's many owners. Around the five-acre plot ranged an ornamental stone-and-brick wall that had been ten feet high. Most of the stones aboveground had been removed by neighbors who needed them for their own walls.

It was too small to be a viable field for any of the farmers, because the footings of the wall were still too high to plow over, and were seated too deeply into the earth to dislodge economically. It was really of no use to anyone in these poor days but someone like Pel, who needed only a small patch of land for healing herbs. The wall would keep animals from wandering across it and destroying precious plantings. A couple of farmers had contributed fruit trees. Pel was especially pleased with the two decent sloes and a wild cherry bush, both old enough to produce next year if he could keep them from going into root shock. But he'd be a pretty poor healer not to prevent that, he chided himself cheerfully.

A few breadths of intact wall still remained, too fragile to disassemble without destroying the lacelike brickwork. In the shade of the widest of these Pel treated laborers with sunburn and a few patients who had ventured outside the city walls in need of his services. A new pipe driven down into an old well dribbled a meager throb of water over his hands as he cleansed the matter from a nasty boil on the arm of an elderly Ilsigi woman. Her blood was slowing, as was the way of extreme old age, and she considered stimulants a plague and a nuisance.

"Try to fool this old body?" she had said, as she rose from the sparse grass with a rustle of skirts and fragile bones. She tapped the side of her head. "It's the old mind you can't trick."

"I bow to your wisdom," Pel said, springing up. She laughed, a dry cackle, and hobbled away.

He wasn't done with physicking just yet. One of the girls detached herself from the group within the garden and made her way over, the tilt of her head just a little too casual, her saunter just a little too deliberate. Ilsei had eaten green berries a few weeks ago that gave her incessant diarrhea. Another youngster who pleaded with him not to tell her parents, she had volunteered for a half day's work to pay for the medication, but the flux had been cured weeks ago. She sent a cocky smile to her friends, then crouched down by Pel's side.

"Healer," she whispered tentatively, after glancing about to make sure no one was listening, "what does it mean when one bleeds twice in the moon?"

A boy Pel guessed to be Ilsei's age came to hover over the two of them. Pel glanced up.

"Can you wait over there a while, please?" he asked, pointing to the remains of a bench against the bricks about twenty feet away, and turned his attention back to Ilsei, but her face was frozen in embarrassment. Pel looked up again.

"I'm not used to waiting," the boy said, putting a hand automatically on the dagger at his belt. Pel recognized him as Raith, youngest of Arizak's three sons. He was a good-looking youngster, graceful in the way of men who have used their muscles.

"I'll go!" Ilsei exclaimed, scrambling to her feet. Pel stood and took her hand. He met Raith's gaze firmly with the confidence of the priest who was used to rambunctious and uncontrollable acolytes.

"He can wait. We will walk over here and finish our consultation."

The expression in his eyes must have surprised the Irrune prince, for he kept his mouth shut. The girl could hardly choke out another syllable as she kept looking over the healer's shoulder at the impatient Irrune. At last, Pel let her go, after she had promised to come to his shop on the morrow with her mother.

"Now, ser," he said, turning to Raith with a pleasant smile. "How may I serve?"

The boy's mouth twisted, as if deciding whether to spit out a sour mouthful. "You've got balls. I came to give you a warning."

Pel raised an eyebrow. "For what?"

The mouthful came out in a blurt. "For my father. I know you were at the palace the other night. Who brought you? What did you do?"

"That," Pel said, with more calm than he felt, "is none of your business."

"Don't give me your Wrigglie evasions," Raith snarled, though he stayed where he was. "My father is gravely ill. I know about you healers. You pretend you have skill, but you keep him ill for your own purposes. You make vegetable soups and stinking pills that do nothing."

"Have you tried them?" Pel asked. "Stop your bristling, young man. I am not being flippant. I will not tell you anything about any patient I have, in the palace or outside it. You would welcome the same discretion if you came in search of my services. Anyone would tell you the same."

"Well, I will tell you something, then," Raith said, his face as red as his hair. "I know how devious you Wrigglies are. If you are attending my father, and if you are thinking about using your skills for anything except healing him, and if he dies before I . . . if he dies and I can trace the reason back to you, you won't need a fellow healer, you'll need a hole in the ground for your remains."

"Ser, there is no need to threaten me," Pel said, gently. "My task is to give aid to the sick. I do not kill. I never sell or use poisons. On that you have my sworn word."

But Raith had made up his mind to be offended. Pel realized he had stepped on a tender nerve. He knew that this youngest of Arizak's three children had no less ambition for the throne than the other two. And he was a boy, no older than the sword-fighting youths who were pulling up roots and raking stones just on the opposite side of the ancient brick wall.

"I will tell you what," Pel suggested, as Raith glared at him. "If you notice that your father is unwell, come to my shop. I would be glad to call upon him at your bequest. If he gives permission, you may even oversee the treatment."

A snort told Pel how likely it was his father would ever let him watch, but Raith was appeased.

"I've got my eye on you," Raith said, pointing a finger at Pel's nose, though he had to point upward to do it. "I have watchers everywhere. If my father dies, you die."

"I understand, ser," Pel replied. Raith swept his cloak in one arm and attempted to retreat in a dignified manner, but the heaps of stones made the stride into a series of tiptoeing hops back to where a man-at-arms waited with the boy's dancing stallion. Raith shot him one more look meant to warn, then spun the horse around. Pel sighed and went back to mixing sun-cure. So he had been followed that night. Raith had wasted a trip warning him to do what he was going to do anyhow.

With Shiprisday safely over, some of Pel's payment-backward patients came out of hiding.

"My spots came back in only three days!" Whido the baker protested, banging his hand on the old stone altar that served Pel as a shop counter, mixing palette, and operating table in one. He plunked himself down on the tall stool to which Pel gestured him. "Call yourself a doctor, eh? The sisters in the ruins up there," he gestured in the direction of the Promise of Heaven, "said it's a condition that goes away in time. Have you been making them come back so you can wring more padpols out of me?"

"Not all acne goes away, you mindless pud," Pel countered, amused. He had respect for the Rankan women who had moved in to aid the unfortunate of Sanctuary. With an eye for a bargain, or just worried about the best care, many a local had tried to play the knowledge of one against the other. Pel found the ladies to be good neighbors. "Sometimes it stays with the victim for a lifetime. It can only be treated, not cured. Didn't they tell you that, too?" The expression on Whido's face told him they had; he was just trying to bring the price down again, for the sixtieth time. Just see what outrage he'd wear if Pel tried to bargain down the price of fresh bread!

Whido shot a glance at the knot of Irrune men loitering casually by the door. "Well, do something! People think I'm infecting my goods." He waggled a hand at his flour-dusted face. The oil from his pores caused it to cake in runnels.

"Oh, I don't know," Pel said, crossing his arms and leaning back thoughtfully. "You look like one of your own crumb cakes. Isn't that a good advertisement?"

"Pel!" Whido sputtered.

The healer couldn't help but laugh.

Once more, he handed over a salve and a draught in a rag-stoppered clay bottle. He didn't need to tell Whido what to do with it, but this time he put out an upturned palm. "Eight padpols. Four for today, and four for last week. I'll get the accounting for your other missed weeks next time I see you."

"Pel!"

The healer folded his long arms and fixed him with a bright blue eye.

"No argument. You didn't come to help yesterday. I don't walk in shite twice on purpose. Payment at the time of service. We'll discuss credit again when you've been up to date for a few months."

Grumbling, Whido felt in his scrip. He plunked down eight blackened shards of silver and stomped out. The brown-cloaked man just inside the door came to take his place on the stool. Pel judged him to be around thirty, silky brown hair and beard framing a weather-bronzed face. He held out a hand. The fingers were swollen and bruised, causing the gash across the back to stand out proud.

Pel began to pick the clods of earth and stone fragments out of the torn flesh and swab it with a cleansing solution. "How'd you do this?"

"New horse," the Irrune gritted. "Bashed me into a wall then tossed me off. Rubbed my glove into my hand. Does that stuff have to sting?"

"Yes," Pel said. "I've never found a mixture that worked that didn't. It'll go numb in a moment. Hold still, this won't take long."

He took a strand of gut out of the bowl where he kept it soaking and threaded it into a needle cleaned and heated in candleflame. The man tensed as the needle went into his skin, then relaxed visibly at the promised numbness. As Pel worked on closing the deep gash, the man's companions wandered about the shop. No other patients were waiting, so they spoke to one another loudly in their own language.

"Eh?"

A brown hand reached past Pel's elbow. He thought nothing of it, until he saw the hand close around the blue stone that Arizak's lady had given him. He glanced over his shoulder and recognized the mustachioed face of the man holding it: Naimun, son of Arizak and brother of Raith.

"Pretty, isn't it?" Pel asked, as the man examined the stone, turning it over and peering into it.

"Indeed it is," Naimun replied smoothly, tossing the stone from one hand to another. He was far taller than Raith, and had a fluidity of movement that went beyond grace, to almost a snakelike sinuousness. "My father's first-wife likes blue stones." His eyes rose suddenly to Pel's. "This one is a great deal like one she has. May I bring her this one as a gift? I will pay you for it."

Pel took up too much flesh in his next stitch, earning a grunt from his patient as he hit a non-numbed portion. He swallowed hard, and dabbed a little more deadening salve on the skin. "I must decline, good ser," Pel said, uneasily. He prayed Meshpri's kindness that the stone would not begin to glow now. "It was a present from a lady."

"Would she be pleased to see her gift used to hold down paper, instead of holding a place of honor in your home?" Naimun asked. "But, I see you live here." He gestured around the renovated temple.

Pel noticed his eyes picking up details of sacks of herbs and grasses, the store of wood, and the multitude of baskets, just the things one might concentrate on if one was planning to wreck or burn a home.

He tied off the knot at the top of the scar, and covered his work with a patch of clean lint that he knotted into place with a length of boiled linen. The man reached into his scrip for a couple of soldats and put them down. Naimun swept up the silver and replaced it with a round, bright disk that glittered unexpectedly in the dimness of the temple. Gold. Pel glanced at the bright coin, then gave the prince a curious look.

"For your services, healer, and maybe for more later on."

"Do you ail, ser?" Pel asked. "How can I help?"

"Not I," Naimun said. He flicked his fingers, and the wounded man strode to the front of the building, out of earshot. "You have heard that my father is gravely ill."

"I had heard he lost a leg," Pel equivocated.

"A foot. But he continues to suffer from the wound. In fact, so much that it might be a mercy if the gods were to gather him into their bosom." Naimun shot him a sideways glance.

"Each man and woman goes in good time," Pel said, knowing perfectly well what the prince was asking of him, and knowing just as clearly that Naimun knew he understood. "Besides, he has healers and magicians in plenty. I have heard stories of the great shaman . . ."

"A fraud," Naimun purred. "But I know your reputation. You are good at your craft. I appreciate that." He tossed the smooth blue stone from his left to his right hand. He set it down where he had found it and smoothed it with deliberate fingers. "A fine tool, perhaps, to be used by the right craftsman. To use toward the right outcome, eh?"

"I am afraid I don't understand, ser," Pel said, his heart rising into his throat. "It's only a stone."

"Of course it is. And you are only an apothecary, a herbalist, who dispenses drugs for the well-being of your patients. But what if they are in so much pain that they wish to die?"

"I never use poisons," Pel stated firmly.

"But the ease into long sleep . . ." Naimun suggested smoothly. "What do you do for the ones whose every moment is a misery? Do you never give them enough poppy to help them go?"

Pel hesitated. "I am guided by their wishes."

"But what if I could assure you that a patient does wish it, but is incapable of expressing such a wish? Whether by infirmity or pride?"

"The patient would have to be the one to tell me," Pel said. "My craft demands I do no harm."

At that moment the blue stone burst into life, radiance shooting out from between Naimun's fingers. They both stared at it. Naimun pulled his eyes away from the stone and fixed them on Pel.

"I don't know why it does that," Pel blurted out, desperately. "I'm sure it's magical, but neither of us knows what it's for. It suddenly lights up, for no reason. I wish it would do that at night."

"You have secrets," Naimun said suddenly, in a low voice. "I know what they are."

Pel's heart stood still. What did he know?

"My father's life is too long. The injury in his leg which will not heal provides the perfect excuse for a dutiful healer to visit him. Perhaps the lady who gave you this stone"—again Naimun fondled the blue rock, the glow reflected in his eyes—"would want you to practice your craft to the best of your ability. But, alas, in this case you were unable to save your patient. Bad luck. The will of Irrunega. No fault to you." He smiled, but his eyes were intent, focused. "Within the week, healer, I expect to hear news. Use this when you visit the palace. It will assure those you meet that you were summoned there by the son of Arizak, your services a gift from his devoted heir." He reached into his pouch and withdrew a heavy bronze-gilt armlet studded with gems and set it beside the gold coin. "The guards will allow you into Arizak's presence. Do not fail me. I will reward you very well. But if you do not"—again the eyes went dead and flat like those of a snake—"you will wish you had poisons to take to avoid the pain that awaits you."

With a swirl of cloak he was gone, leaving Pel to stare at the big ring on Meshpri's altar. It seemed too large for Naimun's arm. The cabochon jewels around which the relief of a dragon twined were worth a fortune. What if he sold it and fled on the proceeds? The summer sea was smooth enough—he could commission a ship with that much money.

But in the meanwhile, a patient awaited him, one in whom the gods themselves took an interest. As soon as he was sure Naimun and his friends had gone, he gathered up his supplies. Just before he closed his bag, he tucked the heavy metal armlet into it.

"Too slow!" Arizak complained, as Pel pointed out the improvement in the raddled flesh of the stump. "Can't you just drain the frogging mess away all at once?"

"No more than I can replace your blood all at once," Pel explained. "It takes time. You should be pleased that it is going as quickly as it is. What are the marks I see here and here?"

Arizak grunted and took a deep draught from his wine. "The others have been cutting away the black flesh. Wouldn't you do the same?"

"Well, ser, if you were a patient in my shop, I'd use maggots to do the job for me," Pel admitted. "They only eat dead meat, and their touch is far gentler than the knife."

"Hah! We Irrune would do the same." His head snapped up and he turned to the silent serving woman. "Go get some maggots out of the kitchens. Don't tell me there are none. I can almost smell them in the bread sometimes. Reminds me of the old days."

The amber-eyed lady escorted Pel back into the secret passage.

"He wants an artificial foot that will allow him to ride the stirrup again. Can you make one that will not hurt him?"

"I believe so," Pel said. "My master taught me how, though I've never fitted one myself. There might be a few trials and errors."

"He accepts that," the lady assured him. "Our customs eschew the dependence upon gold and silver that most of you in Sanctuary prefer," she said. "Our way is to trade directly for what we wish, and to reward those we choose to reward in a tangible manner. What would you like? Anything may be yours, I am so pleased to see my lord mending, in however small a way."

Pel smiled. "Well, if a man came to me in the Avenue of Temples with such a difficult case, I'd charge him the equivalent of a couple of blocks of dressed stone per visit. I'm trying to rebuild my home, and most of my income goes to materials."

"So be it." The lady sounded amused. "Such stone will be delivered to you. I see you still have my globe. May it light your way safely home."

Pel hesitated. "I have a problem, lady, with regard to your globe," Pel began. He told his story of Naimun's visit, and showed her the bronze ring.

"This belongs to my son. It went shortly after he arrived last week. I wondered—" Her eyes met Pel's. "You know who I am, now."

"Yes, m'sera. But I have never heard you say your name, so I couldn't confirm it if anyone asked me."

"You are discreet, healer. I will take care of this myself. That snake will never take my son's place." She tucked the arm ring into a fold of her enveloping cloak. "Farewell."

He didn't have to worry about guiding himself out. The blue globe gleamed brighter when he took the correct turnings, and dulled to a mere flicker when he went the wrong way. It left his mind free to design a prosthetic foot for the lord of Sanctuary. The base would be wooden, covered and padded with leather. Two pieces, one for the ankle to instep, and the other from the arch of the foot forward. Both would be tightly wrapped in the leather so the foot would flex slightly when he pushed off in a step. If his balance was good he would soon forget he was wearing it. Pine was the best choice: light, though not light enough to simulate a real foot. Lint or a silk pad in the cup at the top of the foot in between the straps would protect the stump. The risk was if Arizak used it too much, and rubbed his leg raw. Well, they knew how to summon Pel if he was needed.

He trusted the lady to deal with Naimun, but he would still have to watch over his shoulder for a good long while. Rumors were rife in Sanctuary that those who went onto the middle son's bad list tended to wind up floating in the river, or were just never seen again.

Pel slipped out into the warm night. The blue glow dulled, leaving the globe a simple stone. He looked at it in wonder as he walked toward the long stone lane from the kitchens to the street. No one else was out. What meals might be prepared must be made with foodstuffs brought in during the day. A single lantern told him where to turn for the main street. The stone stayed quiescent. Pel watched it in case Verrezza might summon him to return.

"Thief!"

Suddenly, a hand took him by the throat and slammed him into the wall. Out of reflex, Pel flung his wrists upward, knocking the other's arms away. Scarcely seeing his opponent, he turned to run. More hands grabbed him, punching and clawing at his shoulders. He threw a vicious backward kick. A loud *oof!* came from the man behind him. Pel ducked under the arms and used his shoulder as a battering ram into the midsection of the man on his left. The man on the right reached for him, but got his groaning comrade instead.

Clasping the stone and his bag to his chest, Pel ran. His feet flailed on the hot, wet cobblestones. The sound of booted feet scrambling pursued, coming closer and closer. He dared not look behind him.

He opened up his long legs, wishing he had wings instead. At the end of the lane he dodged across and plunged into the narrow, stinking alley opposite. Constricted by his surroundings, he shoved past or leaped over trash-filled baskets, discarded furniture, and one drunk mumbling to himself against the wall. Pel changed direction, cutting into the next street and ducking underneath the very noses of a couple of burly seamen grinning over the contents of a clay jug. He hit his stride on one long stretch, hoping to make it to the Vulgar

Unicorn before his pursuers caught up with him. The bartender owed him several favors.

Only a few hundred yards to go. The echo of many running feet made his heart pound.

To his dismay, one set of feet came closer and closer. Pel gave his uttermost effort, but the man behind him caught him just steps away from the welcoming door.

An arm around his throat hooked him off his feet and yanked him into the nearest alley. A big face, burned brown by the sun, pressed up close to Pel's.

"Thief! Give me that," per-Arizak growled. He wrenched the stone out of Pel's hand. It burst into light as if glad to see the Dragon. For a moment Pel could see in it an image of the boy per-Arizak must have been. He grabbed Pel's bag and began to paw through it. "Let's see what else you have stolen."

"I didn't steal the stone," Pel protested, as the Dragon's friends caught up with him. "She gave it to me. I'm a healer. It's a loan. She'll tell you!"

"A healer! So my mother did bring in another shite-handed potion-maker," per-Arizak grinned. Pel started to dive past him for freedom, but the big man drew a sharp dagger and put the point to his throat. "Let's see what you have here: leaves, brews, powders . . . trash."

"I do no harm," Pel croaked, rubbing the parts of his neck not immediately adjacent to the dagger point. "She called me."

"I know what she called you for. You do more harm than you know, Wrigglie."

"But I . . ." He hesitated to break confidence, but he couldn't help Arizak if he was dead. He prayed to Meshpri for forgiveness. "I am aiding your father, not harming him."

"That's the wrong thing to do."

"What?" Pel asked.

Per-Arizak leaned close, so that Pel could smell the thick, sour liquor that was on the big man's breath. "You interfere in a natural process. Do nothing. Let him die in his own time, according to the will of Irrunega. It can't be long, not the way I saw the blackness advancing up that stump of his. Better that he had died cleanly in battle."

"But your mother . . ."

"Will do as I say, once I am ruler of this stinking hole," the Dragon stated, plainly. "As you will. When I rule, as I will, if you obey me now, you'll live a long and peaceful life. If you don't"—he reached into his pouch and brought out the gleaming globe of stone—"they'll find this embedded in your skull. Take it. You can return it to my mother when you go to tell her you can help her pervert the course of time no longer."

He pushed Pel against a wall, dismissing him, and gestured to his friends. They shoved past the healer and strode into the Vulgar Unicorn, calling loudly for service.

Pel stood on the pavement, the light from the stone leaking out from between his fingers in the dark of the moonless night. The third and eldest of the sons of Arizak had discovered him and made his demands. What each wanted were all contradictory to one another: heal, kill, or leave alone. He could fulfill one, but not all of their wishes. Any of the three actions would get him killed, not once, but twice. Only one followed the teachings of his savior gods.

Pel turned away from the brightly lit door and started to trudge toward home.

Now what do I do? he thought, praying hard for an answer. He did not want to die, nor did he really want to leave the city he had vowed to help heal.

But there was no answer from Meshpri or Meshnom. His only guiding light on his way was the globe.

Good Neighbors

Lynn Abbey

Chersey felt guilty.

When Dace had arrived at the changing house last winter, crippled and reeking of the Swamp of Night Secrets, she'd welcomed him out of charity. Charity was a godly virtue and Chersey, who'd come of age during the Dyareelan Troubles, had lived comfortably without gods until recently, when she'd warmed to the sensible words and good examples the Raivay SaVell espoused from the ruins along the Promise of Heaven. Charity, the Raivay said, was the path to Paradise.

Chersey didn't worry about Paradise, but charity toward the Nighter had lightened her heart. She'd trimmed his dark brown hair and supplied him with new garments—

Well, not *new* garments. The changing house stored great quantities of secondhand garments. The boy, bless his soul, hadn't cared that his new clothes weren't. Chersey had given Dace a pair of boots, too. He'd appreciated the footgear, but his eyes had sparkled brightest for a carved-wood crutch her husband, Bezul, had dug out of the warrens.

Bezul admitted the crutch was one of the first items his family had traded after they'd descended to Wriggle Way from their former home among the city's goldsmiths. Fools they'd been then: Folk didn't come to a changing house when they needed crutches.

Except Dace.

The youth didn't talk about the swamp; he didn't need to. His life was written in his scars and, of course, in his withered right leg. He'd never used a crutch. What good was a crutch in a swamp?

Between the crutch and boots, Dace's first days at the changing house had been a series of stumbling disasters. Chersey had come within a breath of banishing him from her kitchen. If she had, then neither she nor Dace would have discovered that he was a kettle wizard. The boy need only taste a dish or smell it on the fire to deduce its ingredients. Chersey had been preparing food as long as she could remember, but Dace prepared *meals*.

Dear Bezul had been diplomatic, insisting that no one could make a better stew than his wife, but he'd come around when Dace began doing things that Chersey could never have imagined. Bezul's redoubtable mother, Gedozia, had taken longer, in no small part because Dace wanted to take over the marketing and marketing was Gedozia's domain.

A gimpy Nighter can't bargain! They'll take one look at him, raise their prices, and we'll be on the street before we know it.

Then, overnight, Dace shed his Nighter twang as easily as he'd shed swamp dirt and rags. He spoke common Wrigglie now, and it was easy to forget he wasn't city-born.

That boy is shameless, Gedozia said when the two of them returned from the market; and, coming from Gedozia, that was a compliment.

When the first sultry spell of summer had settled over the city, Gedozia declared that her ankles had swollen and the thrice-weekly trek to market was more suffering than she intended to endure. Dace, whose every step had to be more painful than any Gedozia had taken, leaped at the opportunity to carry the household purse.

The household was eating better and spending less money—because Dace was not only a better bargainer than the old woman, he didn't skim padpols for his own indulgence. Chersey had to tell him to keep a coin or two for himself. Youths his age needed a few padpols and she needed to assuage her guilt.

Like some high-born lady, Chersey consulted with her cook while the family ate breakfast.

"Any ideas for tonight's supper?"

Dace looked up. He was chopping last night's leftovers into the stockpot. Dace wasn't a handsome youth. His grin was lopsided, as if whatever had crippled his right leg had touched his face as well, but his eyes were lively and his gaze was direct as he said, "Depends on what I smell along the Processional."

Chersey laughed. "If I didn't know better, I'd say you were looking for a finer kitchen than this one." When Dace shook his head, Chersey continued in a more serious tone: "Really, you need to be careful—"

"The Processional's there for everyone, Governor's Walk, too. The guards don't hassle me and if the nabobs don't want me sneaking their recipes, they should tell their cooks to close the doors."

"The guards aren't there to protect you, not on the Processional. You'd be wiser to take the Shambles bridge—the way is shorter and if you smell anything around here, we can afford the spices."

"Ser Perrez says not to worry, we'll be rich soon."

Perrez was the only household name Dace hung a handle on. He'd learned that flattery was the way to deal with Bezul's younger brother, Gedozia's favorite son. Chersey had watched Perrez grow from a dreaming youth into a scheming manhood and was wise to his dreams. She wished she could bestow that wisdom on Dace, but there was no putting old heads on young shoulders. If the youth's wits were as sharp as his nose, he'd uncover the truth about Perrez soon enough with no help from her.

The morning chill had vanished long before Dace made his last purchase. Chersey had given him an uncut shaboozh because it was
Shiprisday and on Shiprisday, Dace bought extra bread and cheese.
The mistress didn't demand a precise accounting of expenses and
wouldn't have raised an eyebrow if Dace had come home without a
padpol. She was generous that way, and trusting—totally unlike the
family Dace had left behind.

The changing-house folk didn't pry into Dace's past, and he was
grateful. His kin weren't worth remembering, though Dace hadn't
managed to forget them . . . yet. A year ago he'd *seen* a shaboozh
clutched tightly in his uncle's hand, but he'd never held one, much
less spent it all in a single morning.

Dace took his responsibilities to heart. Gedozia had taught him
to bargain, though, truth to tell, Gedozia was sharp and bitter and
lacked the friendly patience that yielded the best prices. Dace had
memorized each farmer's name, his village and his welfare. He ban-
tered as he bargained, shaving a padpol off the asking price or gain-
ing an extra onion as his reward. Today hadn't been a good day for
bonus produce, but he'd wound up with three leftover padpols.

The broken black bits were knotted securely into a pouch he wore
inside his trousers where it wouldn't come loose or attract unwanted
attention—not that three padpols bouncing on the Processional's
cobblestones would attract attention. Folk on the Processional didn't
stoop for padpols. They scarcely stepped aside for a cripple in secondhand homespun.

Dace sated his curiosity about Sanctuary's richest and best-fed
families with quick sniffs and glances. Someone had dropped a coin
at the feet of a juggler who was putting on a show outside the white-
washed mansion of Lord Noordiseh. Dace stood on tiptoe—a stance
both awkward and painful—at the crowd's fringe. He caught glimpses
of the bright-clad sailor swirling five knives between his rapidly moving hands.

He'd seen jugglers on the streets before, but none who'd added the element of danger to their routine. Each time the juggler caught a knife, there was the chance he'd grasp the flashing blade. Dace couldn't tear away from the spectacle. His ears were deaf to the commotion at the mansion's door until it was too late—

"Make way! Make way!" burly retainers shouted as they shoved through the crowd.

The juggler caught his knives without trouble; Dace was not so fortunate. Already unbalanced on his tiptoes, he crashed to the cobblestones when someone jostled into his crutch. More mindful of his purchases than his bones, the youth clutched his bulging sack to his chest as he fell. His crutch flew and he landed on his back, not hard enough to break anything, but hard enough that he lay motionless, waiting for his body to become his again.

The crowd had vanished like smoke on a windy day.

"Damn insolence! Move him out of the way!"

Dace turned toward the sound and snagged eyes with Lord Noordiseh himself, resplendent in billowing silk and an equally billowed silk-and-feather hat. Three thoughts burst into Dace's mind. The first two—*Find your crutch* and *Get yourself away from here!*—were wise choices, but the third—*He's wearing a fake beard*—was more compelling, at least until one of the burly retainers reached for Dace's sack.

"The little thief's got enough food here to feed an army—"

Dace flailed and found his crutch. With a desperate heave and a measure of luck he lurched to his feet without surrendering the sack. "No army, ser, just my household."

"What family?" the retainer demanded. "Where do you live?"

Dace saw the crack of doom looming before him. He should have listened to Chersey, should have stayed away from the Processional, but bad as things were, they'd be worse if he lied. "Wriggle Way, ser. The house of Bezulshash the Changer."

The retainer wasn't impressed, but Lord Noordiseh showed unexpected mercy: "Let him go."

And Dace went, as fast as his gimpy leg allowed. His heart didn't

stop racing until his feet touched Wriggle Way. Familiar buildings had
never looked so good. He paused to tidy his clothes; no sense walking
into the changing house with his shirt hitched up.

A girl emerged from the Frog and Bucket tavern as Dace swiped his
fingers through his hair. Geddie wasn't the sort to draw much attention. She had a plain face with slightly bulging eyes. Her hair hung in
braids against her back and her skirt was shorter than it should have
been, as if she were in the midst of a girlish growth spurt, though she
swore she was nineteen and a veteran of the Maze brothels.

Dace didn't believe Geddie had worked the brothels and didn't
think she was pretty. In fact, he thought she was so homely that she
might eventually succumb to a cripple's charm. He called her name
and hurry-hobbled to catch up.

"I didn't expect to see you today!"

"It's my day off."

Geddie worked in the palace laundry where she'd risen from
pounding and wringing to the skilled labor of mending.

"So, where're you going?"

"Same place as you. Got me a gift to change." Geddie patted
the pouch slung at her waist. "Then I'm off to see One-Eye Reesch. He
just got a chest of Aurvesh fortune oils. S'not like they're Caronnese,
but my girlfriend says they work real well."

"Can I come with?"

Geddie shrugged and Dace stuck close.

"I can give you twelve padpols—three soldats—for them," Chersey
judged while eyeing the pair of merely serviceable boots.

"You gave a whole shaboozh last time."

Chersey sighed inwardly. She preferred to give her customers what
they wanted and had never hardened to this colder part of changing-
house life. "Last time I didn't have six other pairs of boots on the
shelves."

"I've got to have a shaboozh. Just one until Ilsday. I'll buy 'em
back then, same as always."

"Thirteen." Chersey made her final offer.

The woman was a regular customer who cycled her husband's boots through the changing house the way fishermen cycled their nets.

"We'll starve," the woman insisted, which was merely her way of accepting the offer.

Chersey pulled a thin, baked-clay, double-eyed tablet from a bowl beneath the counter and began writing the details of the trade on it. When she finished, she handed the tablet to the woman who broke it in two, keeping one sherd and returning the other to Chersey who threaded a bit of twine through the eye. She tied the twine to the boots before counting out thirteen good-sized padpols—one of them almost large enough to be a two-padpol bit.

The woman wasn't blind to generosity. She gave thanks and swept the tarnished bits into the hem of her sleeve. Chersey put the tagged boots on the shelf. The changing house always had boots, but eight pairs—she'd forgotten one—were an unusually high number. Something was amiss in the hand-to-mouth segment of Sanctuary society that relied on the changing house to tide them over.

She and Bezul should discuss the problem. The changing house didn't have unlimited padpols. There'd been times in the past when they'd had to stop making exchanges for cash. But Bezul and Pel Garwood were no closer to an exchange for the old Ilsigi ewer someone had given the healer in exchange for *his* services. The healer was a good man—Chersey consulted him whenever one of the children took sick—and a better bargainer. He and Bezul might be at it all day.

The morning was hot. Chersey thought about getting herself a glass of night-cooled mint tea from the kitchen sump. She got as far as the inner door when the brass bell hanging from the open doorway jangled and Jopze—one of the two retired soldiers who kept a lid on things in exchange for clothes for their ever-increasing broods—hailed Dace by name.

Dace didn't usually come through the front door. Chersey wondered why he'd changed his habits and, turning, saw that the youth wasn't alone. She recognized the scrawny girl by sight, not name.

The girl lived above the Frog and Bucket, which was tantamount to saying she sold herself to the tavern's customers. She had some sort of dealings with the palace, too: a job in the laundry, or so she claimed. Chersey couldn't imagine how any laundress could come by the trinkets the girl exchanged without shedding her own clothes.

Chersey wasn't pleased to see the girl with Dace, though she immediately realized she shouldn't have been surprised. Dace might have a crippled leg and a lopsided smile, but he was still a young man at an age when young men had only one thought on their minds. He was being practical, aiming low where his chances of success were high.

Dace began the conversation: "Geddie's got something to change."

So the girl's name was Geddie. Somehow it fit that her name sounded like something stuck to a shoe, but business was business. Chersey returned to the counter.

"Let's have a look."

The girl brought out a cloth-wrapped parcel which proved to contain a small statue of Anen, the Ilsigi god of wine and good fortune. The statue was painted stone, chipped here and there, with hollow eyes where gems had once resided. Three bands confined the god's unruly hair. Two were hollow but the third shone with gold. Chersey could pin a value to ordinary household objects, but when it came to relics, she turned to her husband.

"Bez? Could you take a look at this?"

Bezul seemed relieved by the interruption. He picked up the statue, paying particular attention to its base. "You realize this once stood in Anen's chapel at the Temple of Ils?" he said with a trace of accusation in his voice.

Of course, the Dyareelan fanatics had destroyed the temple. Ils's priests had hidden a few of their treasures before they died. A week didn't go by without someone claiming to have found an abandoned hoard.

Chersey and Bezul heard *all* the treasure rumors, thanks to Bezul's brother, Perrez. Sometimes the rumors were true—that ewer Pel Garwood was determined to exchange had survived the Troubles intact, but the changing house didn't knowingly trade in looted goods. There were dens on the Hill that specialized in covert trade.

"How did you come by this?" Bezul challenged.

"A gift," she replied, sullen and defiant.

"From whom?"

"I got a friend at the palace."

Chersey scowled and flicked her moonstone ring close to her right eye. The ring was minor wizardry. It cast an aura through which Chersey could detect lies and deceit. The girl was full of deceit, but she wasn't lying when she said, "I mended his britches. Them Irrunes, they don't touch money, but they'll give you gifts."

Chersey doubted that mending had anything to do with Geddie's good fortune, but it was true enough that Sanctuary's current rulers refused to handle money. Had it been up to Chersey, they would have sent Geddie and her relic packing. Regardless of how the girl had come by her gift, they weren't likely to resell a stripped relic in day-to-day trade. They'd have to turn it over to Perrez who brokered their one-of-a-kinds to east-side dealers, foreigners, and an occasional rich patron. Chersey would rather have made do without Perrez's contributions. Bezul would have done the same, but his brother's trades turned a tidy profit, when they didn't fall through; and the house couldn't overlook profit.

According to Perrez, Sanctuary relics were all the rage in the Ilsigi Kingdom and the right trade could yield a tidy profit—*could* being the operative word.

Bez set the statue on the counter. "You'd do better at a goldsmith's. I recommend Thibalt in Copper Corner."

Geddie worked her mouth into a sarcastic smile. "Sure. I'm going to walk into a froggin' *gold*smith's. Me an' all my ladies."

"We don't trade in relics. I can only offer intrinsic worth—"

The girl scowled at the unfamiliar word. "Shite for sure, so long as it's four froggin' shaboozh."

"Three," Bezul replied without batting an eye, which told Chersey the statue must be worth ten.

"Three'n twelve."

"Three and eight."

Geddie thrust out her chin. "Done," she declared and held out her hand.

Bezul counted the coins and the girl turned to leave the shop. Dace turned with her, then hesitated. The young man's conflicting thoughts were so obvious that Chersey could read them on his face: The household's supper was hanging in a sack from his shoulder, but he'd rather moon after the girl.

Chersey's mother-wit counseled responsibility. The girl was trouble. On the other hand, Dace was nearly grown and she wasn't his mother. She reached for the sack.

The boy brightened. "I'll be back in good time to start the supper!"

Bezul caught Chersey's eye as the pair left. Chersey shrugged. She liked having someone to do the kitchen chores, but she didn't expect the respite to last forever.

"You should have gone to a goldsmith," Dace said as he kept pace, barely, with the woman of his current fantasies.

Geddie gave a snort worthy of an overheated horse. "And get cheated even worse? When I can dress myself like a lady, then I'll go where ladies go."

"Where's One-Eye Reesch?"

"In the bazaar. With what I got for that statue, I can buy myself some good-fortune oil. I'm telling you, I'm due for good fortune. I'm not spending my life on Wriggle Way."

Dace had never heard of good-fortune oils. At the very least, he'd meet someone new and fill in another gap or two in his knowledge of life beyond the Swamp of Night Secrets. He would have been happier if Geddie looked at him when she spoke, but she wasn't telling him to get lost.

Though Geddie insisted that the bazaar was quiet, almost deserted, Dace was left agog by the sights, sounds, and smells. He didn't dare ask questions, though, lest Geddie get the wrong impression or abandon him among the stalls.

Geddie navigated and brought them to the large wooden stall where One-Eye Reesch both lived and worked. Mostly, the gray-haired, patch-eyed trader sold metal lamps and colorful glass goblets, but when Geddie mentioned fortune oils, he winked his good eye and led her to a wicker chest, maybe two feet on each side, stuffed with straw and wax-stoppered vials.

"Can you read?" Geddie hissed.

Dace winced. Chersey was teaching him Ilsigi letters, same as she taught five-year-old Ayse. He could recognize a few words and enough letters to know that the writing on the bottles wasn't Ilsigi.

Reesch had overheard. "No problem. The blue ones are for money, the red for true love, the green ones will get rid of sickness, and the blacks will break a hex."

Geddie wanted vials in red and blue, but her money wouldn't stretch that far. The smallest red vial was three shaboozh. The blue vials were cheaper. For two and ten Geddie could buy a fist-sized vial of fortune. Geddie bargained Reesch down to two and seven. She slipped the precious vial inside her bodice.

"Fortune comes first," she told Dace as they headed out of the bazaar. "This oil's going to pull me a froggin' rich man. Once I have money, love will follow."

"What if your true love happened to be poor?" Dace didn't add crippled; there was no sense in tempting fate.

"He won't be. I've had my palm read: My love line joins my money line. You want to share?"

"Share what?"

"My fortune oil! Soon as I get home, I'm going to burn some. You want to sit beside me? You need all the help you can get."

Dace agreed. His hopes soared, until Geddie asked—

"Is Perrez rich?"

In self-defense, Dace answered, "No."

"But he looks so fine in his white shirts, and he knows everyone. I've watched him in the Frog."

"Most of the time Perrez works for Bezul. He'll be working for Bezul when he brokers your statue. That means what he gets goes to Bezul—most of it, anyway. He only keeps it all when he brokers something he found—" Dace caught himself on the verge of a secret and clammed up.

Geddie wasn't fooled. "What has he found?"

"Well, he didn't *find* it, exactly. He made a trade—with a fisherman. You've heard the rumors—there's some mystery wreck out on the reef. No one knows anything about it, but the fishermen are picking it clean. Guess the fisherman thought the thing was cursed and wanted to be rid of it. Perrez says it's going to make him rich."

"What kind of thing is it?"

Dace shook his head.

"C'mon—you can tell me. I won't tell anyone."

"It's a black rod, half as long as my arm from elbow to wrist. There's a gold dragon wrapped around the tip and honey amber wired to the base."

Geddie's eyes and mouth widened into circles. "Froggin' sure that's sorcery."

"That's what Perrez thinks. He hasn't told anyone but me. Not even Bezul. He's keeping it—" Dace caught himself again. "Keeping it safe until he can sell it. Not here. He's going to consign it up to Il-sig. Lord Noordiseh's his vouchsafe—'cause he knows Kingdom lords who're richer than all Sanctuary put together. *I* took the message straight to Lord Noordiseh—"

"You've met Lord Noordiseh?" There was new respect in Geddie's voice.

"I saw him this morning."

Geddie stopped short and gave Dace a once-over. He bore her appraisal without flinching. He *had* delivered Perrez's message to Lord Noordiseh's mansion—and waited at the back door all afternoon for an answer that never came. And he *had* seen the nabob on his way back from the market. His heart leaped when Geddie slipped her hand beneath his left arm. Walking close to anyone was a challenge with the crutch but he managed all the way to the Frog and Bucket.

Geddie's room was beneath the tavern's roof and accessible only by a rickety outside stairway. Dace didn't like using stairways, especially when he could see between the risers. He planted his crutch, held his breath, hopped, and hoped. His teeth hurt from clenching by the time he got to the landing and he stayed close to the wall until Geddie undid her latch knot. She ushered him into a stiflingly hot room scarcely large enough for a narrow cot, a couple of baskets, and a tied-together table. For sitting, there was a three-legged stool.

Dace disliked stools almost as much as he disliked stairs, but he wasn't forward enough to sit on the cot, so he stood while Geddie lit the lamp with a sparker, set it on the stool, set the stool by the cot, sat down, and patted the mattress beside her.

Dace didn't need a second invitation. The warmth of Geddie's thigh was palpable against his and she hadn't bothered to tidy her bodice after retrieving the vial. He sucked in a lungful of smoke after Geddie shook a few drops of fortune oil into the lamp, but he already had his good fortune. Her small, pale breast was visible within the cloth. Dace tried not to stare. It was a lost cause, but Geddie didn't seem to mind.

"Take another breath," she urged, leaning toward the lamp.

He could see everything then, from root to nipple. The forbidden sight took his breath away and he choked on the vapors.

Geddie pounded between his shoulder blades. "Shite for guts, haven't you done this before?"

Between gasps, Dace shook his head.

"Want something *easier*? Something *better*?"

Good fortune indeed! Dace nodded vigorously. He wasn't sure what came next, then Geddie shoved a pitcher into his hands.

"Go downstairs and buy some wine."

Downstairs was worse than upstairs, but he'd do it for the reward he thought she'd promised. Except— Except—

"I don't drink much. I have enough trouble staying upright as is."
He laughed, but the joke fell flat.

"You don't have to *drink*. All's you've got to do is dip."

Dace wouldn't admit it, but he didn't understand that remark. He
had another painful confession: "I've only got three padpols."

"That's enough."

Three padpols of the Frog's cheapest wine filled the pitcher halfway.
Four padpols and he'd have spilled some struggling up the stairs a
second time. Geddie had her head in the lamp fumes when he opened
the door. She called him to the cot with a question:

"Ever done *opah*?"

Dace felt like a wet-eared puppy, shaking his head for the ump-
teenth time.

She patted the cot. "I'll show you."

Obediently, Dace sat beside her. Geddie produced a palm-sized
square of dirt-crusted cloth.

"Here. Just dip the corner into the wine"—she demonstrated the
proper motion—"and hold it against the tip of your tongue."

The first sensation was an alarming bitterness, but the second, a
heartbeat later, was a tingling that raced down Dace's throat and
down his arms as well. He pulled away from the strangeness. Geddie
laughed, re-dipped the cloth, and challenged him to stick out his
tongue again. Unwilling to be shown up by a woman, Dace obliged.
The tingling shot down his spine like ice and fire together.

"Now, suck the wine out," Geddie commanded. "Suck hard."

A part of Dace knew that was a bad idea, that nothing that made
him feel so *odd* could possibly be a good thing. But that wasn't the
part he listened to. He closed his lips over the cloth and sucked for
all he was worth.

The bitterness damn near took his breath away and the tingling—
"tingling" wasn't the right word. Dace's flesh quivered and his body
seemed to expand. His eyes watered. When they cleared there new
colors everywhere, colors Dace could taste and hear.

He watched in rapt fascination as Geddie repeated the process for herself. Her eyes closed as she released the cloth and lolled back on the cot. Dace's arm moved toward her breast, which was also the location of the damp cloth. He barely stopped his arm in time and wasn't completely certain which he'd been reaching for.

"So, now you've done *opah*," Geddie told him in a dreamy, distant voice. "Ready to do it again?"

Dace didn't need to think. The unpleasant quivery sensation had passed and he felt . . . he felt better than he'd ever felt. Even the pain in his leg that had been a part of him forever was gone. He reached again . . . for the cloth. Geddie met his hand halfway. Their hands touched. Dace felt the tiny ridges on her fingertips and much, much more. He did the *opah* a second time, and a third, and there was nothing he couldn't have done after that third dosing.

Geddie poured more fortune oil. They knocked foreheads over the fumes and collapsed, laughing, against each other. Dace endeavored to untangle himself, but, as good as the *opah* made him feel, his hands weren't moving quite the way he expected them to. He was still solving that problem when Geddie's hand closed over his shirt and pulled him close.

The brutal heel of midsummer settled firmly on Sanctuary's collective neck. Life slowed especially during the midday hours. Bezul retreated to the warrens where there was always something that needed straightening—and where the shadows were still cool. Chersey retreated to the kitchen. She poured tea from the jug in the sump and sipped liquid, marginally cooler than the air.

The children played in the courtyard under Gedozia's watchful eye. Neither the old woman nor the youngsters seemed to feel the heat as heavily as working folk. Little Ayse laughted as she chased one of Sanctuary's gem-colored bugs and distracted Chersey from other concerns.

Dace hadn't returned from the market. He'd left at sunrise, as usual—or as close to usual as he'd been since taking up with that girl from the Frog and Bucket. Geddie was no sorceress, but she'd

cast a spell over the naive Nighter all the same. The boy's habits now
included evening visits to her room above the tavern. He'd roll in
late, reeking of wine and a bitter perfume Chersey couldn't place.
Even Perrez had noticed the deterioration.

Talk about the pot calling the kettle black!

Perrez had been skulking lately. Something to do with the shipwreck
fishermen had discovered on the reefs where they caught their summer
fish. Chersey didn't know—didn't *want* to know—what Perrez had
gotten himself into this time. So long as he didn't involve the rest of the
household, she preferred to ignore her brother-in-law's affairs.

Chersey took another sip of tea and succumbed to the thoughtless
drowse of a too-hot morning. The next thing she knew there was
noise at the kitchen door: Dace with the sack slung carelessly over
his shoulder and sweat beading on his face.

"The market's frogged for fair." He'd never used language like
that before Geddie.

She replied, "The heat's hard on everything."

"The heat and some sheep-shite nabobs. There wasn't a melon to
be had and the beans weren't fit for pigs."

Dace emptied the sack on the sideboard. The fish were stiff and
glistening with salt, the cheese glowed waxy from the heat, and the
greens were wilted. Not an appetizing array, but unless you lived rich,
you didn't expect appetizing meals day-in and day-out. The palace
wasn't the problem—the Irrune ate like animals: meat, grains, and
wine or ale. It was the city's own aristocrats that bled the markets
dry. Chersey couldn't count the number of times Gedozia had returned from the market with a half-empty sack and curses galore for
the nabobs.

"Don't worry," she reassured Dace. "The weather and the market
will cool soon enough."

"Maybe." Dace picked up a fish by its tail. "Three padpols and
look at the size of it! I had to buy two. You can't tell me that the froggin' nabobs are feasting on salt-fish! Gets any worse and I'm going to
have to go back to baitin' crabs."

"We'll get by. We've always got eggs—"

The changing house's security, when not provided by Ammen and Jopze, came from the flock of geese Bezul turned loose every night. The birds were nasty creatures but the changing house had never been robbed and, come morning, there was always a clutch of eggs for Ayse to gather.

"Oh, I'll find something," Dace assured her. "But a shaboozh isn't going as far as it did a month ago. No change again today."

"We'll get by."

Chersey thought of the folk who wouldn't, the folk who dribbled into the changing house with their precious possessions. This summer was turning into a bad season. Bezul couldn't pinpoint the reason. They'd had a mild winter and moist spring. The farmers were content, notwithstanding the current heat wave. Content farmers were the surest measure of a content Sanctuary. Yet something lurked below the surface, siphoning off the small change.

"We've got sacks of dried lentils out back," she reminded Dace, "and a barrel of pickled congers for emergencies—" Not anyone's idea of an appetizing meal, but better than starvation . . . or overheated prices. "We can live off that for a few weeks."

"No way! I'll find the bargains." Dace put the two fish in a bowl and emptied a ewer of water over them. "That'll hold 'em until I get back."

"You're going out again?"

Dace shrank and didn't reply.

"That girl again."

"Geddie," he corrected and started toward the door. "I'll be back in time to fix the froggin' supper."

Chersey raised her hand to her face and sighted across the moonstone ring. A dark shadow fell across Dace's back. He was hiding something, lying—maybe worse. She waited until he'd left then found Ammen and Jopze dozing over a dice game.

"Will one of you keep an eye on Dace?"

"What needs knowing?" Ammen, the taller, brawnier, and balder of the two inquired. "The bint's gotten her claws into him . . . for now. She'll get bored and cast him off. Her kind's not interested in a boy like our Dace, not for long."

"I don't want him to get hurt."

"Too late for that," Jopze added. "He's shite-faced. Best to let it die natural-like."

Chersey couldn't argue with the soldiers' wisdom, but she couldn't shake the feeling that sex was only part of the boy's problem.

Dace had adapted to the stairs leading to Geddie's room. He bounded up them, knocked once, and lifted the latch before he heard her voice. He embraced her without preamble. To Dace's surprise, Geddie wriggled free.

"You got it?"

Dace let his breath out in a hot sigh. "Yeah, I've froggin' got it. Twelve padpols. More than enough for an *opah* rag and the wine to soak it in."

Geddie frowned. "Not today. Today, I gotta square my debts downstairs. I needed twelve just to cover what we did since Ilsday. I need a whole shaboozh—sixteen padpols—if we're gonna dip today."

"What!?"

"I told you: I don't get *opah* for nothing! I can't afford to share anymore. You gotta pay for your share."

Dace dug the jagged black coins out of his purse and threw them on the cot. "There, I've paid. It's not worth a shaboozh." He headed for the door.

"Wait!" Geddie seized Dace's arm. "You can get *opah* the way I get it. You can do *things* . . . things for Makker. Downstairs. I told him you'd be coming. He wants to meet you. If he likes you, you can buy direct from him. It's half the price."

"What kind of *things*?"

"Nothing much. Run messages—like you already do for Perrez. Maybe sell a book of rags somewhere. Nothing hard. *Opah*'s easy to sell."

Dace tucked the crutch under his right armpit. If he heeded half the wits that got him out of the swamp, he should walk away *now*. He liked the bitter powder altogether too much. By the time he got over here every day, his skin had started to crawl with *want* and *need*.

He'd asked Perrez about *opah*—because Perrez knew the answers to questions Dace could never ask Chersey or Bezul. Frog all, Dace had lied and sworn he'd never touch *opah* himself, only overheard conversations about it in the marketplace.

Opah? *That's nothing but* krrf, *boy, diluted down then made pure again. Don't ask me how it's done, or who, or where, but when it's done, it's cheap as sin and the deadliest poison you can swallow. A sure path to hell, but the hit, now that's Paradise. How's a man supposed to see past Paradise?*

From which statement, Dace had concluded that Perrez sucked a little *opah* himself. And, building on that conclusion, Dace asked himself—why not meet with this Makker fellow? Shite for sure, if Perrez was using *opah*, he would appreciate a cheaper source and— maybe . . . hopefully—consider Dace for tasks more demanding than simply running a message to some under-house door.

By all the gods, Dace wanted to be a man who wore fine clothes, who turned heads when he walked into a crowded room—and not because of a gimpy leg or noisy crutch.

"All right, I'll meet Makker."

Dace had never seen Maksandrus, called Makker, before, but he recognized the type. Was there a gods' law that said all bullies had necks wider than their skulls, squinty eyes, and forearms that could double as pork hams? Dace had a cousin who could have been Makker's twin, save Balor was swamp bred and Makker was a foreigner from Mrsevada—wherever in the seven hells *that* was.

Geddie approached Makker alone. When she whispered in his ear, Makker scowled so deep that Dace expected to be sent packing. Then, Makker said something and Geddie motioned Dace over.

Fear gripped Dace's gut the moment his rump hit the chair.

Makker had serpent's eyes: cold and hard as jet. It was all Dace could do to meet them and, once he had, impossible to look away. He vowed that he'd do the bully's business once and once only—and not for any promise or threat of *opah*.

But Makker didn't ask about *opah*; he asked about the changing house. Early on, Bezul had warned Dace not to answer questions about the business. Dace tried to heed Bezul's warnings and did well, he thought, until Makker started asking about fishermen, shipwrecks, and whatever salvage the fishermen had brought for changing. Dace knew that no fishermen had brought wreck salvage into the shop and said so, but every word had to get past the memory of Perrez's dragon rod.

No way Dace was going to mention that rod to the likes of Maksandrus and he didn't—not directly. Makker's questions were friendly, and lulled by them, Dace let slip that Perrez, not Bezul, handled the exotic trades and that he was running messages to the Processional about an artifact that had, indeed, come from the fishermen's wreck.

"What manner of artifact?"

Dace's blood froze. He realized how much he'd given away. "I don't know," he lied. "Perrez keeps it locked tight. I just run his messages."

"To who?"

Oh, would that the ground would swallow him up! A messenger had to know where to deliver the message, Dace couldn't lie his way around that. "I can't tell," he mumbled. "I'm sworn."

"You hear that, Kiff? An honest messenger!" Makker crowed and Kiff—an enormous man with skin the color of midnight—laughed, revealing a yellow gem winking in a front tooth. "I like doing business with honest men." He slapped the table; everything bounced. "Geddie says you want to work for me."

"Want" was the last word Dace would have chosen, but he didn't have the fortitude to argue. In short order, he found himself agreeing to sell a book of *opah* rags.

"Kiff—" Makker called.

Kiff opened a fist and an *opah* book fell onto the table.

"Seeing as you're an honest man," Makker said with a grin, "here's how it's going down. I give you ten rags, you owe me eight padpols for each—that's five shaboozh, total. Say you sell a rag for more, you keep the difference. Understand?"

Dace nodded but made no move toward the dusty, tied-together book.

"I give you until next Shiprisday, but if you need more before then—more *opah,* not time—you know where to find me."

Dace did calculations in his head. If he could sell the rags for one shaboozh each, he'd have five shaboozh for Makker and five for himself. . . . He'd be rich. How hard could selling be? He was already a good bargainer.

"And—" Makker lowered his voice to a whisper, "you don't have to ask what happens if you don't bring me my shaboozh."

"Shaboozh, or the rags. You'd take back the rags?"

Makker laughed and pounded the table a second time. "I like you, Dace. I'm going to like doing business with you."

Pleased by his cleverness, Dace tucked the *opah* book carefully in his waist pouch. Makker had nothing else to say, and neither did Dace. He and Geddie left the table. They purchased a pitcher of cheap wine and retreated to her room.

"You were right," Dace said.

Geddie nodded glumly. She sat on the cot, twining her hands together, ignoring the wine. Dace asked about her *opah* and was surprised when she said—

"Can't. I'm empty and Makker said, 'not tonight' when I asked. There's no arguing with Makker. Said we gotta use yours."

"Mine?" Dace muttered as the essence of the situation became clear to him: If he wanted to dip *opah* with Geddie he was going to have to dip into his profits. The allure of five whole shaboozh was almost enough to swear off both dipping and sharing.

Almost—but not quite. If he set aside one rag for personal use, he'd still wind up with four shaboozh: a tidy sum. And one rag, prudently parceled out, ought to be enough until Shiprisday. Except it wasn't. When Dace left Geddie's room a few hours before sunset, he left a wasted rag behind, too. The lack didn't bother him . . . half that rag was singing in his head, reminding him that he didn't have to wait until next Shiprisday to claim his four shaboozh. He could sell all nine remaining rags tomorrow . . .

Something had happened. Chersey knew it without her ring. For the last week Dace had been changing, but now the change was complete. He threw supper together. The meal was delicious, but it didn't have the touch of pride. And when the plates were scraped, Dace begged off from playing with the children, preferring to hole up with Perrez.

"We're losing him," she told Bezul as they sat outside the shop, catching the breeze off the harbor.

Bezul looked up from the lantern he was repairing. "He's in love. Whatever we think of that girl, he's in love and love has to run its course."

"Not love—not just love. I watched him prepare the supper. His mind was across the ocean—not dreamy. He's *been* dreamy since she took him in. Now he's determined . . . ambitious. That's not love."

"Not to a woman!" Bezul laughed, "but it's a good sign in a man. I didn't take an interest in the changing house until I'd fallen in love with you. A man accepts certain responsibilities, he rises to them, and makes something of himself."

"What can poor Dace make of himself?"

"A fine cook—like as not, that's why he's gone off with Perrez . . . to press for introductions. We don't know anyone who can pay a cook, but Perrez does. Gods love him, but my brother does get around the better parts of this city."

"I hope you're right."

"I'm sure I am. He wasn't ours forever, he's just passing through, like everything else: one hand to the next. We'll wish him well when he leaves."

"Eyes of Ils! Are you possessed?" Perrez stopped short. The look on his face was not the one Dace had been expecting.

"Ser! I thought you'd be interested."

The private door to Perrez's room was outfitted with an impressive iron lock someone had long-ago brought to the changing house. Presumably it had once been paired with an equally impressive key, but the key had bypassed the changing house. Perrez worked the lock with a bump here, a rap there, and a just-so twist on the movable latch. Dace had watched the sequence so many times he could have performed it himself—though he didn't, out of respect.

Perrez bumped, rapped, twisted, and led the way into his bachelor quarters. He locked the door from the inside—a far easier process— and struck a light for the oil lamp before destroying Dace's hopes.

"I couldn't be less interested. May I remind you that Arizak has stirred his stump and outlawed *opah*? Buyer or seller, it doesn't matter, you'll dance on a rope."

"I've got rags that cost me eight padpols. I could sell them anywhere for a shaboozh . . . but I'm offering them to you for twelve."

"You've used the froggin' stuff, haven't you?"

"No," Dace lied. "It's business."

"How much are you selling?"

"Nine rags."

Perrez surged so quickly Dace backed himself into a corner. "Nine? Nine! Don't lie to me, Dace; don't even try. *Opah*'s handed off in books of ten rags. Nobody's got nine, unless he's used one." He grasped Dace's chin to make sure their eyes met.

"I've stopped." At that exact moment, Dace was telling the truth.

"Eyes of Ils, boy—where did you get it?"

"Makker . . . at the Frog and Bucket."

"Maksandrus!" Perrez spat the syllables out and released Dace's chin. "You don't want to do business with Makker. He'll gut you soon as look at you. Got himself thrown off a Mrsevadan ship for killing two mates—two in one voyage! And if Makker doesn't gut you, his boss will. You've heard of Lord Night?"

Dace shook his head.

"If you turn over the frackin' froggin' rock that's Sanctuary, Lord Night's the biggest bug you find, the one with the biggest bite, the vilest poison. He moves the city's *krrf,* Dace, and *opah*'s just *krrf.*"

"You've told me."

"And you've bogged down anyway?"

"I'm not 'bogged down.' "

"Look at me. Let me see your tongue." For a moment, Dace resisted the command, then he obliged. "You're dippin', aren't you?" Dace didn't move, except to withdraw his tongue. "Dippin's bad, but it's not the worst. Far be it from me to tell someone how to live, but get clear of it, Dace, and stay clear of me until you do. While you're doing business with Maksandrus and Lord Night, I don't want to be anywhere close. Go to my brother, beg the froggin' money you need to buy yourself out and *stay* out. Understand?"

Dace nodded. He understood—understood that he'd made a mistake coming to Perrez and that there was no way that he was going to make a similar mistake with Perrez's brother.

Perrez unbolted the inner door, giving Dace the inner passage to the house warrens. The bolt slammed home behind him: Perrez was taking no chances. Dace hunkered down between a cauldron and a tangle of firedogs. He shivered, despite the heat, and shed a few tears before skulking up to the room Chersey and Bezul had made for him under the eaves.

A cool, harbor breeze stirred the air. Any other night, Dace could have fallen straightaway to sleep; tonight the memories of Makker's grin and Perrez's grasp kept him awake long after Bezul set the geese loose.

Dace's tongue thickened as the *opah* tingle faded to nothing. He wanted wine, ale, tea, even water, but all the liquids were on the far side of a flock of geese. He'd send the flock into a frenzy and, truth to tell, Dace wasn't thirsty, what he wanted was *opah*.

The more Dace thought about *opah,* the more he craved it. Finally, he crawled off his bed, found the nine-rag book, and touched stiff cloth directly to his tongue. For a heartbeat, the experiment was a failure, then his tongue began to burn, and the burning shot through his nerves. Before the fire ebbed, Dace pressed the cloth against his tongue again . . . and again.

His body reeled with sensation just short of agony. True sleep was impossible, but the waking dreams he had instead rose from Paradise.

A dreary sunrise found Dace exhausted. His head throbbed explosively when he sat up and his tongue was raw where he'd abused it. Water helped, but only a little. He'd opened the door and was standing in the courtyard, letting rain spill over his head, when Chersey spotted him.

"What's wrong?"

"Nothing. I couldn't sleep."

He turned toward her and, by her expression, he must have looked a fright.

"What happened? Your mouth is all swollen."

"Nightmare," he improvised. "I bit my tongue."

"I'll make tea."

Tea brewed with one of Pel Garwood's powders was Chersey's solution for every ailment. Obediently, Dace drank from the steaming mug and barely kept from fainting. By then the children, Bezul, and Gedozia (but not Perrez, who always slept late) were in the kitchen and clucking over him. He thought the situation couldn't get much worse until Chersey said he should spend the day indoors.

"You're pale and this rain is sure to give you a fever. We'll make supper with what we've got on hand—"

"No!" Dace countered with an urgency that surprised him. "No—a rainy day like this, there'll be bargains."

Gedozia, a veteran of many rainy market days, gave a mighty snort, but Dace held his ground. As soon as breakfast was over, he headed out.

The market was quiet. Half the farmers hadn't braved the weather; but the fishermen were accustomed to a little wet. Dace bargained for a sizable grouper and, as they neared agreement, mentioned that he had something of his own to sell.

"Like what?"

"Rags of *opah,* one shaboozh apiece."

The grizzled man made the ward-sign against evil. "Go away!" he snarled and refused to part with his catch.

Dace was more cautious at the next monger's. He didn't mention his wares until after he'd slid a fish into his food sack; otherwise, the outcome was the same: fishermen, apparently, weren't interested in *opah*. Neither was a woman selling eggs. The cobbler just laughed, while the old man hawking baskets said he was interested but didn't have the cash. Dace struck gold—in the form of four soldats—when he made his pitch to a hard-eyed milkmaid.

Then the wind changed and the clouds let loose with vengeance. Mongers scrambled and Dace retreated to the old bazaar wall where an overhang tempered the worst of the rain. He hadn't been there long when four youths crowded beside him. In his life Dace had learned to be wary of loud, idle groups. He spotted an opening and tried to escape.

Tried. Failed.

A blue-shirted youth with Imperial hair flashed a knife. Another wearing a leather cap shoved a fist against Dace's shoulder.

"Time to take a walk, Gimp."

It was hardly the first time Dace had been ambushed.

The bravos herded him toward the city gate. A pair of guards stood duty there. Their swords could make short work of the bravos—

"Don't even think about it," Blue-shirt growled with another flash of his knife.

Let it be quick, Dace prayed to Thufir. Another thought crossed his mind. *Let them not find my* opah *rags.*

The club-footed god of pilgrims, travelers, and cripples of all kinds heard the first part of Dace's prayer—they were scarcely out of sight of the guard post when Leather-cap gave Dace a sideways shove into an alley. But the great god missed the second part. The bravos hadn't singled Dace out because he was a gimp; they'd targeted him because he was a gimp selling—trying to sell—*opah*. Between the punches and kicks, they stripped him of his possessions until they found his purse. After they'd liberated his money and his rags, they battered Dace some more and left him in the mud.

Despite the crowded warrens, the changing house's primary purpose was converting the coins of other realms into the padpols, soldats, and shaboozh that other Sanctuary merchants would accept. The man standing on the other side of the counter—a sailor by his dress and salty tang—had a small collection of foreign copper and silver that needed changing before he could buy a drink.

Chersey recognized the silver bits as *soun,* the common coin of Aurvesh. She didn't know the proper name of the copper coins. They were probably Aurvestan, too—not that it mattered. There hadn't been official exchange rates since Sanctuary ceased paying Imperial taxes some forty-five years ago. The changing house converted foreign coins by their weight in precious metals. For copper, the least-precious metal—though still rare enough in Sanctuary that its padpols no longer contained even a smattering of it—the process was a simple evaluation by balance pan. Silver coins were dipped in a jar of magically charged acid that reduced the coins to sinking silver and floating impurities.

Chersey had finished evaluating the sailor's copper coins and was fishing the reduced *soun* out of their acid bath when Ammen approached the counter.

"The boy's coming home, m'ser." Ammen always gave her more honor than she deserved or needed.

Dace was late, and she had been wondering where he'd gotten to, but his habits had become so erratic they scarcely warranted an interruption while she was changing silver.

"Fine. Tell him to start the supper."

"He's limping, m'ser."

"He always limps."

"Your pardon, m'ser, but by the look of him, he's lost a fight."

"Sweet Shipri!"

Every instinct called Chersey away from the counter, but instinct didn't keep the changing house in business. She told Ammen to see the boy into the kitchen before hunting down Bezul, then she went back to weighing the sailor's silver.

Bezul emerged from the warrens cradling a large, dusty box in his arms. "What's the matter?"

Trust Ammen to do what he was told and not a jot more. The man wasn't dim-witted, but decades in the Imperial army had dulled his initiative.

"Dace is hurt . . . bleeding . . . in the kitchen. I need to see to him."

"Of course."

Bezul took the raw silver and the strongbox key. Chersey dashed through the kitchen door.

Dace wasn't as badly damaged as she'd feared. The boy's face was scarcely recognizable and his poor hand was swollen to sausages. She'd been prepared for gaping wounds and protruding bones. He was daubing at his face with a dishrag.

"I'm sorry, Chersey," he said as soon as he heard her. "It's gone— it's all gone. They took the money, even the fish I'd just bought . . . everything!"

"Nonsense!" She took the rag and began a more thorough examination of the wounds. "There's nothing to be sorry about. Were you coming down the Processional?"

"No," Dace insisted until she got squarely in front of him and gave him a silent scolding with her eyes. Then he confessed, "Yes, I stopped to watch a juggler. I wasn't paying attention. I'm sorry."

"Well, you've learned your lesson, haven't you: The shortest way home's the best way, isn't it?"

"Yes, m'sera."

Any mother could see that Dace's conscience hurt worse than his bruises. Chersey washed him off with astringent tea. There was one gouge over his eye that would bear watching, but the tea should keep it clean. She didn't like the way he winced when she ran her fingers over his left ankle—the one that kept him upright. If the swelling wasn't down by morning, they'd be needing Pel Garwood. If Pel didn't have the answers, they'd brave a visit to the Spellmaster, Strick at the Bottomless Well.

She bound a length of cloth tightly around the ankle and sent Dace to sit in Bezul's hearth-side chair, then she dragged Lesimar's high-seated feeding chair over to support his ankle.

"But, Chersey—the supper—I can stand."

"Nonsense! You'll sit and you'll keep that ankle higher than your heart until that swelling goes down."

"But—"

"No arguments. We're your family, and we take care of our own."

If some artist had wanted to paint a portrait of misery, he couldn't have found a better model than Dace just then.

Supper was a poor meal, with no fresh food and not enough time to soften the lentils that formed the bulk of it. Dace slept in Bezul's chair—or tried to. The boy was haggard when Chersey came down to check on him the next morning. The swelling hadn't worsened, but it hadn't subsided, either. Dace insisted he was well enough to return to the market, but Chersey wouldn't hear of it. Gedozia went instead and, prompted by Chersey, brought back fresh honey cakes to brighten the boy's mood.

The cakes didn't help and Chersey feared that the damage done to the boy's confidence was beyond healing.

One day fed mercilessly into the next. Ilsday, Anenday, every day brought Shiprisday closer and, come Shiprisday, Dace would have to gimp to the Frog and Bucket where Makker would peel his head like a ripe grape. He'd prayed that his wounds would fester, but his prayers were no match for Chersey's kindness; and what god would heed the prayers of the liar he'd become?

Several times, Dace had come within a breath of confession. The *opah* wasn't part of him anymore. The fever he'd run those first few days in the kitchen had owed little to bruises and everything to *opah*. Dace knew how foolish he'd been; he'd sworn he'd never touch a rag again. That was an easy oath in Chersey's kitchen.

Shiprisday dawned clear and hot as fire. By afternoon, everybody needed space and Chersey didn't argue when Dace said he was well enough to walk as far as the harbor where there was sometimes a breeze even on a scorching day.

Dace wasn't going to the harbor. He did consider, as he set out on Wriggle Way, that the moment might have come to retreat to the Swamp of Night Secrets. His family wouldn't welcome him, but they wouldn't slaughter him, either.

Inside the Frog, Makker was nowhere in sight. Dace thought he'd been reprieved until the bartender recognized him and sent him into a back room where the Mrsevadan was having his lank hair dressed by two attractive girls. Kiff, the black-as-midnight bodyguard, looked on, as did another man, almost as big, whom Dace hadn't seen before. "Dace! I wasn't expecting you until after sundown. You've got my shaboozh!"

It wasn't a question. Dace prayed to Thufir: O, *Mighty Lord, open the earth and swallow me whole!* But Thufir was elsewhere and Dace spat out the words that would surely get him killed.

"I was robbed, ser. I lost everything, especially the *opah*. I've brought my savings, ser—everything I've got. It's only two shaboozh—"

Dace held out the knotted cloth that contained all the padpols he'd saved from marketing. He intended to deliver the inadequate offering directly into Makker's hand, but Kiff surged and Dace froze.

"Only two?" Makker purred. "And no rags to return?" He sucked on his teeth. "That won't do, Dace."

"I know it won't, ser. I know. I'll get the rest, I swear it. I can squeeze maybe eight padpols a week out of the household. That would be six weeks, if you agree, ser." From the glint in Makker's eyes, Dace didn't think agreement was likely. "Or, I could work for you. Geddie says she works for you."

Makker scowled. "Sorry, boy, you're not cut out for the work Geddie does. And six weeks!? Where would I be if I let six weeks pass between when money was due and when it was paid?"

Dace quivered on his crutch. Fear, shame, terror—they were all coming together. He didn't think he could stay on his feet much longer.

"Ser," he whispered, "ser, I'll do anything."

"Hear that, Kiff? This one knows how to make good. No froggin' questions, no froggin' buts, just plain anything." The Mrsevadan returned his attention to Dace. "There *is* something you can do for me. Something only you can do. I want that wand you told me about— the black one with the dragon—and I want it tonight."

Tonight? Dace's mouth worked, but no sound came out. He forced a swallow and tried again: "Tonight? I can't—"

"Can't, Dace? Can't? You said anything. You wouldn't want to go back on your word, would you?"

Kiff eased forward. He made a fist and stroked it like a lover.

Look at me! Dace wanted to shout. *Do I look like a thief?* Instead he collected his nerves and said: "That dragon's gold. It's worth a lot more than five shaboozh . . . three."

"Shite for sure it is, and if you can find three froggin' shaboozh between now and midnight, bring them here. If not, bring me the froggin' wand." Makker leaned forward in his chair. "Unless you were *lying* about the wand."

Suddenly Dace understood why muskrats thrashed themselves bloody when they were trapped.

"I don't know—"

"Yes, you do. Bring me the froggin' wand, Dace. I'll throw in a book of rags, no charge. Or, we can call it quits."

Kiff unmade his fist. He smiled; the yellow gem glinted.

Dace felt his head bob and somehow he made it back to the hot, bright street. The smart thing to do was hie himself across the White

Foal River. Makker'd never find him in the swamp; he'd send Kiff to the changing house, instead. Dace would sooner die than imagine Kiff threatening Chersey or the children.

Muskrats in a trap—

"Dace!"

Geddie was coming out of the tavern, not down the stairs. Dace wondered where she'd been, why he hadn't noticed her.

"Oh, your poor face! You should've come to me. I could've told you other things to offer Makker."

"Too late now."

"Yeah. You want to come upstairs?"

Dace thought of the cot, of sex . . . of the *opah* they'd shared, and needs got the better of him.

"You figured out how you're gonna steal that wand?" Geddie asked when they were naked and sated.

"I can't."

"You've gotta. Makker'll kill you . . . or he'll have Kiff do it."

Dace could handle the idea of being dead, it was the idea of dying—of being killed—that terrified him. "I can't. They took me in, made me part of their family. I can't steal from them."

"It's not stealing; it's saving your froggin' life." Geddie extracted herself from the cot. She prowled through her belongings and produced an *opah* rag. "Want some? I've got wine left." She brought it and the rag back to the cot.

He hadn't forgotten his silent oaths, but what did oaths matter to a man who'd be dead by midnight? His tongue had healed from the last time he'd used the drug. He didn't get the mule-kick exhilaration when he sucked the wine-soaked rag and eyed an undampened corner. But Geddie had made her feelings known about folks who took their *opah* without wine and, anyway, after a few moments, it no longer mattered. *Opah* was singing through his veins. It took the edge off his despair and told him that if the wand was worth more than five shaboozh, well, then, his life was worth more than any wand—

There was daylight left when Dace made his way down the stairway.

He had a plan, a bright, *opah*-fueled plan that took him to Perrez's iron-locked door.

"You in there?"

No answer—just as Dace had hoped. He imitated Perrez's bumps and raps. It took three tries, but the bolt slid free and, opening the door no wider than necessary, Dace eased into the room. The windows were shuttered. There wasn't enough light to see his hand in front of his face, but Dace didn't need to see anything. He lowered himself to his knees and felt across the floor for a distinctive knot-hole against which he pressed with all his weight. A pressure clasp sprang free and Dace pried up a nearby floorboard.

A cloth-wrapped bundle greeted his fingertips. He unwound the cloth and fit the wand easily into the pocket formed where he tucked his shirt beneath his belt. To make sure it stayed there, Dace tightened his belt until it hurt, then he searched for something wand-shaped that he could wrap the cloth around before returning it to the cache.

A spare candle came to hand. Wrapped in the cloth and laid carefully in the cache, Dace told himself it would pass casual muster. He patted the wand for luck and, with his heart pounding in his throat, slipped out of the room. Bump, rap, twist, and the lock was set.

No one had seen him come or go, he hoped. No one suspected that he was carrying ancient treasure above his belt, he hoped. No suspicion would fall on him when—as would inevitably happen—Perrez realized his fortune had gone missing.

"I'm sorry," he whispered to the lock.

Jopze and Ammen were deep in a game of draughts. They didn't notice Dace until he was in the shop and, as neither Bezul nor Chersey were behind the counter at that particular moment, neither of them suspected he had come from Perrez's room. He thought about taking the wand up to his room, but that would only add complications when it came time to take it to Makker—for that matter, Dace had considered taking the wand straight to Makker, but it was time to put the kettle on for supper.

Chersey surprised him in the kitchen while he chopped second-rate greens. She said he looked peaked and wanted to send him upstairs to rest. Dace could scarcely meet her eyes; she was so concerned and so wrong about what was on his mind. She would likely have given him three shaboozh, if he could have borne the shame of telling her why he needed them.

But he couldn't bear it and he insisted on fixing supper—his *last* supper. Careful as he'd been in Perrez's room, Dace didn't believe he was going to get away with robbery. The dragon's claws and teeth scratched against his belly. The tight belt kept his secret, but not for long.

Dace burned the soup and nearly spilled it all when his shirt hem caught on the kettle's handles. The wand was a few threads from catastrophe, but somehow it didn't fall out and Dace got himself put back together. He excused himself as soon as the dishes were scraped.

"I'm going to the Frog," he told them all, Chersey, Bezul, Gedozia, and Perrez together.

"That girl again." Chersey rolled her eyes.

It wasn't right for Chersey to blame Geddie for every wrong thing, but she didn't know about *opah* or Perrez's black wand, so tonight, Dace let the insults slide. He escaped into the amber light of a summer sunset.

So froggin' far, so froggin' good. Perrez didn't yet know his precious wand was missing. There'd be hell to pay when he discovered the robbery, but maybe—just maybe—he'd blame someone else. *I'd be a fool to run off to the swamp. Run off, and they'll know it was me. Stick around, swear I did nothing, and—who knows—maybe I'll get through this. . . .*

Chersey emptied a basin of dirty water into the sump. Bezul was in the back figuring the day's accounts, Gedozia had taken the children for a walk, and Perrez was skulking in the kitchen. She ignored her brother-in-law. It was usually the best way to avoid his pleas for money and, usually, he got the hint.

Tonight was different. He hadn't asked for money; that was a big difference. He hadn't said much of anything at all until she'd wrestled the basin into its home beneath the sideboard.

"Chersey," he said now that her chores were finished. "I need to talk to you."

She dried her hands and sat on a stool. "About what?"

"Dace. I'm worried about him. Maybe you haven't noticed, but he's changed in the last few weeks—"

"He's fallen in love with that girl above the Frog and Bucket—or he thinks he has."

Perrez shook his head. Suddenly he looked older, soberer than she remembered seeing him. "It's not women. I think it's *opah*."

"*Opah?* That's what—? Some new plague come down from Caronne?"

"In a way. They make it from *krrf* and the best *krrf*—the strongest—comes from Caronne. But I've heard they make it right here, in the villages outside the city. Last week, Dace offered to sell me some. He'd gotten it from Makker . . . at the Frog."

Everyone who lived on Wriggle Way knew Maksandrus, and stayed out of his way. Every few months he or one of his cronies showed up at the changing house, hoping to trade the fruits of his labors. Those were the days when Ammen and Jopze earned their keep. Chersey hadn't made the connection between Dace, the girl, and Makker. Guilt rose within her.

"Let me get Bezul."

"I didn't want to bother him."

"It's no bother. Bez needs to hear this."

She fetched her husband and together they listened to Perrez's account of a conversation he'd had with Dace the day before he'd gotten battered on his way home from the market.

"If you ask me, he got caught selling the stuff—and not by the guard. He's in over his head."

"Why tell us *now?*" Bezul demanded. "We needed to know last week."

"I thought he'd come to me and we could work it out together without involving you!"

"And now you don't. What's come up?"

Perrez writhed his shoulders. "He's hiding something. He's done something—it was all over his face at supper. I *know* that look, Bez—you know I know it. You've got to talk the truth out of him."

"I can't very well now, can I?" Bezul's voice rose. The only time he ever yelled was when Perrez got under his skin. "He's gone off for the evening. Gone to the Frog . . . or do you expect me to walk over there and haul him out by the shirtsleeves?"

In the moments before Perrez framed an answer, they all heard the sounds of footsteps and laughter: Gedozia bringing the children back. Chersey caught Perrez's eye, enjoining him to silence.

Perrez obeyed by flinging himself out of his chair and marching out the kitchen door a half step before the children rushed in.

Makker's thick fingers stroked the shaft of the dragon wand. Dace himself hadn't held the wand long enough to know if the shaft was wood or stone. He'd laid it on the table as though it were a thing on fire.

"You did well, Dace. I admit, I wasn't sure you'd come back—froggin' bad cess for you, if you hadn't. I wouldn't have wanted to break your good leg."

Dace wasn't sure how to respond. A nod seemed the best course: a nod, a smile, and a fervent hope that he could leave soon.

"I've got an idea," Makker said, smiling in a way that dashed all Dace's hopes. "There's a man who wanted this thing—a man I think you should meet. Walk with me to the Maze. You can make it that far?"

He should have said no, but a lifetime of denying his deformity set his head bobbing.

Makker's bodyguards flanked them: Kiff and the other one whose name was Benbir and wore five knives on a baldric across his barrel chest. Dace had never felt so safe—or terrified—as he felt with these three men matching his gimpy stride.

Though Dace had never ventured into the Maze, he knew the names of its more infamous taverns and brothels. There was no mistaking the Vulgar Unicorn, not with its signboard hanging brazen in the twilight.

The tavern stank of stale wine, spilled beer, and charred sausage. The long tables in the middle of the commons—the "cheap seats" Kiff called them—were dotted with men and a few women, all of whom went back to looking at their drinks as soon as they'd taken Makker's measure. There were fewer folk at the smaller tables along the shadowy sides of the room. One of them was a lopsided man— Dace assumed it was a man—with hair on one side of his head, but not the other, and a tongue that lolled out the corner of his mouth. He had a huge hump where his right shoulder should have been and lurched violently as he walked. His arms looked long enough to drag on the floor.

Dace had never seen anyone more crippled than himself and, despite all the cruel stares he'd endured, couldn't take his eyes off the scuttling fellow.

"That one's got a friend," Makker said softly. "We leave him alone, and he does the same for us. Come along now."

Kiff led the way up a flight of stairs to a corridor of shut doors. He paused on the hinge side of a door no different than the rest. Benbir took a similar position on the latch side. Makker knocked once and a man's voice called Makker by name. Makker gave Dace a shove and, leaving Kiff and Benbir behind, they entered.

A ceiling lamp provided the room's only light. Its flame cast long shadows over a seated man's face, making it difficult to fix his features. He was a small man—small, at least, compared to Makker, Kiff, and Benbir—but there was no doubt in Dace's mind that he was in the presence of a powerful man. The stranger's head was bald and shiny, his fingers, long and menacing. Even Makker drew a deep breath before saying—

"He got it."

"You wouldn't be here otherwise," the seated man said with what was both a Wrigglie accent and something more refined. "I'll take it now."

He extended that elegant hand and Makker gave away the wand as fast as Dace had given it to Makker.

"A beautiful thing. Yenizedi. A thousand years old; and still charged. You've done well, Makker, you and your friend. Introduce me to our thief."

Makker motioned Dace forward. "Dace, from the Swamp of Night Secrets. Lord Night."

Dace stepped into the cone of lamplight. He extended his hand; the gesture was not returned. He couldn't see Lord Night's—that had to be a made-up name—eyes but knew he was under close scrutiny and was determined not to blink or quiver.

"You're an insolent lad, for one with but a single leg to stand on."

Dace's breath caught in his throat—not for the insult. He could bear any words, but the word itself was an unusual one. Truth to tell, he didn't know what "insolent" meant, except he'd heard a similar word, in a very similar accent, in a very different place: the Processional when a nabob wearing a false beard had ordered him aside. Lord Night was clean-shaven; that only strengthened the connection.

"Lord Noordiseh," Dace muttered, unaware that his tongue had shaped the words aloud. "Perrez turned to you." Dace's eyes fastened on the object in the nabob's hands. "He told you about the wand. He trusted you—"

A gasp echoed through the room. Dace couldn't say from whose throat it had emerged. Lord Night, who was also Lord Noordiseh, had raised his head and Dace couldn't break the stare of the man whose eyes he could not see.

Oh, Thufir, save me! Dace prayed, but his silence and his prayer came too late. The amber drop at one end of the wand was glowing and a thin wisp of smoke rose from the golden dragon's head.

The smoke first thickened, then divided itself, becoming two airborne serpents with shimmering amber eyes. Makker made a break for the door, but Dace couldn't move to save himself or try. His serpent flew closer, coiled, and raised itself in easy striking distance. Its maw opened: amber, like its eyes.

Oh, Thufir—Dace prayed.

He could not even shut his eyes as the fangs fell. There was no pain, so perhaps Thufir had intervened at the last. The room dimmed and Dace felt as though he were falling from a very great height as he heard a woman's voice say, in Wrigglie—

"Well done, my lord. Your secret is safe with these two—"

Perrez paced the kitchen, full of anger and self-pity, as only he could mix them. "It was worth a fortune. A frackin' froggin' *fortune*. It was going to set me up. I had a deal with Lord Shuman Noordiseh. He was going to sell it to one of King Sepheris's court magicians. I'd sworn him a quarter share, but I swear, the gold alone was worth a hundred royals."

"Maybe Lord Noordiseh wasn't satisfied with a quarter share. Maybe Lord Noordiseh stole it," Bezul suggested with the bitterness he reserved for his younger brother.

Chersey wanted to give them both a hearty shake, but until Dace came home to settle the matter the only thing shaking was her nerves. He'd been gone all night. Dace had never stayed out all night, and for him to disappear at the same time as Perrez's Yenizedi rod. If such a rod had truly been in Perrez's possession . . . Well, it *was* suspicious.

Ammen and Jopze were out on the streets, working their connections, hoping someone had seen Dace. Sweet Shipri, with that limp and crutch, he was easy to notice, hard to forget.

"I never trusted him," Perrez insisted. "He'd stare right at you like he was staring through you, like he was planning something. Planning to rob me blind!"

"You encouraged him," Bezul sneered. "Showing him the rod,

using him as your message boy. He idolized you—the gods only know why—"

Chersey retreated to the shop. The door was barred because none of them was in the mood for business. She was counting padpols for no good reason when she heard a knock.

"Chersey, Bezul—let me in!"

Chersey recognized the voice: Geddie—the scrawny girl from the Frog and Bucket, the very last person she wanted to see.

"We're closed."

"I got to talk to you—it's about Dace."

Chersey hurried to the door. As she opened it she saw the crutch—Dace's crutch—in Geddie's hand.

"Sweet Shipri—"

"Can I come in?"

Chersey retreated. "Bezul! Perrez!" She'd meant to shout their names, but there were tight bands across her breasts. "Where did you get that?" she asked Geddie. "What happened?"

Footsteps signaled that Bezul and Perrez had heard her. Chersey was transfixed by the crutch; she couldn't turn to see her husband.

"Don't know," Geddie answered.

The girl's discomfort was palpable and, to Chersey's eye, not from grief. "How did you get his crutch? Dace wouldn't go anywhere without his crutch!"

"He—he—I don't know. He was where he shouldn't've been and—and—he's *gone*! That's all."

The world spun, taking Chersey's balance with it. She would have fallen if Bezul hadn't caught her. Somehow he supported her and took the crutch from the girl's hand.

"Gone? Gone where?" Bez demanded. "Back to the swamp? Were you with him? Do you know who did it?"

Geddie shook her head and ran from the shop. Perrez started after her. Bezul barred his path with the crutch.

"Leave it. Whatever's happened, it's out of our hands. You were right; Dace was over his head."

"My rod!"

"Wasn't *your* rod."

"He stole it from me and that girl knows—"

"Stop it!" Chersey screamed. "Stop it, both of you! He's gone. Gone! *Dead.*"

The last word tore her throat and stole her strength. They couldn't be sure, of course. They'd never be sure, but they'd all survived the Troubles. They all knew what *gone* meant.

Chersey clung to Bezul for support. He rubbed her back and stroked her hair like a little girl's.

"There, there. It's not your fault. We did everything we could."

Guilt muted Chersey's voice, she could do no more than shake her head while she sobbed.

A week passed. The sea went glassy and there wasn't a breeze to be had in the whole city. Old-timers squinted at the clouds lined up on the horizon and checked the latches on their storm shutters. At the changing house, Bezul asked for help battening down the stock. Perrez heard the call and made himself scarce. He wasn't one for hard labor or sympathy.

The way Chersey mourned, anyone would think Dace was flesh and blood instead of a thief. There wasn't a doubt in Perrez's mind that the Nighter had stolen the shipwreck rod. Perrez hadn't imagined the boy had enough cunning for thievery. Frog all, if he *had* imagined it, he'd never have shown Dace the wand, much less the cache where he kept it.

Frog all.

The day after the theft—the day after the frogging boy vanished— Perrez had made a personal visit to Lord Noordiseh's Processional mansion to confess the bad news. Lord Noordiseh had taken it well, and why not? *His* future and fortune wasn't riding on the sale of a Yenizedi rod.

Damn the Nighter and damn the world . . . Every frogging time Perrez got something put together to get himself lifted off Wriggle

Way, something else came along to ruin his dreams. Something named Dace.

And something called *opah*.

It wasn't Perrez's way to blame himself when there were more worthy targets to hand, but he wished he'd handled that conversation with Dace differently. He'd guessed the boy was tangled in the *opah* trade. Perrez even had a fair idea what had happened: The Nighter had gotten himself in debt—probably to Maksandrus over at the Frog and Bucket—and Makker had put Dace up to the theft.

Perrez could have told Dace that Makker never settled for less than blood. Even money, Makker had killed the Nighter soon as he had the Yenizedi rod in hand.

"What a fracking, frogging waste," Perrez muttered as he strode along Fishermen's Row.

He could have bought the damn rags. The rod would have made him rich, but Perrez was not poor without it, not so poor he couldn't have bought nine *opah* rags. He could have thrown stronger warnings across Dace's bows, but he'd been the recipient of strong warnings all his life and knew exactly how the boy would have received them. He'd thought that disdain would be enough: Respectable folk knew better than to rot their tongues with *opah* . . .

Perrez came to the dock where he'd first met Dace, almost a year ago, when the boy had ventured across the White Foal to sell some cheap jewelry he'd dug out of the swamp ruins. A few gulls bobbed in the water, otherwise the dock was quiet, unoccupied, unobserved.

Perrez stared at the birds until they took flight, then he dug into his trousers and pulled out a wad of cloth. It was another waste, another fracking, frogging waste, but Perrez reckoned that he owed the boy something and slowly, scrap by scrap, he cast his *opah* rags into the water.

Gathering Strength

Selina Rosen

Kaytin feigned sleep as he heard Kadasah slamming around the hovel she called home. She made not even the hint of an attempt to move more silently in order to keep from waking him up.

And he so desperately needed to sleep. He had chased the accursed woman until she caught him, and now . . . Well, she was trying to use his manhood completely and totally up.

He would have liked to believe that she kept him so "busy" because she knew his reputation for being a lady's man, and was afraid he would stray. Unfortunately, he got the distinct impression that when she wasn't using him in one way or another she didn't give a good damn what happened to him, or what he did, as long as he was handy when she needed him again.

Kaytin felt spent, but how could he possibly tell the woman he'd

chased for years that one really could have too much of a good
thing? In fact, Kaytin fully believed that if he begged for mercy she
would find someone in the same minute who she believed could keep
up with her.

Not that Kaytin believed any one man could.

Kadasah's energy seemed to be boundless, and every time she
killed one of the followers of the Lady of Blood, her sexual appetite
became even more insatiable than usual.

And she had killed a lot of them lately. Or at least it seemed like a
lot to Kaytin; of course his fatigue and Kadasah's embellishments
had blurred the actual numbers, but he was pretty sure she'd killed
at least two in the last four weeks.

She would scour the area between the ruins of the Temple of Savankala and the Street of Red Lanterns, hunting for her prey. Sometimes when none of the Bloody Hand had surfaced for a while she
would go into the tunnels after them with a stealth almost magical.
So Kaytin knew damn good and well that she could be quiet when
she wanted to!

Ever since that bloated, silk-clad pud Kadasah called her patron
had given her four times her normal fee for the little added information she'd gleaned from their near-death experience in the tunnels,
she didn't need any encouragement at all to go right down into the
ground. More times than not dragging poor Kaytin right along behind her.

Kadasah seemed to be highly motivated by money—a fact that
defied all explanation, because she never seemed to have any, and
she certainly didn't have anything to show for it. She chose to live in
the decaying outbuilding of an abandoned redbrick estate in the hills
beyond the walls. The roof of this building was only a few half-
rotted timbers with an old oilcloth stretched across it. The door had
ropes where hinges should have been and a hole in the middle of it
big enough to throw a cat through. There was no furniture, not even
a stick. At night the only light was from a red lantern she'd stolen
from the street with the same name. It hung from a tattered piece of

rope tied to one of the before-mentioned half-rotted rafters, and every time she refilled the lamp she had less rope. When Kaytin asked why she didn't just put up a new rope she explained that the one she had still worked.

There was a big stack of old blankets piled haphazardly in the middle of the floor, which she called a bed.

She owned exactly one stew pot, a skillet, a wooden bowl, and a spoon, all of which she kept in a wooden box by the front door of the three paces by three paces structure. She kept their food supplies in there as well, when there actually were any. And she—they—would stay here for days at a time, eating whatever might be in the box and whatever Kadasah could kill. Not, of course, including the cultists, though sometimes he wondered.

Kaytin had given up asking what the current burned animal hanging on a stick might be, deciding it was easier to eat it if he just didn't know *what* it used to be.

Kadasah kept more in her saddlebags than she did in her house, except of course when the saddlebags were *in* the house. What she could pack into those bags never ceased to amaze Kaytin. It seemed that whenever she needed something for her "work" it was always contained within one of them.

Kaytin didn't know just how much her "patron" paid Kadasah for the pieces of skin laden with scars or tattoos she left as proof of her kill—she had certainly never told Kaytin an exact amount—but he had a feeling that they could be living in the lap of luxury in some apartment in Sanctuary instead of out here in the filth.

He wondered just what she did with all the damn money. She gave him only barely enough to jingle in his pocket—Kaytin didn't mind being a kept man at all, but he would have liked to be at the very least *well* kept.

It was true that they ate and drank a lot in the taverns and bars of the city, but they didn't eat *that* much, and he doubted even *they* could drink that much. Besides, she made a frequent habit of sneaking out without paying her bills at all. Sometimes she'd even purposely start a brawl just to keep the barkeep's attention drawn away from the fact that she was leaving.

In fact she stole most everything they needed. The only time Kaytin had ever seen Kadasah willingly part with money was to buy new weapons from the Black Spider.

Kaytin remembered the day well. He had found the shop shortly after it opened and happened to have been there to see the owner's own prowess with the weapons he sold.

When later that day Kadasah had proudly shown Kaytin the new weapons she had bought to replace the ones that had been taken by the followers of Dyareela, he had looked at them, yawned, shrugged, and told her he'd seen better, and at better prices.

She demanded to know where, and he took her straight to the Black Spider.

"Can I help you?" Spyder asked from behind the counter.

She turned to look at him and smiled. "New weapons."

"But your weapons look new," he said looking at her, one eyebrow cocked in suspicion.

"Aye, but my friend tells me they aren't as good as your weapons," Kadasah said slamming a thumb Kaytin's way.

Spyder had smiled at him. "Good to see you again, Kaytin."

From that moment on it was as if Kaytin had gone invisible. As Spyder showed Kadasah all the weapons, she moaned and groaned in damn near orgasmic ecstasy. It was embarrassing to see her gush in such an uncharacteristic manner.

Spyder hadn't even had to work at talking her into the most expensive bastard sword and hand ax in the entire store, with a trade-in of course. She didn't blink an eye at the cost nor did she try to steal the things. And when she had handed over her weapons, paid the difference, and had them fastened to her person, she was in no hurry to leave. She didn't suddenly remember that she had come there with Kaytin and say, *Come on, Kaytin, let's go, and by the way thanks for bringing me here, and I love you with all my heart and soul.*

No, she never even acknowledged his presence. In fact, it soon became painfully obvious why she wasn't showing that she was connected to Kaytin at all as she began to flirt outrageously with Spyder, not that Spyder for his part seemed to take any notice. She engaged him in conversation about weaponry and even played dumb. She started telling him stories, bragging about her riding abilities, all her battles and her talent with both sword and ax. She even, once again, told the tired story about how she'd killed three men with one ax blow.

At first Kaytin had thought it was all some trick, some way for her to get her money back, because he had never known Kadasah to flirt with any man including—maybe even especially—him unless she wanted something. But no, she never once started to steer the conversation into, "You're in a bad section of town, and I am the best bastard sword fighter in all the Kingdom, maybe the known world, and for a small fee . . ." No, she was actually flirting with him as if Kaytin didn't exist at all.

"I'm wondering," Spyder asked, "why you didn't enter the tournament?"

"Tournament?" Kadasah had asked curiously.

Spyder had then told her all about the damnable tournament. In fact, it seemed they might stand there talking all day, but then Spyder's mysterious and beautiful mate came strolling down the stairs, saw Kadasah's rather blatant display, and Kaytin swore he heard the woman growl.

Kadasah took one look at the woman and the way Spyder looked at her and seemed to realize she was wasting her time. She said her good-byes and left. Kaytin had followed her, as he always followed, even though in that moment he had known. . . . Nothing had changed between them. She was using him before, and she was using him now. Kaytin meant nothing to her; he was just, well . . . her man whore.

To add insult to injury she had chided him all the way home for not telling her about the tournament, which she was sure she could have won.

He had been silent, pouting, for all the good it had done him. If Kadasah had noticed at all, she did a fine act of hiding it.

There was very little he could do about the position he had put himself into. His mother had disowned him, and he had no place else to go. As little as Kadasah had, Kaytin had even less. His mother had been in such a rage over his affair with Kadasah—it was so hard to hide things from people with the sight—that she'd thrown him out with only the clothes on his back, screaming after his departing form that she had no son.

Kaytin didn't even have a marketable trade. The only job—if you could call it that—he'd ever been any good at was listening in on other people's conversations, blending in, being relatively unnoticed, and reporting the things he heard back to his family. And now . . . well, none of them were actually talking to him.

So his life was playing decoy for Kadasah, and being her love monkey.

He could probably get a job as a bartender or a dockworker and rent a place in town. There were other women, many women, women who had loved him, who would take him in.

There was only one problem.

He loved Kadasah with every fiber of his being. He would willingly stay with her forever, even in this hovel.

If she didn't frog him to death.

Kadasah belched loudly then yelled—just to make sure he was awake no doubt, "Hey, Kaytin! You want some scrambled eggs?"

"Yes," he said in a small, tired voice, trying not to think about where she had gotten the eggs and what condition they might be in. It hardly mattered. Whatever they had been before, they'd be cinders when Kadasah was done with them. He had heard once that charcoal was good for your digestion. If that was the case, he'd never have to worry about any ailments of the stomach.

He heard her starting to cook. She'd obviously been up long

enough to get the fire going. She was whistling a happy tune as she clanged the one spoon against the one skillet, and it sounded like doom to him.

They had just left the pub after a couple of pints and a bit of bread and cheese. Normally Kaytin would have scoffed at such a bland meal, but after three days of Kadasah's cooking it had been like a little slice of heaven.

"You never listen, or you would have known about the tournament," Kaytin said, wishing this argument wouldn't have started up again. He climbed onto the back of his mule.

"People purposely kept the news from me because they knew that I would win," Kadasah said, now accusing the general population as she climbed onto her red stallion, Vagrant. "Why didn't you tell me?" Kadasah asked as she started riding toward the ruined Temple of Savankala.

"For the hundredth time I *did* tell you. Kaytin talks, and you do not listen." The truth was he hadn't told her about the tournament because he knew she would enter if she had known about it, and although she was a spectacular fighter, even *he* didn't believe she was as good as she thought she was. Since she really did only half listen to him she wasn't likely to catch him in his lie.

"I do listen . . . most of the time," she said, then added, "you should have told me more than once and when I was sober. They said the prize was some jewel worth a lot of money."

"Maybe we could have bought a new tarp," Kaytin muttered with mock enthusiasm.

"What's that?" Kadasah asked.

"Nothing."

"You know, Kaytin, if you didn't prattle on so, saying meaningless nothings and mumbling, I might actually listen to you when you were talking."

"Are you listening now?"

"I am," she assured him.

"Did you hear what those fellows at the table behind us were say-ing about the ship?" Kaytin asked excitedly.

"Yeah, big deal . . ."

"Kadasah, the ship wasn't like anything anyone has seen before. It was in perfect condition. Its cargo was still intact. There was no one on board, not alive and not dead."

"So? It's just a ship, big froggin' deal," Kadasah said as she reined Vagrant to the left as they turned a street corner.

"So . . . you don't find it even a little interesting?" Kaytin asked, more than a little disappointed.

Kadasah shrugged. "Not as interesting as that," she said in a whis-per. She nodded her head to the right where a man was looking around covertly before ducking between two buildings into a narrow alley.

"Who is that?" Kaytin asked.

"That's a member of Naimun's entourage, and he lives in the castle, so what is he doing in this part of Sanctuary just before the beginning of the early watch?" She jumped off Vagrant, who imme-diately came to a complete standstill. Then she looked at Kaytin as if demanding that he do the same thing.

"We never do what *I* want to do," Kaytin mumbled as he watched Kadasah fold herself into the gloom of early evening. "No, no, that's all right. I'll just stay here with the animals, no need to worry about Kaytin." He glared at the horse. "She loves you more than Kaytin," he muttered accusingly, and he could swear the horse smiled. Kaytin sighed. "Even the animal he laughs at Kaytin's pain."

Kadasah recognized the man from her days in the palace. He might have dressed down, but he still stuck out like a sore thumb to her hunter's eye. She might not listen, but she saw plenty well.

She tracked him down the narrow alley and wasn't too surprised at all when he seemed to be taking a back way to the ruined Temple of Savankala. She slung herself into a doorway to hide when she saw him stop as he entered the seemingly deserted temple ruins and looked around, no doubt to make sure he wasn't being followed.

It was nowhere near cloak weather, but she found herself wishing she had her black one just because it would have helped her hide in the shadows. She continued to follow him only when she was sure he hadn't seen her.

If he isn't up to no good, then why is he so worried? she thought. Kadasah was pretty sure that she knew what he was up to.

She'd tried to tell those hardheaded, sheep-shite-for-brains idiots who were holed up in the palace that the Dyareelans were back in force. That they had planted people in Arizak's own court, but none of them would listen. Not to her. She was unstable in their eyes. Kadasah grated against everything they believed she should be. She wasn't a proper Irrune. Whatever the hell that was supposed to mean.

Her quarry disappeared from in front of her. She knew exactly what that meant because she knew about this opening into the Dyareelan tunnels.

She went back to where she had left Kaytin and Vagrant, took the horse's reins, and started leading him back the way she'd just come. Kaytin got off his mule and followed.

"Well?" he asked in a whisper.

"We're going to take a shortcut to the ruins tonight."

"Was it who you thought it was?"

"Yes, I'm sure of it. He turned and I got a good look at his face. It's him all right. I can't remember his name, but it's him—one of Naimun's boys. He went right down into the tunnels, too, so either he's going after them—which I sort of doubt since he was alone—or he's one of them."

"What are you going to do?"

"We're going to wait for him to come up, and then we're going to grab him, take him to Arizak, and make him confess—give up his buddies, too. I'll prove I wasn't just talking shite."

"Kaytin hates when you say 'we,'" Kaytin whined. "You say 'we' and *I* get hurt. My own sweet love, let us not make the chief's problem our own. They will not listen to you no matter what proof you bring, for they have branded the woman with the purest heart in all of Sanctuary as a deceitful, drunken, troublemaker."

"Frogs, Kaytin, I don't have time for your crap. Come on."

Kaytin followed, dragging his mule behind him, his chin nearly resting on his chest. He knew this was not going to end well.

They waited, and they waited, and then they waited some more, until it was pitch dark and near the late watch. Kaytin was convinced that Kadasah had either dreamed the whole thing or the man had left from another opening. Then they heard a shuffling sound, there was a sudden motion, and there he was.

He appeared to be alone, not that Kaytin suffered from any notion that Kadasah would have stayed in hiding if twenty of the Bloody Hand had come boiling up out of that hole.

She struck a match and lit the rag hanging from the bottle she held in her hand, and then tossed the bottle down the hole just to be on the safe side. It wouldn't do any real damage, but it would at the very least stop anyone from coming out of the hole for the next few minutes.

As the man turned to face her she pulled the sword from her back. There was a small explosion, and then a very gratifying plume of flame erupted from the hole at her back.

The man drew his own sword.

"You again," he hissed. "Kadasah, I told them they should hunt you down, but it's just as well they didn't. No one believed you, and now I get to kill you myself. I will go back to the palace holding your head up high, and all will praise me."

"Listen, pud, no man has ever bested me with sword. I've killed everyone I ever intended to kill, but I don't want to kill you. I need you alive, to be my proof," Kadasah announced.

"You live in a dream world, Kadasah. You cannot kill me for I am a servant of Dyareela! I shall drain your blood for the Dark Mother." He ran at Kadasah, and she easily parried his blow. Then she slapped him in the back of his head with the flat of her blade, driving him to his knees, but he jumped up and charged at her again. Kaytin leaped forward, stuck out a foot, and tripped the man. He went flying, landing at Kadasah's feet, and before she could stop herself instinct took over and she slammed her blade through the back of the guy's neck.

"Frogs!" Kadasah exclaimed as she pulled the blade from the wound.

Meral had been sound asleep when he heard the calls for help. In his line of work it wasn't an altogether rare occurrence. He was a healer, and as such was prepared to be awakened at all hours of the night, bright-eyed and bushy-tailed, and ready to go to work. He rose from his pallet, lit a candle, put on his boots, and walked into the middle of the apothecary where the two strangers stood holding a man between them by the arms.

He lit a lantern for better light then walked over to take a good look at the injured . . . very, very, dead man.

"Can you fix him?" the Irrune woman asked as she and her cohort dropped the man on his face.

Meral grimaced and looked up at them. "Was he a friend, Kadasah?" Meral asked guardedly. Kadasah and her friend weren't exactly the sort of people a wise man wanted to give bad news to. She was tall even for an Irrune, and she wore the black leather armor and weapons, not to mention the scars of one who had seen many battles. It was hard to tell what race the man was, Ilsigi maybe. Though shorter than his female counterpart, he was no less capable, and the dirk he wore at his belt looked as if it had gotten plenty of use.

"Nah," she said with a smile. "He's Dyareelan swine, but I need him alive to prove a point, so . . . can you fix him, Meral?"

"I'm afraid he's rather dead," Meral announced after kneeling and taking a closer look just for their benefit.

"Are you sure?" Kadasah asked in a disappointed voice.

Meral stood up and looked at her with a smile. "The blade seems to have both severed his neck from his backbone and cut his wind-pipe in two. In my medical opinion, he's quite dead." Meral marveled at the fact that there wasn't a lot of blood; the blow had managed to bring death without hitting any major blood vessels. "On a brighter note, it's a very clean kill."

"Could you check him again just to be sure? I sort of need him alive," she said.

"I told you he was dead, Kadasah. You don't have to be a healer to see that. You stabbed him through the back of his neck."

Kadasah gave her companion a dirty look then turned to Meral, smiled helplessly, and said with a shrug, "It's a very good sword. Are you sure you can't . . . I don't know . . . make a potion to bring him back?"

"Dead is dead," Meral answered. "I'm a healer not a wizard."

She nodded and sighed. "I was afraid of that."

"He . . . well, he doesn't look like one of the Bloody Hand," Meral said. He'd known Kadasah for a while and it wasn't the first time she'd come to him when she was in trouble. Kadasah was hotheaded and he wouldn't half put it past her to kill some poor soul over a dice game then want to take it back.

"Well of course he doesn't, that's the whole point," she explained. "He's a member of Naimun's entourage."

"They've infiltrated Arizak's court?" Meral asked with astonish-ment and more than a little anxiety.

She seemed to realize then that she might have told him too much. He wondered just what she was up to, and now it looked like she wasn't likely to tell him. She could be making up this whole story right off the top of her head. It would be just like Kadasah to do that, especially if she'd killed this fellow by accident.

"Well, I guess we better take our body and go; sorry to have awoken you, Meral."

"No problem." It was, of course, but no sense telling Kadasah that. For one she wouldn't care and for another it never hurt to have a mercenary of some reputation on your good side.

Kadasah and her friend picked up the body by the arms and started dragging it out.

Meral started to try and stop them, he would have liked to ask them a couple of more questions, but thought better of it. "Sorry I couldn't help," he said, watching them as they dragged the body away.

"Maybe some other time," Kadasah yelled over her shoulder, and then they were gone.

Meral smiled, shook his head, and started back for his bed, but before he made it halfway across the floor a man came screaming into the apothecary brandishing a large dagger. He ran at Meral. Meral stepped aside, and the man ran past him. As he turned to continue his attack Meral pedaled backward, frantically looking for something to use as a weapon to defend himself. He tripped over something of unknown origin and went sprawling. His attacker stood over him ready to pounce, and Meral was sure he was about to breathe his last. He cringed under his arms, and Kadasah seemed to appear from nowhere, sword in hand, screaming a battle cry.

His attacker turned to face the woman and found himself sliced nearly in two for his troubles. She looked down at Meral, smiling helplessly, and shrugged. "Good sword," she apologized. "And bad, bad, evil cultist."

"You . . . you saved my life from that Dyareelan scum," Meral said as Kadasah reached down with her free hand and helped him to his feet. "If there is ever anything I can do for you . . ."

"Ah, it wasn't nothing, but . . . as long as we're talking. You got any potions to . . . Oh, I don't know, make me run faster and jump higher? And I don't want the crap this time, Meral, I want the good stuff."

Meral made up the potion quickly. When he had finished she shoved it into one of three pouches she carried on her belt, then she left, stopping just long enough to reach down and grab the cultist's body by one foot and drag it off with her.

Meral wanted to ask her why she was taking the body. Ask if they shouldn't call the authorities about the attack. But the truth was Meral was a healer of moderate skill. His potions many times didn't work exactly as they were supposed to. He couldn't afford any more bad press, and dead bodies in a healer's office were never good for business. Then there was that other thing—it just wasn't smart to get on Kadasah's bad side, people who did wound up dead.

"Better to have her as an ally," Meral mumbled as he put his herbs away.

They didn't really start talking until they had unloaded the bodies in a remote location next to the Swamp of Night Secrets.

Kadasah started to laugh even as Kaytin stood shaking in his boots and looking all around, expecting some evil haunt to pop out from behind the trees and fog at any moment.

"Meral never even blinked, he just gave me those potions. Hell, I think he'd have given me half the store if I'd just asked. He thought I saved him. It never occurred to him that the bastard had followed us there and that he figured the healer knew too much and was going to kill him just as a forerunner of getting his hands on us."

"The Bloody Hand are on to you. They know now that you're the one who's been depleting their numbers, probably because of all your bragging. They sent an assassin for us, and you somehow find that funny. Well, Kaytin for one is not laughing."

"Would you calm down and quit being such a chicken shite? They didn't have time to send someone after us. That guy had to have seen us take ole-what's-his-face and followed on his own."

"And that's another thing, Kadasah. I saw no one following us, and neither did you. It is the Chaos Goddess herself who has seen what you are doing. That man," Kaytin pointed to the larger of the two corpses, "called out to her in his final moments. She heard and sent another of her servants after us."

"Frogs, Kaytin. If I've told you once, I've told you a hundred times. There are no gods; there are no goddesses. Just stupid people who want to believe that everything that goes wrong in their lives isn't their fault."

Kaytin covered his ears. "Kaytin does not want to hear. Quit saying such things, and especially don't say them here and now." He uncovered his ears and said in a hopeful voice, "Perhaps the Bloody Hand was after the healer and not after us at all."

"Come on, Kaytin, use that little thing you call a brain. Why would a member of the Bloody Hand be after Meral?"

"Because they want to cause pain and destruction, and someone who heals takes away pain and stops destruction," Kaytin answered.

"Ah . . . maybe, but I don't think so. Doesn't matter. Meral thinks I saved him, and I'll be able to go get any kind of potion I want, without paying for quite awhile." Kadasah busied herself stripping the corpses of anything that might identify them—and anything of value. "I ruined this robe and the shirt he was wearing under it," she muttered.

"If Dyareela is on to you, ruined clothing will be the least of your worries and you might need the healer's services to mend your wounds."

"I've blown farts more powerful than this so-called goddess."

"Kadasah, do not taunt the goddess," Kaytin said in a hiss.

She frowned then, and for a second Kaytin thought that perhaps she understood the true seriousness of their situation, but then she ruined the moment by saying, "This one's covered with tattoos and scars, but Naimun's boy doesn't have a single distinguishing mark on his body. Frogs, how can I prove I got two? If these guys aren't going to mark themselves, it's going to make it damn hard for me to collect my reward."

Surprisingly enough, Kadasah never even tried to cheat her patron. Some sort of honor thing Kaytin didn't really understand, considering all the swindling and stealing she normally did.

"Why don't you take two tattoos from the guy who has so many? It wouldn't even be lying, you did kill two of them."

Kadasah nodded and started to do the deed. She slipped the pieces of skin into the pouch she used specifically for that purpose, then she slashed the faces of her victims until they were unrecognizable and tossed the bodies into the swamp. She cleaned up in the muddy water and then they headed back to town.

Kaytin was only too glad to go. Dumping bodies was never one of his favorite things, but the Swamp of Night Secrets gave him goose bumps up and down his spine on the best of days.

There were evil things there; he knew it. Kadasah didn't believe in such things. Kadasah believed in nothing except Kadasah. But despite what she might think, just because she didn't believe in something didn't mean it didn't exist.

Kadasah sent Kaytin ahead to the Vulgar Unicorn as she went to leave the proof of her kill in her secret hiding place for her patron to find. She didn't trust Kaytin to know where that was, and he guessed *that* said about everything you needed to know about their "relationship."

Kaytin sulked up to the bar and ordered a tankard of Talulas Thunder ale. It was getting on toward the middle of the late watch, and the bar was sparsely populated.

"You look more than a little shaken this evening, Kaytin," Pegrin the Ugly said with real concern.

"Were you ever in love, Pegrin?"

He laughed. "Oh, aye, many times," he looked around. "So . . . where is the Irrune wench?"

"On business. She'll be back shortly to drink too much and lie even more. We may even get back home and into bed before daybreak."

"Doesn't sound to me like love is your problem, sounds more like too much of each other."

Kaytin's head shot up and he nodded. "Exactly! The woman . . . she uses Kaytin till there is nothing left."

Pegrin laughed loudly and said over his shoulder as he went to wait on another customer, "You know, in all my years behind the bar I don't believe I've ever heard a man complain about that particular problem."

Kaytin sipped at his ale. "All of Sanctuary is laughing at Kaytin's pain," he mumbled into his drink.

Kadasah awoke early the next afternoon lying crosswise across her "bed" with her head resting on Kaytin's bare stomach and her feet laying out on the dirt outside the door. Her head was pounding, and her tongue felt hugely swollen. Damn! She hoped she'd had a good time.

She sat up and wiped the dirt off her feet. It was drizzling, apparently, because her feet were wet, or maybe they'd just had a very thick dew. No, it was raining, she could see the water dripping from a hole in the roof onto Kaytin's head.

"Hey, Kaytin," she said softly, as much for her head as his.

He covered his face with his arms. "No . . . not again, not so soon, I can't, please, I beg you."

"Whatever are you going on about? I was just going to tell you to move out of the drip."

Kaytin moved his arms, looked up, and a drop of water landed in his eye. He got quickly to his feet and showed that he was at least a little hungover when he staggered and held his head.

"That's it! I've had it. Do you hear me? This is the last straw. Would it be too damn much to ask for a new oilcloth at least, maybe a real door? You're about to get paid, couldn't we have a few comforts for the house? Do you really expect me to just continue to live here in this shack with you without even the simplest of conveniences? Does Kaytin mean anything to you at all, or am I just a convenient frog, a stooge to help you with your dirty work, a lackey to hold your horse and your place at the bar?"

"All right already," Kadasah said, holding her hands over her ears to hold out his yelling. "You can have a new roof, and a new door."

As soon as the rain let up they rode into town and Kadasah sent him to the changing house to swap the sword, dagger, boots, and clothes she'd taken from the two guys she'd killed the night before for the things he wanted.

He should have known it was too much to hope for that she might just hand him money and say, *Go buy what you need.*

Bezul looked at the still-wet clothing suspiciously, and Kaytin, who had stopped to wash the blood from the items of clothing, said quickly, "They got wet in the rain."

"Uh-huh," Bezul said skeptically. "And I suppose your girlfriend takes in laundry for a living."

Kaytin smiled helplessly, and assured Bezul. "She didn't steal them."

Bezul shook his head, a smile on his face. "Get what you need."

Kaytin found what he needed, the whole time wondering why she couldn't just give him the money and come in and exchange things like the clothing and weapons of men she had killed herself. By the time he left the changing house his hands were shaking, and he didn't feel guilty at all about keeping the few coins Bezul gave him in the trade.

The skies were gray and Kaytin was sure he could smell a storm coming. They worked through the rest of the day together to repair the door and lay the new oilcloth over the old one, tacking it down on the edges to what was left of the rafters.

When they had finished Kaytin was surprised at how much better he felt about everything. There was a certain security in knowing he had someplace to go where the wind couldn't reach him and the rain couldn't fall on him.

Besides, he had complained and she had actually cared enough to do something about it, which had to mean something.

They sat around the fire that evening chewing on some burnt animal or another, and Kaytin finally felt like he was home.

"I wish there was some way I could get Arizak and the others to listen to me," Kadasah said.

"Just tell them about the guy you killed. That he came out of the tunnels, that he sang praises to the lady of death," Kaytin said. "Why would you lie?"

"I'm sure they could come up with lots of reasons. They won't believe me any more now than they did before. I don't have any proof," Kadasah said angrily, throwing what was left of her portion into the fire, not that it could burn any more than it already had. "More likely than not they'd string me up for confessing to the murder of ole-what's-his-name."

"You could tell them it was an accident."

"Oh, yes, Kaytin, that will work. I accidentally stabbed him in the back of the neck, and then I accidentally stripped him, disfigured him, threw him in the swamp, and sold his stuff to fix my roof."

"You had plenty of money to fix the roof," Kaytin mumbled. Then he took a deep breath and said, "I heard that the Dragon and some of his people have left Sanctuary and gone off to the wilds to ride horses and play with sheep. And they say that Arizak's taking so many drugs for the pain in his foot that he's somewhat addled . . ."

"You apparently listen for the both of us," Kadasah said with a smile. "But I fail to see of what use that information is to me."

"Kaytin was just thinking that with everyone else so preoccupied, perhaps now would be a good time to approach Naimun, to tell him what you have learned. Without of course telling him that you killed his friend. You could just say that you saw him go down into what you know is an entrance to the Dyareelan tunnels."

"I'm not sure they even believe that anyone still lives in the tunnels. They refused to even go with me to look, remember? Perhaps I should just try talking to my father."

"Your father . . . I thought you said that he was dead."

"Well almost, he's old and he lives in the palace; that's nearly the same thing."

During the night the storm blew in fast and furious. It was so bad that Kadasah found herself glad that Kaytin had whined and that she had caved in to him.

He was sound asleep; she didn't know how. The wind and thunder were loud enough that she wondered if there might be a hurricane in the midst of the storm.

Just before the storm had started in earnest she had gone out to check Vagrant and Kaytin's mule and found them right where she had thought they would be—huddled against a wall in a slightly larger, but less sturdy, stone outbuilding. Kadasah had stacked full logs and tree limbs over the top of it to make a shelter for Vagrant. The first time Kaytin had seen it he had made the observation that the horse lived better than she did.

Vagrant never went into the shelter unless the weather was incredibly horrid, so Kadasah knew right then that they were in for a hell of a storm. She had stroked his nose, assured him that all would be well, and started for the house stopping only a second to say a kind word to the mule.

She'd just reached their newly rebuilt door as the bottom fell out of the sky and the rain started to come down in buckets. In the red light that illuminated the small room she saw Kaytin look up at her with a smug smile.

She smiled right back. "Good idea *I* had to fix the door and the roof."

She was pretty sure that he yelled at her then, but it was hard to tell because amazingly the rain started coming down even harder.

It hadn't let up, and they had gone to bed having nothing better to do. She smiled as the pleasant near-memory filled her head and thought seriously about waking Kaytin up . . . after all, *she* couldn't sleep.

She shook her head. She needed to think, and while that helped her sleep it certainly didn't help her think.

The cult was growing, and she didn't know how. She kept killing them, and they kept coming . . . and what if Kaytin was right and they were on to her? What if they had figured out that she was the one depleting their numbers? There could be assassins at every corner waiting for her.

Not that she couldn't handle it, just that it would be a giant nuisance.

On the one hand, killing them a few here and a few there kept her in good, steady work. On the other hand, she never wanted there to be any chance that the cult could gain control again. She'd heard enough to know that their reign hadn't been a pleasant one. Kaytin had insisted that one of the ones she had killed was speaking in a strange tongue, and she had to admit she didn't recognize it.

She had buried that guy outside the city walls a couple of months ago. Maybe the Bloody Hand was a bigger problem than anyone knew.

The Irrune were in control here now; she was Irrune, and better than that she had grown up in Arizak's court. It should have given her just the in she needed. But it did just the opposite because her father sat at the leader's shoulder and convinced him that every word out of Kadasah's mouth was nothing but a slanderous lie.

Which hardly seemed fair.

The key was getting her father to believe her.

But how?

Then as lightning splashed across the sky brightly enough that she could see it through the cracks in the door, and thunder roared loud enough to make Kaytin jump, she had the answer.

She woke Kaytin up to celebrate.

"What do you want?" Tentinok asked in a slur from where he sat at the corner table in the Golden Gourd.

"You might at least wait for me to sit before you dismiss me outright," Kadasah said, sitting down. "I've brought you an ale—your favorite." She slid the glass toward him, hugging her own in her hand.

"A drink will hardly buy my forgiveness, daughter. I'm surprised they'd let you in here, as much damage as you've done to the place in the past."

Kadasah gave him a curious look. "Now, how would you know that?"

"One hears things. You sent word, I'm here, that's more than you deserve." He spat across the table.

Kadasah sighed, took a drink from her tankard, and then watched as Tentinok did the same, as usual downing half the tankard with his first drink. "I'll keep it short . . . I tried to tell Arizak before, to tell all of you, but no one would listen to me. Well, now I have proof," Kadasah said.

"Proof of what?"

"That you haven't cleaned this city of the Bloody Hand by a long shot . . ."

"Oh . . . you aren't going to start that again."

"They're hiding in tunnels under the Street of Red Lanterns. But it's worse, so much worse than that." She lowered her voice. "They're not all marking themselves anymore. They're walking around with the rest of us pretending to be normal. As I told you before, they have infiltrated Arizak's court."

"What do you hope to gain from these lies?"

"Tentinok . . . Father. I have proof. Only two nights ago . . . no, wait it was three, or four perhaps. It was before the big storm, and it lasted for two days, so I think four days . . ."

"Do get on with it. You said you were going to keep it short, and I'm not growing any younger."

"I saw a man who I recognized as a member of Naimun's entourage. He went down into one of the tunnels. A few minutes later a man in a hooded robe came out of the tunnels. He was one of the followers of Dyareela. I fought with him, and as I fought with him this man you have been sharing the palace with came out of the hole, praised the Dark Lady and attacked me. I cut him, but he and his twisted friend both got away."

"What is this man's name, Kadasah? I have seen no wounded man in Naimun's entourage or in the palace at all, perhaps you didn't hurt him badly . . ."

"Or perhaps I gave him a fatal wound, and he has crawled off to some dark place to die. Perhaps because they failed his brothers have hacked him and his friend to pieces and thrown him into the swamp."

"What is the man's name?"

"I . . . well, I don't remember his name, but I recognized him, I swear."

He laughed at her then. "And your word holds so much weight because . . . you are a creature of virtue? Again, Kadasah, what is it that you hope to gain with your story?" He finished the rest of the ale in his tankard then fell forward onto the table.

When Tentinok awoke the world was dark, and he wondered for a minute if he had died. His vision was blurred, and his head felt . . . well, dusty.

"He's very heavy," a male voice complained.

"I was about to think that not even a six-times dose of the sleeping potion was going to knock him out," Kadasah's voice said. "Then I was glad we had that strengthening potion or I don't think even the two of us could have moved him."

"Maybe you gave him too much. He's not moving at all. Maybe he isn't going to wake up."

"And maybe I'm going to wake up and kill you both," Tentinok roared as he stumbled to his feet, staggering like a drunk.

"Quiet," Kadasah ordered in a whisper, "you'll bring all of them down upon our heads."

"Who, Kadasah? There is no one here. Just some dark, dank," he lifted a foot and shook it, "very wet tunnel."

"They are here, and if you make too much noise we'll have them all to fight at once," she assured him. "Now come on." Candle in hand she moved forward. A young man pressed a candle into his hand, and Tentinok glared at him, sure he knew what this foreign man was to his daughter.

He followed, and as he did so his head began to clear, enough that

he began to wonder why he was following them at all. Especially
when the water started to get deeper and they still hadn't shown him
anything but half-flooded tunnels.

"Kadasah," he said in a whisper, "there is nothing here. No one."

"The storm it must have driven them further in," Kadasah said.

Suddenly a man ran out of the darkness through the mud, and
Kadasah easily took him down. The man fell into the water covering
the floor of the cave, and Kadasah handed her candle to the young
man and dragged the body from the mud. She held the man's tattooed face up for her father to see. "See, Father? Is it not just as I
have said? He's one of them." With her sword she cut one of the tattoos off and stuck it in her pouch—Tentinok didn't even want to
know why—then she dropped the body, took her candle back from
the man, and kept walking.

"One man is not dozens and proves no connection to the palace,"
Tentinok said, but he followed until the water had hit waist deep
and the tunnel in front of them—where it started to go deeper into
the earth—was completely submerged. "Kadasah . . . there is no one
else here. Just one cultist, probably alone."

"No," Kadasah said urgently. "I tell you, these caves are normally filled with activity. They must have gotten flooded out during
the storm and they are temporarily hiding somewhere else."

He wanted to believe her. Not because he wanted to for one second think that the Bloody Hand could get a foothold in Sanctuary
ever again, but just because she seemed so earnest, and she had gone
to all the trouble of . . . drugging him and dragging him here to get all
wet. His patience eroded. He turned around and started stomping—
not at all easy with all the mud—back the way they had come.

The others followed after him. "Father, I swear to you . . ."

"Quiet! Your words mean nothing to me. You drug me and you
bring me here. You tell me stories of one of our own who is a hidden
cultist, and yet you have no proof, you do not even know his name.
You show me one cultist and tell me there are hundreds." He tripped
then, landing in the muck and succeeding in getting himself covered

to the very top of his head. He wiped the water and mud from his face and spit, then he screamed. "Never, never darken my door again! Never contact me. Just leave me be!"

Tentinok walked into the palace slinging mud and water and looking ready to kill.

"What happened to you?" Naimun asked with a smile.

"Don't ask," Tentinok growled back.

"Bad day?"

"You might say that, once again problems with Kadasah. I'm just going to go get cleaned up, get into some dry clothes, and forget the whole sordid ordeal. What brings you to this part of the palace at this hour?"

"I'm a bit concerned. No one has seen Kopal in four days running. You haven't seen him about have you?"

"No . . . which means we might have a much bigger problem."

Kaytin lay quietly, not at all exhausted and still relishing the words he had heard. "Enough, enough!" his beloved had cried out.

"So, I know most of the day didn't go so well, but that wasn't so bad."

"It was amazing," Kadasah said, and she sounded truly sincere, as if all the day's events had been forgotten in their lovemaking.

Kaytin hoped the healer stayed thankful for a very long time. Turned out all he really needed was a little extra strength.

Dark of the Moon

Andrew Offutt

In the final night of its waning the moon was a mere pale sliver that played hide-and-seek among the few blue-gray clouds lounging above the fired old town called Sanctuary. The lone walker under that pallid excuse for a moon was in her late teens or perhaps early twenties.

She did not look nearly as stupid as she did attractive, and yet here she was, a pretty-enough young woman demonstrating a contra-survival lack of intelligence and good judgment by turning down the paved narrowness of an alleged street well shadowed by multistory tenements. Why did not she, even as a foreigner to Sanctuary, at least suspect that she had entered a cul-de-sac forming one of the most dangerous traps any city could provide?

Lurking here in a less-than-savory area of the town named Sanc-tuary and sometimes sarcastically referred to as Thieves' World, the alley whimsically called Sunshine Street existed for two blocks only. Its narrow length was mostly unlit and barely wide enough for the passage of a one-horse cart. Little sound invaded such a narrow walkway between tall tenements. The dying moon was a mere sickle in its final quarter, but happened to be almost directly overhead. Thus it lit the alley well enough to make it possible to distinguish only the brightest colors.

Perhaps that bright light dulled the suspicions of the lone walker—and perhaps also dulled her mind? At any rate, it also created many shadows and lurking places, and they yielded two men.

Chestnut brown of eye and of hair with a mild tendency to curl, the prey was more than comely. The predators were not, and both were considerably larger than her height and build. Both men wore dark clothing and sharp steel and neither was small. The smaller or rather less large accoster was neither good-looking nor ugly of face capped by wispy, hair-colored hair. He wore his soft cap of dark red at a jaunty angle that he probably felt made him rakishly attractive, a belief without foundation. The larger one had a large, dark brown growth of hair that wandered over the whole lower part of his face—not a beard, really, for that implied some gardening. Unfortunately the area concealed by that foliage did not include his nose, an unsightly growth that some might have likened to a truncated sausage.

"Just be a good little dummy and hand over that pretty-pretty bracelet, girl," the larger one said, clutching a gentle moon of breast through her clothing, "and we won't kill you after the rape."

Her valiant struggling was to absolutely no avail against their strength. The night air was ripped by the sound of gasps, grunts, scraping footsteps, and tearing cloth. The outcome of that worse-than-uneven struggle was not in question.

"Damn!" the smaller of the two attackers said—not a small man at all, under his rakishly canted cap, but his hair-faced companion was a veritable bear. That accounted for his nickname, which was Wall. He wrested their prey against his namesake with a heavy sound of the impact of her left shoulder and arm and the squeak that forcible contact brought from her throat. Even so she sent a kick high up between the legs of the cap-wearer and did her best to bite the arm of the one who had the better grip on her.

"That there is gonna cost you the use of that leg for a *long* time," he snarled, close to her ear—which was tickled by his veritable jungle of dark brown facial hair.

Alone in the unlighted street all three participants froze at the sound of a quiet voice from an unseen source. Sounding calm, it wafted down to them from above. Three heads jerked upward and three pair of night-large pupils stared.

"You don't really mean to be doing this, boys," that same voice said, as if stating plain fact that all should know. "You two just stop that nastiness and go along your way and maybe you'll get to see the sunrise."

Adrenaline spurted. Hairs rose abristle on two napes; the fine chestnut hairs on the back of the young woman's neck were already erect. Squatting almost at the very edge of the roof a few feet above them in seeming supreme confidence was a slender youth little beyond his boyhood. Partly because of his squat and partly because his clothing was uniformly darker than that of the assailants, he did not look at all large. The silver slice of moon was high above his right shoulder, making his face a featureless shadow while affording him a clear view of the features, at least, of all three land-bound members of the encounter.

The bigger of the pair of assailants chuckled. "H'lo there, little feller. Careful you don't fall off that there roof. You really think you can handle us both?" Without haste, he reached across the area where his tunic bloused over his belt buckle. There hung a sheath of unadorned old leather. From it he slid a knife as long as his thigh.

The level, quiet voice did not change, nor did the shadow-man move. "I really think I can handle you both without raising a sweat, you big cow."

This time it was the other man who fouled the night with the sound of his voice. "You're talking to *Wall*, and he's a *bull*, not a *cow*, you froggin' piece of shite!"

"Careful. I've heard both those stupid words so damned much in the past few weeks from too damned many copycats. I swore to carve the nose off any fraggin' piece of bat-shite who used both at once."

The big man chuckled again. He had made no move to lift his long knife. "Who in the seven hells are you, boy?"

The chosen victim of the arrogant pair was doing her best to edge away. Shadows beckoned . . .

And yet even she froze at the reply of the would-be rescuer on the roof.

"I am called Shadowspawn."

"Sheeeeee-ite!"

"Not likely. My daddy knowed that oddling called Shadow-spawn. *If* that freggin' super-thief is alive, he's got to be older than rocks."

The youth on the roof was not above theatricality in heaving a great sigh. "You've had your warning, ugly. A wise man once told me that a fool and his life are soon parted. You don't have to go proving that."

The man who was not as large as his companion grabbed their chosen victim by means of hooking a hairy and muscular arm across her throat. From behind her and above her head he glowered up at the accoster.

"I'd say you're the one about to prove it, you fruggin' shike!" he said. "Git far away from here and do it fast, or I break her scrawny neck."

The squatting human shadow on the roof's edge said, "Still making foolish noises, are you? Seems to me it's a very pretty neck. Well, I warned you."

And then in a blurred movement his hand rushed up and back and then forward, his lower forearm just brushing his ear. The result was that the wide-eyed prisoner heard the little humming sound that terminated in a metallic *shing* accompanying a *thud*. Of course she was not able to see the way the forehead below the soft red cap sprouted a silvery-shining steel throwing star. Four and a half points were in evidence, meaning that one and half of another were mostly imbedded. Yes, even in bone.

"Your pond-scum fool of a friend has just joined his dog-relatives in the Cold Hell, big cow," the roof-squatter said, low. "Are you ready to join him and them?"

The big man turned out to be not as stupid as he looked. Without pausing to consider, he ran.

The far from conventional hero of the little affray dropped down just as the victim, released by the fall of the man behind her, also sank to the pave. The shoulder of her mint-green tunic was torn to what most male observers would consider an interesting degree. She stared up at her rescuer from large dark eyes widened by wonder. He was nowhere near the size of the beast he had just frightened off. He was also positively bristling with sharp steel in various lengths.

"You . . . you saved me—a stranger!" She spoke those wondering words in an accent that was not born in Sanctuary.

He shrugged, and squatted beside her to look into a pretty, oval face that tapered down to an almost pointed chin. And oh, what skin! "True."

She gazed up into a dusky face with features that made him appear to be in his teens. Except for the eyes. Strangely *old*, those eyes were, and accustomed to seeing ugliness. He was not a bad-looking youth, her hero, with a sensuous mouth, hooded eyes, and shaped brows. He wore unalleviated black, as if his goal was to be a living shadow, and his jet hair had not been cut in at least two years. It was pulled back into a horse-tail, pulled through a short, narrow sheath of dark leather.

"Did you k— is he dead?"

"Likely."

"Are you really called Shadowspawn?"

"No. Shadowspawn is my mentor. My name is Lone." In the

large-eyed presence of an attractive and grateful young woman with golden skin more beautiful than any he had ever seen, he could not resist adding, "Some call me Catwalker. Are you ready to stand?"

"I . . . think so . . ."

Lone took her hand in a warm one with a rough surface. He noted that it was a small and quite dainty hand, but that it had led no life of leisure. As he rose to his feet in an easy, athletic movement, she saw that his every fingernail had been gnawed. A soul in torment, or the usual dread uncertainty of youth? When he exerted a bit of pressure, she allowed herself to be drawn up just as fluidly—but tottered a bit when she was on her feet. How pale she was, and how *thin*! Her eyes looked deep-set and yet huge—and at a height to gaze directly into his unreadable dark, dark ones. This black-haired boy or very young man was not tall, and looking into those eyes made her think that he trusted no one.

"Give me a name to call you by."

"Janithe. My name is Janithe."

"Janithe. Why were you in this night-dark alley?"

"It—it stinks, doesn't it? Is there a stable just ahead?"

"Does that question mean you don't want to answer mine?"

"I—I wasn't really going anywhere. I am—I am a stranger here."

He already knew the answer, from her accent, but asked anyway: "In this section of town, do you mean, or in *my* town?"

"Yes."

He nodded, without showing teeth. When he said nothing but continued to gaze into eyes little less enigmatic than his own, Janithe was unable to resist providing more information.

"I just arrived from Caronne. I lived with my mother. She has been a widow for over three years. A little over a month ago she took a lover, and the moment she left for work he came after me. I know she likes him, a lot, and I love her and wish her happiness, and so I left. I came here to seek work . . ."

Lone left off saying that the only thing he knew that came from

Caronne was the drug *krrf* and its deadly distillate. He did state his surmise: "And you have no money."

She looked down.

"Lots of people haven't," he said as a kindness, in a voice with a shrug built in. It was so hard not to stare at her, with that beautiful, somehow *glowing* golden skin! "No one remembers the name of this excuse for a street, Janithe. It is used as often for the emptying of bladders as anything else, and hereabouts it's well known as the Drainway. It ends less than a block ahead."

"But it started just over a block back!"

"True." His face did not change. "Do you want to tell me about that bracelet?" He indicated the long and exceptionally handsome ornament, which was at least plated with gold. What a strange set of curlicues it bore, and runes! In seconds her rescuer surreptitiously gave Janithe's one item of jewelry the close examination of an expert thief. "That should bring you the price of lodging until you find work. Just a loan on it, even."

She drew back in some alarm and grasped her braceleted forearm with the other hand. That told Lone that she was horrified or some-thing like, and he decided with a mental shrug that either it had great sentimental meaning to her—or maybe she just could not get the thing off. He turned in the direction whence she had come.

"Coming?"

Janithe hastened to walk beside him along a street that might have accommodated one more person abreast. "I owe you more than money," she murmured in a soft, more composed voice. "Why on earth were you up on that roof?"

Her rescuer made an unextravagant gesture. "Obviously it's safer to travel by roof than by street!"

He was pleased that she giggled. "B—but—aren't you afraid of failing?"

"No. My mentor put it best—'it's not the fall that a person needs to fear, but the sudden stop.'"

He was rewarded with another girlish giggle and was minded to tell her the story that Chance-who-had-been-Hanse had told him, with some relish. The sad tale involved a thief whose talent was definitely less than that of Shadowspawn—but then whose was not?

One morning near dawn this fellow, Therames, Shadowspawn said his name was, truly surpassed himself in laboriously ascending to the very top of a flat-roofed building in a neighborhood peopled by the well-off, and from it leaped to the slightly lower roof of another building, which he had judged unscalable. With great care and little speed he worked his way down to a window, and inside to his goal, which turned out to be a particularly nice evening's take. He was almost discovered, eluded the almost-discoverer, and emerged laden with eminently salable and pawnable booty. So laden that the heavy sack's weight forced Therames to grunt and pant his way back up onto the roof of that building. So laden was he, in fact, that when he made his sinuous pounce back to the first building, his sack of loot o'erweighed him and he fell five storeys to break his neck. Police of the city watch retrieved him and his loot. They kept the latter . . .

But Lone did not relate that to this interesting girl or woman, for she was speaking, posing still another question: "Why did you call yourself Shadowspawn?"

"If those two had any sense, it should have scared the snot out of them. Shadowspawn is my mentor, the greatest cat-burglar in the world, and a ferocious foe in a fight. Terribly good with knives of any length. Oh, fart." He stopped and turned back. "I can be so stupid! I forgot something important! Stand right here where we can be sure you're safe." As he spoke he was tucking Janithe into a deep shadow at the wall of the leftward building. "You're all but invisible in the shadow. I left something back there. I'll be back faster than you can draw three breaths."

That was not quite true, for extracting a death-star from the armoring bone of a man's forehead was no simple task. By the time Lone had wiggled the steel star-shape free and reattached it

prominently to his clothing—incidentally removing the undernourished purse from inside the dead man's tunic—and hurried back to
where he had left her, Janithe was nowhere in sight.

"Fart," Lone muttered, partly because he was impressed, in addition to the dismay he could not help feel. He kept a close eye on the
shadows as he departed the Drainway, but no, that was the way his
mentor of the apt nickname vanished, but it was not the hiding place
of Janithe.

The master mage Kusharlonikas was not at all pleased to receive the
brief letter. Indeed the boy who delivered it should have thanked his
stars that he was well away before the aged mage plucked open the
message with withered old fingers, and read it. It was signed by four
men who were sufficiently well-off and thus powerful enough to ignore or at least pretend to ignore the putative ruler of Sanctuary this
decade, the gr-r-reat noble Arizak: two bankers, a man of the law
who owned not only considerable rental property but a glass manu-
factory as well, and the white mage named Strick and called Spellmaster. Kusharlonikas perceived the "advisory" as an insult and a
challenge. He had now lived into his one-hundred-second year, and
was no fool. He had no doubt that it was that meddling, grotesquely
fat do-gooder Strick who had instigated and probably dictated this
letter.

True; it told him nothing he did not know: that his apprentice was
an incompetent whose attempts at casting spells had caused alarm
and even physical harm to persons and things unknown to him; inno-
cents to whom neither he nor his master meant any harm. Interesting,
Kusharlonikas thought, that this little band of long-nosed do-gooders
knew some specifics, including a couple of events unknown even
to Kusharlonikas until this moment. One or more of these men had
seen weird occurrences in a watering hole he had never heard of, and
the ghastly ruination of a cat and a couple of vendors' stands in the
city market.

The aged master mage was advised to "take action in this matter.

Perhaps he might be well advised to rethink his choice of apprentices?"

His Master Mageship was unamused and unpersuaded, but not unaffected. How dare these turds chastise and challenge him! A while later, in the quiet and ever-shielded privacy of his Chamber of Reflection and Divination, he condemned the message to a slow burning as he stood over it and murmured quiet words while making a series of abbreviated, long-practiced gestures. Oddly, a name he used in his dreadsome incantation was not one of those who had signed the meddlesome letter that so angered him.

By strange coincidence that same afternoon, two young men chanced to come face to face in that same wide-sprawling marketplace. Of course they were far from alone in this sprawling collection of tents and stalls, which was alive with myriad colors and shadings and the mingled scents of food of all kinds and people and the discordant sound of more voices than anyone could ever want to hear—in at least as many accents as the number of fingers on two hands.

Lone had attended the arena games back during the eeriness of the mantling of both the sun and the moon within a few days. He came away with purses numbering rather more than two. He had half fallen in love with the stare-provokingly saffron-skinned warrior maid who called her diminutive, swifter-than-an-arrow-in-flight self "Tiger." But she was no less dangerous than speedy, and Lone realized that it was only lust he had fallen into, not the perilous morass of love. No matter; 'twas a temporary fancy that took not long to pass, while the purses he had so deftly acquired came only from smiling men— and one overly ostentatious woman—who had collected some of the many, many wagers made on the outcome of every contest.

But how the skin of Janithe reminded him of that warrior woman!—and everyone knew that nearly everyone in Sanctuary visited the sprawling market *some*time. So—he stopped at this stall or kiosk and that, and asked about her, and left word that if anyone saw her he would like to know. No one was rude; the never unpleasant youth was too obvious in his cute infatuation with some exotic-to-him girl come here from off somewhere, and what human of any age could resist such a non-phenomenal phenomenon as young love?

And now this confrontation with Komodoflorensal. It was the apprentice sorcerer who happened to be moving the faster of the two, and so the apprentice cat-burglar stopped dead still and allowed the other to bump him. They were not friends and yet not strangers, for they had met once before . . . one night not so long ago, in the Chamber of Reflection and Divination of Kusharlonikas the mage.

The one with the roundish, seemingly ingenuous face wearing a longish tunic the color of bile was Komodoflorensal, apprentice to the master mage. The youth of about the same age with the hooded eyes, several weapons, and more sensible blue tunic over leggings the color of a bay horse was the self-named Lone, who in spite of his swagger and desire for arrogance, was apprentice to the master thief Shadowspawn. Seeming only to be meandering, he had asked several people, both vendor and shopper, about an attractive young woman with golden skin, a foreigner with the unusual name of Janithe. No one admitted to knowing anything of her, even of having seen such a person.

"Uh! Oh! Sorry—"

"Hell-o, sorcerer's apprentice!"

"Uh-oh. You!" Neither of the young men was tall, and Komodoflorensal had to look up only a little above Lone's expensive red-and-beige sash to meet his dark, dark eyes with his own large, round, medium browns.

"Aye. Me. As you and your master know, the name is Lone. I have heard yours pronounced, but am not sure I can imitate the noise."

The smaller youth snapped, "I am Komodoflorensal and you well know it, thief! You of all people have no call to be insulting! Last I saw of you, you were fleeing with goods stolen from my master's innermost chamber."

Lone swallowed the name-calling—after all, it merely described his chosen profession—and his retort. "I don't remember fleeing, but of course you must have got an odd view, considering that you was hiding under your master's spelling table and trying to think of what went wrong with the spell you tried on me."

"Would you two boys mind taking your little chat out of the very center of the aisle so the rest of us can be about our business?"

The pair of "chatters" turned in the direction of the unpleasant voice to see that their accoster was a woman of some years and many pounds, wearing a couple of garishly striped garments that must have contained enough cloth to make a good-sized tent. Her face made her appear to have applied the entire stock of cosmetics of some happy vendor.

"Oh my beautiful lady!" Lone said, accompanying a sweeping gesture with a profound bow. "I apologize most profusely for my younger brother and me for getting in the way of your august self. I can beg only that you forgive us, two men who have not seen each other in all these years since our mother sold us to a hideous catamite with a stenchy stable full of horses fed far better than ourselves were, these fourteen years agone."

Both his alleged brother and the offended woman stared at him, but only one of them turned aside to hide a smile that broadened into a grin.

Looking chastened by such politesse, however exaggerated, and guilty, and charmed—and perhaps smitten—the un-beautiful un-lady apologized for speaking so unkindly to "two poor unfortunates," and Lone apologized again, with florid words and flourishes, and this time Komodoflorensal laughed openly, whereupon *he* apologized, and then Lone made solemn apology for his younger ("much younger") brother and she apologized again and . . .

"Could you three babbling idiots get your buffs out of the middle of the fraggin' aisle so the rest of the world can be about our business?!"

Lone and Komodoflorensal exchanged a startled look at the sound of that rough male voice, before turning their heads in its direction.

They were just in time to see their previous accoster explode her fist into the approximate center of the face of the voice's owner, a large, soft-faced man in his thirties.

"You should long since have learned the virtues of patience!" she stormed as he staggered back, and with a brief but not discourteous nod to the two young men she took for brothers, she bustled on her way.

The large fellow whose nose she had messily flattened flopped backward into a woman who was using a bolt or so of yellow cloth with enormous green polka dots to carry her child of a very few months. The infant's father proved not to have learned the virtues of patience. Turning the offending man with one hand, he gave him a hard backhanded slap with the other. The noise of impact was loud. The yelp of the recipient was not, and this time as he staggered back a tight-clad leg with a pronounced calf muscle was waiting. He was so obliging as to stumble over it. The hapless wight went backward down onto his butt.

"Well done," Komodoflorensal remarked.

"Thank you," Lone said. "And might I suggest that this is a good place to be away from!"

Komodoflorensal agreed, and they made some haste in swerving into a different aisle between tents and stalls and kiosks. In mere moments they had blended into its throng.

"I do admire the way you overdid apologizing to that old bird and charmed her," the open-faced youth said, as they ambled along, inhaling the many, many scents—most of them pleasant. "Were you really sold by your mother?"

"No," Lone said. "She was murdered, with my father."

"Unbelievable!" the mage's apprentice burbled. "That is my story, too!"

The face of the young thief called Catwalker did not change, but his mind did. "Strange," he said, "but believable enough. I was adopted . . . eventually."

"Again, me too!" the excited youth in green said. "Except that it was my great-great-uncle who adopted me. I had seen him but once in my life."

"Kusharlonikas," Lone said.

"Aye. Uncle 'Lonikas. Have you been treated badly? By your adopter, I mean."

"Never by them!" Lone staunchly replied, and it did not occur to him to ask the same question of the ignorant enemy at his side, who seemed so much younger than he was.

After some three steps, Komodoflorensal volunteered the information: "Well I have. I have been tortured in various ways, and even killed."

Lone jerked but did not stop. "What? Killed?"

"Some of it was illusion and some of it was not. The six times I've been killed never really happened."

While Lone's mind wrestled with that spectacular revelation, a smallish red-brown dog with droplets falling from its lolling, oddly spatulate tongue brushed his left leg. Strangely, it was the leg between him and his unchosen companion.

Lone was far more interested in Komodoflorensal's thoughts and memories: While Lone had been tortured and beaten, more than once nearly to death, always the important word had been *nearly*. At last, after swerving around a little girl whose arm was held almost straight up by a mother laden with fresh fruits, he asked, "What's it like, dyin'?"

Since Komodoflorensal was at that moment jostled against him, Lone felt the other orphan's shudder. "Horribler than anything you can imagine."

The survivor of the tortures and mind-assaults of the Dyareelan Pits made no comment on that. What could be more horrible than Strangle and his minions, and their treatment of the children they had worked so diligently to transform into heartless murderers?

But! According to this fellow whose name was the biggest part about him, he had once been strangled not only into unconsciousness—as Lone had been, back when he was called Flea-shit because he was that inconsequential—but to death! The implement of the slow murder of the sorcerer's apprentice *that* time was a serpent-sinuous demon; the reason was that Komodoflorensal had used a Finding Out spell and somehow sucked a bit of information from the lore-stuffed brain of his mentor. No more than an iota of that vast store, true, but Kusharlonikas was not one to observe such niceties as making punishment match offense. As always, Komoetcetera awoke "from death" alive and hale, but never to forget the terror and horror of the experience.

By an hour past noon the two unlikely companions had purchased and shared food and drink and exchanged many words. No, Komodoflorensal had not seen anyone matching Janithe's description; yes, he would be on the watch, and leave word for Lone at the vendor's kiosk they agreed upon.

They were probably the same age, or nearly, as they were similar in height with Lone maybe a finger-width taller; his adoptive mother had assigned him a birthday, more arbitrarily than not. The date made him a few months older than the other apprentice. Strangely and despite himself, Komodoflorensal could not help feeling that he had indeed met a brother and one who was both older and quite respectworthy in spite of his occupation. Later it occurred to him that he had been told not as much as a few lines of the dark Catwalker's life.

They parted because both had business and places to be. By then the same dog had passed close to them twice more.

Lone's destination was not at all far. In the bright sunlight of early afternoon he made his way through the noisy throng. Along the way he enlisted the agreement of several additional vendors to be alert to someone who might be Janithe.

His rambling way led to the permanent stall of a bright and ever cheerful woman who identified herself as Saylulah. Word was that she had once been attached to a Rankan noble and had fallen to this low estate of seamstress-peddler, but who ever knew what was true about the things said about this individual or that?

Especially in the town that all too many people sneeringly called Thieves' World!

Yesterday Lone had picked out a tunic from Saylulah's supply of ready-mades. Naturally most people made their own attire or, if they were sufficiently well off, had their clothing made to measure. Single males did exist, however, and people with other handicaps that prevented them from sewing, and so even in Sanctuary a market existed for serviceable clothing at a moderate price. Or less, for Saylulah also had available a few used tunics and cloaks. The very cheapest were those with patched rents, some "decorated" with brown stains that the new wearer could claim were his or her own blood . . .

Yesterday Lone had chosen a moderately priced item, and bartered a bit of ill-gotten gains for a nice but in no way fancy tunic. It was of a well-woven red fabric that had cleverly been dyed, tedded, and cured so as not to look new. It was a bit long for a tunic—particularly for a young man—but not quite a robe. Lone asked the vendor, also a seamstress, to "fancy it up" as he put it, by sewing a stripe around the garment's hem. Saylulah suggested dark green and he agreed, for the intended recipient was a dull dresser and should welcome a bit of color. Because she was Saylulah, he had committed the strange act of handing over the price in advance, with the agreement that the finished garment would be ready by this morning. No matter that he did not appear at her stall with its green-and-beige-and-yellow awning until after noon.

As a favor today, she also wrapped the additional item he bore.

He carried the packages with him to his regularly scheduled session with the weapon master designated by Chance. Lone and the other orphan boys in the Pits had been inculcated with the concept of remorseless killing without necessity or even reason, but the cluster of trainers had not included a true master of the long blade. According to the man who had been the renowned Shadowspawn, Sathentris from far Ketharvven was the master of swordmasters in Sanctuary.

He and his student parried and swung and dodged and feinted—
and ran!—for a full run of the glass before the swordmaster set up
a quarter-hourglass and Lone devoted that period to left-handed
swordwork, mostly defense. He was not as good this way, of course,
since he had not been born left-handed but persisted in training
himself to be, in emulation of his idol Shadowspawn.

Sathentris the Keth was not a man given to praising those he
taught, but today he was apparently unable to refrain from expressing satisfaction beyond approval. At the end of their approximate
hour and a half together his youngest student went away barely curb-
ing a smile that wanted to be a smirk. With the new tunic and another
smaller, secret package then, Lone went to visit Heliz Yunz.

As he expected, the churlish genius from Lirt greeted him in manner unfriendly—and in the same tired, faded old once-red cassock
made more colorful by buttons of two descriptions and several un-
matching patches, in magenta.

The act of robbing a pitifully few coins from Arizak's keep as a
favor to Strick had been an obscenely pleasurable experience for
Lone. During that dangerous lark the thief in the palace had naturally taken a little something for himself. The slim bronze tablet he
had chanced upon showed four parallel columns of words, each col-
umn in a different language—a sort of dictionary? At once he had
thought of how such an object would light the eyes of one Heliz Yunz
into incandescence, and so Lone added it to his puny loot to take to
the man he thought of respectfully as a better-than-well-educated
scribe—well, and a wise eccentric, too.

After all, Lone had availed himself of Heliz's services more than
once, and with this thing—whichy from Arizak's keep he hoped to
gain a future service or two. To it he had added, for some reason he
could not have stated, the gift tunic. Better to steal the wherewithal
to have it made, he had opined, than to shove at the linguist a tunic
roached from someone else.

"Open this only later, please," Lone bade the scholar, who frowned,
muttered something not quite audible containing the words "silly

youngster"and "nonsense." But he accepted the softer, larger package, gave it a squeeze and Lone a look, and set it aside. His eyes did indeed light up when he beheld the mystery object from the palace, and it seemed to Lone that the man seemed almost worshipful.

He held it in both hands while he studied it, muttering something unintelligible that his visitor thought contained the words "execration text. Most interesting, most interesting," he added, in a normal tone. "I shall study it and consult my sources and advise you as to its purpose and possible worth, Lone."

"You don't know what it is, then?"

"Would I have said what I said if I were sure of its identity?"

Lone looked down. Damn the man! "Sorry, O Red Scholar," he murmured, hoping that Heliz Yunz caught the sarcasm—and with no idea as to how close he was to the truth of the identity of the man from Lirt. "Especially since I have another request . . ."

"Ah!" The scholar made a show of being horrified. "*Another* request from the impatient boy! This soft package had better contain something of value!"

For once Lone remembered the advice of both his mentor and the Spellmaster, and kept silent.

After a long while that seemed longer, "All right, then," the other man said, with no sign of contrition. "What else is it you want to beg of me?"

Lone's head snapped up and in an instant he had reshaped himself into a military posture. "I beg nothing from anyone!" he snapped, and added, "never!"

Heliz Yunz looked startled and more, but did not back-step, either physically or with face or words. "The word 'never' negates the previous statement," he said, as if he expected his meaning to be understood by a youngster who was only just able to read and was barely able to write. "But at any rate . . . what else is it that you would have of me, Lone?"

Aha! He who is a Lirt called me by name rather than "boy"!

"I had hoped you might find out for me anything that might be knowable about a bracelet of gold that looks like this and is this long."

With that the youth drew a quite passable picture of the long ornament that embraced the forearm of the girl he had rescued from robbery and worse. "It looked like beaten gold," he told Heliz, who knew this orphan lad with so much attitude did have an excellent idea for such things.

They arranged another meeting or exchange of messages, and parted with the tunic still wrapped and unidentified. *Damn him*, Lone mused. *He is always so a Lirt!*

After that Lone ambled as if aimlessly, trying to be unobtrusive in looking upward to examine possible targets for a night worker on a moonless night . . .

In the first night of this month's disappearance of the moon above the woods outside Sanctuary a weak excuse for a breeze only just rustled a few leaves of the trees. The trees crowded close against the small waterway that crept through the woods. The breath of air was pallid, and no more significant than the small man who sloshed out of the stream. He bore a good-sized woven sack, laden but not full, and a slim pole hand-equipped at one end with two tines about as long as two sections of his longest finger. In the darkness among the trees, his face was undefined and no one could have named the color of his faded old tunic. He wore no leggings, and his legs, short and knotty, streamed water. He carried the sack as if it was middling heavy. It was swollen here and there, and some among those lumps could be seen to move. Clearly this man had spent some hours in the stream, gigging frogs.

"Looks like you had a good night froggin', Turgul."

At the unexpected sound of that seemingly disembodied voice, the man from far Shitellanor jerked as if in response to the sting of an insect. "Name of the shadow god hisself, Borl, you like to scared me out of a year of my life!"

Borl, a large youth with a total of eighteen digits and fewer than twenty years, treated Turgul the Shite to his imitation of an affrighted chicken.

"Now damn it—" Turgul began.

"Aw come on, Turgul," Borl said amiably. "Didn't know you didn't see me, is all. Wasn't trying to be stealthy, neither. I thought you Shites seen everything of a dark night."

"I see frogs well enough!"

"Looks like you seen plenty. I'll clean 'em for a share of the meat."

Mollified—and outweighed by fifty-something pounds directed by an undeveloped brain unlikely to develop much more—Turgul nodded. "All right. First let's get out of these blasted woods so we don't get no more surprises."

With Borl towering at his side, the frogging Shite resumed his bowlegged gait along the path through the woods. They did not go far before they made camp. There Borl did indeed skin and otherwise prepare the several frogs for cooking before they approached the two men on watch at the gate. The delay was brief and the bribe a heartwarming one to Turgul and Borl; these city-bred men of the watch knew no better than to accept the uneviscerated bodies of four frogs. A few minutes later the friends entered the city, averting their smirking faces. One of the guardsmen made a note of Borl's name and physical description, with a view toward suggesting the recruitment of such a big fellow.

That was not to be. Once Borl and Turgul finished a savory repast of frog's legs and a bit of bread, they parted. Borl was ambling happily along with no particular goal in mind when he saw the young woman turn into the narrow, dark street called Borborygma. With no nearby lights or even a moon, the blackness in there was no less than that of a sorcerer's heart. But the very big fellow named Borl feared little, including mere darkness.

With a little smile on his lips, he followed the sinuous progress of the slender hourglass figure into Borborygma Street. He was discovered there in the morning, not just dead but badly ripped up as by

an animal too totally savage and ferocious to be possible within
the city . . . and mutilated in a way that some folk would call un-
speakable.

Violent death was far from unknown in Sanctuary. But a killing so
spectacular as that of one Borl son of Borl was unusual, and cause
for alarm. Was some sort of wild animal loose in the streets? Add in
the ghastliness of the mutilation, and the news spread rapidly. With
so many retellings by third- and fifth- and then eighth-party sources,
it took next to no time for misinformation and exaggerations to muck
up the story. Business took an upward leap in the farmers' market.
Some people were here to hear and exchange gossip, and to speculate, and others to make certain they were well-stocked with food
for dinner and need not venture out this night.

Among them was a youth who had done physical harm on no one
last night but had gained a few salable items by means dishonest. He
heard much about the man he had never known, but nothing at all
about the very thin young foreign female he sought. He paid off a
short-term debt with coins he had of a changer who asked no questions but was tight as an athlete's butt, and made gifts to three people.
These were jewels, in two cases, and in the third a good dagger in a
nice sheath.

The dark sheath was one that Lone had *acquired* over a year ago;
the dagger one he had carried and used since his adoption. He kept
the newer and thus less sharpened one he had roached the previous
evening, at the same time and in the same third-floor room wherein
he picked up the ruby-and-coral earrings and the matching bracelet—
which now adorned the ears and wrist of two different persons unlikely ever to be in the same place at the same time.

Late that evening in a room on the third floor of an "unscalable"
tenement, he decided not to take anything because it was obvious
that the resident had come upon hard times. He descended empty-
handed but not unhappy. His feet had just come down on the pave
when from the unlit alley to his left he heard the hideous snarling

growls of an animal and then a mingling, high-voiced shriek in a human voice. Hair leaped erect on Lone's arms and nape and he unsheathed a weapon with each hand.

With prickling scalp, he started into absolute blackness.

In two seconds he suffered an attack of intelligence, realizing that the odds strongly favored his immediate death or worse. He decided to wait and see who or what emerged from that obsidian darkness, and sheathed his long blade but kept a firm grip on the dagger and one of his throwing knives. Less than a minute later he heard feet pattering toward him in the alley, and it occurred to him that he'd have been even wiser to have ascended. Then the mad-eyed hideousness with jaws and fangs and claws and streaming hair came hurtling out of the dark. It did not even pause in bowling Lone over, but accomplished that in passing, and raced on.

Lone thought he inflicted a dagger wound, but at the same time as the pavement raised the strawberry of an abrasion on his right arm his head banged into a masonry wall and he and rational thought parted company.

The apparition was of course gone when after a few seconds Lone had got himself together and onto his feet. He bent to pick up his spanking new dagger and saw that the blade was indeed marked with fresh red blood. As he and his staggered brain lurched up the street to the nearest welcoming light, Lone realized that the *thing* he had so briefly seen had been an animal that walked quite erect, on two feet. And the hips, and the bilobed chest . . .

"Among Sanctuary's many troubles is that the bottom of the bottom keeps getting lower." Those words of the white mage Strick were a plague inside his head as Lone hurried away from the bloodiest mess he had ever seen.

Before he went into the greasily lit tavern to order a large dark ale, he thought to wipe his blade on a dirty strip of cloth he found just outside the door. Twenty minutes later he and two large men with a torch retraced his steps and this time entered the alley, which naturally enough surrounded the trepid trio with the odor of ammonia.

It turned out to be a veritable cul-de-sac, narrowing to a passage that would have turned back a man with a real belly, or an extra-busty woman. The doomed young man who had so foolishly entered it had walked all the way to that area. The mark of his urine was still on the wall, but Lone and his companions were staring down at a lot more blood. And horror that proved too much for the stomachs of two of the three men.

Leaving their vomit behind with the victim's blood, they fetched him out of the alley without ever glancing at their burden. A burly man in uniform had turned up in the tavern since their departure. In the name of the City Watch, he commandeered the torn old cloak that had long hung on the back wall. No one should have to look at the ghastliness that had been perpetrated on the slim young man who had sought only to relieve his bladder.

Next day Lone met Chance in a venue that some would have considered unlikely for such men: Chiluna's Green Acre. The place was far from large as an acre, and the only thing green there was the tea. Over a cup apiece, the younger orphan was excited yet carefully quiet in telling the older about how he had found the body of the second murder victim. That did not interfere with their notic-ing the entrance of two strangers. A brief inquiry led them to the table of the two suspicious-looking patrons, who were instantly wary.

The male newcomer was of average height and burly, with dark brown hair and a small beard of lighter brown and ginger. His tunic was off-white with hem stripes in blue, over darkish blue leggings and a handsome pair of buskins, dark brown and worn. His mantle was short, medium brown, and thrown back. He wore both sword and dagger—but of course everyone bore a dagger, the world's all-purpose tool. In cut and style, his hair was . . . just there. This care-fully conservative man, the oldest person present, wanted to be one who faded into any background.

He was neither hurried nor reluctant in showing Chance and Lone the medallion that proclaimed him a representative of the government.

"My name is Taran Sayn," he said crisply. His manner was friendly. "I represent the Sharda. We are investigators in the employ of Judge Nevermind, who is interested in increased citizen safety."

Lone cocked his head to one side. "Judge Nevermind?"

The bland-looking man shrugged. "It's just that he is a magistrate, Lone, a member of government. You need to know my name and that I'm with the Sharda, not his name."

"As you knew mine, already. But—aren't you Ilsigi?"

"Native Sanctuarian, yes," Sayn said, without taking his gaze off Lone's eyes. "Not all of us in government are Irrune."

Lone's head, which had realigned itself, went into cocked mode again. "And you work for an Ilsigi judge?"

"Let's just say that he is a man who believes that we native Sanctuarians have a right to police and judge ourselves. Never forget that most of the nabobs are of Ilsigi descent. This judge's goals are in our interest."

"So," Lone began slowly after a long moment of reflection, "is knowing the name of such a man."

Sayn gazed meditatively at him for about the length of time Lone had taken to process the previous information. Then he said, "His name is Elisar."

"Judge Elisar."

"Right. Now. I am with the Sharda, as I said, and the reason I am here is to ask you questions, Lone, and instead all I have done is answer yours."

"Uh-huh," Lone said, and gestured at the painfully thin young woman standing just aft and to port of the Sharda man. "And who is she?"

Sayn showed his unhappiness at being plied with still another question, but without turning to his companion he said, "This is my associate. Her name is Ixma."

Chance took a turn at speaking. "S'danzo blood in you, Ixma?"

Hair the color of a moonless night shone as the tawny wraith of a woman nodded.

Sayn asked, "And who are you, sir?"

"Name's Chance," he said, and leaned back as if to remove himself from the gathering. "Lone and I happened to meet here a few minutes ago."

"Good for you. Lone: Do you think it's possible that I might get to do my job and ask you a few questions some time before sunset?"

Lone smiled slightly in accompaniment to a solemn nod. "Ask, Taran Sayn."

But now the man of sixty-eight years, longtime foe of authority figures, decided to be contrary. "I think first you should tell us what that odd word 'sharda' means."

By now Lone was impatient to get this incident over with and this pair of law-enforcers out of the neighborhood. "It means some police-types who investigate for Judge Nevermind," he said. "Also known as Elisar."

"Accompanied by a sensitive," Chance added.

Taran Sayn's face showed his reluctance to be amused, just before he laughed. "True. Ixma?"

"A sharda," she said, in a markedly subdued voice that seemed to match her short stature and almost frightening leanness, "is a hound, a hunting dog of the Irrune. A sharda is said never, never to give up the scent."

Lone said, "Are you never going to ask me whatever it is you are going to ask, hunting hound?"

"Yes. Might I sit down?"

Meeting his eyes directly, Lone shrugged.

"Two more cups here," Chance called.

"That's all right," Sayn said. "We won't be here long and don't require anything."

Chance gave him a glare. "*Spend some money*, government man."

Lone was surprised when Chance rose and, leaning on the back of his chair, drew out one of the others for Ixma.

"I never knew my father or mother," he said quietly while she, showing surprise, slid gracefully into the chair, "and she barely knew my father. The nearest to a mother I ever had was a S'danzo, a superb seer named Moonflower. One of the fish-eyes murdered her. I saw to her vengeance. In case you ever wondered, their blood is red." He did not see fit to mention Moonflower's daughter, who had once meant so much to the boy he had been, this man whose boyhood had persisted for so long.

During his utterance Sayn began his questions, nodding at each of Lone's replies. Yes, Lone had discovered the body of the murdered youth last evening. No, to his knowledge he had never seen the victim before. He had been identified as Ticky by some others in the tavern. They said he left alone and no one had noticed anyone leave soon after.

No, Lone had no idea who might have found him even earlier, and no, he had no idea who might have done such a horrendous deed—the same sort of unnecessarily gruesome deed on two successive nights, leaving behind the same sort of blood-soaked victim with his chest ripped open and his lungs missing. It went against the grain to volunteer information, but he did, describing what he had heard and the inhuman *thing* that had bowled him over.

Sayn showed interest in the fact that Lone thought it was female, and persisted with several more queries. Lone and Chance both caught the fact that twice the Sharda man shifted his gaze, very briefly, to Ixma. Apparently she gave no sign that she knew other than Lone's replies, for after a time Sayn bobbed his head and rose to his feet.

Before he could depart, Lone snatched the opportunity to ask Sayn about the phrase "Native Sanctuarian."

"No, it isn't necessary," he was told, and both Sayn's expression and voice were serious and perhaps even portentous. "But I do prefer the phrase to 'Wrigglie' . . . even though a lot of our people have taken over that old Rankan insult as a sort of code."

Chance's brows came down. With incredulity and some anger he demanded, "You mean some *Ilsigi* are actually referring to each other by that insulting word?"

"Yes, but not because some of our ancestors wriggled under the heel of Ranke. They apply the term to themselves as a means of establishing that we are of *Sanctuary,* Sanctuarians, a separate people entirely apart from Ilsig City and not subject to its king. But any of us who use the term still object to its use by others."

The old man chuckled. "So I'm a Wrigglie, and you're a Wrigglie, and it's fine for us to say so, but if a Rankan or an Irrune says it we mess up his face?"

For the first time Sayn showed emotion: He laughed. A little, and briefly. "Exactly! What do you do, Chance of the Ilsigi?"

"I'm retired," Chance said, and the way he declaimed it made the lawman decide instantly that he might as well not ask the next question.

Instead he said, "Lone: Thank you. If you think of anything that might help me uncover the monster who did so much more than *mere* murder on those two boys, please tell Gorbat in the farmers' market, under the sign of the blue-and-white awning."

"I can think of five awnings like that," Lone said, although he had no intention of having more dealings with a representative of law enforcement or indeed anything or anyone having to do with government. "What does he sell?"

"Vegetables from his own garden and a marvelous bread he makes with flaxseed, marjoram, and something he won't reveal."

Lone and his chosen mentor watched the two Sharda amble as if casually across the room, and depart.

"Well," Lone said, "we got our tea paid for, at least. Notice that he did not so much as touch his?"

"Aye—and, I'll bet," Chance said, "they know we were telling the truth. At least I believe that's the purpose of the part-S'danzo."

"You think that's the form her Seeing takes? To know whether people are telling the truth?" Lone looked down to see that the hair on his arm had taken a notion to stand up.

"More importantly," Chance said, "whether people are lying. I hope that's as far as her talent goes, watered down by non-S'danzo blood. Otherwise by now she may well be telling him more about us."

"More than we want policers to know!"

Chance only nodded. He was trying hard to be a proper mentor, and was sure that part of being mature meant being sparing with words. He did make a remark abut how conservative that Sayn fellow was. Lone cocked his head.

"I believe we could ask everyone here what he was wearing and hear at least five different descriptions," Chance explicated. "What does that tell you, roof-hopper?"

"Ahhh . . . people don't notice what they say? Or don't remember?"

"Including you, apprentice who chose me as mentor. Sayn's clothing and hair tell me that he does not wish to be noticed more than necessary. And that is a better than good idea." He paused for a moment of reflection. "And now an admission, Lone. I always had a real need to stand out, to be sure everybody noticed me. It is much in your favor that you do not have such a need."

"Thank you, Master!" Lone said with unfeigned exuberance, and tried to be surreptitious about examining himself, and what he was wearing . . .

This person told that one about Lone's quest, and she told a couple of others, and one of them told fifteen or sixteen others, and some of them spoke to others, and by noon Lone was practically running toward the orange-and-brown-striped roof under which sizzled hot flatbread and savories. Behind the counter was a fellow with an unfortunate nose unaided by his hangdog mustache. Ah yes, the young woman his anxious accoster sought had just made a purchase and departed. The man pointed. Lone's heart leaped as he turned to see the retreating female back below a good deal of lustrous auburn hair. He did not need the glimpse of the ornate gold bracelet to know it was Janithe, despite the fact that she looked fuller of figure than he remembered.

"I owe you," Lone gusted, "but right now I have no time to buy!"

"Later then," the cook-vendor said. "And good luck with that girl."

The elated Lone angered a few people by the callowly careless way he made his way through the multitude, but no one tried to make more of it than an angry yelp or shout. In mere seconds he fell into place beside the girl or woman he had so heroically saved from a fate worse than.

"G'day to you, Janithe of Caronne. Why did you leave me in such a hurry?"

"Good day to you, Lone," she said, turning her face a little his way while still walking. It seemed incredible that she had filled out a bit, in just two days, and was less pale. "I will admit to being fearful and very shaky after you rescued me—and embarrassed, too, for I was in great need of relieving myself."

He gazed ahead as he walked. "You have stopped being fearful of me?"

"I asked about you. You seem well known to the merchants here, and none showed anything even close to fear when they spoke of you."

"Glad to hear it. That rumble you may have heard was my stomach. What are you eating?"

"Beans and rice with onion," Janithe said, waving the fat roll of flatbread and turning his way again as they walked. "Would you like a bite?"

"I would rather have a whole one of my own," he told her. "Are you in a hurry to be somewhere?"

"No," she told him, and they went smiling back to the orange-and-brown vending station.

"I've not stopped here often," Lone told the man with the nose too long and too thin and with a hook besides. "What is your name?"

"Scaff will do. Just Scaff."

"You ought to have a sign, Scaff," Lone said while he waited for his rolled-up lunch. "I'm Lone and this is Janithe."

Scaff did not look up from his cooking. "People charge money to paint good signs, Lone."

"Sorry," Lone said. "I hadn't thought of that."

"That's my mother's recipe for scaff," he told her. "Yes, I'm from Mrsevada and my name is a long one so I'm called after the bread I make—scaff. Here you are, Lone."

Lone paid and the couple walked away, neither with a destination now and both apparently oblivious to everything except each other.

Long view, Lone and Janithe walking hand in hand down a colorful street, chatting and laughing merrily;

Long view, moving steadily in on Lone and Janithe happily picnicking on a grassy sward;

Long midafternoon view, Lone and Janithe happily walking along the beach, hand in hand; then running while giggling happily, her hair streaming behind her like a cloak;

Late afternoon glimpse of Lone and Janithe happily riding in a one-horse carriage, obviously more taken with each other than the scenery they pass;

Sunset scene: Lone and Janithe embracing; kissing . . .

And fade out.

Anyone might have expected a couple so clearly involved with each other not to part at day's end, but to spend the night together. That was not the case. Lone despised the fact that he had a prior engagement, but it was, after all, with his mentor and that man's best friend, at the home of the latter: Strick. Gratifying was the fact that Janithe seemed just as fascinated with him as he was with her, and agreed to meet him at the second hour tomorrow at Scaff's food stand. With little time to spare before he knew Strick's "housekeeper" would have dinner prepared, Lone reluctantly parted her company. He had to rush to the better section of town where Strick dwelled. He had ceased taking a little gift on these more than welcome occasions, for both Spellmaster and Linnana knew where and how he came by them . . .

None of the three in Strick's home could fail to notice how the

quiet and often close to surly Lone *glowed*. He had already told
Chance about Janithe, and now was pleased to tell him and the others that he had found her. Strick asked about the unusual bracelet
Lone mentioned, and he drew the white mage a picture. Clearly,
both the seriously fat mage and Linnana found it interesting, but
gave no indication that they had ever seen it or one like it. Hours
later, as Lone was leaving, she asked him to make an exact drawing
of the design on the ornament.

Lone agreed, and departed, and went home and to bed but lay
awake thinking of Janithe, and was sorry that he had not made late-
night plans that involved his profession. He was early in reaching
the market next morning, where he learned that the *thing* had claimed
another victim, another large young male within the same area as
the others: one within the Maze, two nearby. This one too had been
savagely and nigh impossibly ripped and torn, and bereft of his
lungs. It did seem, after that third consecutive night yielded gory
horror, that everyone in the city knew about the assaults and was
talking about them, and everyone had an opinion, a theory, a "What
if " . . .

That day and the next, on mornings without word of new victims,
the darling couple that included the winsome foreign girl with the
golden skin and the formerly sinister-looking orphan lad with all
the weapons entered the market early and together, and bought
their breakfast from the man nicknamed for his bread. On the third
morning Scaff arrived in the market to discover that someone had
been skulking about his place of business the night previous, but
without criminal intent. Instead, a huge sign had been professionally
inked on heavy sailcloth and clandestinely installed:

SCAFF!
GOOD SAVORY FOOD WITH THE BEST BREAD IN TOWN!

That was also the day when Janithe moved in with Lone. Yes, she
knew what he did for a living. She was surprised to discover that he

had been a virgin until now, but did not reveal that she recognized the fact. Already market regulars had noticed the loving couple and were talking, smiling. A day later, the day when no new corpse was reported and when Janithe appeared wearing a handsome necklace of carved cabochons of amber, Lone asked Scaff if business had improved since yesterday's addition of the sign.

Scaff turned slowly to stare at the dark youth, and was surprised to see that he and his chosen woman were wearing matching new tunics in snowy white with yellow borders on sleeves and hem. Scaff cocked his head.

"Of course business is up. Lone? Did—did you make this sign?"

Lone's smile or response slid into a chuckle. He thrust a clean but nail-bitten finger at the center of his chest. "Me? *Me,* Scaff? I'm no artist, and clearly an artist made your sign! No no oh no, I did not make this handsome sign!"

Scaff looked dubious, but after a while he shrugged and addressed himself to his little stove. "Well, if you ever find the person who did, tell him he will always have a meal here but will never be allowed to pay for it. Meanwhile, you and Janny are such reg'lars I think I'll just *give* you breakfast today!"

And in private Janithe, whose tunic and necklace had not been stolen but which Lone had bought in the market, wondered aloud to her lover how it was that a man who "earned" a living by stealing from others could be so generous. Lone's reply was to lower his head, then turn away, and mutter defensively that it made him feel good.

When they visited his wealthy friend Strick and the S'danzo woman he and she pretended was his housekeeper and who was actually his woman, it was soon clear that Strick and Linnana and Chance liked "Lone's golden girl" and that she was more than welcome. Quietly in the kitchen the S'danzo seer told Janithe what she knew of the ghastly childhood that Lone avoided talking about. Both she and the stricken Janithe allowed as how they could understand that the result of such horror in childhood could grow up to be a monster who hated everyone—or a person unable to resist a desire or maybe a need to give, to do things for others in need—and some who were not.

That night Linnana and the obese Spellmaster examined Janithe's long, ornate bracer. The design, they decided amid their muttering, appeared to be oceanically based. They learned that the work of art, almost the length of Janithe's forearm, was seamless and that she could not take it off. She also could not or would not tell them how it came to be on her arm. No, it did not hurt and no, she did not wish Strick to use his powers to try to discover its origin, or to remove it. He merely nodded. The thing and its presence were sorcerous, of course, but what could the white mage do but accept her wishes?

Sharp-eyed even at his age, Chance noted the odd little slit-like birthmarks just behind/under Janithe's ears. He said nothing about it until she and Lone had left. Strick and Linnana had not noticed, and did no speculating.

The subject of the three mutilation murders did not come up that night, and gradually conversation and speculation on that subject petered out among the general populace of Sanctuary.

On the eighth day after the new moon Lone was happy to move himself and his beloved into new and larger accommodations. By that time it had become necessary for Scaff to hire an assistant, and the business of the seamstress Saylulah was up, too. She knew very well the cause was that Lone and Janithe kept blabbering about Saylulah and her expertise, and soon the charming couple had others talking about her as well. She and others talked about the charming couple, too. People looked their way, smiling. People watched them, and nudged each other, and rolled their eyes, and exchanged winks. Such an attractive couple! So obviously enraptured with each other. No one ever saw them apart anymore. Janithe even accompanied Lone to his lessons in swordwork, and presumably watched, or perhaps merely waited.

The only time Janithe was not present was when Lone in the persona of Catwalker dealt with the husband of the granddaughter of Shive the Changer, a man who exchanged foreign money in quantity for local, and who bought this and that object without asking questions. Business was business.

As usual Strick and Linnana celebrated the full moon by inviting Lone and Chance, and this time they had no thought of trying to find a girl for him. No one need say aloud that the time of the full moon was not good for such night work as practiced by Chance and his apprentice. Linnana, especially, noted that the girl with the fascinating skin seemed paler and thinner than she had a matter of mere days ago. By now she had new earrings, a bracelet, and a luxurious dress too nice for any occasion in her life.

On the twenty-first day they had an argument over nothing in particular and spent most of a day and all night making up and trying to atone to each other.

On the first night of moondark, however, Lone left his woman in their new home while he saw to business, and next morning, for the first time in thirty days and nights, another young man had been lured or surprised in a narrow alley and hideously clawed and bitten, and his lungs ripped out—to be consumed?

Again Sanctuary exploded with horror, anger, fear, and endless exchange of opinions and speculations.

After a month, "everybody knew"—that is, many many regulars in the market—that daily the darling couple bought breakfast or lunch from Scaff. That partially explained the fact that the same pair of Sharda investigators appeared there to, as they told Scaff and others, talk to Lone. They knew he had been out last night, and wanted to know where he had been and what he had done. Sayn and Ixma waited a long time before at last deciding they had been idle long enough, and went away.

Lone and Janithe did not show up until over an hour later; for some reason both lovers had slept both deeply and late.

"I saw the inhuman thing that killed those fellows last month," Lone said, frowning, "and I'm the one found the body, and I told people, and the Sharda man came to question me. Now it has happened again, and however he found out I was not home last night, he did.

Naturally he suspects me . . . and Scaff, I didn't kill anybody—but I can't tell him where I was last night, either."

Scaff understood. "In that case, Lone, Janny—do not turn around. Just walk around my booth and get yourself out of here, fast. A man of the City Watch is heading this way with his hand on his pommel, and it ain't me he's got his eye on."

"Go left," Lone muttered, and Janithe did while he went right-ward, and around Scaff's place of business and across a thronged aisle and between two other vendors and cut left and on a ways far-ther and then left and between two other stalls, and left, and through the crowd, and out of the market. Only then did he unexcitedly say, "Run," and they did.

"Master," a frowning Komodoflorensal said, "look here. That or-nate bracer I learned of . . . it has to do with the daughter of the an-cient beast-god of the sea."

His master turned on the apprentice a frown of his own, almost a murderous one. "Are you speaking of Ka'thulu?"

"Aye, Uncle 'Lonikas! Ka'thulu!"

"Nonsense, idiot! Let me see your alleged work, fool. That fancy bauble could not possibly be—name of Consternatis! A miracle! For once you are right!"

"I'm glad my man found you," a grim-faced Strick told Chance, the moment that man and his cane tap-tapped their way into his office-cum-spelling chamber.

A bit red of face and panting from the effort of hurrying in re-sponse to the urgent summons of his friend, Chance sank down in the chair across the long, blue-draped table that was the white mage's desk. He was surprised to find Linnana also present.

"Rushing across town is not so easy as it once was," he gasped, and accepted the towel Linnana proffered. He wiped his face and set his hand to his chest, a bit left of center. There was that irregular pounding again, damn it. "What is so urgent?"

"We have work to do," Strick said, with no lessening of the deadly seriousness of his face or manner. "Lone has to be warned, and more. That long bracer on Janithe's arm is one the beast-god Ka'thulu gave to his daughter when he proclaimed her the sklamera, chief among the demons of his domain—the sea."

"Ah gods," Strick said, seeming to grow smaller in his chair. "You talk of sorcery! Ach, Ils our Father knows how I hate sorcery!"

Strick only nodded, having heard nothing he had not heard before from this man. "The sklamera never took it off—including in the several hundredth year of her life when she lay with a mortal youth and deceived her father by secretly equipping the lad with gills and becoming his wife. Love, supposedly, true love. The sea-god was outraged and bent on dastardly vengeance, but his daughter persuaded him to forbear. Years passed, and more years, but they were only moments to the beast-god and the demoness. Of course she did not age, while her husband did, and that made him increasingly unhappy. He dealt with his realization of mortality by betraying her, and with a mere mortal woman. Ka'thulu proved so vengeful *and so evil* as to do horrible death on the human. He made the sklamera watch his agony as he died, far beneath the waves."

Chance nodded dully. "He sealed the gills she had given the man . . ."

"Exactly. And then the king-beast of the sea turned on his own daughter, as if she had not been punished enough for having shown a preference for an air-dweller. The spell he cast on her is a particularly nasty one. Without lungs and with her gills sealed, the sklamera can exist only one way—she is forever condemned to imprisonment within the bracer."

"Ah, gods, Strick! Please don't tell me that this sklamera is . . . that it somehow *possesses* Lone's beloved!"

Linnana turned her unhappy face away. Strick nodded. "You saw the mark of the sea-demon on Janithe—the rudimentary gills in her neck. Linnana knows the lore better than I do. Linnana?"

She spoke quietly and seemingly without emotion. "An ancient legend among the Beysib is known too to the S'danzo. Throughout the ages a succession of comely young women has been so unfortunate as to draw the attention of the unhappiest of all females, a demon who exists only by inhabiting a bauble of gold. Their name for her is scilarna. This demon bonds herself to the surrogate, and when a moonless sky renders the sea equally black, she is reminded of a long-ago unfaithful love. She takes revenge on the deceitful male sex by choosing a comely young man each night of the moon-dark, and by ripping out of him that which makes him human, and mortal—"

"His lungs," Chance murmured, staring down at nothing and remembering a long-lost love.

"I need not tell you this is the time of the new moon," Strick said. "A fresh victim was found this morning. No matter how painful for us and Lone, he has to be warned."

"There's more," Linnana said. "The Watch want him."

The three exchanged looks of anguish and alarm, and began to plan.

Taran Sayn and the helmeted, cuirassed man of the Watch who accompanied him reached the apartment recently rented to Lone and Janithe, and knocked, and knocked again, and called out. Then Sayn shouted, and the policer leaned spear and shield against the wall and used his fist to pound the door, and shouted, and suddenly Sayn did a silly thing: He reached out and tried the handle.

The door began to swing open.

"If the occupation of this Lone fellow really is what we more than suspect," Sayn said while the door swung slowly inward, "it's hard to imagine that he fails to lock up when he leaves his own home! Well, inside, Taganall, and let's see what we see."

It hardly seemed necessary for Taganall to draw sword before he entered the darkened apartment, but he did and his companion made no comment. Their search was cursory, since all they sought was a man. They found no one, and no signs of struggle either.

Two blocks away, however, in the direction of that area of town where the four lungless victims had been found, they found a cohort of Taganall's. The uniformed man's left arm was still through the first strap of his shield, and his hand still clutched the second, but his sword was fast in its sheath and his spear lay on the pave. Beside it was his body, which had been gorily ripped apart by talons backed by fearsome strength.

"Odd," Sayn said, ignoring the suddenly bloodless face of his uniformed companion. "His chest hasn't been torn open. That means he still has his lungs. That tells me he was not tonight's intended victim, Taganall. He must merely have run afoul of the thing in pursuit of his normal duties."

"Not normal," Taganall gasped. "Not normal. Every man in the Watch is on the streets tonight. We're all going to be exhausted— tomorrow is likely to be remembered as Crime Day!"

He said it accusingly, as if he held the investigator responsible. But Sayn did not respond, for he was a man not without compassion, and Taganall was busy vomiting.

One person awoke to a foreign presence in his apartment on that night without a moon, and another was not asleep, and the cat-burglar called Catwalker was forced to do some running. Up the facade of a building a floor and a half he forced himself as fast as he was able, every second in peril, and all in silence recklessly raced across that roof unlit even by the few visible stars on this night of sky-prowling clouds. His cloth loot-bag hung silently in one hand because it was padded with cotton fluff against the rattle and clink of precious metals and almost by instinct he launched his black-clad self into blackest night to alight on another roof, to smack into an unyielding slab of brick-hard blacker than blackness, and actually bounce off that chimney to fall and roll on the *almost* flat roof, grunting and gasping but holding back any outcry or curse.

And then he was forced to squint down into pitch blackness and pat the roof with both hands in quest of the bag containing tonight's gleanings, and was on his feet and running again—dodging a second chimney—and again leaping, flying, soaring through moonless darkness under the faint illumination of a few lonesome stars. At last he fastened the bag to his belt, and double-checked the fastening, and began his downward clamber into the narrow space between this building and the next, which was taller.

He had descended past three rows of windows when he froze at the sudden eruption of clamor immediately below: a male shriek, followed by others as well as howls of pain in the same voice, all accompanied by a ferocious bestial snarling. The perilous "route" Catwalker followed down the side of the building was not one that enabled him to go back up. He stayed frozen, clinging to masonry.

Frozen except for his quivering, clinging desperately to masonry, Lone knew what he was hearing, and he did not want to go down. He listened to ripping sounds. And wet sounds. And then a stomach-lurching wet-ripping noise.

He remained hanging there until his fingers gave out, and spasmed, and he fell backward. By that time below him was only silence.

And hard-packed earth, and garbage.

Fortunately, his fall was for the most part broken by the motionless legs of the latest victim of the sklamera.

This time the superb cat-burglar called Catwalker did not try to examine the corpse. He did not even pause, but rolled off the poor fellow's legs, grunted with pain as he lurched to his feet, and headed for the faint light he saw. He did not walk.

That rapid pace swiftly brought him out of the passageway between two buildings, and into the light of a torch set atilt in a cresset thrusting out from the building on the corner. His heart was trying to pound its way out of his chest as he glanced in each direction, decided, and started moving rapidly up Tranquility Street. He was at the next corner and in the act of crossing there when the blood-splashed and smeared thing of nightmares seemed just to *appear* before him, at a distance of some two body-lengths. It snarled in a low voice. It was definitely human-shaped and definitely female, with long stringy hair like seaweed trailing over its shoulders and chest. With feet well apart and arms bent with horribly long claws poised, it stared.

I am dead, Lone thought, filling one hand with nearly three feet of steel and the other with a six-pointed star. He dared not turn his back on this horror to run. He had no choice but to match its stare.

"Lone!" a voice called from behind him, and he jerked spastically at the unexpected sound. "Move aside! You're between us and it!"

Lone was very aware of that fact, but chose not to say so. It was all he could do not to glance behind him. He thought he recognized the voice, but was not sure. He stared into the eyes of the beast, which was no longer snarling but still drooling blood. Now it cocked its hideous head, and the eyes that stared into his seemed to soften.

Impossible, Lone thought, the hand that held the throwing star slowly rising toward his right ear.

He jerked again in startlement when a spear appeared to the left of his waist, its murderously big head aimed at the beast and carried low for impaling. The smooth round pole was thicker than the thumb of a fat banker and tipped with a full foot of pointed, interestingly recurved steel thick as the wrist of a child. Lone recognized the shape and the markings and was even aware of irony; the thief's would-be rescuer was a member of the Watch! The spear was moving slowly past him as its wielder advanced, not yet within peripheral vision.

Suddenly the monster uttered a howl beyond fearsome, and charged.

Lone did not have time even to take a swift sideward step, but his arm flashed forward and down. The star of death whizzed on its way, humming—and skipped ringingly along the cobbled street far beyond the spot where the target had been. The sklamera, however, proved not to be charging Lone, but instead to his left. In a seemingly deliberate act of decision, it impaled itself on the leveled spear.

"*Uh!*" its wielder grunted with impact and effort, while the self-spitted thing of nightmares screamed and writhed and gnashed teeth more horrible than most humans ever saw.

The policer held steady, and twisted his arms and thus the spear, while the sea-beast howled and writhed bloodily on it. And then the hands of the man accompanying the policer enwrapped the far end of the shaft, and savagely rammed it. A freshet of blood burst from the sklamera's back, swiftly followed by inches of pointed steel. Lone swung his sword high, and back.

"Lone!" a shout rose. "Don't!"

Recognizing the voice of Linnana, he arrested his motion and turned his head from the dread scene of an impaled monster. He was surprised to see, behind the policer and Taran Sayn, a horse and the little carriage it pulled. Of course; Strick's home was many blocks from here and he was too fat to walk either fast or far. Four of them had come in quest of Catwalker: the driver Samoff, and Strick, and Linnana, and Chance. Wearing a look of concern deeper than Lone had seen on that face, the master thief was hurrying toward his apprentice.

"Put up the sword, Lone, *please!*"

Lone glanced at the thing writhing and surely dying on the thick shaft of hardwood that completely transpierced its lower torso, and knew that he could deal the death-stroke. But without a word he sheathed his sword.

There on the street called Tranquility in Sanctuary, Chance stood with a hand on Lone's shoulder while they watched the beast-daughter of the god Ka'thulu die—again.

"We could not let you cut her, Lone," Chance said quietly. "You did not slay her and neither did that policer."

"It—just hurled itself right onto my spear!" a sweaty, red-faced Taganall gasped in wonder.

"It did exactly that, and I know why," Linnana said, and came too to stand beside Lone and lay an affectionate hand as seven pairs of eyes gazed down at the spasmodically kicking but dead *thing* on the cobbles. "She just could not bring herself to harm Lone. Oh Lone, we're all so sorry."

Lone was just starting to frown in puzzlement when the dead

thing began to *change*. Over the course of a long, long minute, the sklamera resumed the form of the human whose body and mind it had used. Before the change was complete the long golden bracelet became visible, and the very young man who loved her screamed his plaintive, "No-o-oh!"

That shrill cry of wretched youth echoed and re-echoed off buildings on either side of the stricken gathering of heroes, and raced up and down the length of the street called Tranquility.

Protection

Robin Wayne Bailey

The day promised interesting weather. The bright sun had not yet reached zenith over Sanctuary, yet already the air was warm and uncharacteristically humid. The timid zephyr that blew over the harbor failed to dispel the heat or offer any relief. In the south, however, a low bank of dark clouds mustered on the horizon. Dim flickers of lightning at their roiling edges foretold some turbulence.

Regan Vigeles idly tapped a small jewel-hilted dagger against one palm. Shirtless and in only a brief linen kilt and sandals, he noted the coming storm from the parapet of the apartment over his shop, then returned his attention to the horizon. His thoughts were on the distant Seaweal and his too-brief journey to the strange wreck that hung impaled upon the reef out there. Better traveled than most men, he had never seen the vessel's like before. Yenizedi at a casual glance, to a knowledgeable eye it bore design elements and markings of half a dozen unlikely nations, some of which no longer even existed.

For most of a month since the wreck's discovery scavengers and treasure-hunters had worked to empty its holds and stripped its decks of anything valuable or useful. Among its diverse inventory they'd found a small cargo of weapons—swords and daggers mostly. More than a few of those had turned up in his shop for sale or appraisal, and they puzzled him even more than the origin of the abandoned wreck. As the owner of the Black Spider, the finest weapon shop in the city, Regan Vigeles knew weapons, their quality, their manufacture, and history.

He stared at the dagger again, the latest weapon from the wreck to come into his possession. It looked brand new, without tarnish, wear, or rust. There wasn't even an accumulation of grime around the jewel insets. Yet, he recognized its manufacture, the fold of the blade's metal, and the unusual design of the hilt.

The small blade in his hand was over eight hundred years old.

The dagger and particularly the vessel on the reef were pieces of a puzzle. They represented a mystery in a city where mysteries meant danger. So for a few padpols to a willing fisherman he'd boated out to see the wreck for himself. He still didn't know quite what to make of his observations or how much information to include in his next dispatch to Jamasharem. But the Rankan emperor was keeping a close eye on Sanctuary these days; he would want to know about this.

Turning away from the parapet, Regan Vigeles seated himself on a small couch and leaned over an ornately carved wooden writing table. Setting the dagger aside, he drew a single piece of parchment from a narrow drawer with delicate dragon's-head knobs, then an ink bottle, and a stylus. The breeze fluttered the edges of the parchment as he spread it on the table's polished surface and began to write.

Before he completed the salutation, a loud crashing and shouting rose up the stairway from the shop down below. Channa, his housekeeper, screamed a sharp curse. Then she screamed again, and another crash followed. Grabbing the dagger, Regan Vigeles raced across the roof and descended the steps two at a time. Fleet shadows raced out the shop's door before he quite reached the landing.

Channa lay sprawled on the floor beside her overturned mop bucket. Dirty water soaked her simple dress, and her dark hair hung in wet ropes over her face and shoulders. In one hand she clutched the shattered handle of her mop. The business end of it lay among the wooden shards and scattered small knives of a smashed display case. She waved one bare foot in the air as she sputtered and fumed and tried to sit up.

Bending down beside her, Regan Vigeles caught her by the arm and helped her to sit. Still blinded by her own dripping hair, she recoiled at his touch and swung the mop handle. He blocked the blow without effort and gently relieved her of her makeshift weapon.

"Be calm, Channa. They're gone." He brushed the strands of hair away from her angry eyes and grinned as she looked up at him. He might have chased and caught the thugs, but her safety was more important. "Did you give them a battle?"

Channa wiped a hand over her red face, spat, and wiped her tongue on the palm of one hand. "Indeed I did, Lord Spyder," she answered firmly. "Conked one of 'em good right on his pig-snout, and broke my mop over the back of another. Then someone turned my mop bucket over my head and knocked me down! Me, a helpless old woman that never hurt nobody! Now where's my missing slipper?" Shooting a glance around, he found the shoe under the edge of her hem. It was made of felt and as wet as the dress, but she clapped it on her foot. Then, she snatched the mop handle back from her employer. "If they ever come back again, I'll stick this so far up their arses I'll be pickin' their noses from the inside-out!"

Regan Vigeles, known only as Spyder, took his housekeeper's hand and helped her to her feet. Like many of Sanctuary's women, she was younger than she looked, and also tougher, a lot tougher. Surviving in Sanctuary made a woman that way.

"That's my Channa," he said when he was sure she'd suffered no real damage. "I'll clean up the damage. You take the rest of the day off and spend some time with your daughter. Buy new dresses for both of you, because that one's ruined." He indicated the stains the dirty water had made on her garment. They would wash out with a little effort, but he was always generous with Channa. "Just tell the merchant you choose to send me the bill." He winked as he patted her backside and aimed her toward the door. "Nothing too extravagant, mind you."

Channa shook her mop handle at him as she rubbed her offended rump. "For that liberty, young lord, and for the lumps I just took from those rowdies, I'll buy any dress I want, one that'll make you sit up and beg like a dog, and every sailor in port, too." She leered, then stuck out her tongue and returned his wink. "Though from what I hear, that lot's got dresses enough of their own."

Still clutching her broken mop handle, she departed through the door and headed up Face-of-the-Moon Street toward the ramshackle apartment dwelling where she made her home. Alone, Spyder watched from the threshold until she was safely inside. Then his expression hardened. With pursed lips and narrowed gaze, he studied the old building, noting the cracks in its facade and the black stone-rot, the crumbling outside stairs that led to upper apartments.

Soon, he'd have to acquire that building and the one next to it as well. But not so soon as to attract notice. Like his namesake, the spider, he knew well the value of patience and subtlety. He looked down at the ancient dagger he still held in one hand and tapped the blade on his palm. There were things to tell Jamasharem—and there were things best kept to himself.

He looked up and down Face-of-the-Moon Street, then toward the darkening sky before turning back inside. He had a mess to clean and a shop to set right again. Later today or tomorrow, he would have a visitor or visitors, and he liked his place neat.

Dressed in loose tan-colored trousers and soft brown boots, a white silk tunic that reached nearly to her knees, and swathed in a soft linen veil that draped from the crown of her head over and around her

shoulders, a young black woman made her way with silent, almost regal grace through the throngs of people along the Wideway. On one
arm, she carried a basket filled with fresh-wrapped fish, bread loaves,
and fruit. The thin veil did nothing to hide her beauty, and many
turned to watch as she passed by. Some even whispered her name.

Aaliyah. Spyder's paramour.

Lately, the Wideway had become a second marketplace for Sanctuary, nearly as busy and bustling as the farmer's market. If Aaliyah
heard the whispers, she gave no indication of it. Her green-eyed gaze
darted toward the booths and kiosks and small tents set up along the
sides of the broad street, and toward the swaying masts of the ships in
the harbor beyond them. Her nostrils flared at the many smells and
odors that filled the air, and her eyes lit up at the jugglers and acrobats
busking for coins.

"Feel the wind rising, Milady? We'd better hurry. There's a storm
brewing, and the sellers are starting to pack up their wares."

Aaliyah glanced at her companion. Though small of stature herself, she was yet an inch taller than the heavily muscled, middle-aged
man who carried a second basket at her side. Sweat ran in rivulets
along his temples and down his cheeks. Laying a hand on his broad
shoulder, she paused and set down her basket.

"We really shouldn't stop," her companion said in mild protest.
"It's a long way back home. . . ."

Using a corner of her linen veil, Aaliyah wiped his sweat away
and then smacked him on the nose playfully with the tip of her in-
dex finger. As she moved, the veil slipped from her face to reveal exotic features and a smile that dazzled. Unconcerned, she pushed the
bit of cloth back over her shoulder and picked up her basket again.
A bit of dark cleavage flashed at the neck of her tunic.

"Ronal, get your thoughts back up above your belt," her companion muttered to himself as Aaliyah walked on. He shifted his own
shopping basket into his other hand. With another glance at the gathering clouds, he hurried to catch up. The rising wind snatched at the
edges of his cloak and stirred his iron-gray hair.

Someone hailed him. He waved a hand at young Kaytin, but hurried on without stopping to chat. The coming storm was foremost on his mind now, and getting Aaliyah safely home his only goal. He wasn't at all comfortable with the idea of letting her shop the streets of Sanctuary and didn't understand why Spyder allowed it. She didn't know the city and attracted too much attention. His tastes didn't run to women, but when he let his gaze linger on her, Aaliyah stirred even his jaded blood.

She stopped again, this time to listen to the song of some cresca-playing stranger with an orange cloak spread on the ground before him. A few copper coins shimmered on the bright cloth. Reaching into her purse, Aaliyah tossed down a pair of silver padpols—the foreign kind that came down from the Ilsigi Kingdom. The musician's eyes widened with surprise, but then he smiled and nodded his appreciation without missing a note.

"Outrageous generosity!" Ronal grumbled as he brushed his charge's elbow to speed her along. "You'll have every beggar in town following us!" He glanced back over one shoulder as they walked and watched as the musician ended his song and pocketed the coins. "Besides, he sang like a whale with a congested blow-hole."

The crowds thinned. Everyone sensed the coming storm now. The sun faded, and a powerful gust blew a couple of seller-tents completely off their posts. In the confusion, someone bumped a merchant's vegetable basket and overturned it. Cabbages rolled into the street.

Even Aaliyah picked up her pace. Proceeding eastward along the Wideway, they left behind the booths and kiosks. At the wharves on their right, fishing ships and larger vessels rocked at their moorings as whitecapped waves smashed against their hulls. Men hurried to batten down sails and equipment, paying no attention at all to the increasingly rare passersby.

They reached the Stairs, a long and steep flight of wooden steps that led up the side of the Hill. Aaliyah began the ascent without hesitation, her energy seemingly inexhaustible. Ronal paused at the bottom and stared upward, giving a heavy sigh before he tightened his grip on his basket and followed.

By the time they reached the midway point in their climb, Ronal was puffing. He paused again, putting one callused hand on the rough railing as he cursed the vagaries of age. The wind pushed at his back, but it didn't stop the sweat that stung his eyes. With a glance at Aaliyah farther above, he brushed the droplets away.

Four men appeared at the top of the Stairs. Leaning into the force of the wind, they gripped their snapping cloaks tightly as they started down. The one in the lead looked up and saw Aaliyah in their path. He smiled and waved a hand in greeting while his companions fell politely into a single-file line to give her room to pass.

All seemed friendly, but some instinct raised the hackles on Ronal's neck. Letting go of the railing, he reached beneath his cloak for the short sword he wore on his hip. His fingers curled around the cool hilt, but he didn't yet draw his weapon from concealment. He redoubled his pace, taking the steps two at a time. Clutching his basket with one hand and with his other, the still hidden blade, he called Aaliyah's name.

At the sound of his call, she stopped, turned, and looked down at him. At the same time, the four men reached her. One flung back his cloak, exposing a fisherman's net draped over an arm. With a skilled toss, he ensnared the small black woman. Another wrapped powerful arms around her while a third slipped a coil of rope around her shoulders. The fourth flung his cloak over her head. With their captive secure, two of them lifted her like any piece of baggage and ran back up the stairs.

It all happened with astonishing precision. With an outcry, Ronal flung down his shopping basket. Apples and pears and round loaves of bread bounced back down the Stairs as he drew his sword and charged upward. The remaining two villains blocked his way. One held a long knife, but the other seemed unarmed.

"Thugs and gutter-filth!" Ronal shouted. "I'll make short work of . . . !"

In one smooth motion, the unarmed man swept off his cloak. Just like the fishing net, it sailed neatly through the air and settled over Ronal's head and shoulders. Blinded, tangled, and off-guard, Ronal hesitated. A booted foot pushed against his chest.

Head over heels he fell and fell and fell, unable to stop himself, bouncing like his apples and pears and loaves of bread. His skull banged on the wooden steps, his elbows and knees. A rib snapped. Maybe two or three. And still the damned cloak blinded him! He lost his sword.

Then, before he reached the bottom, he lost consciousness.

With his shop restored to order, Regan Vigeles next secured his rooftop from the approaching storm. Finally, he traded his kilt for fresh black garments. Clad in leather trousers and boots and a high-necked tunic of soft silk, he went back downstairs. For a time, he paced the clean floor and watched the first fine drops of rain fall beyond the Black Spider's open door. The clouds outside grew darker, and dim flashes of lightning played games on Face-of-the-Moon Street.

A deep gloom seeped into the corners of the weapon shop as the rain began to fall with greater power. Face-of-the-Moon Street became a ribbon of mud, and the sky grew darker still. Regan Vigeles listened to the increasingly furious tempo of the rainfall, the moan and screech of the wind, and he felt the energy of the storm coursing through him like blood in his veins.

He thought briefly of Aaliyah and Ronal, hoping they had found shelter, and a frown creased his lips. With a cat's curiosity, Aaliyah had taken to exploring the city, probing its nooks and crannies, sniffing at its secrets. As long as Ronal played chaperone, he hadn't particularly worried, but in light of the last few days' events . . .

From a shelf full of daggers, he picked up a matched set of three and balanced the slim, superbly crafted blades between the fingers of his left hand. He loved knives even more than he loved swords. Knives were subtle weapons, silent weapons. Gripping the trio of darts in the unusual fashion, he moved into the blackest shadows of his shop and perched on a stool to watch the door and wait.

He didn't wait long. A cloaked figure approached his doorway, hesitated on the threshold, then leaned inside to peer through the gloom. Cautiously—too cautiously for a customer—the figure stepped inside and paused again to take off his rain-soaked cloak. He gave it a shake and draped it over one arm. Leaving muddy tracks, he advanced further into the shop.

"Hello-yah?" The man's voice was deep, slightly nasal, unfamiliar, with traces of an Ilsigi accent. "Anyone here? Proprietor?"

Unseen, Regan Vigeles studied the man. Then his left hand made the slightest motion. All three blades flashed through the air to thud point-first at the visitor's feet. With a startled cry, the man jumped backward, tripped, and fell on his overly plump backside. "S-Spy-Spyder?" the man stuttered.

Regan Vigeles drew the shadows closer. From within them, he spoke to his visitor. "I assume you're responsible for wrecking my shop this morning? And for burning my wagon yesterday? And I'm sure it was you and a few cohorts that tried to break in here two nights ago."

His visitor dropped his cloak and rose onto his knees. His nervous gaze fell on the three daggers in the floor, and he swallowed. "I can't see you!" he said, looking all around the shop. He ran a hand over his bald head. "Where-where are you?"

Spyder walked slowly forward. The shadows clung to him like wisps, an effect that wasn't lost on the kneeling figure. Bending, he plucked his daggers from the boards and placed them on a nearby counter. "Thieves' weather," he said without looking at the man. "Nobody on legitimate business ventures out in this kind of storm." Turning, he folded his arms over his chest.

With careful deliberation, making no sudden move, the man rose to his feet and seemed to gain a little courage. "I-I come from Lord Night," he said.

Spyder fixed the man with an unwavering gaze. "No, you

don't," he answered. "Lord Night's business is drugs. Who are you?"

The man inclined his head, blinked, then looked up again. "Topo," he answered. He blinked again and looked confused. He pressed a hand to his head. "Shite me! Why did I tell you that?" A look of panic danced across his face. He turned and started to run.

"Wait," Spyder said calmly as he lifted himself up onto the counter and sat on it. "Please stay, Topo, and tell me what you want. I like to know everyone on the Hill."

Topo hesitated on the threshold and turned back. "Lord Night . . ." He shrugged and made a helpless gesture. "Lord Night heard that you were having these, uh, incidents. These problems. He-he sent me with an offer of—of service. . . ."

"Of protection," Spyder supplied. He had suspected as much. Only Lord Night was not involved, not in anything this petty. He leaned back and reached under the counter for a cash box. He shook it, and the heavy coins within made a harsh rattle. "How much for Lord Night's service?"

Topo stared at the box and licked his lips. "Five . . . uh . . ." He licked his lips again and seemed to have trouble breathing. "Uh, five. Five shaboozh a week."

The lid of the cash box opened, then closed. Spyder leaned back and replaced the box beneath the counter. "Too much," he answered as he turned his empty palms up.

Topo rose on his toes as if he were trying to see over the counter. "Don't play g-g-games with me!" he hissed, emboldened. "You're a wealthy man, Spyder. Everyone knows it. It's the talk of Sanctuary! And . . . and besides . . . !"

Spyder watched Topo carefully. There was nothing physically dangerous about the plump little man. He didn't even seem to be armed. Still, little rats were wily creatures with sharp teeth. "Besides what?" Spyder asked.

Topo lost his stutter as his voice dropped to a whisper. "We have your whore!" he said. "She's our captive! It's five shaboozh a week or we send her back to you a piece at a time. One finger for every payment you miss! And then her toes!"

Spyder felt a stab of rage, the instinctive reaction of any man when his lover was threatened. He glared at the fat little man as his fingers brushed the daggers on the counter. For a brief instant, he considered placing them all in Topo's heart.

Instead, he threw back his head and laughed. "I like you, Topo," he said when he recovered control of himself. "I wouldn't want to be you—but I like you." He took out the cash box again and opened it. One by one, he counted out five silver shaboozh and placed them on the counter by the daggers. "I think we can do business," he continued, beckoning Topo closer. "Let's consider these five coins, shall we say, an introductory fee?"

A fine sweat beaded on Topo's face. He reached with tentative fingers toward the square pieces of silver. Spyder rapped his knuckles, and he snatched his hand back with a confused look.

"Then two shaboozh a week after this," Spyder added. He caught Topo's chin and turned the little man's face up to his own. "Two shaboozh," he repeated, "but only if you bring me useful information."

Topo's eyes glazed ever so slightly as he met Spyder's penetrating gaze. "Wha-what kind of in-in-information?"

Spyder smiled to himself. "You're a criminal, Topo," he answered in a flattering whisper. "No doubt you hear things. You have followers and contacts. A man like you, I'll bet you pick up all sorts of tidbits about Sanctuary's underground." He let go of Topo's chin, but Topo didn't turn away. "I'd like you to share those things with me."

Spyder took Topo's unresisting hand. One at a time, he pressed the silver shaboozh into the little man's palm and folded his thick fingers around them. "No one needs to know about our arrangement, my friend," he added in the same whisper. "You don't even need to remember it yourself."

Topo backed up a step, opened his hand, and stared at the coins. When he looked up again, his gaze was hard and clear. "You're smart to cooperate, Spyder," he said with a sneer. "Lord Night is nobody to play games with." He strode toward the door, grabbing up his cloak on the way. At the threshold, he turned back. "I'll get your woman back to you. She might be a little worse for wear, but I'm sure she'll still love you." He grinned, then tossed his cloak around his shoulders and disappeared into the storm.

Spyder picked up the three daggers and juggled them with a performer's skill. *Lord Night, indeed,* he thought. *You're working for yourself, carving out a little piece of Sanctuary's action. Within reason, I can even admire your ambition.* The blades flew faster and faster. Then he let them go. One after another they thunked into the countertop. Aloud, he added, "But if I were you, I'd pray Lord Night never finds out you're using his name."

He smiled as he drew out the daggers, then bent closer to examine the gouges the points had left. "I'm going to have to take it easier on the woodwork." He clucked his tongue. "Channa will have a fit."

Aaliyah's captors flung her into a dark, windowless room and slammed the door. A heavy lock clicked shut, and booted feet stomped noisily along the creaky floorboards of a hallway. An argument ensued as the men left her alone.

"Why not?" one of them grumbled. "How often do pugs like us get a crack at something that fine?"

"Jus' keep it in yer trousers, boyo!" another advised. "Topo will cut that thing off an' stuff it up yer nose if ye try to touch her. She's business—not pleasure."

"Why can't she be both?" said a third voice. "If you don't enjoy your business you'll never be a success at it!"

In the darkened room, the bundle of netting, ropes, and cloth that covered Aaliyah began to stir and collapse. A moment later, a small shape began to wiggle among the heavy folds. Then from beneath the lower edge of the cloth, a fine-boned white cat poked its head out and looked around.

Green eyes gleaming, it explored the dimensions of its prison on padded paws, finding not a stick of furniture to hide under or perch

upon. A dust ball caught its attention, and the cat attacked, batting
the bit of fluff between its claws until it tired of the sport. After that,
it crept toward the door and sniffed. Its whiskers twitched. Faint
lamplight shone through a narrow gap between the bottom of the
door and the floor. The cat thrust one paw through the gap and felt
around. Then, growing bored, it circled itself three times and curled
up against the wall to lick its paws and wait.

When voices sounded in the hallway again, the cat pricked up its
ears.

"The Citadel of Crime!" The voice was new to the cat, deep and
nasal, vaguely Ilsigi. "That's what we'll call this place from now on,
boys! We'll strike fear into this town, and every petty crook that
wants to work here will have to come to us for licensing! We'll be a
union! A criminals' union! I've got plans, I tell you! Big plans!"

"Citadel o' Crime, my bleedin' arse!" someone sneered. The voices
drew nearer. Floorboards creaked as footsteps approached. "A stiff
wind from the wrong direction will topple this dump on yer head,
Topo. Still, I gotta hand it to ye . . . !"

"No, I'll hand it to you!" the one called Topo interrupted. "Here's
a shaboozh for each of you. And more to come, mark my
words. Once the word gets out that the Black Spider has met our demands there won't be a shop or merchant on the east side of Sanctuary that won't fall into line!"

A key grated in the lock. "Now let's have a look at her!" Topo
said as the door began to open. "I hope none of you were less than
gentlemanly."

The white cat rose to its feet and lifted its tail high. Unnoticed in
the near-darkness, it darted past the pairs of feet that filed into the
room. Down the hall it went, emerging into a common area with a
table and chairs and a few other pieces of crude furniture. It eyed
the shuttered window, then hopped up on the table.

A trio of bowls containing fish stew sat unfinished. The cat dipped
its damp nose into each bowl and licked with a small pink tongue at
the flaky nuggets, finally chewing and swallowing a couple.

Loud shouts and furious cursing sounded from the hallway, followed by pushing and shoving and charging feet. The cat looked up
from its meal, arched its back, and leaped from the table. At double-
speed it loped to a staircase in one corner of the room and raced up
them.

"Her clothes are still in there!" Topo bellowed. "Don't tell me a
naked girl like that one got past three randy louts like you!" A loud
slap punctuated his declaration. "Now what the hell did you do with
her?"

The cat paused only for a moment at the top of the stairs. Then,
spying an open door to another room, it dashed inside. A rumpled
bed stood in one corner. With an easy leap, the cat landed in the
middle of it and sniffed at the myriad of scents that lingered on the
blankets. It twitched its nose and squatted. With the most serious of looks on its feline face, it peed a thin yellow stream on the
pillows.

Bootsteps sounded on the staircase, and the bedroom door thrust
wide open. A tall, rail-thin young man looked inside, his eyes wild
and desperate. A look of surprise flashed over his face. "Hey!
There's a cat in here! Who let a cat in?" Then his surprise turned to
outrage. "Gods' balls! It's peeing all over my bunk!"

He lunged at the cat, diving headfirst with outstretched arms. The
cat sprang aside, rebounded off a chair, hit the floor, and dashed out
the open door. An older man, just as lean as the first, but with a
rougher appearance charged up the stairs. The cat saw him, laid back
its ears, and changed course. It raced down another hallway, finding
another room with another bed.

"It's a white cat!" the young man shouted from the hallway. "I'm
gonna skin it!"

The cat trembled ever so slightly on the blankets of the second
bed and shat a few small turds before it jumped to the floor and
crouched in the dusty darkness beneath a claw-footed wardrobe. A
foot kicked the door wider, and the older man charged inside. The
cat dashed out behind him, but not before he spun around.

"I thought you said it was a white cat?" he shouted as he gave chase. "It's black!"

The younger man stood in the hallway, blocking the cat's path. "The one I saw was white!" he insisted. "Gotta be two of them!" He lunged again, but the black cat sped nimbly between his legs.

"I got it! I got it!" The one called Topo with the Ilsigi accent waited at the top of the stairs. He was already crouched down, and stretched out his hands to grab. "Anybody else around here tired of fish stew?"

The cat hesitated, then let go a sharp wail and showed its teeth. Topo's eyes snapped wide. Too late, he threw up his hands as a black-furred ball of razor-sharp talons landed on the top of his bald head. "L-let-let go!" he cried, stuttering in his panic. "Get it off me! G-get-get it off me!" He grasped at the staircase railing as he pitched backward, but the rotted wood broke in his grip and he slid down the steps on his back, screaming all the way.

The cat rode down on his chest with its claws firmly locked in his flesh. As Topo slammed into the wall at the bottom, it leaped away and dashed to another part of the house, turned a corner, and found itself in a kitchen. It looked around quickly, jumped up onto a counter, sprang onto a shelf, and settled on still a higher shelf.

"It went back here!" called a fourth voice. "You guys pick Topo up before he bleeds to death! Leave the damned cat to me!"

"Cats!" the younger man reminded.

Topo called out in a weak and fearful voice. "That thing's a d-de-demon! It's a d-de-demon among us!"

The fourth man crept into the kitchen. He looked stronger than the others did, in better shape, though his garments were tattered and out of style. "Here kitty, kitty, kitty," he whispered as his dark gaze swept the room. He drew a long rusted knife from a cracked leather sheath on his hip. "Come and get it, kitty. Nice, tasty little puss-kabob!"

A soft purring filled the kitchen. Slowly, the fourth man turned his gaze upward toward the source of the sound. Then he froze. His knees began to tremble, and a wet stain appeared on the front of his trousers. The tip of his tongue darted over his lips, dampening them, as he tried to summon spit.

His womanish scream shook the walls, and he flung himself backward into the common room. On hands and knees, he quickly crawled to the table and hauled himself up again, overturning one of the bowls and a chair. Still clutching his rusty knife, he backed toward the door, wide-eyed with terror.

His companions watched in amazement from the staircase landing with Topo supported between them. "It's just a cat, you bloody coward!" the older one scolded.

"Two cats!" the younger one insisted.

Topo's face was a mass of shallow scratches. "I t-t-tell you, I saw a d-de-demon!"

Unable to find his own voice, the man with his back to the door shook his head and barely managed to point with his knife at the sleek, powerfully muscled leopard that strode from the kitchen. Turning a glittering, green-eyed gaze on each of them, the beast opened its mouth, showed its fangs, then growled.

The man by the door spun and fumbled with the latch, trying to get it open. One of the thugs on the stair landing didn't wait. At a run, he launched himself headfirst at the shuttered windows, crashed through them, and fell with a splash in the mud beyond. The third thug pushed Topo into the cat's path and followed his partner through the window.

The plump gang leader sprawled on the floor with a terrified shriek. As the leopard advanced toward him, he shot a desperate look over his shoulder at the open door. "Traitors!" he called after his fleeing lackeys. "Deserters!" The cat drew his attention back as it playfully smacked his foot with a huge paw. "Nice k-k-kitty!" he said, sucking for breath. "Or . . . or maybe you prefer nice c-c-cat?" The cat locked eyes with him and snarled again.

Topo matched the cat's snarl with a shriek of terror. Rolling onto his hands and knees, he crawled as fast as his bulk allowed straight for the open door. The cat growled again, and four sharp claws ripped through the seat of his trousers to carve furrows in his left buttock. Topo's head snapped back with shock and pain, but he only scrambled faster through the door and out into the storm.

On the threshold, the leopard stopped, licked its paw, and purred with satisfaction.

Drenched to the bone and covered with mud, Topo pushed open the door to the Broken Mast and made his way across the crowded bar to a table at the back. The Broken Mast wasn't the kind of place he frequented, and he cringed inwardly at the way the men at the other tables leered and pointed and laughed at his wounds. He particularly hated the crude comments they made about his torn trousers and his exposed, bleeding buttock. Still, where else was he to go on a night like this? He couldn't show his face in any respectable tavern, much less his usual haunts on the Hill or in the Maze.

Self-consciously, he clutched at his trousers, trying to pull the rent shut with one hand as pulled up a chair. Gingerly and with an audible sigh, he sat down.

"Mate, you look like something the cat dragged in!" laughed a sailor at a nearby table.

"I made an arse bleed like that once!" declared another customer. "That one couldn't sit down for a week, though!" With a loud guffaw, he slapped his table, splashing some of his ale.

"Braggart!" someone laughed. "With that short dirk o' yers, ye couldn't draw blood from a half-dead chicken, an' I'll wager ye've tried!"

Topo did his best not to listen, and with all his scratches stinging and oozing, it wasn't too hard. He winced as he ran a fingertip over his torn scalp, explored his forehead and cheeks, and discovered the tiny tears in his sodden tunic and the cuts in his chest. He gave a low groan as he leaned his elbows on the table and winced. Even those were sore and tender from his fall down the stairs!

Safset, the bar's dusky-skinned manager, glowered as he approached Topo's table. "Don't appreciate people comin' in here an' oozin' their pox all over the furniture," he grumbled. He slapped down a dirty rag and wiped off the top of the table. "This is a 'spectable joint!"

"Respectable, my bleeding . . . !" Topo fell silent. Given his current condition, it really wasn't the cleverest thing to say. He felt inside his waistband, pulled out a silver shaboozh, and tossed it down. Of the five he'd taken from Spyder, he'd given his men one each and kept two for himself. He thanked the Ilsigi gods he hadn't lost his in his narrow escape. "Bring me an ale," he ordered nervously. "And what have you got to eat?"

"Fish stew," Safset answered.

Topo grimaced and instantly regretted it. Any drastic expression made his shredded face hurt! "Nothing else?" he whined.

Safset snapped his fingers under Topo's nose. "This is a sea town, mate," he shot back. "Ye want somethin' special, then try the palace. Maybe Arizak has a banquet all laid out fer ye!"

Topo agreed to the fish stew, and Safset brought his ale. Hunkered down over the mug, he tried not to look around, but his gaze wandered toward the men with their arms around each other, leaning on each other, whispering and grinning. Why were they all looking at him? Even the ones playing dice several tables away kept glancing at him. His hands began to shake. He tried to steady them by locking his fingers around his mug and staring fixedly into the amber contents.

So he didn't see the brown, rain-soaked tabby that squeezed its way through the back door when a pair of customers eased out. Noiselessly, it made its way under a table, then another, weaving among swinging and shuffling feet until it stopped beneath Topo's table. Between his outspread legs, it settled back on its haunches and ran a pink tongue over its furred lips.

Safset brought the fish stew, set the bowl down, and turned away with a grunt as Topo picked up the large wooden spoon. The plump little man could only hope the utensil was clean. He stirred a few of the white, flaky chunks that floated in the creamy broth. It really didn't look bad, but by the gods he was sick of fish! With a look of disdain, he lifted a morsel to his mouth.

Still unnoticed, the cat below his table picked just that moment to attack. Sharp claws stabbed through his trousers as it climbed his right leg like a tree. With a startled cry of pain, Topo shot erect, toppling his chair and overturning his table. Fish stew and ale splattered on the pair of sailors at the table next to him.

"Get it off!" Topo screamed as the wiry feline dug in its claws and climbed up his groin. "Help! Get it off!"

"I'll be happy to help you get off, mate!" said one of the stew-covered sailors. "In this place, you don't even have to ask!" Drawing back a fist, he launched a meaty punch at Topo's nose. The tabby leaped clear a moment before the blow landed. Topo crashed backward over his fallen chair. Multiple hands lifted him up and carried him to the front door. On a count of three, swinging him like a bag of laundry, they chucked him into the street.

One of the sailors linked arms with another as they turned to go back inside. "Don't you just hate it when that kind comes knockin' 'round where they don't belong?"

"Gives the neighborhood a bad name, they do," the other agreed, slamming the door closed.

Topo rose painfully on bruised hands and knees. It was no muddy road that cushioned his landing this time, but the rough cobblestones of the Wideway. Dazed and cold without a cloak to keep him warm, he struggled to his feet and cursed the incessant, damnable rain. He stared at the door to the Broken Mast, thinking of the silver shaboozh he'd left on the table, and wondering if he could brazen his way back inside. Someone would have picked it up by now.

Then he thought of the cat. He didn't know Safset even kept a cat! Acutely aware of the new scratches on his legs and thighs and uncomfortably close to where no man should ever be scratched, he stumbled away.

A low snarl sounded in the darkness behind him. The hair on Topo's neck stood on end. He didn't dare look behind, but increased his pace, limping as he went. He headed east along the Wideway, thinking to return to the crumbling estate he'd claimed for his own purposes on the Hill. He'd be safe if he could bar the doors and windows!

Lightning flashed, briefly igniting the darkness. Thunder smothered Topo's scream as he stared into the road just ahead. Illuminated by the violet fire, a large gray cat blocked his path.

His heart hammered. Desperate, he began to run, turning northward up the street called Safe Haven. But he found no safe haven on the ill-named street. Thunder blasted, and lightning flashed again. In the covered doorway of a candle merchant, a white kitten glared at him and growled.

On the slick cobbles, Topo slipped and fell. Tears burst forth from his eyes, and he sobbed as he looked wildly around. Where was everybody? Was he the only person awake or alive in the entire city? He thought of his men and cursed them for abandoning him. "Help!" he shouted to anyone that might hear. "Help me!" But nobody answered.

He shot another frantic glance toward the shop. A large and muscled black cat sat on its stoop now where the white kitten had been, and its green eyes blazed as if it were hungry for a mouse.

A mouse! That's exactly what I am! Lurching upright, he sped from Safe Haven Street into the Street of Steel. A dim flicker of lightning in the heavy clouds caused him to gaze upward as he turned the corner, and his heart skipped a beat. Poised on a rooftop above him, he glimpsed the shadowy form of the leopard. It stalked him as he ran, leaping easily from rooftop to rooftop.

Still, he ran until his heart threatened to burst and his breathing wracked him. Down the Path of Money he splashed, slipping and falling more than once, and then across the Avenue of Temples. At last he reached the Hill with its steep and narrow streets.

Everywhere he turned, he saw cats or heard their menacing snarls in the rainy blackness. All his scratches stung and tingled, and the cuts on his left buttock burned most of all. But at length, drenched and chilled to the bone, he returned home to his Citadel of Crime, slammed the bar across the door and latched all the windows. Room by room, armed only with a broken chair leg, he searched the interior for any sign of a cat. Only then did he set his overturned table upright and retrieve the one intact chair. He sat down and rested his head in his hands.

A scratching sounded at the door, followed by a plaintive meow.

By midnight, Regan Vigeles was beginning to pace. An hour before, he'd bid good night to the healer, Pel Garwood, who'd spent much of the evening tending to Ronal. But with Pel finally gone and Ronal safe and asleep in his own bed, his thoughts turned to Aaliyah.

Idly, he turned a gold royal over and over between the fingers of his left hand, walking it over each knuckle with impressive dexterity, sometimes palming it, making it seem to disappear. Such minor feats of prestidigitation often calmed him or helped him to think. Tonight, they did neither, and after a while he pocketed the heavy coin and turned the wicks on the lamps higher to fill the shop with light.

He considered going out to look for Aaliyah and decided to wait one hour more. Of one thing he was certain—Topo didn't have her. No man, and certainly not that one, could hold her captive against her will. That meant she was up to something, or wandering the streets to her own purposes. In any city but this one, he wouldn't have worried at all.

But this was Sanctuary, and it was midnight, so he worried.

Just as he was about to grab his cloak, a light scratching sounded at the door. Turning toward it, he heard a soft, familiar meow and rushed to throw back the locks. With a sigh, he eased the door open a few inches and leaned on it. Lightning flashed, outlining Aaliyah's naked beauty.

"You must be lost," he said with a smile as he pointed over her shoulder. "The Street of Red Lanterns is that way."

Aaliyah posed provocatively in the rain, put her hands on her hips, then gave a sudden shake of her head. Waist-length ropes of wet black hair snapped forward, showering Spyder. Putting a hand on his chest, she backed him into the shop, rose on tiptoe, and flung her arms around his neck. She was soaked to the bone, but her green eyes sparkled with mischief.

With a growl, Spyder swept her up in his arms and carried her to their apartments upstairs. *"Shahana,"* he murmured in her language, burying his face against her neck as he bore her. All his worries melted away. Aaliyah was safe, and Ronal resting. For the moment, all was well. How often could he say that? *"Quanali pahabaril maha elberah yora! Quanali muriel maha elberah canta!"*

Each time we part, my heart cries. Each time we meet, my heart sings! For Regan Vigeles, called Spyder, those few words had become as important to him as a prayer.

In their shared quarters, he set her down again and kissed her. "The locks," he said, remembering the front door. Quickly, he descended to the shop, set the locks again, and turned out the lamps. When he returned, Aaliyah was drying herself with a towel. He prepared a basin of water and, kneeling, washed the mud from her feet.

Touching her heart, she made the sign that meant Ronal's name.

"Angry, embarrassed, worried about you," Spyder said as he looked up at her, "and quite asleep, thanks to Pel Garwood's potions. He'll be off his feet for a little while." Taking a fresh towel from a pile, he began to dry her hair. "I think I'll have to find Topo tomorrow and ask him for your boots back."

At Topo's name, Aaliyah turned and gave a soundless laugh.

But Spyder didn't have to track down the little crook. At midmorning, when Spyder threw back the locks and opened his shop for the day's business, he found Topo waiting with a sack. Topo pushed quickly inside and set the sack on the counter.

"Your lady's things!" he stuttered as he wrung his hands. "But I c-c-can't return her, be-because I don't have her anymore! I d-d-don't know where she is!"

Spyder turned away and covered his mouth with one hand in an attempt to appear somber. But the mass of scratches on Topo's face and head and hands! And the rips in his garments! It was all Spyder could do to keep from bursting out in laughter. "She's . . . safe," he answered, turning slowly around again.

Topo's gaze darted to all corners of the shop. "I c-c-can't say the same!" he exclaimed. His stuttering grew worse. "Spyder, you p-p-played straight with me when we made our arrangement, so I f-f-feel I can t-t-talk to you! Some people say some of your weapons are, well, special. You—you know!"

Spyder raised an eyebrow. "You mean enchanted?"

"T-t-that's what some say!" Topo crept to the door, leaned out, and looked both ways up Face-of-the-Moon Street. The rain had stopped, and the storm moved on, but a gray blanket of clouds still hung over the city. He spun back toward Spyder. "You—you got anything g-g-good against d-d-demons?" He rubbed his hands together again. "I'll l-l-let you off the h-h-hook for, say, two months p-p-protection payment!"

Spyder stared at the plump little man for a long moment, then made a subtle gesture. "Did you bring me any information?" he asked.

Topo's bloodshot eyes glazed momentarily, and his stuttering ceased. "There's a *krrf* shipment out of Caronne arriving at the wharves tonight," he muttered. "I don't know who's claiming it, though."

"Demons, you say?" Spyder raised his voice just a little. "No, I have nothing that can ward off demons. My shop is just a shop, and I'm just a humble merchant!"

Topo's shoulders slumped, and he looked crestfallen.

Spyder hid a sly smile. He noted the scratches again and the rip in the seat of Topo's trousers as the little crook turned away. He wondered suddenly, *Why should Aaliyah have all the fun?*

"But I know someone that I'm sure can help you," he added. "Come back tonight after it's dark."

Topo swallowed hard as he looked at Spyder. Hope and fear warred across his features. "After it's dark?" He gulped. "I'll—I'll d-d-do anything!"

Spyder watched as Topo slunk away. He almost pitied the poor little crook. Almost, but not quite. Alone, he looked around his shop, and his gaze fell on the strange little eight-hundred-year-old dagger from the mysterious wreck on the reef. He picked it up and tapped it on his palm again as he made his plans.

"Channa, my love!" he said, when his housekeeper stepped through the door. She was still wearing her old dress, only scrubbed clean. He swept her up and executed a few quick dance turns before setting her down.

Breathless, she looked up into his face. At first nervous, she began to smile a smile that mirrored his own. "Gray eyes," she said, meeting his gaze. "Gray eyes mean trouble."

"But not for you, Mother," he answered. "Not for you."

An hour after nightfall, Topo returned. A drizzling rain had begun to fall, and he shivered under his old cloak as Spyder let him into the shop. His eyes had lost some of the nervous fear he'd exhibited that morning, but his scratches had reddened considerably and looked quite painful. "I c-c-came!" he announced simply. "B-but maybe the d-d-demon is gone. I haven't s-s-seen any c-c-c—"

A fine-boned white cat padded down the staircase from the upstairs apartments. With an easy leap, it settled atop one of the wooden display cases.

"Cats!" Topo shrieked. He backed toward the door. "Cat!"

Spyder laid a firm hand on his shoulder, preventing his retreat. "What cat, my good friend?" he said in a calming tone. "There's nothing there. What are you pointing at?"

Topo stared at Spyder with terror-filled eyes. "You don't see a c-c-cat?"

Spyder turned and surveyed his shop, then hugged himself and faked a shiver. "Now that you mention it," he answered in an ominous voice, "although I see nothing, I do seem to feel some presence, as if we were being watched."

The little crook took a step behind Spyder and, peering under the taller man's arm, watched the white cat lick its paws with indifference.

"We'd better go," Spyder said. "Only a fool keeps Madame Struga waiting."

"Madame Struga?" Before Topo could say anything more, Spyder clapped a blindfold over the little man's eyes. "Ouch! My scratches!" But despite his complaints, he offered no resistance as Spyder tied the blindfold tightly in place.

Tossing his black cloak around his shoulders, Spyder steered Topo out into the night. The white cat followed soundlessly for a short distance, then perched on the street corner as the two men marched up and down Face-of-the-Moon Street, turned a corner, marched back, walked around the shop, then walked around the shop again.

The Black Spider had two doors on Face-of-the-Moon Street, one that led directly into the shop, and another seldom-used entrance that led to private apartments. When Spyder had thoroughly disoriented Topo, he opened this second door, guided his man inside and into one of the rooms. There, he yanked free the blindfold.

"Ouch!" said Topo, clapping one hand to the side of his forehead. A single half-melted candle burned on a small round table at the center of the room. S'danzo cards lay spread upon its surface, and in the middle of the red silk tablecloth, a crystal ball shone. Only a pair of gnarled hands could be seen on either side of the crystal.

Topo stared around and hugged himself. "Gods' balls," he muttered, "it's c-c-cold in here!"

An old crone rose from her chair behind the table. The candle and the reflected light from the crystal ball revealed a shadowed and charcoal-smudged face and wild hair bound in scarves of orange and yellow.

Slightly behind Topo, Spyder smiled to himself. Channa had surpassed his expectations. The room was perfect, as was her makeup. When he'd explained to her that Topo was the man responsible for turning the mop bucket over her head and for harming Ronal, she'd gleefully agreed to play her part. It was obvious, too, that she relished the role.

She let out a cackle, and even Spyder's eyebrows shot up. "You!"

she said, thrusting a finger at Topo. "You have the mark of demons on you!"

"Th-th-they're just s-s-cratches." Topo sounded almost apologetic.

"Not those, you idiot!" Channa shouted. "The mark of demons is invisible to everybody but me!"

Topo forgot his fear and lunged toward the table. "Oh! Oh yes!" he cried. "I do! I'm sure I do!"

"Stay back!" Channa's harsh command froze the little crook in his tracks. In the candlelight, her heavily made-up eyes burned. She fixed Topo with them, then began to wave her smudged hands over the crystal ball, slowly at first, then more wildly, swaying back and forth. "Cursie, cursie, little mousie—cats are playing in your housie!" she chanted. "Cat, cat, bo bat! Bonana fana fo fat!"

Spyder pushed back his hood and nodded. With a grave expression on his face, he joined in. "Fee fi mo mat—*cat!*"

"He knows!" Channa shrieked as she threw both hands into the air and curled her fingers like claws. The candlelight wavered, flickered, threatened to go out, then grew steady again. Her sharp-eyed gaze returned to Topo. "From the wreck on the Seaweal they came, ghosts and demons, a hellish crew from an unknown hell. Demon captain! And the first mate his thrice-damned bitch! Cursed souls and haunted, every crewman, every oarsman!"

Channa's voice rose in pitch and volume as she ran her hands over the cards, stirring them, mixing them. "Now they've come to ground! Freed from the sea! Freed from their ship! Free at last! Free at last!" Arching her back suddenly, she shook her fists toward the unseen ceiling.

Spyder cleared his throat.

Interrupted in the middle of her grand speech, Channa leaned over the candlelight and glared at her employer with one eye squeezed shut. Then, clearing her own throat, she bent over the crystal ball. "I see the wreck!" she proclaimed, waving her hands. "I see the demons coming ashore—horrible things they are, clawed and cat-eyed and ravenous! I see! I see!"

Spyder leaned close to Topo's ear. "Madame Struga sees all."

Topo trembled as he nodded. "So I see."

Channa stirred the cards again and hummed an eerie note as she carefully drew one and turned it over. "There!" she cried, flinging the card at Topo. "The cards reveal you—abuser of harmless women! That's the reason why the demons have chosen you, marked you, and persecuted you! Even the damned cannot abide such a sin!"

"It's true!" Topo shouted, falling to his knees at the edge of the table, but careful not to touch it. He snatched up the thrown card from the floor and placed it carefully back among the rest, his fingers shaking, eager to be rid of it. "I repent! I repent!" He stared across the crystal ball, seeking Channa's grace. Yet, he shrugged. "Well, not of crime, of course. It's my destiny to be a great criminal master-mind!" He waved a hand at the cards. "You'll find that in there some-where, I'm sure." He put a hand on his heart and raised the other hand. "But I'll never abuse another woman again on my climb to greatness, I swear! Just rid me of these demons!"

"I think she's rid you of your stuttering," Spyder observed.

Topo shot a look of annoyance toward Spyder. "I'm not scared anymore—just desperate!" He turned back to Channa. "Don't let the cats get me, Madame Struga!"

Spyder gave Channa a secret nod, and from deep within the folds of her many-layered garments, she drew a small medallion on a leather cord. "Nothing can turn them from their prey!" she informed Topo as she dangled the ornament before his eyes. "But this will hold them at bay if you wear it!"

Topo thrust out his hand. "I'll take it!"

Channa snatched it back and leered at him. "Five silver sha-boozh," she said in an icy voice.

Still on his knees, the plump little crook swallowed as he eyed the medallion. "One," he countered.

A loud cackle, and Channa leaned forward again. "Four!"

Tears began to stream down Topo's face. "No!" he insisted. "I mean, I can't haggle! I only have one shaboozh! I had five, but my cowardly ex-partners took three, and I lost another, and now I've only got one to save my soul!" He clapped a hand to his mouth.

"Poor choice of words," Spyder commented from the shadows.

Channa tapped her lips with the tip of one finger as she considered. "Very well," she said slowly. "But the medallion's power is limited and must be renewed. At the end of each month, return to Spyder with two silver shaboozh. He'll bring your fee and the medallion to me, and I'll restore its magic! If you fail . . ." Sweeping a hand over the table, she turned up a card. It showed the painted image of a cat.

Topo's eyes widened as he stared at the card. "Two silver shaboozh?" The words croaked from his dry throat. "A month?"

Channa dropped the medallion on the edge of the table in front of him. "The price of protection," she said.

The door to the room creaked open a few inches. The white cat walked regally across the floor and sprang up on the table, scattering several of the cards. With a high-pitched shriek, Topo snatched at the talisman. "Agreed!" he cried, slapping down his last coin. Then, leaping to his feet, he shoved Spyder aside and fled out into the rainy night. The cat dived from the table, following close on his heels.

"Did I do well?" Channa asked as she and Spyder watched Topo's vanishing form from the threshold.

"Madame Struga was marvelous!" Spyder laughed as he hugged her and kissed her forehead. "The shaboozh is yours, and all his coins to come."

Now Topo's bound to me even more securely than before, Spyder thought to himself. *Come rain or shine, he'll be back each month with his worthless trinket. And if he fails even once to show, I'll send Aaliyah.*

Legacies

Jane Fancher and C. J. Cherryh

"And the next I knew, the prince was asking for volunteers." Beneath his grizzled hair, Grandfather's pale, staring eyes glimmered with pride. "I could swim, and swim well. I was one of the first to step forward."

Lightning flashed, darting through the smoke vents and every failing seam in the old building. Thunder rattled the shutters on their rotting leather hinges. Kadithe Mur huddled closer to the brazier, holding his breath, knowing well what came next, yet never tiring of his grandfather's heartfelt rendition.

The prince, the golden-haired Kadakithis, had taken a handful of volunteers out on his beloved Shupansea's huge ship. They'd braved the fierce storm to save the fishermen caught in the unexpected squall. Caught and stranded on reefs or drowning. Grandfather and the others had tied ropes to their waists and leaped into the foaming sea, searching for anyone still living. Kadakithis himself had dived with them, a prince risking his life for the humblest of his subjects.

Kadithe sighed and leaned against the cold stone south wall.

Together, Grandfather and his prince (with a little help from the ship's crew and the other volunteers) had fought off pirates attempting to take his lady's ship with one hand and rescued nearly a hundred men that day. Some said the prince had been a fool, had risked two hundred lives to save a handful, that there were always more fishermen, but to him the prince and all those who'd helped him were heroes, heroes of the sort which, with one notable exception, Sanctuary hadn't seen in thirty years.

Not since Kadakithis had kissed Shupansea farewell and headed north to reclaim the Rankan capital, even as the Beysa sailed off to her own destiny.

He knew, even if others didn't, that Kadakithis hadn't deserted the city for the opulent life among the Beysa. He knew because Grandfather had been there. Grandfather had been denied the right to go with the prince. Kadakithis himself had pressed golden coins into Grandfather's hands and told him to stay in Sanctuary, to care for his wife and young son.

And to remember him. To become a great artist and create . . . just a small statue of his prince, so others would remember him as Grandfather had known him.

Grandfather had tried to follow his prince's parting orders, but the gods had deserted him—Kadithe didn't know which gods and cast the blame pretty much equally.

Grandfather's wife had died in the summer of seventy-six—taken away by swamp fever. His son had lived to manhood, fathered his own son (Kadithe sighed and bit his lip) only to have the plague take son and daughter-in-law, leaving him with the howling, ill-tempered infant.

Well, Grandfather had never accused him of such uncivilized behavior, but he'd seen squalling brats enough in his fourteen years to know he must have been a sore trial to an aging, widowed metal-smith, in a city where Dyareela's Hands of Chaos . . . appropriated . . . anything moving that was left unattended.

"Kadithe, dear boy." Grandfather's cane nudged his knee and with a blink, he was back in their tiny home. Squatters, they were, in a rotting wreck of a building no one had yet stepped forward to claim, but "home" it was and "home" it would be for Kadithe Mur, as long as Grandfather filled it with his warmth. "The worst of the storm has passed." And indeed, something that might pass for actual sunlight filtered through the cracks in the wall and roof. "If we're to eat tonight, you'd best stir yourself."

Kadithe. Always Kadithe. Never anything *but* Kadithe. It was a good name, as names went, but sure as he lived and breathed, he *knew* his real name was Kadakithis, that his grandfather had named him after his beloved prince, then called him otherwise, for safety's sake.

Not that his grandfather had ever admitted as much, but his hair had been golden once, and curly. Time had turned it to muddy brown waves and prudence kept it unwashed and so darker and straighter still, but once, he'd been his grandfather's little prince.

"It's Halakday. What do you say to some of Mardelith's cheese? The Gods' Gold would taste mighty fine with a bit of flatbread, don't you think?"

Now . . . he swallowed a sigh and pulled himself to feet gone tingly . . . now he was his grandfather's only hope for survival.

He clasped the arthritic hand extended toward him, pressed it, and kissed the forehead above those eyes whose sight had been burned out five years ago with slag from his own kiln. Payment, so the owners of the red hands had claimed, for his part in the downfall of their bloody goddess.

Better they'd killed him outright, flayed him inch by inch as they had their other victims. But no, they'd let him live—without his soul, his talented hands broken and twisted beyond creation.

"The Gold it is, Grandfather," he said in the low croak of a voice that was all he'd had since that day. "If I have to bed her to get it."

Grandfather laughed. It was an old joke, at least to Grandfather. It was what he had always said when Kadithe made a special request for dinner. What Grandfather didn't know, and what he'd die before he told him, was that one day, perhaps all too soon, it might well cease to be a jest.

But not today. Today, he had something Mardelith might want far more than his own skinny, as yet extremely untried loins. Not today, and perhaps—he closed his eyes, thinking of that strange meeting with Bezul—perhaps never.

A quiver hit his belly, and for once, the feeling wasn't hunger. It took a moment, but eventually he identified that strange sensation: hope. *Two* warm blankets (one for each trip), an iron skillet to cook their flatbread (he'd been using a large rock), a fork for turning the bread . . . a worn velvet pillow for him to sit on by the fire. . . .

He still suspected the changer and his wife of charity, but . . . he thought of that precious roll of glittering wire, the bright ruby he'd been guiltily hoarding for five years . . . *damned* if he wouldn't *make* it worth their trust.

In the meantime, he and Grandfather still had to eat.

He padded his way through the narrow beams of sunlight to the heap of rubble in the corner of the room, rubble scavenged from the ruins throughout the Maze, rubble that was mostly firewood for the small fire he had to keep going for Grandfather's sake, but which also served as camouflage for the far more precious tools. Grandfather's tools. Tools for modeling clay, mallets of all sizes and weights for pounding copper into ornate trinkets . . . everything from the old shop but his kiln and forge.

And, of course, the raw materials: Those had been the first to go.

Copper, bronze, gold . . . statuary to jewelry—even iron and weapons, early on in the prince's employ. If it was metal, Grandfather had worked it; if it was beautiful, Grandfather had made it.

Lifting the loose floorboard, he pulled up a charred, but still-sound box. One day, this salvage might end up in the fire, but for now, it held his own creations: a small handful of jewelry, punched copper lamp shields . . . all made from scraps of salvaged metal. He pulled out the newest shield, tooled with an intricate punch-pattern of his own design, and sand polished until it gleamed in a beam of light coming through a half-rotted plank.

Pride filled him as he remembered the way Chersey had looked at his necklace. Grandfather's eyes were gone, but not his knowledge, and maybe, just maybe, not all of his magic, true magic, that born of hands and clay and bronze and fire, not gods and incantations. Grandfather had had no formal assistants, no apprentices. For fear of the Hand, Grandfather had never let anyone else into that back room where he performed his metal-working magic—and where Kadithe lived.

To the world outside the shop, there'd been no Kadithe. The plague had taken him along with his parents, or so Grandfather told the Hand-plagued world. As an infant, Kadithe lay, drugged to silence, beneath the floorboards. As a child, he'd been the assistant Grandfather had never dared to hire, the apprentice he'd never dared take on. Grandfather had been parent, teacher, and mentor in one. He knew the history of the Empire and Sanctuary, spoke both Ilsigi and Rankene and could judge the temperature of a mold to a nicety and pour a perfect bronze casting by the time he was seven.

But he'd never been outside the shop, never even met one of its infrequent customers, though he'd watched from his bolthole in their home above the shop. He knew Sanctuary's streets, its buildings and gates, but only as maps and drawings. His feet had never been cold or muddy, and he'd known the sun only as shafts of light through cracked shutters.

Grandfather and the shop had been his life, and that had been all he'd needed . . . until, years after Molin Torchholder and the Irrune chieftain had supposedly banished them, the Hands came back.

After the Hands had taken Grandfather's eyes, the shop and all its contents—save those tools, many of them unique to Grandfather and so irreplaceable—had gone to pay the priests and healers who had saved Grandfather's life. What was left had kept the two of them alive for the better part of four years.

After Grandfather had recovered, Kadithe had gone outside the shop for the first time, as Grandfather's eyes and banker. He'd learned the real value of money, had learned how to talk to people and even to bargain, after a fashion. Mostly, he'd learned not to bolt to the nearest shadow at the first hint of bell, footstep, or a voice other than Grandfather's.

In silence lay safety. If the Hand couldn't see you, hear you, and didn't know to look for you, they couldn't take you.

Anonymity and silence remained their allies. They'd become just another set of ragged inhabitants of a city slowly recovering from as black an era as ever it had suffered. But money had been finite and as their small hoard dwindled, they'd had to move into the Maze, where overnight the tangle of streets and alleyways could change. Now it was Grandfather who stayed at home, while Kadithe dealt with the outside world. Alone.

He didn't know what he'd have done these last months without Bezul's repair jobs. It was Grandfather who had suggested he try Bezul earlier that year, after he turned fourteen, old enough, so Grandfather said, for an employer to take him seriously. He had to wonder now if Grandfather hadn't anticipated that turn of fortune. Curious that there'd been no word of remonstrance for his betrayal of their anonymity. In fact, Grandfather had simply smiled and asked to feel the new blanket.

Bezul had given him a whole new perspective on the value of his little creations. He had a few coins still, possibly even enough for Grandfather's cheese for a single dinner. On the other hand . . . he rolled the shield in his hands, watching the light sparkle across its surface, then wrapped it in a scrap of cloth, which in turn he tucked into a ragged drawstring bag. . . .

With luck—and always he needed luck when it came to bargaining—he would be able to get enough of Grandfather's favorite cheese to last a week or more.

Rather less than a week, but it was all Mardelith had left by the time he got to the farmers' market. But he got his pick of her castoff vegetables, and a promise for another half-round of the cheese next week.

It was, he thought, dipping his head in thanks, more than generous. He should object, but he'd left pride behind years ago. Instead he thanked Mardelith, tucked his new treasure into the drawstring bag, and headed through the market, the bag slung over his shoulder. The southern sky promised another round of noise and mud-renewal, but not for a time yet. For now, the sun was warm, the ground still wet, and the light . . . perfect.

For now, the lure of the smells from the neighboring stalls was nothing to the lure of the Prince's Gate. He slipped through the crowds—all of Sanctuary seemed to be taking frenetic advantage of the momentary lull in the storm—and darted through the Gate, barely avoiding an empty cart, the farmer more bent on getting home before the next squall than in avoiding barefooted obstacles.

But his spot behind the guard station was dry and out of the wind. Grulandi, the on-duty guard, greeted him with an indulgent smile, as he checked the departing farmer off his list.

His stash was safe . . . but then who was likely to steal a handful of sticks hidden in a box and buried beneath a rock? It wasn't for fear of theft but rather to salvage every precious moment in this place that he kept the sticks.

Settling crosslegged, his right shoulder to the station wall, he smoothed the damp sand, letting the calm of this place flow up through his fingertips.

Today was the day. He'd put it off too long, wasting his time with textures and perspectives and strangers who passed this busy place. Above the gate was a plaque, a stone carving, two men in profile, facing one another, two crossed swords over a spear . . . there was an inscription, a *dedication* Grandfather had said, but he had eyes only for the profile on the left.

Kadakithis.

It was not, according to Grandfather, a particularly good likeness, but he had dim memories of the time *before* the Hand, of clay busts Grandfather had made, multiple trials to try to catch the prince's elusive vitality. It was time he began his own search, to set those features in his mind while he still had Grandfather to confirm his vision.

He had a lump of clay in the pile at home, carefully protected by oilcloth, regularly dampened. When the time came, when he tried his hand, Grandfather would be able to tell just by touch, if he'd gotten it right.

His (currently) favorite stick, grown dry with time, shattered on the first stroke. Refusing to accept that *accident* as some sort of ill omen, he smoothed the area and selected (and tested) a second stick. First the profile, then, assuming the nose was thus, the eyes thus and thus . . . slowly he began to rotate the head, to make a three-quarter view, then full—

"Not very good, are you?"

The stick jammed into the sand and broke, gouging out Prince Kadakithis' left eye. He winced, lifted shaking hands to his face and told himself, for the thousandth time, it was all ephemeral. It was the practice that counted. Training the hand to be ready for when the time came and he could actually commit his dreams to parchment, or clay, or . . .

He turned slowly toward the owner of the rather shrill, young voice. A dark-haired boy with eyes a touch too limpid stared down his small nose at the drawings in the sand.

"Wha's wrong wid 'em?" he asked, in his outside voice.

"Froggin' shite, doesn't look at all like the froggin' portrait, now does it?"

He smothered a grin. The foul language sat oddly on the boy's tongue and not just because of his youth—he'd heard far worse from much younger Maze-rats. It was the refined Ilsigi wrappings of the filth that called its verisimilitude into question.

"Froggin' carvin' don't look like no froggin' prince, neither," he replied, in his lowest Maze speech, making his own tongue match his clothing as he'd learned to do years ago. "That-there rock-chipper, he made ol' KittyKat's face th' way 'e seed 'im, I makes 'im th' way *I* sees 'im."

"You never! He's long gone. Went to live with the fish, he did. Easy life. Left us all to the Hand and the raiders."

"He did not!" Defense of his hero made Kadithe careless—of his opinions as well as his vowels—and the boy was quick. Suspicion fairly oozed from him, sitting oddly on that heretofore open countenance. Suspicion and (worse) curiosity.

The boy hunkered down beside him, and asked softly, almost . . . conspiratorially: "If he didn't go to live with the fish, where *is* he?"

The unchildlike tone, the sharp-eyed look, made him uneasy. Made him wonder if he was dealing with a boy at all. Some said there were people who could change the way they looked, for real, or just make a person think they looked different. That would be mighty useful for a spy.

Kadithe bit his lip on his desire to defend the long-gone prince, loathe, now, to reveal his stance on that matter, and discovered, to his utter disgust, that he couldn't hold that suddenly keen gaze, and retreated to his drawing, smoothing the damage and restoring the eye.

Grandfather knew this gate well, he'd complained at length and in specific detail about the differences between that image and the real thing.

"I never saw him, of course," he said quietly, dropping the pretense of gutter-speak, but returning to the first, far safer, question. "But I . . . knew someone who did. He's described the man he knew. The stonecarver carved the man he knew, with the tools and in the substance he knew. I'm . . ." How to put Grandfather's teaching into words this child could hope to understand? "I try to imagine how that stonecarver's eyes saw the world as opposed to how I see it, then adjust for the difference, using the first man's verbal description."

"That's . . . dumb."

So much for explanations . . .

"He's *dead,* you know," that childishly ingenuous, non-childishly low voice continued, confident, and rather bloodthirsty. "*Drowned. Just like Chenaya.*"

And so much for avoiding question of Kadakithis' disappearance. The boy had backed off his initial slander, that most popular theory regarding the Disappearance, had shifted to something far more possible, considering the truth he knew. Still . . . dead? like Chenaya?

He refused to believe it.

"How d'you—" He pressed his lips on the angry challenge, which could only bring unwanted attention to him, worse, questions about his own belief, and kept drawing, stabbing the sand viciously, there in the hair, where finesse made little difference.

" 'Cuz I knew someone who knew him, too. Knew him *real* well."

Kadithe couldn't prevent his involuntary twitch.

"Name's Bec. Becvar." A small, ink-stained hand appeared in front of his nose.

He ignored it. Even if this Bec wasn't a shape-changing spy, friends, especially small friends several years his junior and (from his clothing) worlds beyond his current station, were not a part of his life. He had two kinds of peers: those who had been rounded up by the Hands and those who had escaped them. This boy, who must have been born after Arizak took the palace, was neither.

Those he'd met who'd survived the pit kept to themselves, convinced those who'd escaped that life couldn't begin to understand their nightmares. Those who had escaped capture spent a great deal of time and energy trying to match misery for misery; some, the gods only knew why, even pretended they were themselves survivors.

Not that he could remember much about those years. He'd been four when his grandfather had opened this same gate to let in Molin Torchholder, his life to that point little more than darkness, tucked away while Grandfather worked. With the steady tap of a mallet for a lullaby, he'd learned, as Grandfather put it, to hold his peace long before he'd learned to hold his piss.

The ink-stained hand disappeared.

"You got a name?"

Persistent brat. He ignored him, this *Bec*.

No, it hadn't been the reign that had instilled the instincts of the hunted in him, that made him turn to shadows in which to hide rather than extend gestures of greeting. Grandfather had never believed the Hand was gone, had always known a child of his would be a special target, if ever they discovered his part in the so-called liberation. Grandfather had taught him to go up into the bolthole the moment anyone came to the door, to watch and wait until it was safe to come down.

He'd been nine when the Hands took their revenge. He'd watched from the upper floor, through the hole in the wood as they held Grandfather's eyes open with his own tongs and slowly, *slowly* dripped the slag in, a tiny drop at a time.

His grandfather had never made a sound, not in pain, not in betrayal. He'd refused even to cry for help, knowing his neighbors were no match for those animals. And Kadithe? Brave Kadithe? He'd crouched there, barely breathing, as those red hands had smashed every clay model and mold, had seen every wince as his still-conscious grandfather had heard his legacy destroyed around him.

A shadow fell across his sand drawing.

"Why don't you just go away?" he muttered, and thrust himself to his feet.

The neighbors hadn't known about him, but the screams he couldn't contain had been the cock's crow for all of Sanctuary that morning. They'd brought help—and left his voice permanently scarred.

Maybe it hadn't been the Pit, but he'd lived his own brand of hell—still did—and that was nothing to what Grandfather, the kindest, most talented man who ever lived, suffered.

No, there'd been misery enough to go around, as Grandfather was wont to say, and the living had no damn right to complain.

He tossed the sticks into the roadway where passing carts would crush them, and ground his bare feet through the sand, obliterating the images.

"Hey!"

He rounded on the smaller boy. "What did you think I would do? Leave them there for you to laugh at? For the birds to shite on?" He swept up his packet, food for the next week, and headed for the gate.

"But—" A small voice, quivering at the edges and following him. "I *didn't* laugh. I *liked* them."

Laughter, strangely enough of real humor, burst free. "I thought you said I was no good."

"That was when I thought you were copying. And it's not a good copy. But if you were drawing what's—" He tapped his skull. "Up here, well . . . it felt like I knew him, like he was looking at me. A friend. He looked . . . *real*."

Nothing could have disarmed him more. "The rain would have taken them anyway," he said gently with a nod toward the darkening skies, and indeed the first spatters struck his hand as he held it out. "Kadithe."

"Heard ye're hirin'," the one-eyed Ilsigi said, shuffling up to the table, and Camargen gave him a glance. "Name's Pewl," the Ilsigi said.

"Hands," Camargen said, and Pewl, first point in his favor, didn't ask why. He turned them up to the wan daylight sifting through the open window of the taproom, and Camargen read the history in the calluses.

"Foretopman," Pewl said. "Twenty year."

"What are you doing here?" Camargen had learned, that *here* was not a prosperous port, and that it far from abounded in deepwater sailors. Fishermen was more the mark.

Maybe it was the accent. Pewl dug in his ear as if to clear it, and grimaced. "Cap'n died an' the mate took 'er."

"Mutiny, you mean."

"Weren't me, Cap'n."

"Who said I was a captain?"

Pewl shuffled and looked at the table. "Ye sounds it. An' ye're hirin'."

"Haven't got a ship, yet. Will."

"Yes, Cap'n." Easy faith, if there was pay coming.

"Foretopman, able seaman."

"Aye, Cap'n."

"Name's Jarez Camargen. Captain, to you." Easy hire, easily dumped in the harbor if he lied. But there was a simplicity to the man—landsmen could call Pewl stupid, but it wasn't in his answers and it wasn't in those hands. Camargen had met them by the hundreds, illiterate men who could, however, read a ship from her keel to her top, no hesitation about being in the right place, no stupidity at all about going aloft.

No hesitation at all about drinking every copper penny of his pay if he got any in hand. "Mug of ale," he said. "Go get it and sit down. I want to hear the rumors floating this town."

"Mug of ale, aye, Cap'n." Nothing sluggish about the man, either, in his striding over to the bar and giving an order. "On the cap'n's coin," Pewl said, and when Camargen nodded, the barkeep drew it.

Pewl came back, industrious and in his element, sipped at the ale as he sat down in the chair Camargen kicked back for him.

"Rumors," Camargen said. "What's the rumors?"

"Rumors is," Pewl said, "that that bloody great ship wot grounded on the reef is gone wi' this blow. Maybe slid down to the bottom, maybe floated off an' broke up. Rumor is she broke up. Planks an' all been floatin' in. Scavengers is busy."

He'd heard a bit of that one. A ship stuck on the reef. "What ship?" He hadn't been able to understand the barkeep's rendition.

"Some foreign job. Real strange. No sign o' crew nor nothin'. Washed up there three month ago an' then gone wi' th' gale, no one ever the wiser."

There hadn't been any ship there that Camargen had seen, not on his little patch of reef.

That was peculiar.

"An' there was this odd feller, this mornin'," Pewl said, "just kinda wandered down the beach."

"Who?"

"That's the odd part. Silver hair down to here—" Pewl stopped cold at the look Camargen gave him.

"Go on. What about him?"

Pewl went on, very quietly, very respectfully under that look. "Dunno, Cap'n, wish I did to tell ye, but I heard it round the ship-yard."

"There's a shipyard?"

"Aye, Cap'n, but not as to say much of a shipyard. More a breaker's yard. Capper runs 'er, an' I pick up work from time to time, I did, savin' your offer, Cap'n, for which I'm—"

"The silver-haired man. What happened to him?" Damn him. *Damn* him. Things magical had their own way of finding a shore, hadn't he said it to himself, about the ruby, about the rest of the *Fortunate*'s treasure. So had their personal curse, whose last gasp had come with Camargen's hands around his neck, as they went under the waves.

"Far as I know, Cap'n, 'e disappeared into the town. Talk was he was the oddest-lookin' sod wot ever was, an' not answerin' a hail, but nobody wanted to touch 'im."

"Just walked in."

"So's to say, sir." Pewl had a very honest face at the moment, a scared-honest face. One could see all the way to the back of the blood-shot eyes. Camargen knew the look, was relatively sure Pewl wouldn't cross him, not for his life. But it was well to have these things firmly laid out.

"So's you know, Pewl, I'm from foreign parts myself. And I want that man. I want him alive, so I can have the pleasure of killing him myself. And I'll fry the guts of any man who ever crosses me in that particular or any other. Do you hear me clear, Pewl?"

"I hears ye, Cap'n." Marble-mouthed Pewl was, like everybody else hereabouts, but the old Ilsigi was in the rhythms of Pewl's speech, Pewl himself seemingly coming from elsewhere, and Camargen understood him well enough. Likely Pewl understood him better than anybody else at hand. "I hears ye clear." ·

"That's very good, Pewl," Camargen said. "I'll not be hiring many, at first. I'll be looking for a ship, a proper ship, d' ye understand me?"

An animal cunning came into Pewl's eyes, the hint of a grin to his mouth, which was missing a front tooth. "Aye, Cap'n. A deepwater ship."

"That's my notion. And I'm writing you down in the book . . ." Truth was, he didn't have a proper book, but a man like Pewl believed it as holy writ when it was written down and signed. He made one of his sheets of paper do, and took a note. "Pewl, able seaman, foretopman, hired in—what's the name of this port?"

"Sanctuary." Pewl almost thought it was funny, and then decided it was deadly serious. "Sanctuary, Cap'n."

"Sanctuary." Camargen wrote it down. "The date?"

"Why, as it's Produr, the sixteenth, year forty-four of the new reckoning."

"What new reckoning?"

"Well, as it's 3971, in the old Ilsigi."

Not much could make the blood leave Camargen's face. It seemed to for a breath or two, on a rapid calculation. Eight hundred years. *Eight hundred years,* damn silver-hair to an eternal hell!

"Cap'n?"

"Nothing." Camargen finished his entry, turned the paper about. "Sign your name."

"Aye, sir." Pewl made his mark, not an X, but the *Peh,* for Pewl, of which Pewl was probably quite vain. " 'At's fair writ, Cap'n."

"You'll mess here in this inn," Camargen said. "Meat twice a week, duff once, ale two pints a day, the rest whatever the inn's serving, and don't get drunk and don't break the furniture. I'll give that word to the barkeep. You have a knife?"

"Aye." A pleased little slap at the back of the belt.

"Keep it sharp. You take no other work on the side. No hire but mine. None of this working for Capper. You're writ in the book, hear?"

"Aye, Cap'n."

"I'll be looking for a ship, Pewl. I'll be looking."

"First I know of one, Cap'n."

"And first you know of the silver-haired man. Hear me, Pewl? Alive, have you got that?"

"Aye," Pewl said. "Aye, Cap'n."

Camargen said nothing else while Pewl drank his ale, only put the paper with the rest of his accounts, his reckonings what it would take in wood and cordage to assemble a ship, no proper ship being at hand.

Capper, Pewl said. A sort of a shipyard.

But first was a slippery sod of a wizard, who'd killed his crew, sunk his ship, and stranded him here.

The younger boy followed him through the rapidly emptying market, yattering freely about his family, his father's stoneyard, his (apparently very large) older brother, but mostly he went on about *his* grandfather, his very *old,* very *important* grandfather, the one who'd told *him* stories about the old days, who knew *exactly* what had happened to Kadakithis, and whose dreams had implanted this Bec with a dream of his own, a dream to write the *real* history of Sanctuary.

"Which should include *all* the stories, shouldn't it?" Bec asked, his head tilted thoughtfully.

"What do you mean?"

"Well, I've been collecting stories from anyone who'll talk to me, but I've only been writing down those from people who were actually there." A sideways glance. "What people *think* happened is important, too, isn't it? Like you're trying to do with your drawing of Kadakithis, but in this case, maybe writing down the rumors is almost as important as the truth—as long as I write them like they're rumors and not truth. Isn't that what makes rumors part of history, too?"

Kadithe shrugged, more interested than he let on. The kid wasn't just hot air. He had real information and was serious about his dream.

If there was one thing he could appreciate, it was a dream.

"And who do you figure's going to read this history of yours?"

"Everybody. I've already started it in Rankene," he said proudly, "but I'll translate it to Ilsigi—when I learn to write it."

"You write Rankene, but not Ilsigi? Writing's writing, isn't it?"

Bec laughed. " 'Course not. Different letters. Different rules." He sighed, a bit too heavily for credibility. "But Mama's Rankan and proud of it and she gets all upset when I ask about Ilsigi letters. My brother could help, but he won't, so for now, I just collect the stories and write them down in the language I know."

He patted the bag he carried slung across his shoulder—a proper scribe's bag, Kadithe noted with a twinge of jealousy, quickly stifled. But oh! Wouldn't he love to have such a treasure? To keep just one of his drawings, to show—

Funny how after all these years he still longed to share his sand drawings with Grandfather. *Satisfy yourself, my dearest boy,* Grandfather always said these days. *There's no other opinion that counts.*

If only that were true. Bezul's appreciation, his wife's, now Bec's . . . so much in so little time. It was intoxicating . . . and only increased his wish that Grandfather could see, that he could know his efforts weren't in complete vain.

He stopped on the far side of the bridge, ducked under an awning, and pointed with his chin toward the stairway leading to Pyrtanis Street and Grabar's stoneyard.

"Headed home?"

Bec shrugged. "Shite, no." He patted his bag. "Stories to find, you know." And with a big grin: "Got more than ever, now I'm into the made-up stuff, too."

"Be careful of that. For that matter, be careful who you tell about it. Makes no difference to me, but there's a number who'd be fighting mad. Might break those fingers of yours to keep you from writing. Cutting into their trade, you are."

Astonishingly, Bec said nothing, just blinked, confused-looking.

"Storytellers, boy. They don't want some pud's written down history messing with their version, not to mention their drinking money."

Another blink. "I never thought 'o that."

"Well, *go home* and do a little thinking."

A stubborn set to that round chin warned of an upcoming argument.

"Look, pud, I don't care what you do. Write your little stories, for all I care, but leave me alone."

"But—"

"*Go home.*"

"Do you know any?"

He drew back. Startled. "What makes you think that?"

"What you said—" The kid jerked his head toward the Prince's Gate. "Back there."

Why, oh *why* couldn't he keep his mouth shut these past few days? Still, he didn't know any stories, but he froggin' sure knew who did. Grandfather would die happy if he knew his memories of his years in Kadakithis' employment were not going to vanish with him. Grandfather had taught him all he knew; that hadn't included letters.

Anonymity lost to Bezul was one thing. Lost to this undersized pud . . . that was something else. It was a thought, but not one to be entered without consulting Grandfather.

"So, *do* you?" the boy asked again, with just that touch of a whine.

"Might," he muttered, then glowered at the boy. "But not today." The rain began in earnest. "I've got to go—and don't you *dare* follow me."

Bec's soft lower lip disappeared into his mouth, his eyes narrowed in an unnervingly straight stare. Then he nodded. "Okay. I won't follow. But you'll be back. *Promise* you'll be back, and I won't follow."

The whine had disappeared along with the pout.

"I'll be back."

"Tomorrow."

"I can't promise that."

"To the stoneyard. For lunch."

He shook his head. This fine youngster's Rankan mother wouldn't want the likes of him in her kitchen. He smelled. He knew he did, and hated himself for it, but it was the only way. Anonymity. He had a bit of the Rankan look about him, or so Bezul had once remarked when he'd shown up at the changer's too clean. Undersized, undernourished, but still, enough to note, and where he lived, Rankan was not a heritage to flaunt.

"Not lunch. But I'll come to the stoneyard. Maybe not tomorrow, but soon. I promise."

He escaped then, running with long strides down the near-empty Wideway, on feet numb with the rising wind, forcing himself to a pace the boy couldn't hope to match. But there was no sound of pursuit and he skidded to a stop, glanced back as rain soaked his hair, his thin shirt, and the precious bundle cradled in his arms.

There, right where he'd left him, his fine clothes drenched, Bec stood, watching. He lifted his hand in farewell, and that big smile burst out. Bec waved wildly, shouted something, and scampered off toward his father's stoneyard.

It was late, far later than he'd supposed. Far darker, with the ever-thickening clouds, than he cared to be out. The Maze at night was no place for a loner without a knife and no sense how to use it if he could afford (or steal) one.

And now, to top it off, he'd taken a wrong froggin' turn.

Damn that Bec for a pest, anyway.

At least the rain had stopped . . . for the moment. He knew the air: Another squall was on its way.

He wrapped his oversized shirt around his parcel, and slouched his way along, trying to look unpalatable. There were rumors floating in the air lately. Rumors about predators who specialized in young men and boys. That in itself was nothing unusual, but one in particular tended to leave mutilated corpses, which was. If he caught such an eye, a call for help here would only bring more hands to steal Grandfather's cheese. Fortunately he was beyond the age of interest for the worst sort of tastes, but he was somewhat also undersized and in the darkness that dominated these rotting corpses of buildings, he didn't count on discriminating tastes.

He walked as quickly as frozen feet could take him, sighed with relief when the path led (as it must eventually) to the 'Unicorn, and he found himself back in known territory. He kept himself from bolting toward home, a move which would only attract the predators, forced himself to keep his pace, a pace that would still have him home before utter dark took the Maze.

Left turn, right, another left, left again—

A dark form leaped out of darker shadows between two buildings. He dodged, but not quickly enough. Hands closed on him, strong, clawlike. He jerked away, the hands slipped. The shadow sprawled on the ground, taking him with it, those claws biting deep into his leg.

He choked back a cry of pain: It felt as if fire lanced clean to the bone.

He kicked at the hands with his free foot. Strangely, the claws neither let go nor drew him nearer. In fact, the shadowy lump wasn't moving at all. Nothing prevented him standing up and going home— except that fiery, frozen grip.

Was he dead?

Tentatively, he sat up. Still no action. Eyes tearing from the pain, he reached to work himself free, a claw at a time. Not claws after all, but quite normal, if rather long and slender, fingers. And his skin beneath was quite untouched, the pain vanishing with the fingers.

One hand; the other—

Lightning-fast, the free hand caught his wrist. He cried out and scrambled backward, shaking himself free, this time with relatively little effort. The hand dropped, and lay there, limp and bluish in the twilight.

It was an elegant hand. Manicured, clean—at least of the ground-in dirt that marked the perpetually unkempt. The cloak was filthy, but ragged only at the very edges. A good cloak. Warmer than anything he'd ever owned. Kadithe pulled himself to his feet and, giving the still lump as wide a berth as the alley would allow, approached the foot end. He nudged the leg-end lump with his toe, fought the sudden and foolish urge to bury his cold foot in the folds right then and there.

He worked his prod higher on the lump, and when that brought no response, he grabbed the shoulder-lump and pulled, jumping back, out of reach. But he wasn't large enough. The body, too twisted already, flopped back, facedown.

Damn he wanted that cloak. Determined now, he pulled the legs straight, grabbed the shoulder two-handed, and heaved. The lump rolled over; the hood fell back from a face battered and still, but far too fine to be caught in the Maze at night. Long dark hair spilled out, fine and silky, not like any hair he'd ever felt.

He glanced down the alley and up, expecting competition at any moment for this prize, saw nothing, and began searching the very fresh corpse.

The clothing, such as it was, sifted, rotting, between his fingers. He shuddered and shook his hands free of the moldering stuff.

A sigh. A whisper with the *sound,* at least, of a plea for help, though he caught no real words. Not dead yet, then, but soon to be, if he was left here.

Cursing himself for a fool, he patted that wet, stubbled cheek. "Wake up, curse you," he muttered, and shook the man by the shoulders. "Wake up, fool, I damn sure can't carry you."

Suddenly, the not-corpse gasped. Once, twice, and the death-limp disappeared, muscle tensed beneath Kadithe's hands, taking some of the body's weight. Kadithe dropped his hold and backed off, tripped over his bag and scrambled back to his feet, gathering the bag to his chest, ready to run, and he would have then and there if only the rousing corpse wasn't between him and by far the shortest way home.

The corpse pulled itself upright, gasping, head cradled between those fine hands.

Something dark and liquid trickled slowly down the left hand.

He backed away, wrapping the bag's drawstring around his wrist, the only possible weapon he had, trying to think of the best alternate route home, cursing himself for a fool for rousing this stranger *before* extracting his cloak, knowing even as he cursed that he'd have returned it anyway. He wasn't, and never would be, a thief.

A whisper of sound reached him, more words that made no sense, and the man's head lifted, his hand reaching toward him. Asking for help, that much was obvious to the most stupid of fools.

And fool that he was, Kadithe answered.

"Kadithe? Is that you?" Grandfather's voice, filled with worry.

Kadithe's fingers went numb, his hold on the man's wrist gave, and the stranger slipped, bonelessly, to the wooden floor. Kadithe followed, at least as far as his knees, and he knelt there, eyes closed, fighting for breath. The last few steps had been the longest of his life, the stranger a dead weight against him.

He heard the tap of Grandfather's cane, felt its light touch first, and Grandfather's sure, knowing hand second, searching him for wounds. He tipped his head into that touch, silent signal that he was unharmed, and Grandfather's lips brushed his forehead. A moment later, the soft folds of his new blanket surrounded him, and from the glow beyond his eyelids, Grandfather had brought their new oil lamp as well. He huddled in the unfamiliar warmth and light, soaked to the skin, chilled to the bone, following his grandfather by sound as the old man closed and barred (such as they could) the door.

"What's this you've brought home? Has fortune struck twice in one week? I send you out after cheese and you bring home an entire cow?"

Grandfather's voice rippled with the gentle humor that had kept them both sane for fourteen years. His own breath caught on a chuckle and he forced his eyes open, found Grandfather kneeling beside the stranger, straightening his limbs, easing the ties on the cloak that threatened to choke him, his hands telling him more than most eyes saw.

"Is he dead?" he asked, singularly indifferent to the answer.

"Not yet. Come here, child. Be my eyes."

He pulled himself to his feet, froze as he got his first good look at the stranger, at the hair spilling across their floor, pooling around his head. "That's not—" His voice failed him.

"Kadithe? Not what?"

It *had* to be the same man.

"His hair. It was dark—" But that meant nothing to Grandfather. Grandfather couldn't see . . .

"Was?"

"It's silver now." He knelt beside the stranger, and unable to stop himself, lifted those strands, so like the bright metal in color, despite the warm light from the lamp, but liquid soft to the touch. Damp, but not soaked and dripping, like his own. And clean, not a knot or hint of dirt marred the perfection.

Wizardry. He let the strands drop. Or *sorcery*—that devious, bastard craft no mage or priest would pursue. Kadithe tucked his hands around his ribs. Whatever it was, *beautiful* as it was, it was unnatural.

Grandfather's own hands, more finely attuned than his, examined that hair, but, "Curious," was his only comment. Suddenly, his nose twitched. He fingered the cloak, lifted the frayed edge to his face, then dropped it, frowning.

"The Broken Mast," he said, without a hint of doubt, and with a voice suddenly hard. "Who is this person, Kadithe? Where did you find him? Why bring him here?"

Fear filled him. Anonymity. He'd broken their most sacred house rule. Again. Worse, he'd broken it with a denizen of the Broken Mast, the drain-hole of the cesspool of Sanctuary's scum, source of ships' crew (willing and not), boy whores (willing and not), and any drug known to man.

Grandfather's hand caught his arm, demanded his attention. "You didn't go near there, did you, boy?"

Go there? He shook his head, slowly at first, then so hard it made his brain rattle between his ears. "No! I wouldn't, Grandfather.

Never. I came Red Clay and Shadow, like always. I don't know who he is. I—I was almost home, 'tween here and the 'Unicorn, he just . . . fell out of the shadows."

"Fell."

He couldn't lie, not about something this important. "Well, I thought at first he jumped. He grabbed me. Held my leg. His touch burned, but he didn't fight, didn't do anything but hold on. Then he went limp. I thought he was dead. I—" His face went hot, and he mumbled the next words. "I wanted his cloak."

Grandfather squeezed his hand, and his voice, when he answered, had lost the harsh edge. "Only sensible, child. If not you, someone else. Did he say anything?"

He shook his head, remembering those strange sounds, wondering now if they'd been some spell he was casting. "Nothing so you'd understand."

"Well, done is done. You can tell me the whole later. He has no weapons, not much left to his clothes, for that matter. I wonder they stayed together long enough for him to pull them on. If he survives the night, he'll have to kill us with his bare hands, for all the good it might do him. Now tell me: What do you see?"

"Cuts. Bruises. Nothing obvious."

"He's had a bad blow to the head, washed clean; one, maybe even two days healed. Look more closely, boy."

Shamed, he did and found the wound in question beneath its mask of silver hair, and felt the great lump. His hand, when he pulled it away, shone with fresh blood. Holding the lamp over the body, he began a more detailed inspection. Bruises, yes, but nothing compared to the discoloration at his throat. Deep bruises there that spread up the lean jaw and around the ears.

"Strangled," Grandfather said in a voice that said what he saw, confirmed what his fingers had suspected. "Someone tried to kill him with nothing more than bare hands for a weapon."

Strangled. Unusual way to settle an argument in Sanctuary. He wondered whose hands had made those bruises and whether the silver-haired stranger's long-fingered hands, strong and burning, had been more, or less, effective.

"Help me get him over to the fire."

The stranger weighed more than his slight frame would suggest, as Kadithe knew only too well, for all he'd swear they shed a quarter of his weight when they freed him of the water-soaked cloak. He was taller than Grandfather had ever been, and the body increasingly evident beneath the shredding clothing was lean, but well-muscled and well-fed.

They had worn straw pallets for sleeping, and the fire in the brazier, but little else to offer in the way of comfort. He set his new pillow beneath that silver head, and reluctantly sacrificed his blanket as well.

"Keep your blanket," Grandfather advised.

"But—"

"Get the cloak. It's good wool and will only be the warmer for the soaking."

How Grandfather knew these things, he never said, but he'd also learned never to question that tone. He fetched the cloak, which had, at least, ceased dripping and was surprisingly dry on the underside, and spread it across the stranger.

Grandfather had the new skillet heating on the brazier, waiting for him to get home, and not two but three perfect rounds of dough ready for it. Sometimes Kadithe believed Grandfather must have eyes in his fingers.

"Three, Grandfather?"

"I had a feeling you might come home hungry."

A second pan simmered aromatically. If the stranger woke, there'd be mint tea (another gift from Bezul's good wife), flat bread, and cheese. If he didn't waken . . . well, he and Grandfather would just split that third portion.

He moved the skillet over, catching the best of the rising heat and waited, his stomach unfrozen at last and beginning to protest loudly.

He licked his finger, touched the skillet, and got a good hiss. Better, so *much* better than the rock they'd been using this last half-year and more.

He tossed the first round into the pan and retrieved his bag of cheese and the somewhat-worse-for-wear vegetables. He carefully peeled the paraffin from the end of the cheese, salvaging every sliver for his growing collection. Someday, maybe someday soon, he'd have a use for it. Coal. Coal and clay. Wouldn't he give Bezul something to trade then?

So many, so many good things happening, now this. He'd wanted to talk to Grandfather about Bec, had wanted to bring Bec to meet Grandfather, to write down his stories. Everything had seemed so . . . *right*. Now . . . he scowled at the still figure beneath the sodden cloak.

"Time to flip, my dear." Grandfather's voice cut through his daydreams, and indeed it was. He turned the bread, and slid the fine taut wire of Grandfather's one-time block cutter through the cheese round making precise thin slices.

They had plates, bowls, and mugs, of sorts. Salvage, mostly, carved wood and hammered tin, but they functioned well enough. He slid the flat bread with its melted cheese topping onto the plate, folding it over just before it turned crisp, and handed the plate to Grandfather before returning the skillet to the fire. Quiet. Normal. Like every other night. Almost, he could forget about the stranger lying silent beneath his . . .

Silent, but no longer insensible. Eyes, pale, silver-blue beneath strangely dark brows, followed Kadithe's every move.

"Grandfather . . ." Kadithe said, and Grandfather answered: "I know. Since you cut the cheese."

Grandfather heard things, things a normal man didn't consider. He knew when Kadithe tried to fake sleep, had said his breathing changed, and try though he would to control it, nothing had ever fooled him.

He put the next round in the skillet, watching the stranger out of the corner of his eye. A tongue appeared briefly between his swollen lips, and his throat worked in a swallow that must go hard past the bruises.

Those pale eyes left his hands and the skillet, lifted to his . . . except . . . they weren't as pale as before. Now, they were a light hazel, darkening with each passing heartbeat.

Kadithe fell back, caught himself, and pushed to his feet, back to the wall, staring as the pale stranger with the silver hair changed before his eyes—darkening—skin, hair, eyes, until his eyes were hazel—like Kadithe Mur's; his hair dirty brown, like Kadithe Mur's; and his skin, were he to put his hand on the stranger's, would blend, one into the other.

"Kadithe?" Grandfather's voice, and another, the stranger's echoed, "Kadithe?"

"Kadithe, tell me what's wrong." Grandfather again, calm, commanding.

"Chameleon," he whispered.

"Explain, Kadithe," Grandfather said.

"He . . . he's changed again, Grandfather. Skin, eyes . . . hair. All brown now. Like mine. *Exactly* like mine."

Startlement in those newly hazeled eyes. A hand, slowly freed from the cloak's folds, lifted for self-examination. Could he possibly not know?

Smoke rose from the pan. With a cry, Kadithe darted to the brazier, flipped the bread, and scowled at blackened spots. Not ruined, but damn, he hated that taste. Damn if he wouldn't give this one to the chameleon, who should be thankful for anything . . .

He thought of those eyes, wide and shocked one moment, twisted with pain the next, as one fine-boned hand lifted to that bump on his skull, and thought, maybe, he'd keep that burned one after all.

As it turned out, his sacrifice made little difference. The stranger sat up and accepted the plate, but seemed far more interested in the tea than his food. Kadithe scowled at his own, picking off the burned bits and tossing them into the fire, thinking generally unpleasant thoughts at their silent, unasked-for guest. Grandfather was no help at all, sitting there in the one chair, sipping and nibbling slowly, thoughtfully. Listening. Waiting, damn him, for his *grandson* to take the lead with this stranger he'd brought into their home.

"Kha-deet?"

That whisper, painfully produced past the bruised throat, shook Kadithe free of his dark thoughts, and when he looked up, he saw the stranger extending his plate with one hand, pointing toward his with the other.

Offering to trade.

Shamed, he shook his head. "No. Thank you. I'm fine." And he forced himself to eat a charred bit, washed it down with a large mouthful of tea.

A silent chuckle, and the man leaned forward, very carefully, to set the plate on the floor between them, pushing it toward him. Then, simply, held out his hand for the other plate.

"I'd suggest you complete the transaction, Kadithe," Grandfather said, and he was smiling.

Kadithe sighed, handed the older man the plate, and fell to eating with less enthusiasm than he might have had, as the guest proceeded to eat the charred piece with all the enthusiasm he lacked, chewing carefully, as if, maybe, some teeth had been damaged along with his face, and sipping tea before swallowing. When he'd finished, even to licking the crumbs from his fingers, he handed the plate back to Kadithe with a soft, slow, "Thank you."

"So, you can talk," he said sourly. "How 'bout a name?"

Which only earned him a confused blink.

"Who are you?" he asked. "Where did you come from? What are you doing here?"

More confusion.

"Try Rankene," Grandfather suggested and Kadithe repeated the questions in that language of his ancestors, but the response was the same.

"Khadeet," the stranger said, dipping his head toward Kadithe, then pointing with his chin to Grandfather: "Who?"

Ilsigi, then, if broken.

"Grandfather."

Eyes narrowed, confused. "Grandfather? Name?"

"Yes," Kadithe said firmly. And echoing the man, he gestured with his chin and asked, "Who?"

Confusion lit those hazel-but-not eyes, then fear, before they dropped to study hands turned palm up. Fear turned to intent concentration, as he turned those hands slowly, examining them from all angles. "N-n-nai . . . jen," he said at last and still hesitantly, and slowly the color drained from those hands, leaving them with the pale, slightly blue cast they'd held when he was asleep, and his eyes, when he looked up, were silver-blue. "My name is Naijen Mal."

Firmly. In Ilsigi. Without a hint of hesitation or what Grandfather called Sanctuary's peculiar slant on the language.

"Where are you from?" he asked, slowly and in his best Ilsigi. "Who tried to kill you?"

No question of understanding this time. Mal's pale eyes dropped, avoiding his. A shaking hand lifted to finger that knot on his head, the bruises at this throat. He swallowed, hard and painfully. Finally, "I don't know."

"Don't know. You mean you didn't recognize him?"

Fear, panic, finally, resignation. "I mean I don't remember. Anything."

Malediction

Jeff Grubb

Here's what Little Minx did right before she went to hell:

She picked up four heavy ceramic mugs, two in each hand, and with a minimum of sloshing delivered the watered ale intact to one of the booths in the back. She dropped the ale and retired quickly as one of the drunks made a half-hearted lunge for her. She managed a false smile in recognition of the attention but would rather have had a few padpols by way of a tip instead.

Crossing the main floor, Little Minx nodded as a barrel-maker tried to flag her down to order the same rot-gut ale he always ordered these days. She dodged out of the way of another groper along the back aisle and pulled a meat pie of dubious provenance from the cook's counter, delivering it to the third table on the right, where a group of dark-haired men stopped talking the moment she arrived.

Dropping the meat pie, she retreated, hearing the conversation kick in again in sharp whispers behind her. She orbited out of the range of a ham-handed swat at her backside and pointed to a bleary red-haired drinker two tables up who had clearly had enough. She announced his bar tab, padding it for a tip, and left him to sort through his change as she wound her way back to the bar. She stepped neatly out of the way of Big Minx, who was herself loaded with a heavy tray for the Ilsig party in the back room.

A firm hand grabbed a good section of her posterior, squeezing a full cheek. She wheeled, smacking the offending paw away, the worn smile on her face turning suddenly feral. She let out a string of curses sufficient to blister the tattered wallpaper and spun back out into the main aisle, heading for the bar, still snarling a blue streak.

Two steps later the floor opened up beneath her feet in a wide hole, perfectly circular. The pit within glowed with the light of burning embers, and smoke billowed upward in an acrid puff. Everyone in the Vulgar Unicorn who could look up did.

Little Minx had enough time to hurl one more epithet, then plunged straight into hell.

I'm in hell, thought Heliz Yunz.

The Linguist of Lirt blinked and tried to force himself awake as the merchant continued to elaborate on the wide variety of stock that had been broken, lost, or obviously stolen from his most recent caravan. Heliz bridled against the fact that he should be researching but instead was parked in the marketplace writing letters for padpols and the cost of paper. Across the way, a street conjurer cadged for loose change by presenting wilted flowers out of thin air and appearing to drive nails through her hands—simple tricks that would fool no child over five. Yet the street conjurer was doing better business than Heliz.

Indeed, Heliz looked like an object of pity as opposed to commerce. His hair was a black bowl-cut tilted at a slight but noticeable angle, the result of self-inflicted barbering. His faded and patched robe was now even more faded and patched than it had been when he had arrived at this gods-forsaken town, and of the thirty silver buttons that once closed it, not a single one remained—all had been replaced with wooden disks.

In truth, Heliz had a newer robe, no fancier than the one he wore but of similar cut and more contiguous material, given to him by the youth called Lone as payment, but felt that the merchants he had to deal with deserved no better than pure poverty-stricken Heliz Yunz. They prattled their petty concerns into the ears of a man who was no mere scribe, but a true researcher, a man who sought out the words of power that created the universe itself, and had mastered a few such words along the way: A verb that softened the earth for plowing. An adjective that created a small flame. A turn of phrase that would ease a lamb's birth.

And a particular noun that was very, very powerful indeed. No, these merchants and mendicants had no idea of the true power of such words.

This particular merchant, a weasel-faced Rankan, was no better or worse than the rest of Heliz's clients. Just from the cadence of his voice Heliz could tell what claims were valid and which were false. There was a catch in his throat just before declaring some crate of his had gone missing, a slight vagueness in the description of the damage to a particular piece of statuary. Heliz had no doubt the missing crate was resting comfortably in the merchant's back room, and from the way the merchant circumspectly described it, the damaged statue itself was of an extremely erotic nature.

Through it all, Heliz felt the heavy lump of bronze in his breast pocket of his worn and over-patched robe. He would rather turn his attention to the tablet than to Weasel-face, but the current path of his life led in this less-appetizing direction.

A shadow appeared at the corner of his eye, a shadow both large and dull. Heliz didn't need to know who it was and had no desire to show that he recognized it. Instead he narrowed his eyes and tried to look like he was listening more intently to the Rankan merchant. Perhaps the bulky shadow would take the hint.

The shadow did not, but Weasel-face, suddenly aware he had an audience, did. The Rankan stopped, stumbled over a word or two, and finished up his dictation with a crusty demand for reimbursement from the letter's recipient that Heliz had no doubt would be ignored. A few coins ransomed the official-looking letter from the Heliz's hands, and the merchant was gone.

The linguist-turned-scribe sighed deeply, gathering his strength. The monotonous drone of the merchant had left him more tired and petty than normal. He tried to remember a time when he didn't feel so, but he came up empty.

He looked at the looming shadow and tried to conjure a suitably nasty greeting. Nothing came to mind, so he settled on, "What are you doing here, besides chasing away my clientele?"

Lumm the staver cleared his throat and said, "It looked like he was wrapping up. I didn't want to intrude."

Heliz managed another hopefully obvious sigh. "He was wrapping up because the weight of your shadow was enough to drive him away. It's hard to prevaricate effectively when a barrel-maker's shade is resting athwart one's shoulder blades."

Lumm didn't respond. Heliz wondered what words the big man was having trouble with.

The linguist took advantage of the silence to press on. He shook his head. "Bad enough I have to sit here in the marketplace, in the blistering sun like some relic of a bygone age, writing letters for any fool that passes by because I have to get you a new house."

"A new business," said Lumm quietly. "You destroyed the old one. I mean, it was destroyed because you were there."

"A new house that *includes* space for a business," snapped Heliz. "One that has a hearth large enough for small iron-smithing, a source of water for shaping the staves, an anvil, of course, and all manner of space for storage of staves, hoops, and finished barrels. No, it's not bad enough that I bleach myself on this barren expanse to pay off a debt of my life (not that I forget such things, I want you to know), but now you come into what can laughingly be called my place of business and scare away my patrons, patrons I need to pay for the new house with the et cetera and so forth. So forgive my effrontery when I ask, what are you doing here?"

The side of the large man's mouth twitched, and Heliz knew the cooper was trying to phrase a response in a manner that would prevent, or at least minimize another tirade. For a brief moment, a moment shorter than the orgasm of a moth, he felt sympathy for Lumm. To be saddled with a set of slow thought processes and trapped in a ponderous form would be more than Heliz could bear. That was another breed of hell entirely.

But the moment, like the moth, came and went. Heliz scowled at the barrel-maker.

"There's a problem," said the cooper at last.

Heliz grunted. "Linking verb, missing the proper pronoun. Not 'I have a problem,' nor 'You have a problem,' nor even 'We have a problem.' Merely a recognition that a problem exists. You're next going to tell me what the problem is and why it is going to become *my* problem."

"I was at the Vulgar Unicorn last night," said Lumm.

"And you didn't come home before I left this morning," noted the linguist. "Not that I am your mother. I thought you could not get blotto on rot-gut ale and cabinet wine, but I am no barfly and have been wrong on such matters before."

"I was consoling . . ." The cooper's words failed him, and he reddened. Then he shook his head and said, "Let me start at the beginning."

Start he did, laying out in plodding detail his evening after their late supper (hard cheese and bread eaten in their current quarters: an upper-room flat with a communal well in the atrium, a communal privy, too). A short walking tour to collect debts and seek orders, then an evening at the 'Unicorn, watching the lowlifes in their natural habitat. Heliz noted that Lumm apparently spent a lot of time watching two of the staff, the Minxes (Big and Little), because their actions wove through the commentary regularly, right up to the point where the floor opened up beneath the smaller, fox-faced one and plunged her into hell.

"And then what?" said the linguist.

"And then everyone left," said Lumm. "I mean mostly everyone. Some of the staff stayed, and me, and few of the curious. But most cut and ran. You don't smell brimstone and hang about. Some left quickly, and some left slowly, but most just left and haven't come back. There were attempts to pound on the floor looking for a hollow spot. There are tunnels everywhere else, it seems, but where Little Minx disappeared, the floorboards rest on solider-than-solid rock. And some of the staff was afraid, and I spent the night . . ." His face reddened again.

"Consoling," finished Heliz. Lumm nodded, and a moment of silence passed between the two. Finally the linguist said, "So?"

"So, what?" said the cooper.

"Exactly," said Heliz. "So what? Why does this pyrotechnic disappearance have anything to do with me and my life, penurious as it seems?"

"Well, people are saying it's very strange."

Heliz snorted. "Strange? This rattletrap of a town occupies the corner of Odd and Weird. I don't doubt that it already has half a foot in four separate dimensions, so a mere flaming chasm opening shouldn't surprise anyone."

Lumm regrouped, "Well, there's an idea that it was because of a curse."

"Curses are three-a-padpol here," said Heliz, his mind wandering. He felt the weight of the bronze tablet again over his heart, the tablet set with lines of five languages, two of which he had never seen before, all threatening dire curses on the one who violated the tablet's sanctity. He could take a rubbing of the tablet, of course, but it seemed a pity to have to give it back to the young man who asked for the translation.

"No," said Lumm. "It was because of her curse. I mean, her cursing. She was cursing like the devil's dam right before, and suddenly the ground opens up beneath her."

Heliz looked hard at the cooper. "And you think it's because of her cursing that she disappeared?"

"Not me," said the big man. "But others are talking, and when they talked, the idea sort of evolved, if there are powerful words . . ."

"And there are," said Heliz.

"Then there's a chance that someone might stumble onto them, and . . . you know, work a spell."

Heliz looked out across the marketplace, then took a deep breath. "That," he said, "is the *stupidest* thing I have ever heard."

"Hold on," said Lumm. "You work with words. I mean, those type of words. You know what I mean. And I've seen what you do with them."

"Do you think that's it?" said Heliz. "That if you utter a few choice phrases, suddenly you're a magician? The words of power, the words the gods used to build the world, are slippery things. The human mind isn't made for them. Indeed, you can look right at one without seeing it, you can hear it spoken and not remember it a moment later, because your mind doesn't want to recognize it. Words of power aren't something that a cursing doxie would suddenly stumble upon in mid-tirade. And even if she did, without recognizing what they were, without some base understanding, she couldn't work an effect that large. That is stupid beyond belief. Even for the crowd at the 'Unicorn."

"That's what I thought," said Lumm, "I didn't say anything at the time, because I could be wrong, but that's what I thought. What you just said."

"Were that true, a combination of common words, the most common words usually uttered in this town, would cause such damage," continued Heliz, shaking his head, "that the entire Maze would be filled with fiery chasms, and every bar and tavern from here to the docks would be in flames. Who would be dull enough to put forward such an idea?"

"There was this Irrune warrior that told me," said Lumm. "Ravadar, his name was."

"I wonder who told *him*," muttered Heliz. The linguist shook his head and took a deep breath. "No. No. You have an odd occurrence. You have a bizarre theory that I have now thoroughly debunked. Why is this still my problem?"

Lumm was quiet for a moment, such that to someone other than Heliz, he would look deep in thought. At last he said, "I thought you would be curious."

"Curious, yes!" said Heliz, now packing up his pens, stylus, inks, and tablet. There would be no more writing this day. "Curious enough to get involved, no! The curious do not survive here, in case you haven't noticed!"

"And I thought you'd be able to help," said Lumm, "because you always seem to be asking the questions that no one else thinks of."

"Flattery is not your strong suit," said Heliz. "And you ended that bit of praise with a preposition. But your words ring true. However, regardless of my abilities in the matter, why is this your problem? And by this I mean to ask, why is it *my* problem?"

Lumm was quiet for a moment, and Heliz knew that now the cooper would speak the truth. "There is talk that this particular curse is one that only worked in a specific place. In the tap room of the Vulgar Unicorn."

"And?" pried the linguist.

"Well, people are now a little wary of cursing in the 'Unicorn. You know, in case it happens again."

"And . . . ?"

"No one likes to go to a bar and not be able to curse," said Lumm.

"And once more: Why is this . . . ?"

"It's *my* problem," said Lumm, "because people are staying away from the 'Unicorn now. And if people stay away, they don't spend money."

Heliz's eyes lit up. After the long night, understanding finally dawned like the morning thunder. "And they owe you money," he said, simply.

Lumm the staver nodded. "They need barrels, and it's good steady work until we have a place of our own."

"And that Talulahs Thunder swill you quaff is gratis, I'll bet," said the linguist with a grin. "Part of the deal. You wouldn't drink that swill if you had to pay for it."

The cooper shrugged.

"So," said Heliz, "bad things at the 'Unicorn equals no money at the 'Unicorn equals no money for us equals me sitting here for an even *longer* period of time writing other people's letters. Have I finally got that clear?"

"Clear enough," said Lumm the staver.

"And should I to make this *my* problem," said Heliz, "you will forgive my remaining debt to you?"

The cooper was quiet, then said, "Half—"

"Two-thirds."

"Done."

"Done." Heliz rose. "Then we should go."

"To the 'Unicorn?" said Lumm.

"To our temporary digs first," said Heliz. "If you want me to play a professional investigator, you should let me look the part. And you should bring something that looks like a weapon. You salvaged something sufficiently wicked from the wreckage of your old shop, am I correct?"

"A hand adze has a good, tempered blade."

"Too small to impress," said Heliz. "Didn't I see a big mallet in your collection?"

"The long-handled bung hammer?" said Lumm. "It's hardly a real weapon, heavy headed and all. It has no balance."

"I didn't say you should *bring* a weapon," said Heliz, "I said you should bring something that *looks* like a weapon. Let's go."

As they left the market, Heliz's brow furrowed. "So why is 'Unicorn hiring you to make barrels? They serve ale and wine. And those horrible little dry fish. They should be codpiece-deep in barrels!"

"You see!" said Lumm the staver, smiling. "That's why I came to you. You ask questions that no one else thinks of!"

"Nice robes, by the way," said Lumm as they paused at the main door to the Vulgar Unicorn, as though he hadn't noticed that Heliz had changed his garments until they were lit by light from the tavern's reeking interior.

"A payment," said Heliz, already preoccupied. "Possibly a bribe. From a lone youth who confuses literacy with power. I hope that there are a few others like that in the common room tonight. I don't know what's going to happen, if anything, but if I tell you to do something, do it. No questions. Pretend that you believe I know what I'm doing."

Lumm nodded grimly, as if the cooper had been summoned to some higher calling. Heliz touched the bronze tablet in his breast pocket for luck, and they entered.

The common room was mostly empty, a testament to the barrel-maker's concerns. Usually at this time of day there would be a brace of bravos whooping it up in one corner, and at least three plots unspooling in the back booths, not to mention a regular clientele of sailors, fishermen, pickpockets, snatch-purses, grafters, grifters, bilkers, smugglers, con-artists, tin changers, coin biters, ladies of easy virtue, and lords of no virtue at all. Now the majority of the previously listed had decamped to less-auspicious climes, leaving a double-handful of individuals gathered around a clear spot where the tables had been pushed back and a large chalk circle scribed. Along one side of the circle a list of foul words and phrases had been chalked and crossed out.

The air smelled of stale beer, wood smoke, pine dust, and vomit. And just a touch of brimstone.

Someone shouted Lumm's name as they entered, and Heliz was almost knocked over by a charging water buffalo. In this case the buffalo wore a low-cut gown, copious bracelets, and enough perfume to gag a minor devil. Other than that, the comparison was accurate. The water buffalo embraced Lumm tightly, and the big man peeled her off as delicately as he could.

"I said I would bring help," said Lumm, his face blushing furiously. He held out a large hand to steady the teetering linguist. "This is Heliz Yunz, of Lirt. He knows about these things."

The buffalo wheeled on Heliz, and for a moment the linguist feared that she would embrace him as well. Instead she said, "Oh yes, your little friend." She smiled and Heliz noted that her heavily kohled eyes were red from crying and lack of sleep.

The towering bar wench had stressed the word "little," and despite himself Heliz stiffened his spine, which did him no good— his chin barely cleared the tattered lace decking of her bodice. Irritated, he turned toward the circle and the motley collection gathered around it.

He pretended to examine the chalk circle, but cast glances as well at the surrounding group. There were other employees—two of the kitchen servers and one of the cooks. Everyone else apparently had been sent home. No sign of anyone who looked like an owner. A gray-robed man sat calmly to one side; his very demeanor screamed bureaucrat. To the left of the bureaucrat was the Irrune warrior Lumm had mentioned, Ravadar, flanked by two bored-looking mates of similar tribal origins. (Heliz wondered why he never saw such a warrior alone—did they travel in flocks?) Across from them perched a dark-haired young person of indeterminate gender, playing with a long, delicate knife.

S'danzo, or at least S'danzo blood, Heliz thought. *A people known for their curses.*

Two drunks were splayed forward on tables, who might have been sober when the incident first happened but now were no longer conscious. One drunk was blond, while the other one had brilliant red hair. Big Minx, Heliz, and Lumm finished out the numbers of those in the not-quite-empty common room.

"Who's the 'little friend'?" said the warrior Ravadar with a challenging chuckle. "Not a frogging spell-caster, I hope."

"Hardly," said Heliz, trying not to rise to the bait. "I just know a lot about words. Someone told me that words were involved here."

"Aye, cursed words," snarled the Irrune, punctuating his comment with a hawking spit that missed the spittoon by a good foot and a half. "She stumbled into a spell and damned herself."

"Evil eye," muttered the S'danzo, apparently re-engaging a conversation their entrance had interrupted.

"Cursed words," the warrior huffed. "She damned herself."

"She had the evil eye put upon her," said the dark-haired youth. "My mother's brother, he had the evil eye put upon him, and he fell down a well. A well that had not been there the night before."

"Your uncle got drunk and lost his way," said Ravadar, and his allies laughed. The S'danzo-blooded youth gripped the knife more tightly but said nothing.

"What's this?" said Heliz, toeing the list of phrases.

One of the kitchen staff, a blond girl with blackened streaks in her hair, said, "Those are the curses Little Minx used, best as we can remember them. One of them may have done this."

"So you spoke the words?" said Heliz.

"Do we look like fools?" thundered Ravadar. "We described them and wrote them down so we could all agree with them. Words have power. Curse words most of all."

"Who told you that?" asked Heliz, trying to keep his voice as neutral as he could for the moment.

The big warrior's eyes flickered. "I always heard it was so." Heliz remained silent. "It's common knowledge," the Irrune warrior added after a moment.

"Evil eye," repeated the dark-haired youth.

"And you are?" said Heliz to the youth.

"I am . . ." Feminine features twisted beneath hard, masculine brows. "Merely curious."

Ravadar let out a chuckle, "S'danzo won't tell you it's raining out even if they come in soaking wet." His companions laughed in agreement.

Heliz ignored the comment, and instead looked at the scrawled list. "The first one reads . . ." He tried to sound it out. "Puh-ed-knawk . . . ?"

The Irrune leaped back as if burned, along with his two companions and the kitchen staff as well. Big Minx let out a squeal. It was the S'danzo's turn to let out a laugh, harsh as a northern winter and sharp as a knife blade.

"Don't say it!" bellowed the Irrune. "You would call down ruin on us all!"

"So what do you refer to it as?" said Heliz dryly. "This first epithet?"

The gray bureaucrat said, "We're calling it Engaging with a Ilsigi Woman." His voice was whisper-quiet. "An ill-kempt Ilsigi woman."

"And the second?" Heliz looked around.

"A S'danzo not of her father's issue," said the youth in a flat voice.

"And the third?" said the linguist. He looked hard at the Irrune.

"Eating one's dinner a second time," said the big warrior. When Heliz said nothing, he added, "It's a common curse in the north."

"I do not doubt that it is," said the linguist. He scowled at the writing, and said, "They're not very readable."

"Best that could be done," said the gray man, "under the circumstances."

"So you are the scrivener of this list?" said Heliz.

"I am."

Heliz squinted at the list. "You're not very good at it."

The gray man's tone grew sharper. "A workman is only as good as his tools."

"A poor workman blames his tools," said Heliz, pulling his tablet and writing kit from one of the new robe's deep pockets. He opened it on the table and produced a quarter-sheet of papyrus and a charcoal stylus. "Show me."

"Show you what?"

"That you can write." The linguist nodded toward the phrases.

"Write what?" said the bureaucrat, his brows knitted.

"Anything you like," said Heliz. "Recopy this mess." He tapped his toe against the eighth epithet, which involved unwilling engagement with a barnyard animal. "Or just write 'I know how to write,' in the language of your choice. Don't worry, I can read any language you put down. If your penmanship is up to snuff, that is. I need to know whether this mess on the floor is accurate."

The gray little bureaucrat glared at Heliz, looked briefly at Lumm, then picked up both the stylus and the challenge. As he scratched the papyrus, the linguist said to the others, "Have you all been in Sanctuary long?"

"Three, four weeks," said Ravadar, looking at the others. They nodded.

"Just passing through," said the gray man, not looking up.

"I live here," said the youth. The kitchen staff nodded in agreement, though it was unclear if the youth was claiming Sanctuary or the Vulgar Unicorn as his home address.

"And you all saw the same thing?"

The Irrune recapped the points, similar to what Lumm had told him before, and the S'danzo put in a few comments, but there was nothing that Heliz has not heard before arriving.

"Here," said the gray bureaucrat, shoving the bit of reed paper toward him.

"*I know how to write,*" read Heliz aloud. "Not horribly original, but a good hand. I apologize for my impeachment of your ability, Master . . . Gobble, it says here?"

"Gothal," said the gray man frostily.

"Close enough."

Heliz lifted the piece of paper and spoke a word, an adjective of power that he knew. The word was strange and arcane and those that heard it would not be able to repeat it if they tried, so slippery was it in their mind. He felt the forces of the universe twist around him, and despite himself, he allowed himself a small grin.

The piece of papyrus burst into flames.

Big Minx and the staff leaned away, frightened. Lumm and the gray man both scowled. The dark-haired youth's eyes brightened.

The Irrune warrior's hand dropped to his sword, "You *are* a frogging wizard!"

"Hardly," lied Heliz. "That's a street-corner trick, a bit of rough-treated paper that ignites when rubbed against itself. And that's what I think all this is, a bit of street-corner mummery."

"Nonsense!" snapped Ravadar. "She spoke cursed words!"

"Evil eye," said the youth.

"She cursed," said Heliz, color coming to his face. "So has every man and woman that's ever come into this nasty little hellhole." He saw Big Minx bridle at the description, her brows knitting. "There's nothing here," he tapped the chalked words with a boot, "that hasn't been said within these walls at least a thousand times, and probably by the little round-heeled trollop herself."

The knitted brows of the large tavern wench deepened, but Heliz pressed on. "These words on the floor are harmless, a bit of misdirection. Street-corner stuff. Only a fool would believe them dangerous."

Heliz would have gone on, but Big Minx interrupted. "If you think they're harmless, then you speak them."

Heliz looked up, stunned by the challenge.

"Go on!" The buffalo was in full-charge mode now. "If you think they're harmless, do it!"

The others around the room nodded, and the red-haired drunk shifted in his chair.

Heliz stammered for a moment, "Well . . . I . . . That is . . ."

"Here!" She shoved him out of the circle and pointed at the top of the list. In a loud, clear voice, she announced, "Pudknocking bastard!"

Half the group leaned back, the other half leaned forward. Lumm took a step forward, but Heliz lifted a hand and the larger man froze. The cooper's brow was furrowed in concern as well.

Big Minx would not be denied. She rattled off curse after curse, her voice rising. She used the fifth word three times, and the sixth term in a rattle of different tenses. She took a deep breath for the seventh.

And the ground opened up beneath her feet as she opened her mouth. It was a circular hole, limned in flame, that suddenly yawned underneath her heavy feet. With the seventh curse on her lips, she vanished into the hole.

Lumm let out a cry himself and took two steps forward, but Heliz held him back, watching the others. The Irrune, Ravadar, was wide-eyed but nodding, his two comrades rising to their feet and craning their necks to see if they could get a better view. Gothal the Gray shook his head. The curious youth looked suddenly ashen. One of the drunks snorted.

"What did you do?" shouted Lumm, his face now twisted in anger.

"Told you!" said Ravadar. "Told you that it was a cursed word. This word! This place! I told you! This place is cursed now, for sure! You should burn the building and let no one build upon the ashes!"

"I trusted you!" said Lumm. "I trusted you, and now Big Minx is gone as well!"

"Hush," hissed Heliz. "Act like I know what I'm doing. And be ready with your hammer."

To the others the linguist said, "What did you see?"

"What did we see?" said the Irrune warrior. "We saw that poor woman use the cursed words, and fall into hell!"

"You goaded her," said the gray man, softly.

"Goaded," picked up the warrior. "You goaded her into using the cursed words! And now she's lost as well."

"She's not lost," said Heliz, "merely misplaced." He turned toward the man in gray. "You can bring her back now."

Gothal scowled, "What do you mean?"

"Misdirection," said Heliz. "Street-corner magic. Everyone was watching Big Minx, but I was watching the rest of you. And your lips were moving."

The others were silent. Lumm hefted his bung-hammer. The warriors' hands trailed toward their blades. The ashen-faced S'danzo gripped the knife tightly. The gray bureaucrat kept one hand on the table, the other in the pocket of his own robes. The man was too calm, Heliz thought, and with that realization, all the pieces fit into place.

"Words were involved," said Heliz. "But not hers. Yours. A spell? A trigger word? A mantra? It doesn't matter. Here's what happened: I think you made a grab for her, and one or more of her insults struck a little too close to home. So you decided to get vengeance. That was very stupid."

The gray-robed man gripped something tightly in his pocket and shouted his words this time. His phrases were alien and mystic, but Heliz had heard worse, and he threw himself to one side as the pit to hell opened beneath his feet.

Before he hit the ground, Heliz shouted, "Lumm! Keep the hole open!"

Heliz twisted as he fell, slamming a chair aside as he landed. The linguist's shin and thigh rang from the impact, but he stood up quickly, and saw that the barrel-maker had been ready. His long-handled bung-hammer reached across the width of the sudden pit and hooked against the far end. Lumm strained to keep the pit from snapping shut on him. Ravadar, the big Irrune warrior, joined him, leaning onto the hammer, which was already starting to bend under the force trying to shut the pit again.

The other two Irrune swordsmen were at the sides of the pit, reaching down into it.

The gray man pulled something golden and roughly spheroid from his pocket, and held it before him. The object had runes carved on it. Only Heliz would notice the runes at a time like this; they displayed fluid curves, intriguingly similar to the ancient Yenizedi alphabet.

Gothal snarled the alien words again, and Heliz danced to one side, almost tangling himself up in another heavy chair. The linguist pushed it aside, and the chair fell into a brimstone-scented pit and disappeared when the hole closed over it a half-second later.

The Irrune were pulling the two Minxes out of the pit. Lumm and the big warrior leaned into the hammer, the haft of which now arched like a bow from the pressure.

"What was it?" said Heliz, taunting the spell-caster, his words gasping. His chest was tight and his leg throbbing, but he needed to keep Gothal's attention on him and not the others. "Which of the insults got under your skin? Pudknocking bastard? Toading shite-sucker? Misbegotten foulsnatch? Which one is most accurate?"

Heliz gave a false laugh. "I know—small-codded frog-raper! That was it, correct?"

The gray man snarled inhuman words, and Heliz took three steps backward. The table in front of him disappeared, taking a platter of ceramic mugs into the abyss.

There was nothing else between him and the gray spell-caster. The cluttered tavern floor had been cleared by suddenly appearing, suddenly disappearing chasms. The women were almost out of the first pit. The force trying to close it had bent the haft of the hammer almost double.

Heliz needed a weapon. Anything would do. He remembered the heavy bronze tablet in his breast pocket. He smiled and casually reached his hand into the pocket over his heart—

His fingers closed on empty space.

The linguist looked around furiously. The bronze tablet must have fallen from his pocket in all the dancing around. It could be any-where by now, including at the bottom of one of the vanished pits.

Gothal the Gray smiled. Sweat streamed down the side of the bu-reaucrat's face in broad rivulets. Whatever magic he was using strained him. His face was in a rictus grin, but he knew he had Heliz trapped.

Heliz started to say, "Before you do anything rash . . ."

The gray man opened his mouth to conjure, but for a second nothing came out. Then a trickle of blood appeared at one corner of his mouth, and his eyes went glassy and as gray as the rest of him.

Then, slowly, Gothal started to deflate, his knees going and his body falling backward. He twisted as he fell, and Heliz saw a thin S'danzo knife sticking out between his shoulder blades. He gripped the golden spheroid tightly as he collapsed—

And toppled over the edge of the first and last pit. He descended into hell.

Lumm let out a warning shout and the haft of the bung-hammer finally snapped under the eldritch pressure. Pieces of kiln-dried wood shot across the common room and imbedded themselves in the far wall. The head of the hammer was lost with the gray mage when the hole snapped shut. The entire floor roiled like an oil-filled wineskin, and then stabilized again.

Heliz let out a sigh, this time of relief, and dropped down onto a chair. Unfortunately, the chair he thought was there wasn't, and he fell, ass over shoulders against the wall, and knocked himself out cold.

Much of the room had been restored, minus a few tables and chairs, when Heliz came to. The images of the Minxes' faces, one wide and bovine, the other thin and vulpine, swam in front him.

He raised a hand to swat them off like bats, and they retreated a few steps. Lumm was nearby, as was the young S'danzo. Heliz still could not discern the youth's gender, but he/she seemed greatly shaken by the events.

Lumm the staver gave a weary smile and said, "How did you know?"

"I didn't," said the linguist weakly. "I figured that if it was a one-time thing, there would be no hope for her. Things like that do happen around here, you know. But if it were something that could happen again, there would be three types of people who would still be here. The first were those who hadn't seen it and wanted to see if it would happen." He looked at the youth and received a hesitant nod in return.

"The second were people who thought they had the answers." Heliz waved a hand toward the warriors, who had already opened the bar and were celebrating. "That lot picked up the story about the curse early, helping to clear everyone out. But then they liked being experts so much, they hung around to tell anyone they could. The third group that would hang about . . ."

"Would be those responsible," said Lumm.

Heliz nodded. "I think it was a magical amulet or something. Foreign, probably from Yenized, though it used an older language. Needed a phrase to activate it. Such a device would be like a spell but with one word missing. When the word was in place, it opened the hole. A hole into another place, warmer, but not nearly as warm as the various hells are supposed to be. The little one angered him, so he opened a pit under her. Then he had to do it a second time to the big one to keep his story intact. He was waiting for everyone to leave so he could open the hole and probably pull them out, hungry and tired and maybe unconscious. You knew him?" Heliz asked the women.

Little Minx gave a shrug. Big Minx shook her head. Lumm said, "So the amulet was like a key?"

Heliz ran a hand along his head, trying to dispel the fuzziness in his mind. "If it was, we've locked the key in with him. That means he's going to get hungry and thirsty and unconscious fairly quickly, and there is nothing anyone can do about it. Least of all him."

"Then you knew it was him," said Lumm.

"I knew that your Irrune warrior could not think up something like this on his own," said the linguist. "His eyes moved toward the gray man when I pressed him for details. And I knew that Gothal was hiding something—he wrote exactly what I told him, but his handwriting was much more careful than what he had scrawled on the floor. But other than that, no, I was just throwing accusations around and hoping that something hit."

To Big Minx he added, "Sorry to have put you in danger." Heliz knew he didn't mean it and thought she knew it as well.

Big Minx held out something. "This is yours, right?" she said. "Onoe the kitchen girl found it."

It was the bronze tablet. It was an execration text, heaping curse upon curse to the wicked in five languages. Yet none of the curses were as colorful as those the Minxes had used earlier. And one of the scripts he hadn't quite recognized looked very much like these curving runes on the Gray Mage's amulet . . .

Heliz allowed himself a smile. At least something worthwhile came out of dueling with a sorcerer in the Vulgar Unicorn.

"More good news," said Lumm. "The young ladies are most appreciative of what we did, what *you* did, for them."

The two women were back, flanking the linguist.

"We have a place," said Little Minx, leaning forward.

"Belonged to a friend," said Big Minx, leaning forward as well.

"He had to leave town," said Little Minx, giggling.

"We could use a man around," said Big Minx, smirking.

"And you're welcome to stay as well," said Little Minx, brushing against one side.

"You might be cute to have around," said Big Minx, brushing against the other.

"If you put a little muscle on," said Little Minx, pressing tighter.

"And started dressing like a real man," said Big Minx, pressing tighter still.

Crushed between the two women, Heliz thought, *I'm in hell. But given a choice, it is one of the more pleasant hells.*

The Ghost in the Phoenix

Diana L. Paxson and Ian Grey

Something is rustling . . . wood grinds . . . impending pressure weighs on the air. A girl sits in her bed, knuckles white as she clutches worn sheets to her chest.

"Taran?" she whispers, as shadows shift about the room.

On the wall a mask of a face is smiling, white as ivory, painted hair twining to either side. Its eyes cast desperately about the room and perspiration beads its brow. But still—it smiles. The girl wraps the blankets around herself more tightly.

"Taran?" she whispers again, knowing even as she speaks that he is far far away. From the face on the wall comes a noise as if teeth are grinding, and then a girlish giggle.

Water leaks in beneath the windowsill. Beyond it, the girl sees fish swimming through dim sunlight filtered through endless blue. The grinding noise grows louder, and the face on the wall, still smiling,

looks afraid. A body floats up to the window, unblinking, hair a co-
rona of reddish-blond, its skin peeling and green.

"Taran!" the girl screams, "TA . . ."

". . . RAN!" Sula rolled upright suddenly, her heart pounding
sharply. Slowly she recollected who and where she was, and *when.*
Another nightmare, she thought angrily. *Is there no end to them?*

The gray light of the hour before dawn filtered through the window. She got out of bed, draping a shawl across her shoulders, and
peered out. In the murk little could be seen. It didn't matter—even
the reassurance that it was only the sleeping city, and not that endless expanse under water, was enough to let her heartbeat slow.

She could still hear a faint grinding noise. She'd like to think it
was simply the wind pushing against the inn, or perhaps a guest's
thunderous snoring, but after the last few weeks she knew better. An
uninvited guest had come to the Phoenix, and its presence filled the
inn like the stench of a dead rat in the wall. None of them knew
what it was or how it had come there, but for the past month it had
persistently driven out every guest her family had taken in, and she
kept having the same dreams.

It was really too bad, when they had begun doing well enough to
start making repairs and restoring the house to some of its former
glory. The carved cabinet that stood now in the dining room, for in-
stance, was just the thing, said her mother, to give it a touch of class.
It had come from a ship that had grounded on the Seaweal reefs a
few months ago. The purchase had taken a good bite out of their
savings, and now there were no guests to make it up again.

Why Sula was the only one who seemed to be having the dreams,
she did not know. The Presence subjected the rest of the inn's inhabitants to waking torments—thumping at odd hours, cold spots by
doors, blood seeping through the walls. . . . It was enough to frighten
all but the most stalwart souls into a hasty departure. There was
magic in her family, but until recently, she'd thought her twin brother
Taran had been the only one with a sensitivity to the supernatural in
her generation.

Was this some kind of sending from Taran? It seemed unlikely. When they were little they had been so close they hardly needed words. She shivered as a memory of using that silent communication to escape a squad of Dyareelans hunting for stray children tried to surface and was suppressed again. But the stresses of puberty had driven them apart, and besides, Taran was far from here. She had not expected she would miss him so.

Last spring her restless brother had signed on as a caravan guard. *He* had said he wanted to travel to Ranke to see their father's homeland. Their mother said he'd just lost his head over that Rankan woman they'd rescued, but exposing Taran's real motive for traveling had only strengthened his resolve. Would he ever return? He'd been gone less than six months, but it felt much longer.

Sula heard a creaking from the bed in the next room as her mother turned over. Soon Latilla would be up, badgering the rest of them to get on with the day. If she too had trouble sleeping she would never let them know. When the first manifestations had occurred, Latilla had announced that this was their home. They had survived the Dyareelans and a dozen other external horrors, and she was not about to let a common domestic spook scare her off now.

Holding to that thought, Sula twisted her fair hair into a knot, lit the candle that sat by her bedside, and carried it into the dark hallway, keeping her eyes averted from the pale face that smiled at her from the wall. Its tortured gaze followed her until the light of her candle was gone.

The caravan from Ranke moved slowly toward Sanctuary beneath the summer sun, dust puffing up behind it in an amber haze. Bronze bells clanked dully as the line of mules and pack ponies clopped past the bored guards who watched the Gate of Triumph. As the caravan moved off, two weary travelers separated from the steady procession of wagons to rest a moment in the shade of the city wall. The guards shouted at the urchins who scampered beneath the feet of the horses, then leaned back against the cool stone.

"So this is Sanctuary?" asked the smaller of the two. His accent earned a second look from one of the guards, but this town had seen everything at least once, and the fellow didn't look threatening.

The second man, broad-shouldered and at least a head taller, pulled back the hood of his light cloak to reveal a face younger than his size would have suggested, and a mop of reddish hair bleached almost blond from the sun. He took a deep breath and coughed. "Yeah, smells like home."

The smaller man looked about as his eyes adjusted to the shade. Unlike his companion, he was meticulously groomed: his black hair cut short, his skin pale and clean. His clothes were a mix of dark colors, a deep burgundy tunic and trimmed cloak giving a faint impression of wealth, despite their simplicity. Most curious were his eyes, which seemed thin, as if he had squinted too long against the desert's glare.

"Come now, Taran," he smiled, "it is assuredly not as bad as all that?"

Taran couldn't help but smile back. "Sanctuary redefines the word, G'han. Trust me. One hand on your purse, another on your sword— that's the sort of pit we're in."

"But it is 'Home and Hearth,' yes?" G'han laughed. "The place of one's birth can never be left completely behind. Come; let us find your home. Be it amid riches or squalor, any place with a roof, a meal, and a bed would be a palace after so long on the road."

Taking a step or two from the wall, Taran stretched. "That it would. The 'Phoenix' has all the amenities you mentioned, and my mother can likely tell you where to go if, through some miracle of fortune, she's already got a full house."

His companion laughed, and resting a hand on the larger man's shoulder, accompanied him through the assemblage of unloading carts and milling people. "Worry not, my friend, for fortune fits G'han the Wanderer like a well-worn pair of shoes. They may look ugly, but they are snug, and even in tatters they protect the soul."

"Sula! Were you asleep, girl? What's wrong with you?"

Her mother's voice jerked Sula upright and the bowl of peas she had been shelling rocked dangerously. She grabbed and felt another force shove her hand, sending the contents rattling across the floor.

"Now look what you've done—"

"You startled me!" Their voices clashed and Sula began to cry.

"Don't we have enough troubles here without you mooning—" Latilla began, then stopped herself with a sigh. She had a flyswatter in her hand. "All right—I didn't mean to startle you, but really, child—"

"I wasn't *mooning*," Sula answered sullenly. "And if I was asleep, is it any wonder, when I haven't had any rest at night since that *thing* started haunting us all?"

"Nightmares?" her mother asked more quietly.

"Every night." Sula sniffed. "There's this *face* . . . and sometimes there's water." She stopped. The vision of her brother's drowned body was a terror she dared not share. Especially with her mother.

Latilla sighed. "I'm sorry." Something brightly iridescent buzzed by and Latilla slapped it down. "Got to do something about these things. Get enough of them to grind down for dye and we might make a few padpols," she said absently.

"*Mother,* why are you standing there swatting flies when we've been *invaded*?"

"Because I can," Latilla said simply. "Because though they may be magical, they're real, and when you hit them, they fall down. I've tried to use the magic your father taught me against this haunting, but Darios, bless him, was always more interested in perfecting his own spirit than in controlling others. He knew spells for protection, and I've used them, or we might have worse manifestations to deal with. But that's all I can think of to do." She sat down with a sigh. "And whacking these—" her eye followed a spark of crimson and purple that was circling above the fallen peas, "is practically a family duty. Your grandfather invented them, after all." She turned, frowning, as someone knocked on the front door.

"It might be a lodger—" said Sula when her mother didn't move. Latilla's scowl deepened.

"Maybe . . . maybe not. Go to the window and see."

Sula peered through the curtain, grimacing as she recognized the fleshy shoulders and the heavy haunches encased in a pair of striped trousers.

"It's Rol . . . I assume we're not at home?"

What was that pig's ass doing here? They had met the man shortly after Taran left, when Latilla was looking for bargains to refurbish the house. Even then, Sula had thought him a slimy character.

Latilla sighed. "No—I'll have to face him sometime. Stay here and finish the peas."

Sula heard the front door open and then a murmur of voices. Her mother did not sound happy. With a sigh of her own she pushed back her chair and moved softly down the hall.

"Yes, of course I will pay you!" she heard Latilla say as she eased open the door from the passage to the entryway. "All I am asking is a short extension."

From the front Rol was no more prepossessing than he had been from behind, his muscular frame run now to fat, and his dark hair stringy above unshaven jowls. He dabbled in a number of things, serving as a go-between for those who still aspired to respectability and Sanctuary's underworld.

"Now there's no need to look so fierce at me, darlin', though yer a fine sight when angry, for sure. Haven't I been a good friend to ye, after all?"

Sula stilled. She hadn't realized that her mother still *owed* him.

"Even among friends, financial dealings should be kept on a business footing," Latilla said more quietly. "I would not be any more beholden to you."

Well thank goodness for that! thought Sula. She started to close the door. There had been times when she feared that her mother might be taken in by Rol's florid compliments. Sometimes older women could be . . . vulnerable.

"Ye know that I would be more than a friend, Tilla me dear, but what am I to do?" Rol took a step closer. "If it's business only that's between us, I must have *somethin'*—I have creditors of my own, you see!"

That, thought Sula glumly, *would not surprise me at all.* Rol had the reputation of being involved in a variety of shady dealings, and a sore on his tongue that looked like a *krrf* ulcer to her. For all she knew, the man was dealing in that drug, or even in *opah.* If so, it was *suppliers,* not creditors, that he was worried about paying. Not very forgiving people, from what she had heard. Taran, with all his contacts among the street gangs, would have known. She stifled a spurt of very familiar anger at him for leaving them with no man in the house but her uncle Alfi, whose own encounter with the Dyareelans had left him crippled both in body and in mind.

"You can take back that cabinet you sold me," Latilla said unhappily. Sula, remembering her mother's delight in its intricate carvings, could understand why. She was the limner's daughter, after all, and the cabinet, like all the wonders that had come off that strange ship, had a beauty of a kind no one in Sanctuary had ever seen.

"Ah . . . no," responded Rol. He took a step closer. "The silver clink of soldats, that's what me creditors want to hear. . . ."

"Then you'll have to seek it elsewhere. The rest of what you gave me went for nails and lumber. I can hardly tear the house apart to give them back to you!"

"Nay—the house is worth more in one piece, both to you and to me," Rol said softly. "There's moneylenders who'd give a goodly sum with the Phoenix for security."

"No!" Her mother's exclamation brought Sula, fists clenched, into the room.

"But if ye were to wed me, it might not be needful. . . . They'd know I *could* pay them, once business gets a bit better here . . ." Rol laid a beefy hand on her shoulder. "Ye know I love ye, Tilla darlin'. Won't ye turn to me?"

"You take your hands off her!" Sula's voice squeaked, but she continued to advance.

"Just like yer mother, ain't ye?" Rol let go of Latilla and looked Sula up and down with a leer that would have made her blush if she had not already been flushed with rage. "But I like a girl with spirit!"

Sula felt her skin crawl and wondered what he liked such girls *for* . . . She shut her lips against the retort that trembled there as Latilla gripped her arm.

"I'll have to think—" Latilla said, her voice shaking with what Rol might take as fear. "It's a big decision. I can't answer sensibly right now!"

"Well now, that's just what I'm askin' for. I'll give ye a night, Latilla, to choose the *sensible* thing!" The ulcer on his tongue winked red as he grinned.

"Faugh!" exclaimed Sula as the door slammed behind him. "That man makes me want to fumigate the room and scrub the floor!"

"Are you volunteering?" Latilla asked with a tired smile. Just now she looked every year her age.

Sula shook her head. "Come back to the kitchen. I'll make you a pot of tea."

The pot was just coming to a boil when they heard the front door bang open and the thump of footsteps.

"Has that shite come back again?" Latilla reached for the heavy frying pan, but Sula rose to her feet, a wordless *recognition*, one that brought hope thrilling through her veins.

"No—" she whispered as it distilled to knowledge and a new voice echoed from the hall.

"*Mother*, where are you? I've brought you a customer. Do you have any room?"

"It's Taran! He's come home!"

Taran shook his head, torn between consternation and laughter. Of all the Sanctuary sights G'han might have asked to see once his bags had been stowed in the first-floor front room, he wouldn't have expected that pit of pits, the Vulgar Unicorn.

"But friend Taran, it is you yourself who has inspired me . . ." G'han had chided when Taran had tried to argue. *"You have been telling me stories about this place for lo these many months. I cannot withhold my curiosity . . ."*

Thus, before rest and bed they'd made their way through the Maze to this place. The minstrel who was singing some endless ballad about a man from Shemhaza was new, but Stick the barkeep looked as if he had not been off-duty since before Taran left town, and the clientele were the same unsavory sweepings he remembered, eyeing him with a familiar predatory gleam. He tried to tell himself that he had survived for nearly half a year on the roads—surely he could make it through his first night back in town. But his gut did not believe it.

Not a half day back into Sanctuary and I'm going to die . . . Taran thought to himself, smiling stupidly as he watched G'han laughing across the table at some joke one of their "new friends" had made.

"Oh, but it's true . . ." chuckled G'han to a scruffy man in his middle years with a bald pate, but infested with curly grayish-black hair everywhere else. "I am an adept of sorts. Oh, not as flashy as those Blue Stars you tell me of, but we do have some talent for magic."

"I thought yours was a Warrior's Order?" Taran asked when his friend paused to drink more ale.

G'han shook his head, "No, no, one should not assume a sword and a skilled hand for its use doom one to war. It is a tool of my trade, little more."

"And what, pray tell, is that?" drawled the goon, who had named himself Khut, Taran thought, though he had drunk just enough so that he was not quite sure.

"I hunt demons," G'han said cheerfully.

"Shite, but only a fool'd be doin' that!"

"Oh, but it's true—demons, spirits, ghouls . . . It is a sideline to my true calling, but it keeps me supplied with food and ale." G'han drank again.

"Well then," laughed Khut, "you've come to the right place— Sanctuary may be a poor city, but she's rich with work for one such as you." The older man pushed himself up, swayed for a moment, and then swaggered toward the door.

"If there's a back way," murmured Taran, "perhaps we should use it."

"Nonsense, my friend," laughed G'han. "The people here seem friendly enough. Why, look at that poor misshapen creature at the far table. Even he seems to have a kind and gentle disposition."

"Oh yes, if you think well of a pervert dwarf whose favorite pastime is to expose himself to every girl at every tavern and inn that's fool enough to let him in . . ." Taran growled.

"You've encountered him before, I see."

"He flashed his 'dragon' at my sister Sula once." Taran turned away.

"She is your twin, yes? Interesting girl—" G'han threw up his hands in mock defense as Taran rounded on him. "No, no, I do not attack maidens. I mean what I say—there is a gift in her I think, but hidden. Even she does not know. . . ."

Taran eyed him uneasily. He had thought he knew the man, but he thought he knew his sister as well. He wasn't sure whether the idea that G'han might court her or that Sula might have magic disturbed him more.

"So, what did you do to this 'dragon-flourisher,' eh?" G'han said then.

"I wanted to kill him, or at least pummel him a bit—gathered Griff and the rest of the gang I hung out with back then, but Griff talked us all out of it. Word has it he's a lackey for some zombie magician living outside of town, and Griff figured messing with him would get us skinned alive—"

G'han sat back, a smile playing faintly on his lips.

Taran recognized that look, and shook his head emphatically. "No. G'han, you can't just show up, kill a handful of ghouls, and expect a grateful mob to hand you a sack of coin! Appearances are deceiving, and even a mage's kindness can be a curse . . ."

"You've said so before, friend Taran," his companion murmured reassuringly, though whether he had given up that line of thought or merely filed it away until later Taran had no clue. "But why you should have such sentiments remains unclear, when I can see that it is not magecraft itself that bothers you."

My father died because he was a mage . . . thought Taran, though to be sure, a great many other people had died during the Dyareelan interregnum as well. He sighed.

"Let's just say that Sanctuary is haunted by magic. . . ."

Sula rinsed a porridge bowl and set it into the dish drainer to dry. She would never have expected to miss the mountain of dishes that were the usual sequel to breakfast at the inn, but it was scarcely worthwhile to heat water to wash only three bowls. There should have been two more, but by the time her brother and that strange friend of his had rolled in, dawn was breaking. Already wakened by her nightmares, she had heard them come in, and hoped that the stranger was drunk enough to sleep through any daytime disturbances.

She could hardly believe Taran was really home. She realized now that she had given up on ever seeing him again. Her grandfather had disappeared into that vast world beyond Sanctuary's walls—he'd promised to be back in a year, but they had never heard from him again. Why should Taran fare any better? But now that he was here, his presence filled a hole in her heart she had not allowed herself to admit was there.

Stifling a yawn, she picked up the bowl and began to scrub. The backlogs of blackened pots were more than sufficient to use up the dishwater. . . . It wasn't fair that Taran should be sleeping in while she had to slave out here.

"We'll just take advantage of all this spare time to catch up on a few tasks we never could get to when the house was so full," her mother had said. "Remember, 'every misfortune hides an opportunity if you look it in the eye!'" *And the inevitable proverb as well,* Sula thought in exasperation.

There were a lot of jobs on her mother's list, and a good number of them had been put off "Until your brother gets home." Sula's frown turned to a slow smile. Taran couldn't stay in bed forever, and when he did get up, Latilla would be waiting for him. . . .

The temperature of the dishwater shifted suddenly to blood-warm and she jerked her hands from the basin with a cry, staring at the red liquid that filled it now.

It's just blood, she told herself. *I've seen it before.* But the last time the dishwater had turned to gore had been three days ago, and she had hoped that whatever was haunting the inn would find some other manifestation to trouble them.

Taran woke from a dream in which his mother had set him to re-paint the Phoenix Inn with a bucket of blood, and he lay for a moment, wondering why he had come home. Even his bed felt strange, smaller than he remembered and sagging in places that no longer fitted him. But the sunlight was flooding in through the window at an angle that told him the hour was well past noon.

The pounding in his temples was familiar, too, but that, he had expected. His mother made a tea that might fix the hangover, if he could persuade her to make it for him. She hadn't seemed very pleased when he and G'han had left without even waiting for dinner the night before.

He headed down the hall, encountering G'han, whose clothes, as usual, seemed to have been newly refurbished by some invisible minion. He grunted, half-listening as G'han continued some story about the best way to dispose of rainbow snakes, when both the tale and Taran's attempt to make sense of it were interrupted by a scream from outside.

Taran peered through the window that lit the stair, and saw his uncle Alfi on the ground, his nose a bloody mess, while beyond him a fat, unshaven man was yelling at Latilla.

Taran flew down the stairs and out the door. Months of driving mules across the miles between here and Ranke and learning to hold his own among the caravan guards had given him muscles and a knowledge of how to use them. The world kaleidoscoped into a narrow tunnel at whose end two figures were struggling.

Latilla saw him first, her eyes widening. Her assailant, seeing her sudden distraction, turned, his jaw positioned at an angle that lined up perfectly with Taran's incoming fist. An audible crack, and the man fell, his filthy hand loosing its prey.

Words buzzed around him, but the incessant pounding in his ears overwhelmed them. Instinct impelled his foot into the man's rib cage as he fell.

Crunch! stated Taran's fists as the man made the mistake of getting up again.

"Taran!" came a distant cry.

Taran staggered as his tunnel vision cleared. A very familiar face was looking up at him, murmuring comfort, and then his mother's arms enfolded him in a fierce and protective hug. Beyond her he glimpsed his sister, her eyes shining with a fierce approval he did not remember ever seeing there before.

The stranger's face was now redecorated in crimson, his torn shirt spattered with the remains of the lunch he was retching up into the road. G'han helped him up, speaking quietly. The fellow cast a quick look at Taran, his face growing pale, though whether from fear or blood loss Taran couldn't say. The man took a step, discovered he'd developed a painful hunch, and settled for a comical shuffle down the street. Taran's instinctive surge after him was checked by G'han.

His mother grasped his face firmly between her two hands, forcing him to look into her eyes.

"Taran! Taran! It's all right, we're all right! You're home!"

He coughed as a shift in the wind brought him the uric reek of the fuller's bleaching vat. Interested neighbors averted their eyes from his bloodshot stare.

"Breathe, boy—did they turn you into a berserker out there?!" That sounded like his mother, all right.

"Sula, help your uncle up and put him to bed," said Latilla. "Then come back to the dining room. We have some talking to do."

Taran let her take him by the arm and lead him back inside. The house smelled of baked bread, and those funny herbs she liked to tuck into stew—the familiar smells of home. Why, he wondered, did his skin crawl?

They had not stayed long enough for him to notice anything when they first arrived, and he had been too drunk to feel *anything* when they came home from the Vulgar Unicorn. But the energy of the fight had dissolved whatever insulation his hangover might have supplied. There was definitely something wrong at the Phoenix Inn.

As Latilla finished her (rather expurgated) account of who Rol was and what he had been after, Sula poured tea into mugs and handed them to the two men, eyeing her brother uncertainly. Taran had been getting into fights since they could walk, but she'd never seen him fight like *that*!

"But I don't understand—" he said when his mother was done. "If you didn't have money, how did you buy that thing?" He pointed toward the carved cabinet that stood in the corner. Latilla had placed it where the afternoon light would caress each swirling curve of the carving, and strike gold sparks from the brass studs. After a moment G'han got up to inspect it more closely.

"It's beautiful," Taran said then, "but why—"

"It is *strange*," said G'han. "I have seen work like this before, but where . . . ?" He shook his head. "Where did this come from?"

"Last Sperraz the fisherfolk found a strange ship washed up out on the reefs," said Sula. G'han turned to look at her and she flushed beneath his intent stare. It wasn't a leer; she felt as if he was trying to look into her spirit, not through her clothes.

Her mother had seen the look, too, and was surveying G'han with a frown. Sula took a breath and plunged on.

"It wasn't Beysib or Rankan or anything anyone had ever seen. It looked old, but the stuff in the holds was fine. There were all kinds of rumors about it, but no one really knows. Anyway, it's gone now. By the time last month's storm washed the wreck away, the treasure-hunters had picked it pretty clean. The cabinet came from the ship. It was empty too, when Mother fell in love with it—" She smiled.

Latilla grimaced. "I bought it from Rol. It just goes to show, 'Even good food is spoiled if a rat drags it in!' "

"True," replied G'han, "but even the fruit of a healthy tree can hide a worm—"

Sula met Taran's exasperated gaze and both sighed. Their mother's proverbs were bad enough—but if she and their guest were going to *compete* with them, maybe both Sula and Taran should run away from home.

"All right—" Taran attempted to get the conversation back on course as G'han took his seat again. "Why couldn't you pay the man back? Even when times were at their worst we've always had *some-one* staying here. Why are G'han and I the only ones sleeping on the second floor?"

"Ah . . ." Latilla sat back with a sigh. "Well, the fact is, we do have a visitor—"

"We have a *ghost*, who drives our paying guests away!" Sula interrupted her. She glared at her brother. "Did you have bad dreams last night, or were you too anesthetized to remember?" She stopped, sensing the change in his awareness, but before he could speak, his friend sat up with the smile of one who has discovered a silver soldat glinting in a muckpile.

"Ah! So that is it! I felt energies, whispers, in my chamber, and I did wonder if that was normal, after what you have told me of this town."

"No. Even for Sanctuary, this kind of haunting is strange," Latilla said tiredly. "In the old days I would have gone to a wizard for help, or to the Mage Guild, but the Irrune have forbidden all such things now."

"Not all!" grinned G'han. "Now I know why the divine forces direct me here. I am Master of the Fourteen Spirits, a destroyer of demons, a hunter of ghouls. Whatever the nature of the being who haunts you, I will undertake to banish it in gratitude for your hospitality!"

Sula suppressed a snort as Latilla raised one eyebrow. "If you do banish it, I will certainly be grateful," she said tartly. "If not, I hope you have money. Even after the rough welcome my son gave him, or maybe because of it, Rol isn't going to take no for an answer for very long. . . ."

"Not to fear," G'han said grandly. "You show me where the spirit resides and I will show you what I do!"

"Well, that's just the problem," observed Sula. "We've had cold spots in the hall and blood in the dishpan. Levitating tables in the guest rooms and leering pictures in the hall. Wherever it came from, it's all over the house now."

"In the day or the night is it most active?"

The man appeared to be impervious to her irony, and Sula began to hope that perhaps he did know what he was doing after all.

"The manifestations can occur at any time," said Latilla.

"But every night they visit me in my dreams . . ." added Sula.

"So then, I lie in wait for it, like a hunter at a water hole," said G'han.

"Not alone—" put in Taran, eyeing Sula with a worried look that made her want to cry. With relief, she thought. She and her mother had been facing this without help for too long. "I'll watch with you."

At half-past the midnight hour the whispering began.

Struggling in the throes of dream, Taran dimly recalled something about battling alongside an assortment of heroes and gods, up north near the wintry passes where the Nisibisi witches rained down horrendous spells that turned men's bones to jelly. The fact that the entire war was taking place in both the kitchen and main hall of the Phoenix was immaterial, as was the struggle up the stairs, littered with dead. The Nisibisi held the top, and if Taran was ever to get the tools to fix the sign out front, he would have to lead the charge.

But now. . . . Now the dream had become more . . . real.

A stranger stood next to him, wearing clothes and a hat of most peculiar design. It turned, displaying a smiling mask, its laughter deep and frightening as the groaning of timber.

Somewhere upstairs his sister Sula screamed.

Taran started awake, and was up and into the hall before he realized he was not in his bedroom. He all but tripped over G'han, as the smaller man, who had been sitting by the fire, leaped up from the hearth, sword still sheathed but ready to hand. In moments they had cleared the stairs and were spilling out onto the upper landing.

A face poked out of the wall, a pale mask twisted in amused contempt. A low growl came from the walls about them, and his grandfather's old paintings shook as a tremor rolled through the inn.

"Sula! Mother!" Taran shouted from the top of the stairwell, bracing himself between wall and banister. "Where are you?"

G'han slipped past him, drawing his well-oiled sword in one fluid motion and discarding the scabbard. He brushed the two middle fingers of his left hand across the flat of the short blade and sank into that peculiar fighting stance Taran had seen him use once before, hunting ghouls in the small town of Khava. Whispering a short prayer in a singsong alien tongue, the small man burst into action.

With a short leap he was across the hall, fingers sliding from hilt to tip of his blade. As he landed in front of the phantom face, his fingers skipped from the top of the sword, acquiring a sickly green luminosity quite unlike that of the sputtering lantern hooked above them as he touched the apparition's brow.

"*Haj-nak! Iilaa Iilaa!*" he shouted. "Naming the Fifth Spirit I ban you now from wood and stone! Cower not in shadows but fight me openly, maleficent shade!"

Taran watched in horror as the wall around the face swelled and splintered, fragments spraying through the air. The apparition dis-limned like a fog, filling the hall. Taran could barely see G'han danc-ing and weaving about. A barely discernible shadow moved with him, bending in inhuman ways.

"Taran!" he heard his mother shout.

"Stay where you are!" he cried, keeping his back to the wall. "G'han's putting steel to your ghost now! We'll be safe soon!"

"*You fool!*" Latilla shouted back, nearer now in the mist. "Tell your sword-crazy foreign friend to stop hacking up the place! I can't find Sula with him swinging that glorified knife of his around!"

G'han's dry laughter stopped their bickering cold. "No need! I am much sorry to say Mistress Sula has found me."

As the mist faded Taran glimpsed him dancing backward, sword held tightly behind him with his right hand while he blocked his op-ponent's reckless swings with his left. After another shocked mo-ment, he realized that the attacker was his sister. But it didn't move like Sula, and on the face beneath her madly fluttering golden hair was the same distorted smile he had seen on the mask.

G'han's foot slid on a smashed board and only a quick twist saved him from her flashing fists. A titter of laughter accompanied each blow.

"Sheep-shite!" Taran threw himself across the span between them in a full-bore tackle. "Leave her *alone*!" he screamed as he caught his twin in his arms and the two slammed into the wall, and he did not know if he meant the warning for G'han or the thing that had pos-sessed her. A portrait of an old man in purple robes holding a large, weird-looking crab fell to the floor.

Before Sula could break free Taran straddled her, pinning both arms to the floor. "Mother, get rope! I don't know how long I can hold on."

They had wrestled like puppies when they were children, but he had never, even when he was running with Griff's gang, tried to mas-ter anything that fought with the contorting, fluid energy he gripped now. And throughout the struggle she kept screaming. Taran could only be grateful he couldn't understand the words. From the tone, it had to be something obscene. G'han stared down at her with widening eyes.

"What's she saying?" muttered Latilla as the girl began to convulse.

"Not sure—never heard it spoken," whispered G'han. "But I've seen such words in old scrolls. They come from Yenized, lady. It was an ancient empire with great magic far away."

Taran rolled away, panting, as Latilla finished the binding and forced a piece of leather between Sula's teeth to keep her from biting her tongue. Then she sat back on her heels and glared at G'han, who had picked up his sword and was sliding it into its sheath once more.

"Then we have a clue where the demon came from, and we know where it is now," she said tartly. "How do you plan to get it out of my child?"

Taran's heart sank as he realized that for the first time since he had known G'han, the little man was at a loss.

"Those of my Order are ghost-killers—" he said unhappily, setting his hand on the hilt of his sword. "The only way I know is to strike evil spirits with my blessed blade."

"Not while it's in my daughter, you don't!" Latilla glared at him.

"Taran . . . what's happening?"

Taran sat up, eyes widening as he realized those words had not been spoken aloud. They were in Sula's voice, though. He looked at their prisoner and flinched from the fury in its glare. "Sula? Where are you?"

"I think I'm seeing through your eyes. . . . Ugh—does my body really look like that?"

Taran blinked. "Not when you're in it. But it's *your* body! Can't you just shove the ghost aside?"

"There's some kind of wall around it. Don't let them kill me, Taran!"

"Taran!" His mother's voice broke in. "Who are you talking to? Has that thing got you as well?"

"No. It's Sula. She's in my head somehow."

"Oh, that is good, then!" exclaimed G'han. "Her spirit is not lost."

Taran shuddered. He loved his sister, but he didn't want to share his life with her.

"Good?!" Latilla snorted. "Now it's not my home but my daughter that's haunted! Don't *any* of your fourteen spirits have a useful suggestion?"

He shook his head, frowning. "No, lady, unless—let us take the girl downstairs to the room with the cabinet. The spirit raves in Yenizedi. Maybe the cabinet came from there as well. . . ."

"I should have expected this," muttered Latilla as G'han and Taran lifted Sula's jerking body off the floor and carried her down the steps to the common room where the cabinet sat. "We all saw the manifestations, but Sula was the only one who had nightmares. I should have sent you away." She looked from Sula's body to Taran and back again, as if uncertain where to direct her words. "You—her, I mean. Can my daughter hear me?"

"It's not your fault—" said Taran, and realized he did not know whether he or his sister had replied.

"Maybe not," his mother said grimly, "but it's surely my responsibility."

"You have an idea, lady?" G'han sounded almost humble. "I sense that it is not only from their father that these two have inherited ability. There is power in you—"

"I know a thing or two," Latilla said absently, rolling up her sleeves. "Listen," she added in an undertone, "I'm not sure what will happen, but it may sound as if I've gone crazy, too. Don't lose faith, either of you, whatever I may say or do."

Sula's body had ceased to jerk, but there was still hate in the staring eyes. With a quick twist Latilla pulled the leather from her jaws.

"Listen, you!" she snapped. "This is an inn, and anyone who stays here has to pay." For a moment they traded glares, then she turned to G'han. "You know Yenizedi—talk to it. Where did it come from, and what restitution will it pay?"

G'han frowned for a few moments, then managed a few rippling syllables that were answered by another spate of invective.

"That won't do," said Latilla. "Threaten it with your sword."

Taran could feel Sula's unease, but he held still. *"Mother said to trust her—do you? You've been here all the while I was gone—"*

"Yes . . ." came Sula's slow reply. *"I do. But I'm afraid."*

"That makes two of us—" He returned his attention to G'han.

The sword gleamed oddly in the oil lamp's flickering light. Taran's breath caught as it came to hover above Sula's throat and G'han spoke again. This time the response came more slowly.

"He is a Yenized sorcerer. An Enlibrite wizard cursed the ship eight hundred years ago. The spell took him by surprise, but when it wore out he was ready, and in the moment when the ship returned to time and his body turned to dust he transferred his spirit into—that cabinet—" G'han looked at it with new appreciation. Then the spirit spoke again.

G'han's face darkened and as he translated once more the sword dipped until its edge brushed the smooth skin. "He says that when I banished him from wood and stone he was free to find a new home, and the girl was closest. He says," G'han added distastefully, " 'She was a good choice. This girl's body is young and sweet. I will enjoy my new life as a sorceress . . . ' " The words trailed off into manic laughter that echoed around the room.

"How dare he! No—don't interfere!" screamed Sula as Taran started forward.

"Not if you don't have a body—" observed Latilla, frowning as the sorcerer spoke once more.

"He says you won't kill your daughter—" said G'han.

"But that's not Sula," Latilla answered him. "She wasn't much use when she was in her body, and her body without her is no use to me at all. You don't seriously expect us to unbind you, do you?" She addressed the sorcerer directly. "Even if you won't speak our language I can see that you understand me," she added as the girl's features spasmed. Uneasily the eyes followed her as she paced up and down.

"Yes—" she said to the others, "I think the thing to do is to make this body so uncomfortable that he'll want to leave it. And if that doesn't work, well, there's always your sword. . . ."

"No, not the peppers! Please, no more. . . ."

Even from the kitchen, Taran could hear his sister's voice quite clearly. So could she. They had never imagined their mother could be quite so . . . *inventive,* even though she'd done no permanent damage to Sula's body, so far. He was unpleasantly reminded of the potions Latilla used to force down him when he was sick. He'd been half convinced she meant to poison him.

She was making progress, though. The ghost had admitted he could speak Ilsigi. He had become accustomed to being lonely, but he had forgotten how to bear physical pain. And the girl's body was a prison as well as a refuge, in which the spells G'han had cast on his bonds kept him from working his sorceries.

The ghost had already tried to bribe them with the gold in the cabinet's secret drawer. Only this afternoon, that would have solved their problems, but the stakes were higher now.

"But if you banish me I will go mad!" came the cry. Taran raised an eyebrow. Outside, dawn was breaking. Was the ghost breaking as well?

"Go back in there—" said Sula. *"I want to see."*

"It does sound as if he's giving up," Taran agreed. But when he opened the door, what he heard was a girl's hopeless weeping. "Sula, keep talking to me so I know you're here—" he murmured, "or I'm the one who'll go mad."

Latilla looked down at the limp body with the burning eyes. "No madder than you were," she said persuasively. "The cabinet kept you safe before—you can dwell there again. Isn't that better than drifting without place or name?"

"I can't . . ." the ghost gasped. "The spell only worked for that moment when we were outside time and between the worlds."

There was a short silence, and for the first time Taran glimpsed defeat in his mother's eyes.

"Taran . . . it's not going to work . . . I'm sorry. I know you can't carry me forever. I'll go. . . ."

"Don't you dare!" whispered Taran as he felt her presence begin to withdraw. "I can get used to it. Sula, you have to stay!"

They both stiffened at the sound of G'han's dry laugh.

"I am the Master of Fourteen Spirits, and the first of them toys with time like a toddler his blocks. With such gifts I can carve a way into Paradise and scar a sliver of time for you to slip through. Taran, come hold up our friend, and you—" He addressed the ghost, "Leap out of that body and go back where you belong!"

As Taran heaved up his sister's body, G'han settled into his odd, balanced stance once more. For a moment everyone was absolutely still. Then the sword flared, sending a flicker of dawn-light across the interior of the cabinet and leaving a glowing wake behind it that outlined a passage into shadow.

"Now *go!*" snarled Latilla. "Or his next stroke will pass through that pretty neck!"

Taran felt Sula sag in his arms as with a fading howl the ghost obeyed.

G'han slammed shut the cabinet's doors and slashed a sigil across the wood to bind it. Carefully, Taran laid his sister's limp body down. Her fair skin was blotched and her hair straggled around her face. Her breast rose and fell with her shallow breathing, but Taran did not need to look into her empty eyes to know that no one was home. In his own mind he still felt Sula's fear.

"She must return to that body," said G'han. "It can exist on its own for a little while, but without a spirit, soon it will begin to fail."

"Sula—it's all right. He's gone. Go back into your body now," said Latilla, but Taran shook his head.

"He pushed her out. She doesn't know how to return."

"Ah—then there is one thing left for me to do." Latilla had never seemed so tired, so old. "I bore you two in my womb, and welcomed your spirits," she said then. "Maybe what you need is for me to hold you again. Lie down, Taran, and take her in your arms. Lay your heads in my lap, and I will sing to you. . . ."

Even yesterday Taran would have balked, but the hours in which he had shared Sula's mind had changed him. He put his arms around her body as he would have held his own. There was a comfort in his mother's soft lap, and a healing in the lullaby she sang, that took him back to the days in which he and his sister and his mother had all been one. Exhaustion overwhelmed him then and his eyes closed.

When Sula woke, morning light was pouring into the room. She was lying on the floor of the dining room with a pillow under her head and a blanket over her, and she hurt everywhere. For a moment she could not imagine how she came there. Clearing sight showed her brother curled up beside her and her mother asleep at the table with her head pillowed on her arms. Only G'han was still awake, sitting cross-legged by the door like a sculpture of some exotic god.

"What happened to me?"

"Oh, many things—maybe your mother should tell—" G'han began, but his next words were drowned out by a sudden thunder of knocking at the front door.

"You open up in there, Latilla, or we'll break it down! Don't think yer son can save you this time. My men'll break him as well!"

"It's Rol!" gasped Sula as the others sat up. "He'll kill us! He'll take the house—"

"No he won't—" With clothes awry and hair askew, Latilla looked like a harridan, but a fey light danced in her eyes. "I can pay him, remember?" She scooped half of the gold pieces that lay scattered on the table into a leather bag and tossed it in her hand. "All I owe him, and—" Her gaze paused at the cabinet and she smiled. "I can return his merchandise as well. Taran, G'han—pick up that thing, and follow me."

Though every movement was an agony, Sula managed to get to her feet and follow them. Apparently the sight of G'han's sword had been enough to gain Latilla a hearing, and the gold worked a miraculous cure on Rol's lacerated pride.

"Ah well, me darlin', this is another story—" He beamed up at her. "There's no need to be giving back yer furniture too—"

"When two have been as 'involved' as we, the break should be a clean one," Latilla said sweetly. "I'll not keep in my house so much as a memory of you." She motioned to Taran and G'han, who manhandled the cabinet down the steps and thrust it into the arms of the two hulking brutes Rol had brought to protect him.

They managed to get back into the house and close the door before they started laughing.

"But what happened?" wondered Sula. *"Why did she give the cabinet away?"*

"That's not all she gave him! Wait till he gets the cabinet home and that sorcerer's ghost starts popping out of the walls!" Taran replied.

Sula stopped short as she remembered that neither of them had spoken aloud. She could see her brother's gray eyes rounding in wonder as he realized it, too. But aching muscles provided assurance that her spirit was firmly seated in her body. *I never meant this to happen,* she thought. *Will Taran hate me?*

But he looked stunned, not angry. Sula offered a tentative smile. This was going to take some getting used to, but at least she was no longer alone.

The Man from Shemhaza

Steven Brust

Pegrin wandered over and said, "Hey. How are things?"

"Splendid," I told him. "Couldn't be better."

He grunted. "You about ready?"

"Almost. Just tuning."

"Why?"

I grinned and didn't answer. My cresca was a pretty thing, with a stained maple neck supporting a teak fretboard, a top of maple, and back and sides of reddish-brown prectawood; but there was an extraordinarily thick steel truss rod running all through the neck, so it was far, far stronger than it looked. It held a tune remarkably well. Me, too, I guess. I mean, about holding a tune remarkably well.

I touched it up a little, then gave Pegrin a small nod and a big smile. "Ready," I said.

He gave me a half-hearted glower. "Do you have any idea how

annoying it is to be around someone so perpetually cheerful?"

"Can't help it," I said, grinning. "That's the beauty of the cresca; it's a naturally happy instrument." That wasn't strictly true. The cresca can be mournful just by keeping the low drone going and ignoring the high drone; but I rarely play that way. Who wants mournful?

"Uh-huh." He gestured to what passed for a stage in the 'Unicorn—a place under the rear balcony near the front of the room. "Go," he said.

I went. I flipped my orange cloak over my shoulder (yes, orange. Shut up.) and sat down on a hard, ugly chair. My cresca snuggled into my lap. The audience eagerly awaited my first note. Heh. I made that part up. Actually, one old lady who was leaning on the bar like she needed to gave me barely a glance, and a fat little merchant flicked his eye over me with an expression of distaste. He'd either heard me before and didn't like it, or else didn't care for my taste in clothing. Kadasah and Kaytin were enjoying another of their spats, Perrez was scanning the room for anyone stupid enough to fall for one of his deals (I'm not that stupid. Anymore.), and, to my delight, Rogi was nowhere in sight. Believe me, the only thing worse than no one singing along is Rogi singing along. I started the drones going, thumb and forefinger, then started in the comp for "The Man from Shemhaza," which is a great opening tune. Two gentlemen who looked to be Rankan at the table nearest me (which meant I could have knocked one of their heads with the neck of my cresca) glanced at me, then went back to their conversation.

"In the hills of far Shemhaza lived a man both weak and strong
Who lived in a house both big and small on a road both short and long
His hair was dark and fair and red, he was both short and tall
He was skinny, fat, but more than that he was not a man at all

So sing me of Shemhaza and the man who couldn't fail
And I'll keep singing verses until you buy me ale."

And then back into an instrumental that my fingers carried without me having to think about it, just as my mouth didn't have to think about the verses. The two Rankan noblemen didn't have to think about them either, they continued a conversation in which the rotting leg of our ruler figured prominently. And so into the second verse. No one sang along, but the 'Unicorn isn't a singalong-on-the-chorus sort of place. And so on for about an hour and a half.

The second verse drove away the Rankan nobles, which was almost enough to hurt my feelings, but three drunken dockhands replaced them by the time the third verse started, and dockhands will occasionally tip.

I made a few padpols in tips and was bought a drink, and got a meal into the bargain—spit-roasted nyafish with pepper. I packed up my cresca, slung the case over my shoulder, and, with a grin and a wave to Pegrin, headed out into the Sanctuary night.

While I was walking through the Maze, I heard, "Tor! Wait up." I turned and smiled, though I have to say I don't enjoy hearing my name abbreviated. My name is Tord'an J'ardin, or Tord'an, which is already shortened from Tordra Na Rhyan, or, "One who follows the Old Ways." It is not Tor. But cutting names down until they are meaningless is the custom in Sanctuary, and nothing good can come of bucking custom.

"Tor! How are things?"

"Wonderful, Dinra. As always. How is your evening?"

"Good enough. Where are you going?"

"Land's End."

"Private party?"

I nodded.

"Oh, lucky you!"

I nodded and grinned. Private parties are one of the few chances a songster has to make any real coin. And one can lead to another, if you're both good and lucky.

"Who are you playing for?"

I shrugged. "In the End you're always playing for Lord Serripines, even if someone else is playing, and even if he never shows."

He nodded. "Yep. Among the Ilsigi, you're always playing for the princes and nabobs, even if they never walk into the room while you're playing."

"But in the palace you make more money."

"Same artistic satisfaction, though," he said. "That is to say, none."

I grinned and nodded. We'd been over this before. He had his connections among the Ilsigi, I among the Rankans.

I smacked him lightly on the back of the head and said, "Where are you off to?"

"I'm going to pay another visit to Pel."

"Your wrist again?"

He nodded.

"You play too fast," I told him.

He chuckled. "I keep telling you, lessons are available."

"I haven't forgotten. How is Mirazia?"

He smiled. "Wonderful, as always. She asks about you."

"Well, why shouldn't she?" I punched him lightly on the shoulder and winked. "So, what else is new?"

He smiled. "You want to know?"

"Oh? Now I'm suddenly intrigued. Tell."

He stopped walking and glanced around in order to make sure no one was watching us. Fortunately, there was no one on the street, because I can't think of a better way to attract attention. Then he untied his belt pouch of some really ugly off-white fur, opened it up, and dug around in it. What he showed me was a flat, rectangular piece of what looked like dull gray metal, small enough to fit into his palm (and, for a musician, he had rather small hands).

"We need more light," I said. Dinra grunted and led us around until we spotted a streak of light leaking out from a shutter overhead. He showed me the object again, and now I could see various scratches on it, like glyphs, and the glitter of three red jewels set in a triangle.

"It's a pretty thing," I said. "What is it?"

He chuckled. "My fortune, with any luck. And yours as well, my friend."

"Mine?"

"It was something you said that led me to it, and, with all you've done for me, I think you des—"

"I've done nothing for you," I said, laughing. "Though you're welcome to think I have."

"Uh-huh. Right. Teaching me to play is nothing?"

"I didn't teach you. You learned."

"Heh," he said. We'd had that argument before, and neither of us were ever going to win it. He started to say more, but I shook my head and led him away from the light, indicating he ought to put the thing away.

"Tell me," I said, dropping my voice, "what I said that led you to that thing, whatever it is."

He graced me with one of his, "Are you joking?" looks. "You said there are still artifacts around from when the Hand ruled."

"Well, yes."

"And you spoke of one in particular, for which the right people would pay a fortune. You said it was being passed from hand to hand by those who didn't know what it was, and was presently in the cache of a fat little merchant—"

"Kakos!"

"—who kept it somewhere in his back storeroom. Yes, that's right."

"I told you about that? I mean, that's all true, but I don't remember telling you about it. I can't believe I'd have been so stupid."

"You were a little drunk."

"Oh. But—" I frowned and stared at him. "Wait—is that . . . ?"

He nodded. "The Palm of the Hand," he said.

I don't know if I actually turned pale, but it felt that way. "Put it away, for the love of—"

"Relax. No one—"

I screamed a whisper, if you can imagine such a thing. "Put it away. Now!"

He put it away, giving me a sort of hurt look. Our feet carried us past Carzen the wheelwright's, now closed and shuttered and locked, but with some signs of life. I said, "I did not spend four years teaching you to play in order to watch you get your bloody throat cut. That thing—that isn't us. We sing. We play. We entertain people. We drink a lot. We don't mess with—"

"But I have it already."

Light came flooding out from a doorway, a small public house called the Bottomless Well. I don't know much about it because they don't encourage musicians. When we were out of earshot of the place, I said, "Yes, you do. You survived getting it—and no, I don't want to know how, or from where—but how are you going to survive keeping it?"

He started to answer, but I cut him off, because we'd reached the Processional, and I needed to head east and out the gates to Land's End. "Look," I said. "Keep it out of sight, and stay safe. I'll talk to you later."

I left him there with a puzzled look on his face and went to do what they pay me for. Finding Land's End is easy; finding this particular residence within its walls was a bit of a challenge, but I managed.

His home was in the country in the middle of a town
A simple square with three fine walls it was completely round.
It rested in a valley, high up on a hill
It burned down many years ago so it must be there still

So sing me of Shemhaza and the man who couldn't fail
And I'll keep singing verses until you buy me ale.

The Enders spent the night not listening to me, and then told me how good I'd been. Enders—at the least the ones that hire musicians—come in three styles: dirges, fugues, and jigs. Dirges just scowl at you as if you were terrible and that's why they aren't tipping you. Fugues beam at you, telling you how wonderful you were, and calculate that you'd rather hear that than receive a tip. Jigs figure that, if they're going to say you were wonderful, they have to back it up with a soldat or two. In no case, as far as I can tell, does it have anything to do with how well you've played. Dinra said that playing for the Ilsigi is similar, but they are a little more willing to listen, now and then, and will occasionally even admit they enjoyed the music.

Lord Serripines had appeared briefly, but so far as I could tell, hadn't spoken more than three words to anyone or spared a glance in my direction. The story was that his hatred of the Dyareelans was deep and abiding. What would he say if he knew that I'd just seen a powerful artifact of theirs in the hand of my best friend? I very much did not want to know.

In any case, the Ender who acted as host that night was a jig, so in addition to meaningless praise I had a nice pair of soldats warming my pocket as I packed up my cresca and prepared to head for home.

A servant escorted me to the back door, where there were two uniformed guards. Their eyes pounced on me, and they moved forward on the balls of their feet as if ready to start chasing me. I blinked at them.

"Tordin Jardin?" said the skinny one. Well, he was mostly skinny, but he had big shoulders that looked like they had a lot of muscle under them.

I nodded. "Yes, sir. I am Tord'an J'ardin. May I be of service?" I gave them a smile.

The skinny one nodded brusquely. His partner, who was a bit taller and had amazingly thick, shaggy eyebrows, just stood there, still looking like he was ready to leap if I took off.

I didn't take off.

Skinny said, "The Sharda has some questions for you. Come along with us."

The Sharda? I'd heard of the Sharda. I tried to remember where, and in what context.

I smiled again. "Sure."

I know being cheerful to the City Watch just makes them suspicious, but I can't help it; it's how I am.

They positioned themselves on each side of me, but didn't hobble me or anything, so there was a limit to how much trouble I might be in. As we walked, I said, "I don't suppose you can tell me what this—"

"No," said Shaggybrows.

I chuckled. "I hadn't really thought you would." They like to have you on their own turf before they start on anything. There was no point in speculating, but I couldn't help it. When they come and get you, it's something more than to ask if you happened to witness a day laborer ducking out on a bill at the 'Unicorn.

I said, "So, how are you gentlemen doing this evening?"

Skinny grunted. Shaggybrows didn't. This completed the conversation until we reached the post.

It was a long walk, made longer by the conversation, of which there was none whatsoever. They brought me to the Hall of Justice, near the palace, and deposited me in a chair in a room full of blank walls with a single chair. Skinny indicated the chair, and I sat down. They left, and when they closed the door I heard a bolt being shot.

The fact that they hadn't taken my cresca, or, indeed, searched me, was a good sign. And more than a good sign, it also gave me something to do while waiting for the dance to begin, so to speak. Of course, I'd have had something to do anyway: If they'd taken my cresca, I'd have whistled. I whistle very well. But I opened up the case, tuned the instrument, and began running through some scales. I also wondered at the evident cooperation between the City Watch and whoever the magistrate was who was investigating this matter.

Sharda. . . .

Right. They work for the magistrate, Elisar. They investigate crime. Crime important enough to warrant attention from those in power. Therefore, this matter involved the nobility of Sanctuary, in some way, for some reason.

This matter.

What matter?

Who or what could I know that could attract the attention of a magistrate, and was so important the magistrate would enlist the City Watch?

I played my cresca and tried not to speculate.

Presently the door opened, and a fellow with muscles on his muscles, a massive gray-brown beard all over his face, and not too many teeth appeared. "Strip, please."

"Excuse me?"

"You are to be searched."

"For what?"

Evidently, he didn't feel it was his job to answer my questions. I won't go into detail, but my clothes and even my cresca case were searched thoroughly. He kept me there while he searched, and every time they started searching something, he glanced at my face. It was a little comical, to tell you the truth. In any case, nothing they found was even worth a question. I asked him if he were with the City Watch, or the Sharda, and he didn't answer. When he was done searching me, he grunted and left me to dress again, after which I did more scales.

It wasn't too long before a pair of officers appeared.

"I am Sayn," said the man. "This is my colleague Ixma. We work for the magistrate." He didn't bother to add a name.

I smiled at them both and said, "A pleasure. How may I be of assistance?"

Neither of them wore any sort of uniform. Sayn was big across the shoulders, with a bull chest, and a neatly trimmed beard. He might have had some Rankan in him. Then again, maybe not. Ixma was more interesting. Short, tiny, with big black eyes that dominated most of her face, and if she weren't all or partly S'danzo, my eyes were failing me. From my first glance at her, I wondered if she were a liesayer, one of those who can hear a lie the way I can hear a missed note. I'd heard of such among the S'danzo, and been told that sometimes the magistrates employed them. The concept fascinated me.

What is a lie, anyway?

If I sang to them of the man from Shemhaza, would such a person hear it as a lie? How about if I claimed not to remember a song that I *almost* remembered? Would that be a lie? How about an exaggeration? An understatement? I thought about asking if that's what she was, but thought better of it. The oddest thing was that I was filled with the temptation to lie for no reason, to test her. All of my training—control of voice, control of body language, even control of breath, could be a direct challenge to such powers. I wanted to know if I could tell a direct, bald-face lie that she couldn't detect.

And I knew very well that making such a test would be the height of stupidity when dealing with those who have the power of life and death. I sat on the temptation until it whimpered and went away.

Sayn said, "You are Tordin Jardin?"

I smiled. "Tord'an J'ardin," I agreed.

He stood over me and said, without preamble, "You were seen earlier this evening with a certain Dinrabol Festroon."

He seemed to be waiting for a response, so I nodded. He still said nothing, just looked at me in that way those in power have, so I added, "He's a friend of mine."

"A friend."

I nodded.

He glanced at the one called Ixma, then turned back to me.

"When and where did you see him last?"

I frowned. "I . . ."

His lips tightened. That's something else they do.

I said, "If he's in trouble, I wouldn't want to be the one—"

"Answer the question, please."

I sighed. "It was a few hours ago, before I headed out to Land's End. I was just headed out of the Maze."

He nodded. "Yes, that's where he was found."

I stared at him. "Found?"

He nodded again, and went back to waiting for me to say something. It's the way they have, where they're looking for you to give something away, and even if you have nothing to give away, you feel like you've confessed.

I said, "What happened to him?"

"He's dead. Stabbed. One thrust from under the chin up into the brain."

I winced. He'd given me a better image than I wanted.

"Robbed?"

"Interesting question," he said. "He had a purse with a few padpols in it, and various personal items. These things weren't taken. Did he have anything else worth stealing?"

"Everyone has things worth stealing, Sayn. May I call you Sayn? In his case, well, I don't know."

"You don't know? How well did you know him?"

"He was my best friend," I said quietly. "I taught him to play, and to perform. I worked with him on his voice and his stage presence. We'd spend hours together, mostly drinking, or walking around. We—"

"I get the idea. If it wasn't robbery, who wanted him dead?"

"No one," I said. "If there was ever someone who didn't make enemies, it was Din."

He frowned, and tilted his lead a little, staring at me. I guess it was supposed to make me uncomfortable, and I have to say it did. It doesn't matter how innocent you are when you're interrogated by someone who knows how to do so; you still get nervous, uncomfortable, and start feeling like you ought to confess to something, just to stop the ordeal.

He said, "You were the last one seen with him, you know."

"I know. Well, except for whoever ki—whoever did it."

"And we only have your word for it that there is such a person. Did you kill him?"

I felt myself flushing. "No," I said.

He gave an expressive nod. What it expressed was, *I don't*

necessarily believe you, but I'm not going to push it now. He glanced at his partner, I guess for confirmation. She still had not said a word, and her eyes had never left my face.

He studied me a bit, then said, "You weren't born here, were you?"

I shook my head. "A place called Shemhaza, a few hundred miles inland."

"When did you arrive in Sanctuary?"

"About eight years ago."

"Why?"

"If you'd ever seen Shemhaza, you wouldn't ask."

He was polite enough to chuckle, then said, "Seriously. Why here? Why then?"

"I had played all my songs for all six people in Shemhaza. I wanted an audience. I'm not kidding; I need an audience. I need to play for people. It's what I live for."

He nodded as if he was willing to believe me for the moment. "Do you have a wife, or a lover?"

"Not anymore."

"Oh?"

"I had a woman named Mirazia, but she stopped seeing me a few months ago and took up with Din."

He stared at me. "She left you for your best friend?"

I met his stare. "Yes."

"You know, that does nothing to make me less suspicious of you."

"I know. But what if I'd said nothing about it? You'd have found out anyway, and then you'd be asking me why I didn't say anything."

I was hoping that would get a chuckle and a nod from him. It didn't.

"How did you feel about that?"

"In truth? It hurt a little. But with Mirazia and me, well, it was never one of the great passions of which ballads are made. I got over it pretty quickly. I will say . . ." I bit my lip. "I'm not looking forward to having to tell her."

"You needn't. I already have. Before I spoke to you."

"Then you knew—"

"Yes."

I nodded. "I'll still need to see her."

He shrugged. "That isn't my concern." He gave me a thoughtful look. "I'm not done with you, J'ardin. But for now, you may go. Don't stray too far."

I nodded. Any other response seemed like a bad idea.

He escorted me out of the building. I tried my best to pick up what I could from the bits of conversations, just as I do when I'm playing. One of the guards was having troubles with a girl, another couldn't decide what to eat tonight, and a third wasn't sleeping well of late; then I was outside once more.

I made my way to Mirazia's walk-up, which was in the east side of town—in the 'Tween off the Wideway. No one followed me, but I hadn't expected anyone to. What happened to Din mattered to me, and to Mirazia, and, I'm afraid, it just didn't much matter to anyone else.

Except, of course, if that were true, why was the Sharda interested?

And even as I asked myself that, I had the answer: He had played for the Jlsigi nobility. He had even performed in the palace. Someone liked him, and someone was unhappy that he was dead.

Well, I was unhappy that he was dead, too.

Mirazia let me in, and instantly had her arms around me, her head in my chest. We just stood like that for a while. She made no sounds, no motions.

"Cry if you wish," I told her.

She shook her head against my chest. "I'm all cried out for now," she said very quietly.

A few minutes later she said, "I'm sorry. Do you want something to drink? Are you hungry?"

I almost chuckled. That was so like her. I didn't, but I let her get me some watery wine and some cheese, because she needed to be doing something.

We sat on the couch and I held her. I said, "I'm suspected of doing it, you know."

"You?"

"Yes. Apparently I was jealous, because you and I used to—"

"They're such idiots."

I shook my head. "No. From their perspective, it makes sense. They don't know us."

"That means they won't be looking for who really did it."

I exhaled slowly. "Mirazia, they aren't going to investigate. People like us, like Din, don't matter. If anyone is going to find out what happened to him, it will be me."

She stared at me with reddened eyes. "Torrie, don't!"

I think we stopped seeing each other because I couldn't get her to stop calling me "Torrie" but now wasn't the time to object. I said, "Nothing will happen to me. I'll ask a few questions—"

"Wasn't it just a robbery?"

"Not just a robbery, no."

"What do you mean?"

I sighed. "Din did something foolish," I said.

"What do you mean?" She sounded like she wanted to get angry, which perhaps would have been good for her.

"He stole something. I don't know how he got it, I didn't want to ask, but—"

She glared. "He'd nev—"

She stopped in mid-outraged denial, stared into space for a bit, then looked down.

I said, "What?"

"I knew something was up. He's been acting funny for the last week."

"Funny, how?"

"Excited. I asked him about it and he'd, well, you know how he'd get when he had a surprise planned, like when he wrote that song about you and sprang it on you at the 'Unicorn."

I nodded. "For the last week?"

"Yes. What did he steal?"

"The Palm of the Hand."

She frowned. "What is that?"

"I'm not sure exactly. Perhaps it is magical, perhaps it has some other significance, but it's important to those who worship Dyareela."

She looked at me like I'd just turned green and grown wings. "The Hand?" she said at last. "Are you sure?"

I nodded.

"How can you know that?"

"Mirazia, think who you're talking to. I'm a musician. I sing in taverns. I listen to gossip. I know songs and stories from everywhere about everything. That thing he showed me is an artifact of the Bloody Hand."

"Did he know that?"

"He knew."

She started crying again.

A little later, she said, "What are you going to do?"

"Find his killer."

"The guards—"

"Will arrest him, if they see proof, and they feel like it's worth their time. They're half-convinced I did it, and they didn't even hold me."

"But—"

"I'll be careful," I said.

She rested her head on my shoulder. Her hair was wavy, and that color that looks red in some light, and almost black in other light. I put an arm around her, but did nothing else; didn't even think of doing anything else.

"How will you find his killer?"

"I don't know," I lied. "I'll think of something."

I held her, and a little later she said, "Tor, tell me a story?" When we'd been together, she had often said that after we made love. I'd tell her old stories, or funny stories, or ballads taken out of verse until she fell asleep. I wasn't about to make love to her tonight.

"All right," I said. "One day a man set out from Lirt to find Shemhaza. He had a mule, enough food for a year, and just kept walking inland. Every night, he'd stop and build a fire and eat his dinner and sleep and get up early the next morning and continue walking. One night he stopped in the middle of a forest, but when he woke up, it was raining. He was too wet and cold to want to continue, so he built up the fire thinking to stay as warm as he could until the rain stopped. The rain didn't stop that night, so he found a dead tree, cut it up, and added it to the fire. The rain continued the next day, so he took branches that he hadn't burned, and his spare clothing, and built a sort of shelter. The rain continued, day after day, and he was determined not to leave until he was dry. One day a pair of travelers came along on their way to Shemhaza and asked to share his fire. He agreed, and they made a good meal together.

"As the rain continued, one of them went out to hunt, and was able to snare a coney, out of which they made stew. They constructed a better shelter together, and cut down trees for firewood and shelter, and the rain continued.

"Soon more travelers arrived and joined them. When the rain finally stopped, winter had begun, and so they remained. When spring came, some of them planted corn and rye, and others hunted. By this time they had made a large clearing in the forest, with a dozen homes made of wood. There were a husband and wife there, and by the time the roads were good for travel, she was great with child, so they all stayed to help her and to care for the child. By the time she and the child could travel, the rains had begun again, and the crops were ready to be harvested, and so they stayed another year, and more joined them.

"One day, a stranger arrived and asked the man if he could stay to get out of the rain. The man said of course he could. The stranger said, 'What is the name of your village?' 'Shemhaza,' said the man. And it is there still."

I stopped talking. She was asleep. I half carried her to her bed, undressed her, and covered her up. Then I went back into the other room and fell asleep on the chair.

The next morning, I puttered around her pantry long enough to eat some of her bread and cheese, and left some out for her. I felt stiff from sleeping in the chair and rather unclean from sleeping in my clothes. I put both feelings behind me and went out into the bright Sanctuary morning.

Somewhere in or around the city were those who still followed the way of Dyareela—probably several groups, in fact, none of whom agreed with each other about what exactly the Mother Goddess wanted. All of them happy to cut each others' throats, in a city happy to cut all their throats. I had to find one of those groups. I glanced down at my unstained hands, thinking about dying my nails red, but I rejected the idea as soon as I thought of it; getting myself killed by some outraged citizen would do no good, and a musician cannot hide his hands for very long.

I took myself back to the 'Unicorn. It wasn't especially busy—just a few of the hardcore drunks—but that was okay. Pegrin wasn't working. The man behind the counter was a fellow called the Stick, whose permanent bad temper matched my permanent good mood. The Stick didn't mind if I played a little; I told him I felt like practicing in front of an audience. He muttered something in which I caught the word "audience" and pointed to the stage.

It was funny, because it remains one of the longest shows I've ever done: I just sat there, mostly running through instrumentals, and tried to pick up pieces of conversation around me. I'm pretty good at that—at least, when there's something to listen to. It is the hardest thing there is . . . playing, and at the same time trying to put together scattered bits of overheard conversation into the one piece of information you need.

His third son was short and tall, the second thin and fat
And ten years after he was dead his first son was begat

He grew to fine young manhood, till at midnight one bright morn
He came to Shemhaza before his father had been born.

So sing me of Shemhaza and the man who couldn't fail
And I'll keep singing verses until you buy me ale.

But it is, after all, what I'd been trained to do. It took me three days.

Outside the western walls of Sanctuary, you'll find the Street of Red Lanterns, which is where the brothels grow, among other things. Between two of the older buildings there is a place where you can duck between them, slide through an alleyway, climb over a low fence, and look behind a moderately heavy barrel to find a rusted grating. You move the grating aside, climb down, and go through a sort of hatchway. You'll find yourself in an old sewer system, that is no longer used except by a curious species of rodent that doesn't bear describing. You can walk upright in it, and if you don't mind the smell it isn't too difficult. You may want to bring a rope, in case the iron ladder down to the lower level has finally rusted away. Better still, don't go.

But I went there, cresca case slung over my back, following bits of footprints in the slime and bits of half-heard conversation, until I came to a place where there was a sort of niche. I went through it, and waited.

Presently they appeared, in just the way they were supposed to— they remembered that much at least. A weak, rather pitiful man from the front looked as if he wanted to talk, and a larger and stronger man (judging by his hand) from behind. Both of their nails were dyed red. The one from behind went for the grip, but I'd been expecting it and caught his hand the way I'd been taught, pressing my thumb into the weak spot on the back of his hand. He went down to his knees. Yes, he was a big man indeed, full of lank black hair and pale skin. He didn't look so big as he knelt, whimpering, however. The wall was close, so I could put a finger into each of the little man's nostril's and pin him against the wall without losing my grip on the other's hand. The little man held perfectly still, his arms off to the sides, which is about all you can do when someone is holding you that way. The big man whimpered.

I addressed the little man. *"Tr'kethra ircastra'n cor leftra, stin!"* I told him.

He swallowed. "I . . . do not speak the Mother Tongue," he said.

I grunted. "You recognize it, at least. Take me to the leader of this *ircastra*, at once."

"Ircastra?"

I rolled my eyes. "This group. This enclave. Do it, or I'll rip your face off your skull."

He whimpered like his friend. I applied a little pressure, and he yelped. "All right!"

I loosened my hold on the big man long enough to get the grip on him he'd been trying to get on me. When he was sleeping, I relaxed my hold on the other, switched to his elbow, and hurt him just enough to let him know how much more I could hurt him if I chose.

"Go."

It was ugly and damp and smelled like mold and the droppings of small animals.

The *ircastra'n* was a man, which I had been warned to expect. He was in his late thirties, with sunken cheeks, wisps of brownish hair, and pale, watery blue eyes. He was sitting in a sort of parlor full of badly made wooden chairs at a makeshift desk. He stared at us and his mouth fell open. I could see him recognizing the grip I had, so his first words were, "Who are you?"

"I am Tord'an J'ardin of Devrith."

"Devrith!"

"Yes." I didn't ask his name. I didn't yet know if it mattered. "The good news is, you have not been forgotten by the Mother Temple. The bad news is, you have not been forgotten by the Mother Temple."

"I don't believe you!"

"From now on, I will be taking charge here. First this *ircastra,* then the others. You may assist me, or join the Mother."

"You lie! Who are you?"

"Shut up and listen, *nief'kri.*" He knew enough of the Mother Tongue to recognize the insult—he blanched, bit his lip, started to get angry—and listened.

I said, "You and those like you held Sanctuary, a place the Council of Priestesses badly wished, and then you gave it back."

"Priestesses? But—"

"Priestesses. Things have changed. You might say that the feminine side of the Mother has emerged. Things are different now. And the Priestesses are not pleased with what has happened in Sanctuary. You have lost it for us for at least a generation, with your bickering and squabbling, with your blindness, and with your stupidity. Neither the Council nor the Mother has any wish for rivers of blood to be spilled for no purpose. We are here to cleanse the world. Not to satisfy the bloodlust of fools. The power we crave is to serve the Mother, not to gratify the egos of little men. You will spend the rest of your life trying to get us back to where we were fifteen years ago in this puss hole of a city. Or you may die now. I don't care. But from this day forward, it will be Priestesses who rule. Through me, until another arrives."

"You can't have come from—"

"You need convincing?"

There was fear in his eyes, but stubbornness in the set of jaw. He nodded.

I let go my grip on the little man, who stepped quickly away from me, rubbing his arm.

I unslung my instrument case, set it on the desk, and opened it. Then I took out my cresca, raised it, and brought it smashing down on the desk, leaving me holding the fretboard, with a bit of the truss rod sticking out the end. Some of the splinters hit the *ircastra'n,* which pleased me though I hadn't planned on it. I searched among the remains of my instrument, and found it. I held it in the proper way and showed it to him.

"You recognize this?"

He turned yet another shade of pale. "The Palm! You have the Palm!"

I touched the Palm with the fingers of my left hand, letting them tickle the gems as I'd been taught. Lights flickered among them.

"Any questions?" I asked him.

He stared at me with his mouth hanging open. "Who *are* you?"

"I gave you my name. I was trained from childhood in the main temple of Devrith."

"Trained . . ."

"I'm a Conversant, of course."

He stared. He was, it seemed, not so far removed that he didn't know at least something of what that meant—the hundreds of hours in memory training, in knowledge of the history and lore of the Temple, learning to listen to four conversations at once and being able to recite every tone and nuance of each one, and then mastery in singing, composition, and musical instruments thrown on top of it almost as an afterthought, because tongues are never looser than in a good inn with loud music. He was impressed, and that was good. But none of that really mattered, because, after years of work, I had the Palm. Without it, he had no reason to listen to me. With it—

He stood up from his desk, stood before me, knelt, and bowed his head. "Your orders, *ircastra'n?*"

I studied the flickering gems and thought to them, *"It is Tord'an, and the work is begun."* The gems flickered more in answer, and the warmth I felt from it filled my soul. I put the Palm inside my shirt, against my skin, until I could find a thong to hang it from my neck.

Then I nodded to the man who knelt in front of me. "For starters, you'll fill me in on what you know of the other *ircastra'i*. Then we'll make plans. To begin, you'll all wipe that silly paint off your fingernails. We'll move slowly, this time. There is a healer named Pel who may be able to help Arizak. If so, the person who brings the healer will have a nice entry to the ear of those who rule. That will save us a few years. What is your name?"

"Rynith."

I nodded. "We have a lot of work to do," I told him. "Let's be about it. Oh, and as soon as someone has cleaned off his nails, have him go buy me another cresca." I chuckled. "Killing my best friend was easy, but I hated to lose the instrument."